VIENNESE
NOVELETTES

Viennese Novelettes

by

ARTHUR SCHNITZLER

WITH ILLUSTRATIONS BY
KURT WIESE

SIMON AND SCHUSTER · NEW YORK · 1931

CONTENTS

INTRODUCTION

By Otto P. Schinnerer

I

In every noted creative artist there is a fundamental unity of his life and his work, and each throws light on the other. In some instances indeed, where the author's experiences have not been sufficiently sublimated, the congruity is so obvious that it casts doubts on his title to greatness, and in extreme cases amounts simply to a public washing of soiled linen. Needless to say, Arthur Schnitzler has never been guilty of such indiscretions. His work is, nevertheless, in a very real sense, an embodiment of his experiences, his views of life, his personality.

Two outstanding factors have left an indelible mark on his work. First and foremost, he is thoroughly Viennese; secondly he was, and is still at heart, a physician. His native city—and it is primarily the pre-war Vienna that figures here—has long been noted for its light-hearted gayety and its subdued melancholy. While racially and linguistically it is predominantly German, culturally it has always drawn heavily on Romanic civilization. Vienna, furthermore, is the meeting-point between East and West, the last important outpost of Western culture. Bordering on the Balkans, it has absorbed among its population many diverse elements from the Slavic states.

These facts serve to explain the vast difference, say, between Berlin and Vienna. Berlin, the business metropolis of efficient, industrialized Germany, has a sterner, harsher note. Its people are more ponderous, more absorbed in the economic problem of living. Not unnaturally, therefore, it was in Berlin that the naturalistic drama, with its undertones of hunger and revolt, rose and prospered. Vienna, on the other hand, heir to an age-old culture, has made a fine art of living itself and produced a lighter, gayer, more vivacious art. In this respect it resembles Paris more than it does Berlin. A certain Gallic sprightliness in Schnitzler, which on occasion makes him seem more French than German, is due, not to his dependence on French models, but to the spirit of Vienna which lives in his soul.

With but few exceptions, the scenes of all of Schnitzler's stories and plays are laid in Vienna or in those sections of the Austrian Alps where the well-to-do Viennese spend their vacations. The present volume represents the cream of the Viennese stories, the perfect expression of the Viennese spirit. In Vienna we encounter primarily the quaint and ancient inner city with its patrician houses, its little quiet squares and lovely fountains, its old churches; the magnificent Ring Boulevard with its large hotels and cafés, with the Opera, the Court Theatre, Parliament, City Hall, the University, and the former imperial residence with its extensive gardens; the elegant residential section of villas where the author himself lives; and last but not least the lovely wooded hills and mountains just outside the city, so dear to the heart of all Viennese. The proletariat, to be sure, is conspicuously absent. The characters the author depicts belong largely to the upper middle classes, especially to those professional and artistic circles with whom he has associated all his life. He knows them intimately. They are one hundred percent Viennese, with all their charm, but also with all their foibles. Seldom has a writer of renown identified himself with his native city so completely as has Arthur Schnitzler with Vienna.

Schnitzler, moreover, is a physician, possessed of that combination of cold objectivity and warm-hearted sympathy for which many successful physicians are noted. Though a keen, almost inspired, diagnostician, he is interested primarily in the soul of man, in the complex of human emotions. It is his uncanny understanding of the human soul, combined with the grace and charm and simplicity of his style, the perfect blending of form and content, that place him in the front rank of living authors.

Not only is the author's profession apparent from his manner of portraying his characters, but he has in addition projected himself into a notable array of physicians. Besides the hero of *Rhapsody,* the somewhat pathetic Dr. Graesler, and the splendid gallery of medical men in *Professor Bernhardi,* he has created more than a score of doctors, most of whom embody his own high ideals of his profession. Many of them play only a secondary rôle, usually they stand somewhat aloof from the current of life about them, looking on with a sense of wistful resignation, but they are imbued with a deep sense of responsibility and exhibit that broad and tolerant understanding of their fellowmen so characteristic of the author himself.

The fact finally that Schnitzler is of Jewish extraction may have had an appreciable influence in shaping his outlook upon life. Spending his entire life in a rabidly anti-Semitic community, he has been exposed not only to hostile criticism, but to an incessant barrage of bitter invective and downright abuse. This has undoubtedly intensified his perception of the mean and vicious qualities in human nature and probably accounts to some extent for the occasional strains of pessimism and cynicism to be found in his work.

2

Schnitzler's paternal grandfather, Joseph Schnitzler, was an illiterate joiner who plied his trade in the small Hungarian city of Gross-Kanizsa. His name had originally been Zimmermann, a German word that actually means carpenter or joiner. Apparently he was a rather shiftless character, not averse to drinking. Having fortunately contracted a marriage with a woman of some means, he was enabled to give his son Johann the advantages of a higher education. The latter, born in 1835, received his M.D. degree from the University of Vienna in 1860. Devoting himself to laryngology, he became in the course of time the favorite specialist of the leading operatic and theatrical stars, and later also of the aristocracy and plutocracy of Vienna. The position of eminence obtained through his medical practice was greatly enhanced by his activities as editor of medical journals, as professor at the university, and as director of the General Polyclinic founded by himself. The government recognized his accomplishments by conferring upon him the title of Privy Councillor. In many respects Professor Johann Schnitzler was the direct opposite of his son Arthur. He was rather pompous and vain-glorious, fond of parading his decorations from the King of Greece and other crowned heads, whereas the son is a man of great modesty and

humility, upon whom outward honors make not the
slightest impression. The father, furthermore, was
strangely deficient in that penetrating knowledge of
human nature in which his son so excels.

There is every reason to believe that, like Goethe,
Schnitzler inherited his artistic and creative talent from
his mother, whose maiden name was Louise Markbreiter. She was born in Güns in Hungary in 1840. Her
father, Dr. Philipp Markbreiter, later made a name for
himself as the founder of the first medical journal in
Vienna and as editor of several other professional peri-
odicals. Although trained as a pianist, she early became
her father's editorial assistant, especially as translator
of scientific articles from foreign languages. She never
abandoned her great love for music and to her very last
days spent hours at the piano almost daily. In 1861 she
was married to Dr. Johann Schnitzler, and the first
issue of this union was Arthur Schnitzler, born on May
15, 1862, in the former Jägerzeile of Vienna, now called
Prater Street.

3

Young Arthur grew up in an environment of ele-
gance, even of luxury. At his father's home which was
later transferred to the exceedingly fashionable Burg-
ring, the élite of Vienna's artistic and theatrical circles
were regular guests. There can be no doubt that the
early and intimate contact with these people had a definite influence on Schnitzler's latent talents. He pursued, however, the normal course of education for
young men of his social class, graduating from the
Academic Gymnasium in 1879, matriculating at the
University of Vienna as a student of medicine, and tak-

ing his degree in 1885. During the next few years he was assistant physician in the clinic for internal medicine under Professor Standhardtner, then in the division of psychiatry under Professor Meynert and finally in the clinic for skin diseases under Professor Isidor Neumann. In 1888 he spent several months in London, making a study of the facilities for medical education and especially of hospital conditions in that city. His impressions are recorded in a series of three "London Letters," published in the *International Clinical Review* (*Internationale Klinische Rundschau*). Shortly after taking his degree, he began to review books on medical subjects for the *Vienna Medical Press* (*Wiener Medizinische Presse*), the journal founded in 1860 by his father who had remained its editor ever since. At the end of 1886 his father severed his relations with this journal, due to some misunderstanding with the publishers. A new medical journal was launched at once, however, the *Internationale Klinische Rundschau* just mentioned. As the father hesitated to sign as the responsible editor, Dr. Bèla Weiss and Dr. Arthur Schnitzler appeared as the nominal editors. Beginning with the second volume the latter became the sole responsible editor, but in 1889 his father again assumed the editorship-in-chief.

At first the son simply reviewed those books which his father handed out to him, but now that he figured as an editor he could exercise greater choice. Consequently we now find reviews on diseases of the nervous system, neurasthenia and hysteria, psychotherapy and hypnotism predominating, studies that had a marked influence on his later writings. It is interesting to note in passing that he also discussed two books by J. M.

Charcot, rendered into German by Sigmund Freud. In both he extols the masterful translation. One of the most interesting of these reviews (1890) is that of a book on sexual hygiene in which he scores the author for his condemnation of writers like Zola, Strindberg, Garborg, Maupassant and Ola Hansson. Schnitzler displays an intimate familiarity with the works of these authors and makes some striking comparisons between this group on the one hand, and Boccaccio, Casanova, Faublas, Paul de Kock on the other.

In 1889 Schnitzler also contributed a research article, entitled "Functional Aphonia and its Treatment by Hypnotism and Suggestion." Here he reveals the method he applied to induce the hypnotic state, which was that of the Bernheim school. Continuing, he gives all the essential details of six case histories, in all of which his treatment was more or less successful, in most of them even strikingly so. These experiments with hypnotism later found reflection in the first *Anatol* scene and in *Paracelsus*.

After the death of Professor Schnitzler in May, 1893, the entire burden of responsibility in editing the journal again fell on the shoulders of his son. The latter's name again appeared on the title page as editor until September 9, 1894, when he definitely withdrew.

Finally, the poet also collaborated with his father and his brother-in-law on a *Clinical Atlas of Laryngology and Rhinology.*

It is frequently asserted that Schnitzler is still actively engaged in practicing medicine. This is erroneous. He has preserved his old love for his profession, but for the past thirty years has devoted himself exclusively to writing.

4

The boy Arthur early became a voracious reader and when no more than eight or nine years old already tackled such ambitious works as Schiller's *Robbers* and the like. His earliest literary compositions date back to these same years. At nine he had completed a full five-act tragedy. In order to elude the watchful eyes of his father who frowned upon such efforts, they were written in ordinary school composition books. During the ensuing years work after work, of almost every conceivable type of literary form flowed from his pen. His unpublished writings from his boyhood and early manhood would almost suffice to fill a five-foot shelf.

It is rather amusing that Schnitzler first saw his own name in print in a clerical, conservative paper of Munich, the *Free State Messenger* (*Der freie Landesbote*) in 1880. He had made no attempt to get his work published, but when a former schoolmate who had secured a position on this paper requested some contributions, Schnitzler—he was just eighteen—accommodated him by forwarding two of his literary endeavors. No one was more surprised than the author when a poem, "Love Song of a Ballet Girl," and a rather sceptical sketch "Concerning Patriotism" actually appeared.

Six years were to elapse before Schnitzler again published anything. During this period he became so engrossed in his medical studies that his literary work remained a mere hobby for idle hours. In 1886 a new periodical was founded in Vienna, *By the Beautiful Blue Danube* (*An der schönen blauen Donau*), which soon became very popular. Schnitzler ventured to submit three poems to the editorial staff, but instead of being either accepted or rejected they were turned over to the clever and witty editor of a correspondence column, who published one of them with rather disparaging comment. From 1889 onward, however, Schnitzler became a more or less regular contributor to this middle-class family journal in which his poems and novelettes alternated with illustrations of Austrian archduchesses, songs of spring, riddles, and questions of social etiquette for young girls before their first ball.

In subsequent years Schnitzler also became a sporadic contributor to some half dozen other publications. Altogether there are between thirty-five and forty of these contributions up to 1895, none of which has ever been republished in book form. About half of these early works are poems, most of them signed "Anatol." A large number of them deal with the theme of woman's infidelity and the lover's jealousy of his sweetheart, jealousy of her past, her present, her future. From this disbelief in woman's faithfulness it is only a step to a general disillusionment which often leads to cynicism or wearied resignation, a note that repeatedly recurs. During these years Schnitzler was, as a matter of fact, passing through a mental and emotional crisis. It was the time when he had to come to a decision whether to give up his chosen calling, the medical profession, or to launch out on a literary career, and the resulting conflict was only intensified by his father's sceptical opposition to his literary ambition.

Several one-acters with sparkling witty dialogue and a few short stories which foreshadow the perfection he was later to attain conclude this early period. It was largely an experimental stage in which he endeavored to master the technique and to discover the mode of expression most in consonance with his native genius.

5

Schnitzler's first published book was *Anatol*, which appeared in 1893. Most of these scenes were written in the late eighties. Originally there were some ten separate scenes, all centering in Anatol, but only seven were finally included in the book. Some of them appeared separately at the time in periodical form. When they were finally offered to publishers, they were invariably rejected, most of the publishers refusing even to read them. Even S. Fischer who has been his regular publisher for the past thirty-five years, considered them too insignificant to be profitable and turned them down. Finally Schnitzler had them brought out by the Bibliographical Bureau in Berlin at his own expense, borrowing the money from a friend.

Anatol, like the majority of Schnitzler's lovers, is a mere philanderer, bent on adventure. He is interested solely in the dramatic side of love, in conquest, and not in its epic element, permanence. Both parties embark upon a love affair with the distinct understanding that it is to terminate as soon as either feels so inclined. Furthermore, in his portrayal of love-relationships, the author shows a predilection, not for the flowering of love or the height of passion, but for its declining stages and the effects of its termination. Anatol's seven love affairs are analyzed in a delightfully keen and subtle vein, with a plentiful dose of irony and scepticism. A second male character, Max, Anatol's friend, is a *raisonneur* who comments objectively on the various episodes, whereas Anatol experiences them subjectively. It would be a mistake to assume that Schnitzler is either Anatol or Max, for he has projected himself into both.

One of the striking features about this book is the complete absence of those crudities of form and style we often associate with the initial effort of an author. The dialogue is so bright and natural, so elegant and graceful that it at once attracted the attention of critics, some even comparing the author to the best masters of French dialogue. As we have seen above, however, *Anatol* was not the sudden blossoming forth of a unique literary talent, but the crowning-point of a long period of apprenticeship.

On the other hand, there is a tendency among critics and the reading public to overestimate the importance of *Anatol*. While full recognition is due to the unusual qualities of these playful and slightly sentimental sketches, it must not be overlooked that after all they form only the starting point of a long and distinguished career during which Schnitzler's technique has been constantly refined and his problems have deepened and broadened.

6

Schnitzler's path in launching out on a literary career was not strewn with roses. First he had to contend with the passive resistance of his father. Besides it was not an easy matter for himself to renounce the medical profession to which he felt so devoted. But even more disheartening was the amused and sceptical attitude of the great majority of his friends and acquaintances who simply refused to take him seriously. This young doctor, this well-groomed man of the

world, who seemed most at ease in fashionable draw-
ing-rooms—no one was surprised that he should also
dabble in literature, compose waltzes and take part
in amateur theatrical performances, but it was obviously expecting too much to consider him more than
a dilettante. In the early nineties Schnitzler made the
acquaintance of some kindred literary souls, and his
closer association with these men, among whom were
such outstanding lights as Hugo von Hofmannsthal,
Richard Beer-Hofmann, Felix Salten and Richard
Specht, undoubtedly contributed toward restoring his
confidence in himself. But his first efforts to find a
publisher for his works were, as we have seen, doomed
to disappointment. Also the expenses for the publication of his second play, *The Fairy Tale* (*Das Märchen,*
1894) were defrayed by himself. Nor was he more
successful in getting a hearing on the stage. Although
Anatol was favorably received by the majority of critics, it did not attract unusually wide attention. With
the exception of a few isolated scenes on two or three
occasions, it was not performed at this time. Its victorious march across all the important stages of Central Europe, extending also to London, New York and
Chicago, was destined to wait until 1910 and 1911.
The production of *The Fairy Tale* on December 1, 1893
was a flat failure and it was withdrawn from the boards
after only two performances. The critics surpassed
themselves in hostile and denunciatory reviews. It was
not until after the successful performance of *Light-o'-
Love* (*Liebelei*) at the famous Burgtheater in Vienna
on October 9, 1895 that Schnitzler's reputation as an
author was definitely established.

In *Anatol* the love episodes were treated frivolously,
but in *Light-o'-Love* they have a tragic ending. The

first act reads like a scene from *Anatol,* but when Christine Weiring learns that Fritz Lobheimer, the man on whom she had bestowed all her love, is killed in a duel with another woman's husband, without ever having taken her into his confidence, she commits suicide. Theodor Kaiser and Mizi Schlager serve as a foil to these two central characters. Just as Fritz is the counterpart of Anatol, sentimental and subjectve, so Theodor is a replica of Max, cynical and objective, while Mizi is the type of the "sweet little girl" who has no illusions about her amours. With them love-relationships are initiated without much ado and terminated without shedding of tears. Christine's father, Weiring, the old violinist, is endowed with the noblest human qualities, wisdom, tolerance and understanding. He does not interfere with his daughter, because the experience with his sister has taught him a bitter lesson.

Both in style and structure this three-act play is of the utmost simplicity, and yet in it inheres a poignancy and power seldom equalled. It is unquestionably the masterpiece of Schnitzler's early creative period. He has created profounder and more brilliant works, more searching and important works, but never anything that surpasses the broad and universally human appeal of *Light-o'-Love.*

7

For a time, perhaps under the influence of Ibsen and the naturalistic school in Germany, Schnitzler strayed into the field of the social problem play. The first of these, *The Fairy Tale* (*Das Märchen*) mentioned above, is an indictment of the conventional at-

titude of society toward a girl—in this case a sincere
and gifted actress—who in her youthful passion has
violated the moral code. The author Fedor Denner
flatters himself that he is sufficiently emancipated not
to condemn a woman who has yielded to her erotic
instincts outside of matrimony, and in the first act he
makes an eloquent appeal for these social outcasts
and pleads the cause of equal rights for women in
the sexual sphere. But when he discovers that Fanny
Theren, the girl he loves and hopes to marry, is one
of these "fallen" women, the old prejudices reassert
themselves and he is unable to convert his theories into
practice. It is the tragic situation of a person who has
emancipated himself intellectually, but whose emotional reactions still follow the conventional pattern.
Fanny, on the other hand, has the courage of her con-
victions and scores her sister for entering a loveless
match merely to be respectably provided for. When
first produced, the ideas put forward in the play
seemed too bold and revolutionary to find general
approval. Amusingly enough, when revived in 1907,
the theme was felt to be too obvious and old-fashioned
to arouse interest. In 1910 it had a successful run in
Chicago under the title *The Tale* with Nazimova in
the principal rôle.

Free Game (*Freiwild,* 1898) illuminates the theme
of honor and is directed not so much against the duel
as such, as against the social conventions that make
it compulsory. For a time the play was forbidden by
the censors because in it an officer is slapped in the face.
Moreover, Schnitzler incidentally presented here such
a realistic picture of the sordid conditions prevalent
in provincial theatres, that many actors, feeling self-
conscious, refused to take a part in it.

The Legacy (Das Vermächtnis, 1899) has been aptly called "The Pillars of Viennese Society." The problem is that of the unmarried mother and the heartless cruelty she suffers from the very people who would be expected to extend to her sympathy and love. When Hugo Losatti is killed by a fall from a horse, he implores his parents on his deathbed to take his common-law wife and his son into the family and to treat them with the same consideration as they would their daughter-in-law. They assent somewhat grudgingly, but Toni Weber is sensitive to the cold and somewhat hostile atmosphere surrounding her. When her child dies, there is nothing more to hold her and she commits suicide. The situation is frankly summed up by Hugo's sister in the concluding speech of the play: "We were cowardly, we did not dare to love her as she deserved. We extended favors to her, favors—we! —and we needed only to be kind, Mother!"

These three plays are a high tribute to Schnitzler as a man for the sincerity and courage he displayed in thus boldly attacking intrenched prejudices and conventions, but from the point of view of dramatic technique they have certain flaws. The author begins by setting forth a certain thesis, but instead of carrying this through consistently, his objectivity and sense of fair play cause him to see the other side of the picture, so that in the end he almost proves the opposite of what he set out to do. He seems to have had an experience here somewhat similar to that of Professor Bernhardi. During his imprisonment the latter started a book in defense of himself and in denunciation of his opponents. But he gave up this idea, explaining: "When I began writing it, in the contemplative seclusion of my cell, I still felt the heat of anger, but in the course of work this evaporated more and more. The denunciation of Flint & Co. became—I can hardly say myself how it happened—perhaps in recollection of a certain incident—something in the nature of a philosophic treatise. . . . All at once the problem was one of broad ethical issues, of responsibility and revelation, and in the final analysis of free will."

8

Hitherto we have discussed exclusively Schnitzler's dramatic works, but from the very beginning his prose fiction has occupied an equally important place in his creative work. Even before the publication of *Anatol* he had completed a novelette of about a hundred pages entitled *Dying* (*Sterben,* 1890), the first of the narrative works in the collected German edition. Since its first appearance, critics have pointed this out as one of the magnificent achievements of Schnitzler's genius. To be sure, it lacks the richness and saturation of many of his later creations in this field. One might almost say the characters here are two-dimensional compared with the full-bodied living persons that stalk through the pages of his later novelettes. But as a profound psychological study of the emotions of a man who knows that he is doomed to die of tuberculosis within a year it is unequalled. Although here again we meet with a lover, Felix, and his mistress, Marie, it is not their erotic relationship with which the author is concerned, but rather their changing reactions in the face of the dread fate that awaits Felix. When first apprised of his doom, the latter offers Marie her freedom, but Marie vows that she will never desert him. As the fateful months pass, however, Felix clings to life more and more tenaciously. He cannot bear the thought of dying alone and so at first he suggests, then demands that Marie accompany him on his journey into the great unknown. She remains with him, to be sure, loyally and patiently, but she becomes slowly estranged from him, the call of life becomes ever more insistent, and when at last he menacingly demands the fulfillment of her promise, she flees from his bedside in horror.

Everything not strictly relevant to the one problem the author has set himself is scrupulously excluded. The souls of these two characters are revealed to us with the calmness, but also with the inexorableness and inevitableness of a medical case history. Both in subject and in manner of treatment Schnitzler is here preëminently the physician.

In 1898 five additional novelettes were published, the collection bearing the title of the first story *The Sage's Wife* (*Die Frau des Weisen*). The themes and situations are frequently reminiscent of the *Anatol* scenes, but they usually have a tragic ending. They are characterized by a delicate lyrical quality, and pervaded by a subdued melancholy atmosphere that lends them a rare charm.

At the end of the nineties a turning point in Schnitzler's creative career is clearly discernible. *The Sage's Wife* and *The Legacy,* discussed above, may be looked upon as concluding the period of his early work, the outstanding accomplishments of which were *Light-o'-Love* and *Dying.* From this time on we find him abandoning the treatment of social problems as such and confining himself to the creation of human beings. We note a constant deepening and broadening of his art, an increasing refinement in his techique.

The external action as a rule means little to him; primarily he is interested in getting at the hidden motives for human actions and beliefs, at the illusions by which men live, and at the interaction between different personalities.

Before continuing our account, however, we must consider a work which, although published at a later date, distinctly belongs to the period we have just traversed. This is *Hands Around* (*Reigen*) which has certain points of resemblance to *Anatol*. But whereas the latter work has spread Schnitzler's fame throughout the world and has been extolled far beyond its deserts, *Hands Around* has been denounced and suppressed with almost religious fervor and has caused the author untold annoyance. Yet it is by far the more serious, the more artistic and the more noteworthy of the two plays. Each of the ten scenes is a dialogue between a man and a woman: a prostitute and a soldier, the soldier and a servant girl, the servant girl and the young man of the house, the young man and a young married woman, the married woman and her husband, the husband and a sweet little girl, the sweet little girl and a poet, the poet and an actress, the actress and a count, the count and the prostitute of the first scene. Thus all the various social classes are linked together by the common bond of sex. The author shows, as has been aptly remarked, that "the Colonel's lady and Judy O'Grady are sisters under the skin." It is not, however, the culminating point in these promiscuous relations that is of interest to Schnitzler. The play is a psychological study of the typical reactions of the male and the female before and after the gratification of their libido. In *Anatol* such amours were treated in a playful, tolerant mood and enveloped in an atmosphere of poetic sentimentality. Here in a spirit of disillusionment the author ruthlessly tears the veil from the many shams and pretences that enter into the most intimate of human relations. The keenness of observation and the deftness of characterization, the almost appalling revelation of the subtlest nuances of the human psyche, coupled with so much brilliant wit and biting irony, possessed only by him who has a superior vantage point, make this work one of the foremost contributions to the psychology of sex in any literature.

When these scenes were written in the winter of 1896–1897 the author fully realized that despite the seriousness of his purpose they might easily be branded as pornographic by the average reader and critic, and so for the time being they remained buried in his desk. In 1900 he had two hundred copies printed in manuscript for presentation to his personal friends. It was not until 1903 that he gave his consent to have the work issued through regular publishing channels. Even at that date its publication caused general consternation. The book itself was never molested in Austria, but in Germany it fell foul of the censor and was confiscated. Despite numerous requests Schnitzler consistently refused his authorization for a public presentation of these scenes until after the war when he yielded to the persuasion of Max Reinhardt. Consequently the play was staged in Berlin with a run of more than a year, culminating in a sensational trial in which the producing directors and participating actors were acquitted. In Vienna and other cities the production caused theatre rows and riots, but in all cases the courts eventually gave *Hands Around* a clean slate. Only in New York the book, not to men-

tion public performances, is still under the ban of
Mr. John S. Sumner.

9

In his dramatic productions Schnitzler is at his best
in his one-act plays, although his longer plays, artistically less perfect, are often more revealing of his own
deepest thoughts. In 1899 there were published in book
form three one-act plays, *Paracelsus, The Mate* (*Die
Gefährtin*) and *The Green Cockatoo* (*Der grüne Ka-
kadu*), for which the title "Trilogy of Illusion" has
been suggested. *Paracelsus* is in verse and reflects
Schnitzler's early interest in hypnotism. Although the
time is the beginning of the 16th century, the theme
is essentially that of woman's real or potential infidelity. The play reveals to us, to quote from *Rhapsody,*
"those hidden, scarcely suspected wishes, which can
produce dangerous whirlpools even in the serenest and
purest soul." The armorer Cyprian is so smug and self-
complacent that he boasts of the faithfulness of his
wife Justina. But he is simply deluding himself. Hitherto a loyal spouse, Justina had consistently repulsed
Junker Anselm's advances, but when Paracelsus en-
joins her, while under his hypnotic spell, to tell nothing but the truth, she admits the tenuousness of her
marital bonds.

The Mate, a transformation of a short story published in 1894 in the *Wiener Allgemeine Zeitung* entitled "The Widower," is an ingenious variation of
the familiar triangle.

In *The Green Cockatoo* we are introduced into a
somewhat questionable tavern in Paris on the eve of
the French Revolution, which the degenerate French

aristocracy frequents in order to get a thrill. The inn-keeper has engaged a troupe of actors who pretend to be criminals and who titillate their audience with the impromptu recital of their imaginary crimes. The most brilliant of all is Henri who has just married the actress Léocadie, a notorious courtesan. Henri invents a blood-curdling story of how he has murdered the Duke of Cadignan, one of the habitués of the place, after having discovered him in his wife's dressing room. His recital is so realistic that even the inn-keeper believes it to be true and warns him to flee, for he knew that Léocadie had deceived him with the duke. Henri stands aghast and when the duke actually enters a few minutes later he stabs him and is cheered by the mob that has just stormed the Bastille. *The Green Cockatoo* is generally considered one of Schnitzler's most brilliant plays, teeming with life. With the utmost economy of means he gives us a vivid and faithful picture of conditions in Paris just before the revolution, at the same time introducing, long before Pirandello, one of his favorite themes, the border-line between dreaming and waking, play and reality. With a few strokes he has created a variety of characters, all of them convincingly real.

Four additional one-act plays appeared in 1902, *Living Hours* (*Lebendige Stunden*), *The Lady with the Dagger* (*Die Frau mit dem Dolche*) *Literature* (*Literatur*) and *The Last Masks* (*Die letzten Masken*). The subject of all four of these plays is more or less the artist's utilization of his personal experiences for his work. But there is a vast difference between the really creative artist who transmutes these experiences into genuine art, and those would-be artists to whom experience is merely so much "material" to be exploited. On the latter class Schnitzler has repeatedly heaped his scorn, as he does so effectively, with such delicious humor and such biting satire, in *Literature*. Margaret and Gilbert are the Greenwich Village type of writers who had had a love affair in Munich. Margaret is now engaged to Clemens, an aristocratic sportsman "with cultivated hands and an uncultivated brain." When Gilbert unexpectedly calls on his former mistress in Vienna, it develops that both have written a novel in which their former love letters are literally incorporated. But a public scandal is averted. Clemens who frowns upon Margaret's literary ambitions has had the whole edition of the novel suppressed, unaware of the compromising evidence contained in it.

In *Living Hours* the invalid mother of a young author has committed suicide so as not to be a stumbling block in his literary career. Heinrich of course assumes that she has died a natural death. But her closest friend Anton Hausdorfer, a pensioned official, gives vent to his grief and irritation by betraying her confidence and revealing the brutal truth to him. Heinrich is momentarily cast down with grief, but then pulls himself together, with the firm resolution that he must show himself worthy of her sacrifice and prove by his work that she has not died in vain.

The Lady with the Dagger is one of those playful experiments in artistic creation to which Schnitzler occasionally surrenders himself and which must not be taken too seriously as an expression of his innermost nature. The heroine lapses into a trance in a picture gallery and becomes identified with the figure portrayed in one of the paintings. She relives the experiences suggested in the picture, but at the same time these parallel and forecast her fate in her real life.

The intricate blending of the doctor and poet in Schnitzler has brought forth fine fruit again in *The Last Masks*. The scene is in a hospital where Karl Rademacher, a humble journalist, is on the point of death. His one remaining desire is to vent his spleen upon his former friend Weihgast, who has apparently reaped the full harvest of money and fame from his successful authorship, by crushing him with the revelation that in the early days of their marriage the latter's wife had been his mistress. He gloatingly rehearses the scene with an actor, a fellow patient. But when Weihgast has nothing but petty cares and disappointments to relate, Rademacher realizes the futility of his revenge and takes his secret with him to the grave.

10

Schnitzler's most ambitious attempts in the field of drama are the two huge canvases *The Veil of Beatrice* (*Der Schleier der Beatrice*, 1901) and *Young Medardus* (*Der junge Medardus*, 1910). The former has some thirty-five, the latter some seventy-five characters, not to mention numerous supernumeraries. Each is a lengthy five-act play. *Young Medardus* has in addition a prologue and each act is subdivided into several scenes making a total of seventeen. Even with considerable cuts it requires five hours to be played. *The Veil of Beatrice* is composed in fluent and polished verse and is an outstanding contribution to the modern poetic drama. *Young Medardus* is written in un-

usually effective and characteristic prose. Both works
are historical dramas, the former taking us back to
Bologna in the year 1500, with Cesare Borgia before
the gates about to capture the city, while the scene
of the latter is Vienna in 1809 with Napoleon victori-
ously approaching, and establishing himself in the
castle at Schönbrunn. Neither Borgia nor Napoleon
actually appears on the stage, but they loom all the
more ominously in the background. Both plays transport us most vividly into the spirit and atmosphere of
their respective times. This, however, was only an inci-
dental object. Schnitzler's purpose was rather to create
human beings and to portray the infinite complexities
of the human soul; and by placing his characters in a
remote period, the essential human traits stand out
in bolder relief.

Four additional full-fledged plays, a group of mar-
ionettes and a one-acter were written by Schnitzler
within the first decade of the present century. Of these
The Lonely Way (*Der einsame Weg,* 1904) and *The
Vast Country* (*Das weite Land,* 1911) are justly considered two of the finest products of his genius. It
grows increasingly difficult in the case of the author's
maturer plays to summarize their content or to convey any adequate notion of the richness of their tex-
ture, the profundity of their wisdom, their emotional
appeal and the delicacy of execution. As Richard
Specht has pointed out, the concept of the dramatic
"hero" disappears more and more, not only in the
sense that the plays are mostly concerned with un-
heroic people, but because a single person no longer
occupies the center of the stage, and because in reality there are as many dramas as there are characters
in the play.

The Lonely Way is principally a tragedy of senescence, a theme we also encounter among others in *The Vast Country,* in *Bertha Garlan* and *Doctor Graesler* and especially in *Casanova's Homecoming.* Intimately related to this is the utter loneliness which is the mortal lot of all human beings. It is the life-like characters and the autumnal atmosphere tinged with poignant yearning and melancholy resignation that lend the play its value and rare charm.

The Vast Country, a study of sexual infidelity, is one of the most effective stage plays Schnitzler has composed, but a much more searching analysis of marital relations is *Intermezzo* (*Zwischenspiel,* 1906) for which Schnitzler received the famous Grillparzer prize in 1907. The musician Amadeus Adams and his wife Cecilia, an operatic star, have contracted a superior kind of marriage, one based on absolute sincerity and truthfulness. For six or seven years this proves entirely successful. Then Amadeus begins to succumb to the charms of a countess, one of his pupils, while Cecilia is attracted by a prince who pays attentions to her. In utter frankness, but somewhat reluctantly on the part of Cecilia, they agree to part company for the summer, each to enjoy the fullest freedom, but they see no reason why, having so many interests in common, they should not continue in the fall to live under the same roof as friends and comrades. Amadeus of course has no compunctions about profiting by his liberty, whereas Cecilia is somehow deterred from taking the ultimate step. But she has returned with her senses deeply stirred and is radiant with a new beauty. Amadeus woos her like a new sweetheart and is successful in winning her love for one night. But then to his consternation and grief she insists on a complete separation: they were neither made to be forever true to each other, nor strong enough to keep their friendship pure. Brilliant as this play is in ideas, sparkling in wit and superior in dialogue, somehow the psychological subtleties seem to be carried too far and the solution does not seem entirely convincing.

The Call of Life (*Der Ruf des Lebens,* 1906) deals not only with the instinct to live at all costs, but suggests that the value of life is determined by the variety and intensity of our experiences. Only those who have much to remember will rest quietly in the earth, says young Catherine Richter, who is doomed to an early death. It is one of the motifs that run through *The Veil of Beatrice,* the concluding words of which are: "It is not time that measures life, but fullness." There is here much mellow wisdom and an unqualified affirmation of life as the supreme good.

II

Until some half-dozen years ago Schnitzler's fame in this country rested almost exclusively on his dramatic productions. This was due primarily to the fact that his prose works, with a few minor exceptions, were not accessible to American readers, whereas *Anatol, The Fairy Tale, The Green Cockatoo* and other works had been successfully staged at various times and places. But as we have attempted to point out, from the very beginning of his career Schnitzler has devoted himself with equal zeal and success to prose fiction. In the collected edition narrative and dramatic works are about equally represented. Seldom has a writer of genius so distinguished himself in both fields with such signal honors as has Arthur Schnitzler. It was only when the present publishers initiated the formidable series of prose translations that this fact was brought home to American readers. Now, however, there is danger that the excessive emphasis on the author's fiction will eclipse his reputation as a playwright.

At the beginning of the present century Schnitzler wrote and published a story which European critics have long considered one of his early masterpieces, *None but the Brave* (*Leutnant Gustl,* 1901), included in this volume. Here the author presents to us with astonishing veracity the entire stream of consciousness of a young lieutenant during one fateful night in his career. His most intimate thoughts with all the relevant and irrelevant associations of ideas are set down by the author so vividly and convincingly that the reader almost shrieks with delight.

The publication of this story in the Christmas supplement of the *Neue Freie Presse* in 1900 at once provoked indignation in military circles. Shortly afterwards proceedings were instituted against Schnitzler by a military court of honor. The author, however, firmly and consistently declined to appear before it or to submit a statement in defense òf himself, as he considered his literary activity beyond the jurisdiction of the military authorities. Several months later he was formally deprived of his commission in the medical branch of the reserve for having disparaged the army and for his failure to challenge a denunciatory newspaper critic.

There are certain superficial points of resemblance between *Bertha Garlan* (1901) and *Beatrice* (*Frau Beate und ihr Sohn,* 1913), the latter included in this

volume. Both novelettes are revealing and sympathetic
analyses of a woman's psyche. Both of the titular hero-
ines are widows and both have a son. Both women
have passed the prime of youth, but they experience
a belated flickering of the flame of erotic passion,
which, however, proves illusory.

After a loveless match with a distant relative, Bertha
Garlan is eking out her meager income with music
lessons. In her drab existence in the provincial town
where she now lives she is stirred with the memories
of a harmless love-affair from her conservatory days.
The fame of Emil Lindbach, now a celebrated violinist, has reached even her secluded retreat, and acting
on a sudden impulse she dispatches a letter to him.
The latter gallantly replies, arranges a rendezvous
with her in Vienna, and unhesitatingly reaps the fruit
of such an easy conquest. Shocked into a realization
that the passion of this one night was the only interest
he had in her, she returns to the monotonous round
of her life in the small town.

Again it is not the plot as such that is of striking
interest, but the delicate and yet ruthless dissection
and portrayal of the soul of Bertha Garlan. Incidentally
the author has sketched in a half-dozen episodic characters in this small town so skilfully and convincingly
that the very atmosphere of the place seems to vibrate
with life.

The problem in *Beatrice* is entirely different. In a
most subtle and delicate fashion the author here depicts among other things a mother-son complex which
verges on incest. It is partly the mother's jealousy that
induces her to intervene between her son and the
wicked enchantress. It is because her son is becoming
more and more identified in her mind with the image

of her deceased husband that the temptation to which he is exposed also rouses her slumbering passions. It is this intimate blending of the maternal and the erotic instincts that ultimately cause her tragedy. Although written in a subdued tone, this relentless probing of the murky abysses of even such a pure soul as Beatrice inspires the reader with a disconcerting apprehension.

The analysis of *Doctor Graesler* is also more depressing than exhilarating in its pathetic revelation of the essential poverty of this man's emotional life. With consummate artistry, with admirable objectivity, and yet with a gentle touch of irony, the changing moods and the self-delusions of this mediocre personality are disclosed. Despite the general drabness of background, in keeping with the author's purpose, all the figures stand out in plastic relief.

There is a striking parallelism to be found between Schnitzler's own life at a given period and the prevailing type of characters he has created and the general themes that attracted his interest. At the outset of his career young men of the world of the type of Anatol predominated. The amours of these more or less irresponsible young men were simply taken for granted and the paramount problems were those of jealousy and infidelity, in endless variations. After the turn of the century when the author crossed the threshold of forty and himself contracted a marriage, his characters are as a rule of maturer age and the problem of matrimony frequently comes to the fore. With advancing years it was only natural that the approach of age too should claim his attention as a subject for poetic treatment. It will suffice to point to *Bertha Garlan* and *Beatrice,* to Friedrich Hofreiter in

The Vast Country, to Julian Fichtner and Stephan
von Sala in *The Lonely Way,* and finally to *Doctor
Graesler* as illustrations of the author's absorbing interest in this phase of man's life.

The most superb treatment of this theme, however,
is to be found in *Casanova's Homecoming* (Casanova's
Heimfahrt, 1918), a novelette which has attained unnecessary notoriety because of the exceptional moral
sensitiveness of Mr. John S. Sumner. We meet Casanova in his old age, keenly aware of the fact that his
days of glory are over. But instead of resigning himself philosophically to his fate, he rebels against it in
impotent rage. Unsuccessful in his wooing of the
lovely young Marcolina who experiences merely a
feeling of loathing and disgust, he resorts to a despicable
deception to gain his ends. His delusion of being
superior to the ravages of time is horribly shattered
and he emerges from this adventure only a more piti-
able and pathetic character.

12

From 1905 to 1907 Schnitzler labored over his first
full-length novel, *The Road to the Open* (*Der Weg
ins Freie*), which appeared in 1908. In composing the
work he was spurred by the ambition to produce the
outstanding novel of Viennese life. Opinions may
differ as to whether he has succeeded in realizing his
ideal, but there can be no doubt that the book con-
stitutes one of his most important works. It is perhaps
the most personal work he ever created. Into it he
poured all his pent-up thoughts and emotions concerning the most vital problems of an intellectual in
Vienna, and more specifically of a Jew living in a

hostile, anti-Semitic community. With his keen perception Schnitzler illuminates every angle of this complex problem without personally committing himself to any one solution. If there is a single work of Schnitzler that may be considered in the light of a personal confession it is *The Road to the Open*. Furthermore, the author has utilized his friends and acquaintances as models for the majority of these characters, which lends the book an additional aspect of verisimilitude and conviction.

Anti-Semitism and Austrian politics again play an important part in *Professor Bernhardi* (1913). The play is unique in that of twenty characters there is only one female rôle, and that an unimportant nurse. The erotic element is completely lacking. What we have here in its larger ethical aspects is not the conflict between science and religion, not an anti-Catholic polemic, and not an exposé of the anti-Semitism rampant in Vienna. The play is rather a treatment of the problem of personal responsibility.

Dramatically it is a character study in the form of a comedy. Professor Bernhardi at once calls to mind Dr. Stockmann in Ibsen's *An Enemy of the People*. Both are animated by the noblest motives, both are unnecessarily tactless and obstinate. Schnitzler here glorifies the self-abasing devotion of a high-minded man to his chosen profession in contrast with the petty, self-seeking machinations of a politically oriented group. Similarly young Dr. Stauber in *The Road to the Open* has decided to give up politics and return to his old love, bacteriology. It's a cleaner occupation, he remarks. The play is a devastating commentary on political conditions in Austria under the old regime. How accurately Schnitzler had depicted these was revealed in 1921. The notorious riots in connection with the performance of Schnitzler's *Reigen* clearly showed that even the revolution had not brought about any fundamental change.

In Vienna, as was to be expected, *Professor Bernhardi* fell under the ban of the censor, but it was successfully produced in Berlin, Budapest, Zurich, Berne, Stockholm, and other cities in 1913, and in the old Irving Place Theatre in New York in January, 1914. After the censorship had been abolished by the revolution, the Deutsches Volkstheater in Vienna, which had originally sponsored the play, hastened to redeem its pledge, and in December, 1918 scored a signal success with it.

During the first year of the war Schnitzler completed a cycle of three one-act plays bearing the general title *Comedy of Words* (*Komödie der Worte*). All three deal with marital infidelity, not merely with that of the husband which in Schnitzler's works is usually taken for granted and not considered to constitute a problem. In two of the plays it is the unfaithfulness of the wives that causes the complications. In the third the wife is only tempted to do likewise as a result of the flagrant, unprincipled amours of her actor-husband, but she is deterred from taking the ultimate step. In his mellow wisdom Schnitzler seems to point out that mere infidelity does not exclude genuine love and is after all a minor consideration in the institution of matrimony, that its ultimate value and significance lie in the community of interests between the partners. Especially the wives in these plays hold a firm conviction that their husbands' need of them to encourage and sustain them far transcends any other considerations. These plays excel in their finesse of workmanship and their dramatic effectiveness on the stage. On this score they not only rank with the best work Schnitzler has produced, but it would be difficult to find any one-acters in all of modern German literature to surpass them.

Five additional plays were launched by Schnitzler since the war. None of these has been translated or produced in this country, nor have they found great favor abroad. *Fink and Fliederbusch* (1917) is a journalistic comedy which abounds in clever dialogue and has some amusing situations, but is not one of his major achievements. *Casanova or the Sisters in Spa* (1919) is in verse. In a delightfully light and yet significant manner it deals with another window-climbing escapade of Casanova in his prime. The *Comedy of Seduction* (*Komödie der Verführung,* 1924) and *The Forest Pool* (*Der Gang zum Weiher,* 1926) contain some of Schnitzler's most mature observations on a variety of subjects, but they are too heavily freighted with ideas and too top-heavy in construction to make a wide appeal. Finally, in *The Play of Summer Breezes* (*Im Spiel der Sommerlüfte,* 1930) the dramatist reverts to the relative simplicity of content and technical execution of some of his earliest plays. If not a masterpiece, it is a noteworthy addition to the many brilliant works of his genius.

13

During the war Schnitzler's reputation as a playwright began to wane. This can be easily accounted for. In the first place, the war-conscious people of Europe demanded, not artistic creation, but works which dealt with their immediate problems. This atti-

tude was even more pronounced in the years directly
following the war when economic misery and political
questions occupied the center of the stage, and when
the expressionists dominated the literary field. Schnitzler refused to compromise with the demands of the
moment and continued to develop his art in accord-
ance with the laws innate in his artistic personality.
In recent years, however, his fame as a writer of prose
fiction has grown by leaps and bounds. This is particularly true in America where in the last decade his
reputation as a dramatist has been almost completely
eclipsed by his renown as a novelist.

Fräulein Else included in this volume, was published
in German in 1924. It was Schnitzler's first narrative
work in six years. The germ of the story extends back
to a much earlier period. While the author was dining
in a fashionable hotel, an unusually beautiful woman
entered the dining room. The thought flashed through
Schnitzler's mind, what would happen if the lady
suddenly stood there completely nude. As a doctor
he told himself that such an occurrence might be
motivated by a pathological condition, but this was
rejected as too commonplace and unpoetic. The idea
was merely jotted down for the time being. It did not
become fruitful until many years later when a financial
crisis in the family of a relative, similar to the one de-
scribed in the novelette as overtaking Else's father,
provided a connecting link. However, another period
of years was to elapse before the story was finally composed. This is entirely typical of Schnitzler's usual
method of creation.

In technique *Fräulein Else* is a continuation and
refinement of the method that proved so successful in
None but the Brave, slightly modified in that we also

have occasional bits of dialogue interspersed with
Else's stream of consciousness. With almost incredible
veracity the author reveals to us not merely Else's outward position in life, her state of mind and her emotional conflicts, but in addition the members of her
family, her relatives and friends, and mere casual acquaintances stand out in sharp relief. The ability to
combine with this astounding knowledge of every
cranny of Else's soul such sheer power of narration,
such sustained emotional suspense, is nothing short
of virtuosity.

Of less sparkling brilliance and less dramatic intensity, but of more abiding interest and more poetic
charm, *Rhapsody* (*Traumnovelle*, 1926), included in
this volume, takes up again a theme that had repeatedly
occupied Schnitzler, the borderline between illusion
and reality, dreaming and waking. Furthermore, it
points out once more the tenuousness of marital bonds.
The dual nature of human beings, the resulting in-
stability of human relations, and the unpredictability
of human conduct are here subtly set forth in a delicately wrought and superbly polished tale.

As early as 1891 Schnitzler had contributed to a
Viennese periodical a gambling tale entitled *Wealth*
(*Reichtum*) which, on the occasion of Schnitzler's
sixtieth birthday, Hugo von Hofmannsthal singled out
for especial commendation. Naturally in the two works
dealing with Casanova, playing for stakes also figures
prominently. But by far the most perfect treatment of
this theme is to be found in *Daybreak* (*Spiel im
Morgengrauen*, 1927), included in this volume. There
is reason to believe that Schnitzler has drawn heavily
on personal experiences of his earlier years in depicting
the feverish excitement of thus matching yourself

against the whims of fate. *Daybreak* is more a novel
of incident than one of subtle psychological analysis.
Once the reader exposes himself to its insinuating
charm, he is irresistibly carried along by the succession
of thrilling events. The author merely presents his
characters without comment. Yet there is implied in
this calm and even tolerant portrayal of Lieutenant
Willi Kasda a criticism of certain pre-war officers and
their code of honor more telling even than in *None
but the Brave.*

Theresa (1928), finally, occupies an almost unique
position in Schnitzler's creative work. It is his only
full-length novel except *The Road to the Open.* But
novel is not the appropriate term for this book. The
author himself designates it as "A Chronicle of a
Woman's Life." Its genesis dates back to 1892. At that
time the author published a short sketch entitled *The
Son (Der Sohn)* in the *Freie Bühne* of Berlin, thus
incidentally initiating his contact with his later publisher S. Fischer. With minor modifications this sketch
contains the essential facts of the two concluding chap-
ters of the chronicle. The novelist has merely supplied
the whole antecedent history of Theresa.

Theresa's harrowing experiences are an appalling
commentary on the futility and misery of the average
human life, and on the shocking lack of the most ele-
mentary human kindness in the more fortunate members of the human family. Schnitzler may be decried as
a pessimist, but any honest investigation would undoubtedly reveal that he has not been given to exag-
geration, that Theresa's lot is a typical one. To some
readers the book may seem slightly monotonous, but
obviously the apparent repetition of similar scenes and
experiences was deliberately designed by the author

to produce the cumulative effect he wished to achieve. In many respects *Theresa* is the crowning achievement of his long and distinguished career.

14

Looking back, it is indeed a long way from *Anatol* to *Theresa*. During these forty years of creative effort Schnitzler composed and published approximately fifty separate works. His reception by the public was marked by many disagreeable and discouraging experiences. Almost every new work called forth a flood of savage denunciations because of his alleged immorality or his subversive, anti-patriotic tendencies. In a number of cases he came into actual conflict with the civil and military authorities. On the other hand, there was no lack of favorable and even enthusiastic comment, and compensations of a more substantial nature. His books were translated into almost every civilized tongue, including the Japanese. In the theatre he soon became a figure of international importance. Up to the war the distinguished Burgtheater in Vienna with its extensive repertory gave over two hundred performances of plays by Schnitzler, more than double the number of those by any other Austrian playwright. In 1908 he was awarded the famous Grillparzer prize, in 1914 the Raimund prize, and in 1920 the Volkstheater prize of Vienna. Several years ago he was elected Honorary President of the P. E. N. Club, and in 1926 he became a member of the Prussian Academy of Arts.

The hostilities Schnitzler encountered left him undaunted, the signal honors bestowed upon him failed to corrupt his artistic conscience. Unperturbed he pursued his work with an eye ever single to the artistic requirements of his subject. He labors over his works with incredible patience. Before a play or a novel leaves his hands it has been recast, revised and filed, not once, but innumerable times. Even after publication he views his works with complete objectivity and is his own most severe critic.

Since the war Schnitzler has frequently been assailed abroad for not dealing with the pressing questions of the day. This is not due to lack of interest, for he is fully abreast of his time and keenly alive to all the insistent problems that face the world. But in the very nature of things these problems of the moment are very transitory and change from decade to decade and from generation to generation. Schnitzler is no politician or economist or social reformer. He is a psychologist interested in the mysteries of the human soul which is more or less the same at all times and in all countries. For that reason he has no need ever to become didactic or polemical. He does not want to preach or propagate some pet idea, but merely presents human beings as he sees them. Even though the setting and atmosphere in his works is intensely local, it is because of the universality of his themes and the life-likeness of his characters that he has been able to win such a large international following.

It may not be amiss to say a word about Schnitzler's relations to Freud. That he knows Freud goes without saying. But that he merely absorbs Freud's teachings and then applies them in his writings, as is sometimes asserted, is a mistaken notion. The most that can be said is that Schnitzler and Freud are psychic twins. Both, however, proceed independently. As we have seen, early in his career Schnitzler, like Freud, experimented with hypnotism. Two of the chief

Freudian principles, the wish-fulfillment of dreams and the so-called catharsis or abreaction of the psychoanalytic method were clearly expressed by Schnitzler in *Paracelsus* and *The Veil of Beatrice* before the appearance of Freud's *The Interpretation of Dreams.* For the greater part of his life Schnitzler has kept a record of his dreams and analyzed and interpreted them according to a method of his own. On many important points he differs from Freud who, contrary to Schnitzler, sometimes goes to absurd extremes. In Schnitzler it is the combination of the clarity of vision of the man of science and the intuition of the artist that enables him to peer so deeply into the human soul.

Schnitzler may not have the range or the power of some of the other great figures in the world's literature, but within his chosen field he has well-nigh achieved perfection. If he has not ventured beyond the limits which he has deliberately set himself, he has also avoided the pitfalls that have entrapped many another author. He has always preserved his artistic and intellectual integrity. Besides enriching us with more than a score of brilliantly executed works of art, he has in addition greatly extended the boundaries of our knowledge of human nature.

New York
January first, 1931

DAYBREAK

Translated from the German of
SPIEL IM MORGENGRAUEN

by

WILLIAM A. DRAKE

I

"Lieutenant! . . . Lieutenant! . . . Lieutenant!"

Only after the third call did the young officer move, stretch himself, and turn his head toward the door. Still drunk with sleep, he muttered among the pillows: "What's up?" Then, having roused himself, and seeing that it was only his orderly standing in the shadows near the half-opened door, he shouted:

"What the devil do you want, so early in the morning?"

"There is a gentleman below in the court, Sir, who wishes to speak with the Lieutenant."

"What kind of a gentleman? What time is it, then? Haven't I told you often enough that I don't wish to be disturbed on Sundays?"

The orderly stepped over to the bed and handed Wilhelm a visiting card.

"Do you take me for an owl, you blockhead? Do you think I can read in the dark? Put up the shades!"

Even before the command was finished, Joseph had opened the inner shutters of the window and drawn up the dirty white curtain. The Lieutenant, half sitting in the bed, was now able to read the name on the card. He let it fall on the covers, looked at it again, ran his fingers through the morning dishevel of his blond, close-cropped hair, and considered hastily:

"Send him away?—Impossible!—There's no occasion for that. If I receive a person, that certainly does not imply that I am intimate with him. Anyway, it

3

was only because of debts that he had to quit. Others simply have better luck. But what can he want of me?"

He turned again to the orderly:

"How does he look, the Lieut— I mean, Herr von Bogner?"

The orderly replied with a broad, but somewhat melancholy smile:

"If I may be permitted to say so, Sir, the Lieutenant looked better in his uniform."

Wilhelm was silent for a moment. Then he sat up more comfortably in the bed:

"Well, ask him to come in. And beg the Lieutenant to be so good as to excuse me if I am not yet quite dressed. And see here—this applies to every one!—if any of the other gentlemen should ask for me—Lieutenant Hoechster, or Lieutenant Wengler, or the Captain, or anybody at all—I am not at home. Do you understand?"

As Joseph closed the door behind him, Wilhelm quickly pulled on his blouse, arranged his hair and, crossing to the window, looked down into the still deserted courtyard of the barracks; and as he saw his former comrade below, walking up and down with bowed head, his stiff black hat pressed down on his forehead, in an unbuttoned yellow overcoat, with brown and somewhat dusty oxfords, he grew sick at heart. He opened the window and was almost on the point of beckoning to him and greeting him aloud; but at that moment his orderly approached the waiting man, and Wilhelm observed, on the painfully drawn face of his old friend, the emotion with which he awaited the answer. Since it was favorable, Bogner's features lightened in a smile, and he disappeared with the orderly through the door beneath Wilhelm's

window—which the latter now closed, as though sur-
mising that the coming conversation would doubtless
make such a precaution necessary. And suddenly the
odor of the forest and of spring was gone—an odor
which permeated the barracks courtyard on such Sunday mornings as this, but, curiously enough, could
hardly ever be noticed on the week-days. Let happen
what may, thought Wilhelm—and what could happen, anyway?—I'm going to Baden today, and I'll
have luncheon at the Stadt Wien—that is, if they
don't keep me to dine at the Kessners', as they did the
last time.

"Come in!" And with a rather exaggerated cordial-
ity, Wilhelm held out his hand. "How are you, Bogner? I'm delighted to see you. Won't you take off your
coat? Yes, look round; everything the same as ever.
The place hasn't gotten any larger. 'But there's room
in the smallest hut for a happy . . .' "

Otto smiled politely, as if he were aware of Wilhelm's embarrassment and wished to help him out
of it.

"I hope," he said, "that your quotation about the
'smallest hut' usually fits better than it does at the
present moment."

Wilhelm laughed, more loudly than was necessary.

"Unfortunately, not often. I live quite simply. I assure you that, for six weeks at least, there has not been
a woman in this room. Plato was a rascal, compared
with me. But won't you sit down?" He took some
linen from a chair and threw it onto the bed. "And
mayn't I offer you a cup of coffee?"

"Thank you, Kasda, don't trouble yourself. I have
already had breakfast. . . . A cigarette, though, if you
don't mind . . ."

Wilhelm would not permit Otto to use his own case, but pointed to the smoking stand, where lay an open box of cigarettes. Wilhelm offered his guest a light. Otto inhaled a few draughts, when his glance chanced to fall upon a well-known picture which hung on the wall above the black leather divan—an old-time representation of an officers' steeplechase.

"Well, now, tell me of yourself," said Wilhelm. "How have you been? Why has no one heard from you in such a long time? When we parted, two or three years ago, you did promise that, now and then—"

But Otto interrupted him:

"It was better, perhaps, that I did not let anybody see or hear of me. And it certainly would have been better if I had not been obliged to come here today." And—rather surprisingly, Wilhelm thought—he sat down in a corner of the divan, the opposite corner of which was filled with a clutter of books. "For, as you may well imagine, Willi"—he spoke rapidly and sharply—"my visit today, at this unusual hour—I know you like to sleep late on Sundays—my visit has, of course, a purpose. Otherwise, I should not have permitted myself—to be brief, I have come in the name of our old friendship, since unluckily I can no longer say, 'our comradeship.' You needn't grow so pale, Willi. It's not so dangerous. It's a question of a few gulden, which I simply must have by tomorrow morning. Otherwise, there is nothing left for me but to do that"—his voice rose in a military harshness—"that which I should have done two years ago, had I been wise."

"What utter nonsense!" Wilhelm observed, in a tone of annoyance, tempered by friendly embarrassment.

The orderly brought in breakfast and disappeared. Willi poured the coffee. He was sensible of an acrid taste in his mouth, and it vexed him that he had not been able to complete his morning toilet. However, he had planned to take a Turkish bath on his way to the station. If he reached Baden by noon, there would still be time. He had made no definite appointment; and if he were to arrive late, even if he were not to come at all, nobody would think it strange—neither the gentlemen at the Café Schopf, nor Fräulein Kessner; though perhaps her mother, who was not at all a bad sort, would wonder why he had not come.

"Please, please go on," he said to Otto, who had not yet put the cup to his lips.

The latter took a hasty sip, and began at once:

"I shall tell it briefly. Perhaps you know that, for the last three months, I have held the position of cashier in the office of an electrical installation company. But how should you know that? You do not even know that I am married—that I have a four year old boy. You see, I had him already when I was still here. Not a soul knew of it. Well, I did not have such a fortunate time of it. I fancy you will understand. And particularly this last winter. The boy was ill. The details can't be of any interest to you—but then, on several occasions, I was forced to borrow a little out of the drawer. I always put it back at the proper time. But this time, as my luck would have it, the circumstances were quite exceptional, and . . ." —he paused for a moment, while Wilhelm stirred his coffee with his spoon—"and, to make matters worse, by mere chance I have learned that a thorough inspection is to be made, beginning with the factory. The auditor will come Monday, that is, tomorrow. We are

a branch, you understand, and we take care of only
very small accounts. As a matter of fact, it is only a
mere nothing that I owe—nine hundred and sixty
gulden. I might say, a thousand—that is about the
same. But nine hundred and sixty is the amount. And
I must have them by tomorrow morning, at half-past-
nine. Otherwise . . . Well, in any case, you would
be doing me a really tremendous favor, Willi, if you
could spare me this sum."

Suddenly he could go no further. Willi was a little
abashed for him, not so much on account of the petty
infidelity or fraud—for it was really fraudulence!—
of which his former comrade had been guilty, but
rather because the sometime Lieutenant Otto von Bogner, who, only two years ago, had still been a smart,
popular and well-situated officer, now sat, pale and
crumpled, leaning against the end of the divan, unable to continue on account of his tears.

He placed his hand on Otto's shoulder. "See here,
Otto," he said, "you must not abandon hope so
quickly!"

And, as Otto, with a desolate, frightened air, looked
up at this somewhat inauspicious beginning, he added:
"That is, I am myself somewhat low in funds just now.
My whole fortune consists of about one hundred
gulden. One hundred and twenty, to be as accurate
as you have been. It goes without saying that the
entire amount is at your disposal, down to the last copper. It isn't enough, of course. But if we set ourselves
to it, we shall certainly be able to think of some
way out."

Again, Otto cut him short:

"You may be sure that I have just about exhausted
all the possible ways. We must not waste time racking

our brains unnecessarily—especially, since I already
have a definite suggestion."

Wilhelm looked at him intently.

"Try to imagine, Willi, that you yourself were in
just such a difficulty. What would you do?"

"I don't quite understand," Wilhelm replied, a little
stiffly.

"Naturally, I know perfectly well that you have
never taken money from a stranger's cash drawer—
that is something that can only happen to a man in
civil life. Agreed! Still, for the sake of argument, if,
for some less criminal reason, it became absolutely
necessary for you to obtain a certain sum of money, to
whom would you go?"

"I beg your pardon, Otto, but I have never thought
of such a necessity arising, and I hope . . . Of course,
I have sometimes had debts. I do not deny that. Only
last month Hoechster had to help me out with fifty
gulden, which, of course, I paid him back on the first.
That is how I chance to be so short just now. But a
thousand gulden—a thousand!—I certainly do not
know where I could lay hold of such an amount."

"You really do not?" said Otto, looking him squarely
in the eye.

"That is what I said."

"And your uncle?"

"What uncle?"

"Your Uncle Robert."

"What makes you think of him?"

"Why, it is perfectly natural. He has helped you
out on several occasions. And you have a regular allowance from him, as well."

"There has been no allowance for a long time,"
Willi replied, annoyed by the hardly appropriate tone

of his former comrade. "And not only has there been no allowance. Uncle Robert has turned out an eccentric. In point of fact, I haven't set eyes on him in a year. And the last time I asked him for a little something—as a very special accommodation—well, he practically threw me out of the house."

"Indeed, is that so?" Bogner passed his hand across his forehead. "So you would consider that possibility absolutely ruled out?"

"I hope you don't doubt my word!" Wilhelm replied, somewhat sharply.

Suddenly Bogner forsook the corner of the divan, pushed the table aside, and went over to the window.

"We must take a chance," he declared, with assurance. "Yes, pardon me, but we must! The worst that could happen would be that he may refuse, and it is possible that he may not be too polite about it. I grant you that. But, as compared with what will probably happen to me if I do not succeed in gathering together a few paltry gulden by tomorrow morning, that is only a minor annoyance."

"Very likely!" said Wilhelm, "but an annoyance absolutely to no good purpose. If there were only the slightest chance—well, I certainly trust that you have no doubt of my good intentions. The devil take it! There must be other possibilities! For example—you mustn't be angry; I just chanced to think of him!— how about your cousin Guido, who has the estate near Amstetten?"

"I assure you, Willi," Bogner replied, calmly, "that there is no possibility of getting anything from him. If there were, I should not be here. In other words, there is not a person on the face of the earth—"

Willi suddenly lifted his finger, as if an idea had come to him.

Bogner gazed at him, in eager expectation.

"If you were to try Rudy Hoechster! Only a few months ago, as it happens, he received an inheritance! Twenty or twenty-five thousand gulden! Something must be left of all that!"

Bogner's face clouded, and he answered, with some hesitation:

"I have already written to Hoechster. Three weeks ago, when the situation was not yet so serious. And I asked him for much less than a thousand. He didn't even answer me. So, you see, your uncle affords really the only way out." And, as Willi shrugged his shoulders, he added: "I know him, Willi—a very sympathetic, charming old gentleman. We were at the theatre together several times, and at Riedhof's—he no doubt will remember! Good God, you certainly cannot tell me that he has suddenly become another man!"

Willi interrupted him, impatiently :

"And still it seems that he has! I myself don't know what has really happened to him. But it's not uncommon for people in their fifties and sixties to change very conspicuously. I can say no more than this—that for fifteen months or more, I have not entered his house, and that, moreover, I shall never enter it again, under any circumstances."

Bogner stared fixedly ahead of him. Presently he raised his head, gazing beyond Willi as if the latter did not exist, and said:

"Well, I am sorry to have troubled you. Good-bye!"

And, taking his hat, he turned to the door.

"Otto!" Willi cried, "I have had another idea!"

"Another! What does it matter!"

"But you must listen to me, Bogner! I am going to
the country today—to Baden. There, on Sunday afternoons, in the Café Schopf, we sometimes gamble a
little—a friendly break at Vingt-et-un or else Baccarat, one or the other. Of course, I take only a very
small part in the game, or perhaps I even stay out of
it altogether. I have played three or four times, and
then only for the fun of it. The banker is Tugut, the
Army Doctor; Lieutenant Wimmer is usually there
also, and Greising, of the 77th. . . . You don't know
him. He is detailed in Baden on some outside work—
on account of an old scandal. And then, there are a
few civilians—a local lawyer, the manager of the
theatre, an actor, and an old man, a certain Consul
Schnabel. He is having an affair with a musical comedy
singer—a chorus girl, in fact. These are the regulars.
Two weeks ago, Tugut raked in three thousand gulden at a single sitting. We played on the open veranda
until six o'clock in the morning—the birds gave us a
musical accompaniment to our play. I have only my
endurance to thank for the hundred and twenty that
I now have—otherwise, I should be quite penniless.
Now, do you know what I am going to do, Otto? One
hundred of this hundred and twenty gulden, I shall
risk for you. The chance is not overwhelmingly favorable, I know, but only a few days ago, Tugut sat down
with fifty and got up with three thousand. And there
is still another point: in the last few months, I have
had no luck at all in love. Perhaps we can place more
reliance upon a proverb than we can in people."

Bogner said nothing.

"Well!" Willi demanded. "What do you think of my
idea?"

Bogner shrugged his shoulders.

"Whatever may come of it, I thank you. I thank you very much. Of course, I do not refuse. Still—"

"Naturally, I can't make any guarantees," Willi broke in, with a brave flourish of vivacity. "Still, I'm not risking very much. And if I win, if it's only one thousand—at least one thousand of it belongs to you. And if I should happen to make an extraordinary killing—"

"Don't promise too much," Otto remarked, with a melancholy smile. "But I mustn't detain you any longer. And for my own sake, too! Tomorrow morning, I shall take the liberty—rather . . . I shall be waiting, tomorrow morning, at half-past-eight, over there, near the Alser Church." As Willi attempted to reply, Bogner silenced him with a gesture, and added quickly: "Besides, I do not propose to be idle, upon my own account. I still possess a fortune of seventy gulden. I shall risk them this afternoon, at the races."

He crossed over to the window with quick steps, and looked down into the courtyard of the barracks.

"The air is very clear!" he said, and his mouth was twisted in a smile of bitter sarcasm as he spoke. Then, having given Willi his hand, he departed.

Wilhelm sighed softly, pondered for a moment, and then began to prepare himself to go out. He was not very well satisfied with the condition of his uniform. Should he win today, he was determined to buy himself at least a new cape. Because of the lateness of the hour, he abandoned the idea of a Turkish bath. But in any case, he would take a fiacre to the train. Two gulden, more or less, did not really matter today.

2

WHEN, at noon, Wilhelm left the train at Baden, he was in excellent spirits. At the station in Vienna, he had had an extremely cordial conversation with Lieutenant-Colonel Wositsky, who, when on duty, was the most disagreeable of men; and in his coupé there had been two young girls, who had carried on such an animated flirtation with him that he was relieved when they did not get out at his station, since otherwise he would not have been able to carry out the program which he had determined upon for this day. Despite his amiable mood, he was still inclined to hold some reproach against his former comrade, Bogner, not so much because he had taken the money from the drawer—an occurrence which, since it was due to his unfortunate circumstances, was to a certain extent excusable—but more particularly because of the stupid gambling scandal by which he had, three years before, cut short his promising career. An officer, certainly, ought to know just how far he can let himself go. For example, three weeks ago, when ill-luck dogged him, he had simply gotten up from the card table, in spite of the fact that Consul Schnabel, in a most charming manner, had offered him his purse. In fact, he had always known how to resist temptations, and he had always contrived to make ends meet on his small salary and the petty allowances which he had received, first from his father, and, after the latter's death as a Lieutenant-Colonel at Temesvar, from his Uncle

Robert. And when these additional remittances had ceased to come, he had known how to conform to his slighter means—he had diminished the frequency of his visits to the coffee house, cut down his purchases, saved on cigarettes, and determined that women, in the future, must not cost him anything. Only three months ago, a little adventure, which had begun most auspiciously, had ended in disaster, for the sole reason that Willi had been absolutely unable to pay for a dinner for two people.

He became truly sad, as he mused. He had never been quite so conscious of the narrowness of his circumstances as he was today—this beautiful, spring day!—as he wandered through the fragrant gardens of the country estate in which the Kessner family lived and which they doubtless owned, and considered that his cape was a little shabby, that his trousers were beginning to shine somewhat at the knees, and that his cap was too low, much lower than the newest officers' style. And today he realized, too, for the first time, that he was ashamed of the fact that he hoped for an invitation to remain to dinner; or rather, he was ashamed of the fact that this expectation should have presented itself to him with the urgency of hope.

Nevertheless, he was by no means displeased when his hope was fulfilled, not only because the meal was delightfully appointed and the wine excellent, but likewise because of Fräulein Emily, who sat at his right, and who made an exceedingly agreeable neighbor at table, with her friendly glances and her familiar touches, which might, however, always be considered as merely accidental. He was not the only guest. There was also a young attorney, whom Herr Kessner had brought from Vienna, and who understood how to

lead the conversation into light, gay, and somewhat
ironical channels. Toward Willi, Herr Kessner was
polite, but somewhat cold; he was not greatly pleased,
on the whole, at these Sunday visits of the Lieutenant,
who had taken entirely too literally the casual invitation to stop in some time for tea, which the ladies
of the house had extended to him when he had been
presented at a ball during the last Carnival. Even the
still pretty Frau Kessner apparently retained no recollection of the fact that, two weeks ago, seated on a
secluded bench in the garden, she had neglected to
withdraw herself from the Lieutenant's bold embrace
until the sound of approaching footsteps on the gravel
path had been heard. The first subject of conversation
at the table had to do with a suit, concerning some matter which the lawyer had been administering in behalf
of Herr Kessner's factory; and the Lieutenant was
annoyed because he had not been able to understand
all of the legal expressions. Then the talk drifted to
country life and summer travel, and in this Willi was
able to take part. Two years ago, he had participated in
the Imperial manœuvres in the Dolomites, and he now
told of camping out in the open, of the two dark-
haired daughters of an innkeeper at Kastelruth, who
had been called the Two Medusæ, on account of their
unapproachability, and of a certain Field-Marshal,
who had, as it were, before Willi's own eyes, fallen
into disgrace in consequence of a bungled cavalry attack. And, as ever after his third or fourth glass of
wine, he grew more and more unaffected, sprightly,
even witty. He could note how he gradually conquered
Herr Kessner, how the lawyer's tone gradually became less ironical, how Frau Kessner's face began to
glow with a certain memory, and how the thrilling

touch of Emily's knee no longer was at pains to dissemble its intimacy as the grace of chance.

Punctually with the black coffee, an elderly, rather corpulent lady appeared, accompanied by her two daughters. Willi was presented to the newcomers as "our dancer at the Industries Ball." It soon developed that the three ladies had also resided in South Styria two years ago; and was it not the Lieutenant whom they had seen galloping past their hotel in Seis one beautiful summer day, on a coal-black horse? This Willi was reluctant to deny, although none knew better than he how unlikely it was that an obscure Lieutenant of the 89th Infantry might have been seen galloping on a proud charger through any village, in Styria or elsewhere.

The two young ladies were attractively clad in white. Fräulein Kessner, in a light, rose-colored frock, was between them: and thus all three ran mischievously over the lawn.

"Somewhat like the Three Graces, aren't they?" the lawyer observed. His tone was again ironic, and the Lieutenant was strongly tempted to demand: "What do you mean by that?" But it was easy to pass over the remark, for Fräulein Emily, out on the lawn, had turned round and was beckoning him to join her. She was blonde, slightly taller than he, and it was presumable that she might expect quite a considerable dowry. But it was still a long way to that; even to the imagining of such agreeable possibilities: and meanwhile, the thousand gulden required by his unfortunate comrade had to be procured before tomorrow morning.

So there was nothing left for him to do, in the interests of the former Lieutenant von Bogner, but to make his excuses at the very moment when the entertainment was becoming most diverting. He was made to believe that they would sincerely have liked him to remain, and he assured them of his own regret; but, unfortunately, he had made an appointment, and he felt compelled, moreover, to visit a comrade who was taking a cure in the Military Hospital for an old case of rheumatism. Again, the lawyer laughed ironically. With a smile full of promise, Frau Kessner asked if the visit must take up the whole afternoon. Willi shrugged his shoulders uncertainly. At any rate, everybody would be happy to see him again this evening, in the event he should manage to get free.

As he left the house, two elegant young men rode up in a fiacre. This did not please Willi at all. What might not happen in this house, while he was forced to sit in a wretched coffee house, earning a thousand gulden for the sake of a broken comrade! Would it not be much more wise to abandon the whole affair, and to return in half an hour, after his pretended visit to his sick friend, to the Three Graces in the beautiful garden? All the more wise, he reflected, with some complacency, since, by the law of the adage, his chances of winning at cards must assuredly have been considerably reduced by the exploits which still left their triumphant flush in his heart.

3

A YELLOW poster of the races stared out at him from the advertising column, and it occurred to him that at this hour Bogner must be at Freudenau, at the races; perhaps at this very minute he was engaged in winning the redemptory sum upon his own account. Was it credible that Bogner might remain silent about such a fortunate occurrence, and in addition, possess himself of the thousand gulden which Willi in the meantime would have won at cards from Consul Schnabel or Army Doctor Tugut? Why, certainly!—When one has fallen so low as to take money from a stranger's drawer . . . And within a few months, perhaps even a few weeks, Bogner would be in precisely the same fix that he was in now. And then what?

Willi heard music. It was some Italian overture, in that half-forgotten style which is preserved only by these resort orchestras. But Willi knew this piece very well. Many years ago, he had heard his mother play it, four hands, with some distant relative. He himself had never been privileged to be his mother's partner at duet-playing; and when she had died, eight years ago, there were no more piano lessons, such as there had been before, when he had gone home from the military academy on his vacations. Softly and poignantly, the sounds rose on the tremulous spring air.

He crossed the little bridge over the muddy Schwechat and, after a few more steps, he reached the spacious terrace of the Café Schopf. It was always crowded on Sundays. Lieutenant Greising, looking pale and malicious, sat at a little table near the street. With him sat Wiess, the fat theatre manager, in a somewhat wrinkled, canary-yellow suit, with the eternal flower in his buttonhole. Willi had some difficulty in pushing his way among the tables and chairs to reach them.

"There is nobody here today!" he observed, extending his hand.

And he reflected with relief upon the possibility that the card game would not take place. But Greising explained that they two had merely been sitting in the open air in order to recruit their energies for the "work." The others were already playing, inside. Consul Schnabel had arrived, having, as usual, come from Vienna in a fiacre.

Willi ordered an iced lemonade. Greising demanded to know where he had overheated himself, that he already needed a cooling drink, and remarked, with no further preliminaries, that the girls of Baden were decidedly pretty and temperamental. He then recounted, in not particularly choice phrases, the incidents of a trifling adventure which he had begun last evening in the park and which he had, that very night, brought to a successful conclusion. Willi drank his lemonade slowly; and Greising, who noted the tenor of the latter's thoughts, responded with a little burst of laughter. "That," he said, "is the way of the world. You may take it, or you may leave it!"

Lieutenant Wimmer, of the Transport Corps (whom the unadvised often mistook for a cavalryman) suddenly appeared behind them.

"What do you say, gentlemen," he said. "Shall we worry ourselves to death, all alone here with the Consul?"

And he extended his hand to Willi, who, in his

singularly conscientious way, although he was off
duty, had saluted his ranking comrade.

"How are things going inside?" Greising asked,
suspiciously and brusquely.

"Very slowly," replied Wimmer. "The Consul is sitting on his gold like a dragon—on my gold, at that.
So up, gentlemen, and into battle, Toreadors!"

The others rose.

"I am invited elsewhere," Willi remarked, lighting
a cigarette with feigned carelessness. "I shall just stay
round for a quarter of an hour."

"Oh, come!" Wimmer laughed. "Hell is paved with
good intentions."

"And Heaven with bad ones," added Wiess, the
manager.

"Well, said!" exclaimed Wimmer, and clapped him
on the shoulder.

They went inside the coffee house. Willi glanced
back regretfully over his shoulder out into the open,
across the roofs of the villas, towards the hills. And he
swore to himself that, in less than half an hour, he
should be sitting in the Kessners' garden.

Together with the others, he entered a dark corner
of the place, where the light and the spring air could
not penetrate. In order to indicate that he had absolutely no intention of joining in the game, he had
pulled his chair away from the table. The Consul, a
lean gentleman of uncertain age, with a mustache
trimmed in the English style and with reddish, partly
gray, thin hair, immaculately clad in a light gray suit,
was scrutinizing, with his peculiar thoroughness, a
card which Doctor Flegmann, the banker, had just
dealt him. He won, and Doctor Flegmann drew some
crisp, new notes from his wallet.

"Didn't bat an eye!" remarked Wimmer, with ironical appreciation.

"Batting one's eye won't alter accomplished facts," Flegmann answered calmly, his lids half closed. The Army Doctor Tugut, on detail in charge of the Military Hospital in Baden, laid down a bank of two hundred gulden.

The actor, Elrief, a young man from one of the leading theatres, but more celebrated for his parsimony than for his talent, allowed Willi to look at his cards. He risked small sums and, when he lost, shook his head, as if he were quite bewildered. Tugut soon doubled the capital of his bank. Wiess borrowed a small sum of money from Elrief, and Doctor Flegmann took more money out of his pocket. Tugut was on the point of withdrawing, when the Consul, without counting, cried: "Play the bank!" He lost and, with a swift glance into his wallet, he calculated his debt, which amounted to three hundred gulden. "Again!" he said. The Army Doctor refused. Doctor Flegmann took charge of the bank and dealt the cards. Willi declined to take a hand, but, purely in jest, "just to bring him luck," upon Elrief's continued pleading, he placed a gulden on the latter's card—and won. In the next deal, Doctor Flegmann tossed him a card, which he did not refuse. He won again, lost, won; he pulled his chair up to the table between the others, who very willingly made room for him, and won, lost, won, lost, as if Fate could not quite determine how she should conduct herself towards him today. Wiess had to leave to go to the theatre, and he neglected to repay his debt to Elrief, although he had already won back much more than enough. Willi was a little ahead of the game, but he still lacked nine hundred and fifty gul-

den to make up the thousand which his friend so
urgently required.

"There is nothing in this!" Greising insisted, dis-
satisfied.

The Consul took the bank again, and in a moment
every one knew that the play was at last about to become serious.

Hardly anything was known of Consul Schnabel,
except that he was the representative of a small free
state in South America and a "wholesale merchant."
It was Wiess who had introduced him into the officers' circle, and the manager's relationship with him
originated in the circumstance that the Consul had
known how to interest him in the engagement of a
minor actress, who, immediately upon her appearance
in a small part, had become very friendly with Elrief.
The company would have enjoyed engaging in the
good old custom of making sport of the deceived
lover, but when the latter, his cigar between his teeth,
would ask Elrief briefly, without looking up from the
cards which he was dealing: "Well, how goes it with
our mutual lady friend?" then it became clear that
jests and sarcasm would be lost upon such a man. This
impression was substantiated by a remark which he
had made to Lieutenant Greising. Late one night, between two glasses of cognac, the latter had once in-
dulged in certain offensive observation with regard to
the Consuls of unknown countries. "Why do you stare
at me, Lieutenant?" the Consul had replied. "Have
you already made inquiries as to whether I am of a
sufficiently high rank to give you satisfaction in a
duel?"

A long silence followed this speech, and thereafter,
as if by a tacit agreement, no further eventualities were

risked, and it was unanimously decided, although by no concerted arrangement, that the Consul must be dealt with very carefully.

The Consul lost. No one objected when he made a new bank after he had lost his first one, and, losing that as well, made up a third, although this was against the usual custom. The other players won, and especially Willi. He put his original capital, the hundred and twenty gulden, back into his pocket; these were not to be risked again, in any case. Then he laid down a bank himself. Soon he had doubled it. Then he withdrew, and, with a few aberrations, his luck held with him against the other bankers, who followed one another in quick succession. The sum of one thousand gulden which he had undertaken to win—for some one else—he had exceeded by several hundreds; and since Elrief had just risen to go to the theatre, to present himself for the rehearsal of a rôle of which he would say nothing despite the sarcastically inquisitive questions of Lieutenant Greising, Willi availed himself of the opportunity to accompany him. The others were soon deep in their play again; and when Willi turned to look at them as he reached the door, he saw that only the eye of the Consul had left the cards to follow him with a quick, cold glance.

4

Not until he stood in the open air, with the sweet night breeze sweeping his brow, did Willi fully realize the enormity of his good fortune—or rather, as he immediately corrected himself, Bogner's luck. But even when Bogner had been provided for, he would have enough left over for himself to buy a new cape, a new cap and a new sword belt, just as he had dreamed. And in addition, a sufficient surplus for a few delightful suppers in some pleasant society, which would be easily found. And without counting the fact that he would have been plentifully compensated solely in being able to turn over to his old comrade, at half-past-eight upon the morrow, in front of the Alser Church, the sum required for his salvation. Here were a thousand gulden; yes, the celebrated golden thousand, which heretofore he had only read of in books, and which he now actually had in his wallet, together with several other one hundred gulden bank-notes. Well, my dear Bogner, here they are. I have won these thousand gulden. To be absolutely precise, one thousand, one hundred and fifty-five. Then I stopped. Self-control, what? And I hope, my dear Bogner, from now on— No, no, he could not permit himself to preach. Bogner would himself adduce the necessary lesson; and it was to be expected that he would be sufficiently tactful not to make a precedent of this so happily terminated episode, and that he would not assume that he was now qualified to continue upon a friendly relationship with the Lieutenant. Still, it would perhaps be wiser, and even more correct, if he were to send his servant to the Alser Church.

On his way to the Kessners', Willi wondered if they would ask him to remain for the evening meal. Well, fortunately, the meal itself was of no importance to him now. He was rich enough to take out the whole company, if he chose. It was a pity that there was no place where one could buy flowers. But he passed a confectionery shop which was open, and decided to buy a box of bonbons; and as he reached the door, he turned back to buy another, still larger box, reflecting how he should properly divide them between the mother and daughter.

When he entered the front garden of the Kessners', a housemaid met him with the information that the entire company had gone riding in Helenental. They had probably gone to Krainer Lodge. The company would no doubt dine out, as they generally did on Sunday evenings.

A mild disappointment was visible on Willi's face, and the maid smiled at the two boxes which the Lieutenant was holding in his hands. Now what should he do with these! "Please present my respects, and—and please . . ." He extended the packages to the maid. "The larger one is for your mistress; the other, for the Fräulein. And say that I was very sorry."

"But perhaps, if the Lieutenant were to take a fiacre —the company is doubtless still at Krainer Lodge."

Willi looked at his watch, pensively and a little self-consciously.

"I'll see," he remarked carelessly, and, with a humorously exaggerated deep bow, he took his leave.

Now he stood alone in the evening street. A small

company of happy tourists, ladies and gentlemen, with
dusty shoes, passed by. In front of a villa, an old gentleman sat on a wicker chair, reading his newspaper. .
Further up the street, on a first floor balcony, an
elderly lady sat crocheting, conversing the while with
another lady in the house across the way, who was
leaning out of an open window, resting her arms on
the sill. To Willi, it seemed as if these few people
were the only ones in the town who had not fled at
this hour. The Kessners might have left some word
for him with the housemaid! Well, he had no intention of intruding. There was really no occasion for
that. But what should he do with himself? Should he
go back to Vienna? Perhaps that would be best. But
he would let Fate decide.

Two carriages stood before the casino. "How much
to Helenental?" One of the drivers was already taken;
the other one unblushingly demanded an exorbitant
fee. So Willi decided in favor of an evening walk in
the Park.

The Park was still quite crowded at this hour. There
were married couples and pairs of lovers, which Willi
had no difficulty in distinguishing apart. There were
also young girls and women, walking alone or in
twos and threes, who passed by him gaily. He encountered several smiling, even encouraging glances.
But one could never be sure that there was not a father,
a brother, or a fiancé walking behind, and an officer
must needs be twice, nay, thrice careful. He followed
a slender, dark-eyed lady, who was leading a boy by
the hand. She ascended the steps of the terrace of the
casino, seemingly looking for some one; at first, without result, until somebody eagerly beckoned to her
from a distant table: whereupon she bestowed upon

Willi a quick, triumphant glance, and joined the large company assembled there. Willi also looked round, as if he were expecting to find a friend; then he passed from the terrace into the restaurant, which was almost deserted, and went thence into the lobby, and then into the reading room, which was already lit up. There, at a long, green table, sat the solitary occupant, an old, pensioned General, in uniform. Willi saluted, bringing his heels smartly together. The General nodded with a bored expression, and Willi turned sharply round. Outside, in front of the casino, the unengaged fiacre was still waiting; and the coachman, unasked, declared himself willing to take the Lieutenant to Helenental.

"Thank you, but you are too late," Willi observed.

And, with rapid steps, he took himself off in the direction of the Café Schopf.

5

THE players were still sitting there, just as they had
been before, as if not a minute had passed since Willi's
departure. The green-shaded electric light outlined the
little group in a glare of livid brilliance. Consul Schnabel was the first to take any note of Willi's entrance,
and Willi thought that he could detect a sarcastic
smile on his lips. No one expressed the slightest surprise when Willi took his empty chair and pulled it
forward again in its old place among the others. Doctor
Flegmann, who was holding the bank, dealt him a
card, as if it were the most natural thing in the world
to do so. In his confusion, Willi put down a larger
bank-note than he had intended. He won, and pro-
ceeded more carefully. But his luck had changed, and
soon there came a moment when his thousand gulden
seemed to be in grave danger. What do I care? thought
Willi; I shouldn't have had anything from it anyhow! But now he began to win again, and he did not
find it necessary to change the bill. His luck remained
with him, and at nine o'clock, when the game ended,
Willi found himself in possesion of two thousand
gulden. A thousand for Bogner, a thousand for myself! he thought. Half of my portion I shall reserve as
a gambling fund for next Sunday! But he did not feel
as exultant as, in the nature of things, he ought to have
been.

The entire company adjourned to the Stadt Wien
for dinner. They sat under a shady oak in the garden

and spoke about gambling in general, about famous
card sessions played, for enormous stakes, at the Jockey
Club. Flegmann, the lawyer, said, with great seriousness: "Gambling is, and will always be, a vice." Everybody laughed, and Lieutenant Wimmer diverted himself by extending the remark in a queer light. That
which was possibly a vice to lawyers, he observed, was
far from being a vice to officers. Flegmann declared
politely that one may be depraved and still remain a
man of honor, and cited many examples, such as Don
Juan and the Duc de Richelieu, to prove his conten-
tion. The Consul expressed the opinion that gambling
was a vice only when one was not in a position to
pay one's gambling debts. And in such cases, he added,
it was not really a vice, but became a fraud, and a fraud
of a particularly cowardly type. There was a moment
of silence at this. But then, fortunately, Elrief appeared, with a flower in his buttonhole and with victory in his eyes.

"And did you fly so soon from the ovation?" Greising asked.

"I did not appear in the fourth act," the actor replied, and carelessly stripped off his gloves, as if he
were rehearsing for the rôle of a Viscount or a Mar-
quis.

Greising lit a cigar.

"It would be better for you if you did not smoke,"
Tugut observed.

"But, my dear Doctor!" Greising replied, "there's
nothing the matter with my throat any more."

The Consul had ordered a couple of bottles of Hungarian wine. Toasts were drunk. Willi glanced at his
watch.

"Oh, I'm so sorry!" he exclaimed. "I must go. The last train leaves at ten-forty."

"Finish your wine," said the Consul. "My carriage will take you to the train."

"Thank you, Sir, but I can't . . ."

"You can too!" Lieutenant Wimmer interrupted.

"Well, what do you say?" Doctor Tugut demanded. "Shall there be anything more doing tonight?"

No one had doubted that the session would be resumed after the evening meal. Such was the order of every Sunday. "But not for long," the Consul said. Lucky devils! thought Willi, and he envied them the prospect of sitting down at the card tables to try their luck once more, and possibly win thousands. The actor Elrief, whose wine invariably went promptly to his head, transmitted to the Consul a greeting from their mutual friend, Fräulein Rihoschek, smiling as he did so, with an inanely impudent expression on his face.

"Why didn't you bring the young lady along with you, while you were about it?" Greising demanded.

"She will come to the café in the evening, to spend a little time with us," Elrief replied. "That is," he added, mischievously, "that is, if the Consul will permit it!"

The Consul made no sign.

Willi finished his wine and rose from the table.

"Next Sunday!" Wimmer warned. "We shall take a little weight off you then!"

In that, thought Willi, you are mistaken, my fine fellow! There is no such thing as losing, if one is cautious!

"Will you be so kind, Lieutenant, as to send my coachman immediately back to the café?" the Consul asked. And, turning to the others, he added: "But, gentlemen, we must not play so late, or rather, so early, as we did the last time!"

Willi once more saluted everybody in the circle, and turned to go. He was pleasantly surprised to see the Kessner family, with the corpulent lady and her two daughters, seated at an adjacent table. Neither the ironical lawyer nor the two elegant gentlemen who had arrived at the villa in the fiacre were present. The Lieutenant was joyfully greeted. He remained standing at the table, gay and unaffected, a chic young officer, in comfortable circumstances, not to mention the three glasses of strong Hungarian wine which he had imbibed, and, at the moment, without rivals. He was invited to sit down, but he declined, thanking them and excusing himself with a vague gesture toward the entrance, where the carriage awaited him. He was asked to answer one question: who was the handsome young man in civilian attire? Ah, an actor? Elrief? Nobody knew the name. The theatre here, Frau Kessner asserted, was quite mediocre; there was not much more than operettas to be seen. And she continued, with a glance which encouraged delectable expectations, that, the next time the Lieutenant came, they might go together to visit the Arena.

"I think the nicest thing," Fräulein Kessner observed, "would be to take two boxes, next to one another."

And she smiled in the direction of Elrief, who smiled back at her.

Willi kissed the hands of all the ladies, saluted the officers at the next table once more, and, a minute later, he was sitting in the Consul's fiacre.

"Quickly!" he said to the driver. "You shall have a good tip."

Piqued by the indifference with which this promise was received, Willi reflected that the coachman was considerably deficient in respect. Still, the horses maintained an excellent pace, and in five minutes the station was reached. But at precisely the same moment, the train, which had arrived at the station a minute early, began to move. Willi leaped from the carriage, started after the lighted coaches as they began to move slowly and cumbrously over the viaduct, heard the whistle of the locomotive splinter in the night air, shook his head, and was not quite certain whether he was the more angry or pleased at his mishap. The coachman, perfectly unconcerned, sat on his high seat, stroking one of the horses with the handle of his whip.

"Well, I suppose there is nothing to be done about it!" Willi finally declared. And he turned to the coach-man.

"Back to the Café Schopf!" he directed.

6

It was pleasant to whirl through the town in a fiacre; but it would be more pleasant still, on such a mild summer evening, to be driving out into the country in the company of some attractive girl, and then to have supper, either in Rodaun or at the Rotan Stadt, out in the open. Ah, what bliss, not to have to gaze twice at every gulden before making up one's mind to spend it! Careful, Willi, careful, he said to himself; and he made a firm resolve on no account to risk all his winnings, but only half, at the most. And, moreover, he determined to employ Flegmann's system—to begin with small bets, not increasing until having won, and never to put the entire winnings back into play but only three-fourths of the total amount, and so forth. Flegmann always began with this system, but he was never able to carry it through. So, of course, he got nowhere with it.

Willi swung himself down in front of the café, before the coach had quite stopped, and gave the driver a noble tip—so much that he might have hired a carriage for the amount. The coachman was still reserved, but his thanks were friendly enough.

The company was assembled to the last person, including the Consul's friend, Fräulein Mitzi Rihoschek —a stately little person, with excessively black eyebrows, but otherwise not too highly made up, and wearing a light summer frock, with a flat-brimmed straw hat with a red band on her brown, curly hair. Thus she sat next to the Consul, one arm thrown across the back of his chair, watching his cards. He did not glance up as Willi approached the table, yet the Lieutenant could feel that the Consul was at once aware of his presence.

"Missed your train!" Greising observed.

"Half a minute late!" Willi replied.

"Yes, that's how it goes!" Wimmer remarked, and dealt the cards.

Flegmann excused himself, since he had just lost three times running. Elrief was still looking on, although he had not a kreuzer left. A heap of bills lay in front of the Consul.

"There are big doings here!" thought Willi, and he put down ten gulden instead of the five which he had actually planned to risk. His boldness was rewarded. He won, and continued to win. Fräulein Rihoschek took a bottle of cognac from the sideboard, poured out a small glass for the Lieutenant, and handed it to him with an engaging smile. Elrief begged for the loan of fifty gulden, to be repaid the next day at twelve sharp. Willi passed him a note. An instant later, it had wandered over to the Consul. Elrief arose, perspiration standing out on his forehead. Attired in the glory of his yellow flannel suit, Weiss, the manager of the company, entered at this moment and, after a low-toned conversation, was persuaded to repay the money which he had borrowed that afternoon. Elrief lost this also and, quite unlike the gallant Viscount whom he was accustomed to play on such occasions, he shoved back his chair in a rage, got up, muttering an oath, and left the room. When he did not come back after a certain time, Fräulein Rihoschek stroked the Consul's hair with a delicate and abstracted gesture, and left as well.

Wimmer and Greising, and even Tugut, had become careful as the end of the session approached; only the theatre manager still displayed some boldness. But gradually the game took the form of a duel between Lieutenant Kasda and Consul Schnabel. Willi's luck had shifted, and he had scarcely a hundred gulden left above the thousand reserved for his old comrade, Bogner. When these hundred are gone, I'll positively stop! he swore to himself. But he did not credit his own determination. What is this Bogner to me? he thought; I owe him nothing!

Fräulein Rihoschek reappeared, humming a melody. She stood before the big mirror and arranged her hair, lit a cigarette, took up a billiard cue and essayed a few shots, put the cue back in the corner, and amused herself by spinning alternately the white and the red balls on the green cloth. A cold glance from the Consul summoned her from this diversion. She began to hum again, took her place at his side, and rested her arm on the back of his chair. A student's song, shouted by a passing group of mixed voices, rose out of the silence outside. How are they going to get back to Vienna today? Willi wondered. And then it occurred to him that they might be students of the local gymnasium. Since Fräulein Rihoschek was sitting opposite him again, his luck was slowly returning. The song died out in the distance; a bell struck in a church tower.

"A quarter to one!" said Greising.

"The last bank," the Army Doctor declared.

"A bank all round?" Lieutenant Wimmer suggested. The Consul indicated his approval by a nod of his head.

Willi said not a word. He won, lost, drank a glass of cognac, won, lost, lit a fresh cigarette, won and lost. Tugut held the bank for a long time. The Consul finally relieved him of it with a high bet. Curiously enough, Elrief came back, after almost an hour's absence, and, still more curiously, he had money again. With a noble insouciance, as though nothing had occurred, he sat down, the living pattern of that Viscount whose rôle he would probably never play; and he had added a new attitude of superior indifference, which he had really copied from Doctor Flegmann, with his weary, half-closed eyes. He put down a bank of three hundred gulden, as if that were the most ordinary thing one could possibly do, and won. The Consul, without emotion, lost to him, to the Army Doctor, and especially to Willi, who was now the possessor of not less than three thousand gulden. That meant a new military cape, a new sword belt, new linen, patent leather shoes, cigarettes, suppers for two and even three, rides in the Wiener Wald, and two months' leave of absence, in addition to the time due him! At two o'clock, he had won four thousand, two hundred gulden. There they lay before him; a concrete reality which could not be doubted—four thousand, two hundred gulden, and something over. The others had all fallen to the rear, and scarcely played any more.

"That is enough!" said Consul Schnabel abruptly.

Willi did not quite know how he felt. If they stopped now, then nothing more could happen to him, and that was well. At the same time, he was possessed of an uncontrollable, an absolutely fiendish desire to play on; to conjure a few more, or even all, of those crisp thousand gulden notes from the Consul's wallet. That

would be a capital with which one could make one's
fortune! It did not necessarily always have to be Baccarat—there were still such things as the horse-races
at Freudenau and the Trabrennplatz, and there were
gambling houses as fine as at Monte Carlo on the
shore of the sea in the south. With beautiful women .
from Paris! . . . While his thoughts ran on, the Army
Doctor was attempting to rouse the Consul to one last
bank. Elrief acted as if he were the host, and served
the cognac. He himself was drinking his eighth glass.
Fräulein Rihoschek swayed her body and hummed
a soundless melody. Tugut gathered the scattered
cards and shuffled them. The Consul remained silent.
Suddenly he called the waiter and ordered two fresh
packs of cards. Everybody's eyes lit up. The Consul
looked at his watch.

"At half past two," he said, "we shall stop. That is
final!"

It was five minutes after two.

7

THE Consul put down a bank larger than any that this company had ever experienced—a bank of three thousand gulden. There was not a soul in the café, apart from the players and the single waiter. The morning songs of the birds drifted through the open door. The Consul lost, but he still maintained himself as banker. Elrief had completely recovered his losses, and a warning glance from Fräulein Rihoschek caused him to withdraw from the game. The others, who were all somewhat ahead, played modestly and carefully. Half of the bank still remained intact.

"Play the bank?" Willi suddenly proposed, and at once he was frightened at his own voice. Have I lost my mind? he thought. The Consul won, and Willi was fifteen hundred gulden the poorer. Now, remembering Flegmann's system, Willi put down a ridiculously small sum, fifty gulden, and won. How stupid! he thought. I might have won the entire sum back in one trick! Why was I so cowardly?

"The bank, again!"
He lost.
"The bank, once more!"
The Consul seemed to hesitate.
"What has come over you, Kasda!" the Army Doctor cried.

Willi laughed, and felt the intoxication rising to his head. Was it the cognac which was dulling his reasoning faculty? Evidently! Of course he had made a mistake. He had had absolutely no intention of wagering a thousand or two thousand on a single play.

"I beg your pardon, Consul! I really meant—"

The Consul did not permit him to finish. He remarked, in an amicable tone: "If you did not know what sum was in the bank, of course I will take your retraction into consideration."

"What do you mean, take it into consideration, Consul?" Willi said. "A wager is a wager!"

Was it really himself that was speaking? His words? His voice? If he lost, then it was all over with the new cape, new sword belt, the suppers in the company of amiable women. There would remain, then, only the thousand for the defrauder, Bogner—and he himself would be the same poor devil that he had been two hours ago.

Without a word, the Consul uncovered his card—nine! No one uttered it aloud, yet it could be heard all over the room, in a kind of ghost-tone. Willi felt a strange moistness on his brow. God, that went quickly! At any rate, he still had a thousand gulden lying before him; in fact, a little more. He would not count it—that might bring him ill-luck. He was still richer than he had been upon leaving the train at noon. *Today* at noon? There was nothing to compel him to risk the whole thousand at once. One might begin with a hundred, or with two hundred, Flegmann's system. Only, there was so little time left—hardly twenty minutes! Everybody was silent.

"Lieutenant?" the Consul began inquiringly.

"Certainly!" Willi laughed, and folded the thousand gulden note. "Half, Consul," he said.

"Five hundred?"

Willi nodded. The others also placed bets, but merely out of formality. The coming disruption was already apparent. Lieutenant Wimmer was standing up, with his cape round his shoulders. Tugut was leaning over the billiard table. The Consul uncovered his card—eight!—and half of Willi's thousand was gone.

He shook his head, as though there was something amiss.

"This rest," he said. I am really quite calm! he reflected. He uncovered his cards slowly. Eight! The Consul had to buy a card. Nine! And the five hundred were gone, the thousand were gone. Everything gone! Everything? No! He still had the hundred and twenty gulden with which he had come away in the morning, and even a little over that. Queer! Now he was suddenly only a poor devil, as he had been before. And the birds were singing outside . . . just as before . . . when he had been able to go to Monte Carlo. Well, it was a pity, he had to stop now; these few gulden he certainly could not afford to risk. . . . He had to stop, although there was still a quarter of an hour remaining. What shameful luck! In a quarter of an hour, he might win five thousand, just as he had lost them.

"Lieutenant?" the Consul asked.

"I am very sorry," Willi replied, in a high-pitched, grating voice, and pointed to the few miserable bills laying before him. His eyes were actually laughing, and by way of a jest, he placed ten gulden on a card. He won. Then twenty. And won again. Fifty—and won! The blood mounted to his head. He could have wept with rage. Now his luck had come—and it came too late! And with a sudden, bold resolve, he turned to the actor, who was standing behind him with Fräulein Rihoschek.

"Herr von Elrief, will you be so kind as to lend me two hundred gulden?"

"I am very sorry," Elrief replied, shrugging his shoulders with a noble gesture. "You yourself saw me lose everything, down to my last copper, Lieutenant."

It was a lie, and everybody knew it. But it seemed as if everybody thought it quite proper that the actor Elrief should lie to Willi. The Consul thrust a few notes across the table, seemingly without counting them. "Please help yourself," he said. The Army Doctor, Tugut, cleared his throat audibly. Wimmer warned: "In your place, Kasda, I should stop!" Willi hesitated.

"I don't wish to persuade you, Lieutenant," said Schnabel. He still held his hand spread lightly over the money.

Willi made a hasty movement toward the money, and then began to count it.

"There are fifteen hundred there," said the Consul; "You may be certain of it, Lieutenant. Do you want a card?"

Willi laughed.

"What else?"

"Your bet, Lieutenant?"

"Ah, not all of it!" Willi cried, his brain again becoming clear. "Poor folk must be economical! One thousand, to begin!"

He uncovered, imitating the Consul's habitual, exaggerated deliberation. Willi had to buy a card, and added a three of spades to his four of diamonds. The Consul also uncovered. He too held a seven.

"I should stop!" Lieutenant Wimmer warned once
more, and now his words resounded almost as a command. And the Army Doctor added: "Now, when
you are just about even—!" Even! Willi thought. He
calls that even! A quarter of an hour ago, I was a well-
to-do young man; now I am a pauper, and they call
that "Even!" Shall I tell them the story of Bogner?
Perhaps they would understand!

There were new cards on the table. Seven! No, he
did not wish to buy. The Consul did not even ask if
he did; he simply uncovered his eight. A thousand
lost—the figures buzzed in Willi's brain—but I shall
win them back! And if I should not, it will not make
any difference. I am just as incapable of paying back
one thousand as two thousand. Nothing matters any
more! Ten minutes still remain. I still have a chance
of winning back all of the four, or even five thousand.

"Lieutenant?" the Consul inquired.

The room was full of reverberations, for every one
was absolutely quiet, audibly quiet. And no one now
ventured to say: I should stop, if I were you. No,
Willi thought, no one dares to do that! They realize
that it would be stupidity for me to stop now. But
what sum ought he to wager? He had now only a
few hundred gulden left. Suddenly he had more. The
Consul had thrust two thousand more over to him.

"Help yourself, Lieutenant!" Assuredly, he helped
himself! and put down fifteen hundred, and won.
Now he could pay back his debt, and still have something left.

There was a hand on his shoulder.

"Kasda!" said Lieutenant Wimmer. "No more!"
His voice was hard, almost severe. I am not on duty
now, Willi remonstrated to himself, and outside the

service, I can do what I wish with my money and my
life. And this time he wagered modestly, only one
thousand gulden, and uncovered his card. Eight.
Schnabel still took his time, playing with funereal
slowness, as if he had all the time in the world. There
was still time; they were not obliged to stop at half-
past-two. The last time, they had played till six. The
last time . . . that beautiful, distant time. Why were
they all standing round him? Just as in a dream. There,
they were all more excited than he; even Fräulein
Rihoschek, standing across from him, with her straw
hat and its red band surmounting her curly hair, had
curiously shining eyes. He smiled at her. She had a
face like the queen in a tragedy, although she was
little better than a chorus girl. The Consul uncovered his cards. A queen! Ah, the Queen Rihoschek and
a nine of spades! Damned spade! it always brought
him ill-luck. And the thousand fared over to the Consul. Oh, that did not matter; he still had something
left. Or was he completely ruined? Not at all! . . .
Why, there were a few thousand again! Magnanimous
Consul! To be sure, he was certain of getting them
back. An officer had to pay his gambling debts. Such
a person as Elrief remained Elrief in any case, but
an officer, unless he happened to be called Bogner . . .
    "Two thousand, Consul!"
    "Two thousand?"
    "That is correct, Consul!"
    He did not buy a card; he held a seven. But the
Consul had to buy. And this time, he did not bother
to be ceremoniously slow; he was in haste, and added
an eight—the eight of spades—to his one, which made
nine. There was no doubt about that. Eight would
have been sufficient, and the two thousand traveled

back to the Consul, and thence back to Willi again. Or was there more than that? Three or four? It was best not to look; it brought ill-luck. The Consul would not cheat him; besides, everybody was standing round and watching closely. And since he did not know any longer just how much he owed, he put down two thousand again. The four of spades. Well, one had to buy to that; the six, six of spades. So that made one too many! The Consul did not have to trouble himself, and had only a three . . . and the two thousand wandered over, and wandered back again. Why, this was ridiculous! Forward and back. Back and forward. There! the clock in the tower struck—the half-hour. But no one gave any sign of having heard. The Consul dealt the cards quietly. Everybody was standing round; all the gentlemen, except the Army Doctor, who had disappeared. Yes, to be sure! Willi had noticed, a little while ago, how he had shook his head with rage and mumbled something between his teeth. Doubtless he could not bear to look on, while Lieutenant Kasda was playing for his existence. Strange, that a doctor should have such feeble nerves!

There were cards in front of him again. He made his bet—he did not exactly know how much. A handful of bills. That was the new style: to let Fate take care of the amount. Eight! Now his luck had to change!

It did not change. The Consul uncovered nine, looked round the group, then pushed his cards away. Willi opened his eyes widely.

"What's up, Consul?"

The latter raised his finger and pointed toward the outside. "It has just struck the half hour, Lieutenant!"

"Really?" Willi cried, pretending astonishment.

"Might not one play another quarter of an hour?" He looked round the circle, as if he sought approval. Every one was silent. Elrief looked away, in his most aristocratic manner, and lit a cigarette. Wimmer pressed his lips together. Greising nervously whistled an inaudible refrain. The manager, however, remarked, somewhat rudely, as if it were a small matter: "The Lieutenant has certainly had a run of bad luck tonight!"

The Consul had risen and called for the waiter, as though the night were like any other night. Only two bottles of cognac appeared on his bill, but, to simplify matters, he wished to take care of the entire check. Greising refused, and paid for his coffee and cigarettes. The others accepted his hospitality indifferently. Then the Consul turned to Willi, who had remained seated, and again pointed to the door, just as he had when he had verified the striking of the clock. "If you like, Lieutenant," he said, "I will take you back to Vienna in my carriage."

"That would be kind of you," Willi replied.

And at this moment, it seemed to him as if the last quarter hour, as if, in fact, the whole night, with all that had happened in it, had become inadmissible. The Consul apparently regarded it in the same light. Otherwise, how would he invite him into his carriage?

"Your debt, Lieutenant," the Consul added, in his most friendly manner, "amounts to exactly eleven thousand gulden."

"That is correct, Consul," Willi replied, with military briskness. "It will not be necessary to have it in writing, will it?"

"No," Lieutenant Wimmer interposed gruffly. "We are all witnesses!"

The Consul paid no attention either to him or to the tone of his voice. Willi still sat at the table. His legs had become as heavy as lead. Eleven thousand gulden! Not so bad! Approximately three or four years' salary, including bonuses. Wimmer and Greising were speaking together, in low, excited tones. Elrief was revealing something evidently very amusing to the theatre manager, since the latter burst into laughter. Fräulein Rihoschek stood near the Consul, and addressed a question to him in a low voice, which he answered in the negative, shaking his head. The waiter helped the Consul into his cape, a wide, black, armless cape with a velvet collar, which Willi had seen once before, and which had struck him as extremely elegant, though perhaps a little eccentric. The actor Elrief poured himself another glass of cognac from the almost empty bottle. It seemed to Willi that they were all avoiding him, as though they did not wish to be troubled with him, did not even wish to look at him. He rose with an abrupt effort. The Army Doctor, Tugut, who, most surprisingly, had returned, suddenly stood before him. At first he seemed unable to find words.

"I hope," he at last observed, "I hope, Lieutenant, that you are in a position to procure it by tomorrow morning?"

"Why, of course, Doctor!" Willi replied, with a broad, vacant smile. Then he went over to Wimmer and Greising, and shook hands with them.

"Until next Sunday!" he said lightly. They did not even answer; they did not even nod.

"Are you ready, Lieutenant?" the Consul asked.

"At your service!"

Now he took leave, in a very cordial and animated manner, of all the others; and, very gallantly, he kissed Fräulein Rihoschek's hand—it could do no harm!

Everybody left. On the terrace, the tables and chairs glowed a ghastly white; night still covered the city and the fields, though not a star was to be seen. In the direction of the station, the edge of the sky had begun to lighten. The Consul's carriage was waiting outside; the coachman was sleeping, his feet on the dashboard. Schnabel touched him on the shoulder. He awoke, raised his hat, shambled up to his horses, and took their blankets off. The officers touched their caps once more; then they sauntered away. The manager, Elrief, and Fräulein Rihoschek waited until the coachman was ready. Willi mused: Why does not the Consul stay in Baden with Fräulein Rihoschek? Why does he keep her, anyway, if he does not stay with her? It occurred to him that he had once heard a story of an old gentleman who had been struck with apoplexy while in bed with his mistress, and he glanced obliquely at the Consul. The latter, however, seemed both fresh and cheerful, not in the least ready for death; and it was patently in order to annoy Elrief that he took leave of Fräulein Rihoschek with delicate caresses, which somehow did not seem quite in accord with his usual disposition. Then he invited the Lieutenant into the carriage, offered him the place on the right side, spread a light yellow robe lined with brown plush over Willi and himself, and thus they drove off together. Elrief lifted his hat once more, with an elaborate, sweeping movement, not devoid of humor, according to the Spanish custom, just as he intended to do it at some little subsidized theatre during the next season, while enacting the rôle of a grandee. As the carriage wheeled round to cross the bridge, the Consul turned and waved a farewell to the three, who, arm in arm, with Fräulein Rihoschek in the middle, were just strolling away, and, engrossed in lively conversation, were not even aware of the Consul's parting gesture.

Not a sound was to be heard except the rhythm of the horses' clattering hoofs, as they rode through the sleeping city.

"It is rather cool," the Consul observed.

Willi had little desire for conversation; still, he realized the necessity of a reply, were it only in order to preserve the Consul's friendly attitude. So he said: "Yes, in the early hours of the morning it always freshens up a bit. We soldiers learn that in our encampments."

After a short pause, the Consul began, in a pleasant tone: "We need not be so exact about that matter of twenty-four hours."

Willi breathed more easily, and promptly availed himself of the opportunity which this remark afforded.

"I was just about to beg your indulgence, Consul," he said, "since, as you can well understand, I do not have the whole sum at hand at this very moment."

"Of course not!" the Consul interrupted. The hoof-beats rattled on, awakening echoes as they rode under a viaduct and out into the open country. "If I were to insist on the usual four-and-twenty hours," the Consul continued, "you would then be required to pay me your debt tomorrow evening, at half-past-two, at the latest. That would be inconvenient for both of us. Let us then set the hour"—he pretended to be considering the matter—"say, Tuesday at noon, at twelve exactly, if that suits you."

He extracted a visiting card from his wallet and handed it to Willi, who examined it attentively. The morning darkness had so far disappeared that he was able to read the address—Number 5, Helfersdorfer Strasse. Only five minutes' walk from the barracks, he reflected.

"Then tomorrow at twelve, Consul?" he said, and he could feel his heart beating faster.

"Yes, Lieutenant, that is what I mean. Tuesday, at twelve sharp. I am in my office from nine o'clock on."

"And if I were not in a position to pay it at that hour, Consul—if, for instance, I could not satisfy you until the afternoon, or until Wednesday . . ."

The Consul interrupted him. "You shall certainly be in a position to pay your debt, Lieutenant. Since you sat down to play, you were naturally prepared to lose, just as I had to be prepared; and in the event that you did not dispose of a private fortune, you have, at any rate, no reason to fear that your parents will not support you!"

"I have no parents," Willi answered quickly, and Schnabel allowed a sympathetic "Oh!" to escape him. "My mother," he continued, "has been dead these eight years; my father, a Lieutenant-Colonel, died four years ago in Hungary."

"So your father was also an officer?" The tone was sympathetic, actually warm-hearted.

"That is right, Consul. Who knows if I would have selected a military career, in other circumstances!"

"It is remarkable"—and the Consul nodded his head —"when you come to think of it, how some people's existence is, so to speak, planned out for them, while others don't know what they are going to do from one year to the next, sometimes not even from one

day to the other! . . ." He paused and shook his head.
This general, sober, unfinished sentence somehow
struck Willi as reassuring. And, in order to make
still more certain of this new relationship between
himself and the Consul, he too attempted a somewhat
generalizing philosophic phrase; and without reflection, as he was immediately aware, he remarked that
there were officers, too, who were obliged to change
their career, now and then.

"Yes," the Consul replied, "that is true; but that
generally happens upon compulsion, and then they
are, or at least, they feel themselves to be, ridiculously
degraded, and it is usually not possible for them to
go back to their former profession. On the other hand,
such people as myself—I mean, people who, through
no prejudice of birth, or rank, or anything else, are
prevented—I, for example, have been at least half a
dozen times above and below. And how far below!—
ah, if you and your comrades knew how low I have
been, it is hardly possible that you would have cared
to sit with me at table. For that reason, you have all
preferred not to make too careful inquiries concerning my position!"

Willi did not reply. He was very deeply touched,
and not quite decided what attitude he ought to take.
Of course, if Wimmer or Greising were here in his
place, they would doubtless have found the right
answer. But he, Willi, had to keep quiet. He did not
dare to ask: What do you mean by "far below," and
just what do you imply by "inquiries"? Oh, he could
imagine what was meant. He himself was now far
below, as low as one could possibly be. Lower than,
a few hours ago, he had imagined any one could be.

He was dependent on the Consul's state of disposition, on his willingness to meet him half way, on his mercy, however degraded socially he may once have been. But would he be merciful? That was the question! Would he consent to partial payments extending over a year—or over five years—or to a revenge match the next Sunday? He could not expect that— no, just at present he was not expecting that. And if he were not merciful!—well, there would be nothing left but to go begging to Uncle Robert. Still— Uncle Robert! It would be an extremely painful, actually a frightful resort, but none the less, it would have to be attempted. Absolutely! . . . And it was really unthinkable that his uncle would refuse to help him, when his career, his existence, his life—yes, to put it simply, the life of his nephew, the only son of his dead sister—depended upon his help. A man who lived on his income, who lived very modestly, but was nevertheless a capitalist, and who had merely to take the money out of the bank! Eleven thousand gulden! that wasn't one-tenth, not even one-twentieth of his fortune! In that case, it would be just as well if, instead of asking for eleven, he asked at once for twelve thousand gulden. And thus Bogner would likewise be saved. This thought put Willi in a more optimistic mood, somewhat as if he felt that Providence owed him a special consideration in recompense for his noble intention. But this was merely an alternative which he would keep in view, in the event the Consul was obdurate. And that still remained to be tested. Willi threw a quick glance sideways at his creditor. He seemed to be lost in memories. He had taken off his hat; his lips were half open, as if in a smile; he looked older and less severe than formerly. Was not this the right moment? But how should he begin! Confess frankly that one was simply not in a position—that one had let oneself into a situation without thinking—that one had lost one's head—in short, that, for a quarter of an hour, one had simply been incapable of lucid calculation? And, even then, would he have dared to go so far, would he have dared to forget himself so completely, if the Consul—there was no reason why he should not say so!—if the Consul had not, unasked, without even the slightest hint, placed the money at his disposal; in fact, passed it over to him; in a certain sense, forced it upon him, although in the most charming fashion possible?

"A ride like this, in the early morning, is quite marvelous, isn't it?" the Consul observed.

"Splendid!" the Lieutenant answered, sedulously.

"But what a pity," the Consul added, "that it always seems necessary to purchase such a ride by staying up all night, either gambling or doing something still more stupid!"

"As for myself," the Lieutenant observed eagerly, "it very frequently happens that I am up and in the open at this early hour, without having spent the night awake. The day before yesterday, for example, I was down in the courtyard of the barracks with my company at half past three. We drilled in the Prater. But, of course, I didn't ride down in a fiacre!"

The Consul laughed heartily, which raised Willi's spirits, although his gayety had sounded somewhat forced.

"Why, I've occasionally had such experiences myself," the Consul said. "To be sure, not as an officer, nor even as an enlisted man—I never got that far. Imagine, Lieutenant, I did my three years' service long ago, and never rose beyond the rank of Corporal. I

was such an uneducated person—at least, I was then!
I have caught up a little during the passage of time;
one gets the opportunity to do that on long voyages."

"I suppose you have seen a great deal of the world,"
Willi remarked obligingly.

"Indeed I have!" the Consul replied. "I have been
almost everywhere—except to that country of which
I am Consul. I have never been in Ecuador. But I
have decided to drop my title of Consul very shortly,
and to go away." He laughed, and Willi joined him,
although a little wearily.

They were riding through a tedious, wretched district, among plain, drab, dilapidated houses. In a little
front yard, an old man in his shirt-sleeves was watering the bushes; a young woman, in somewhat shabby
clothing, stepped out into the street with a pail of
milk purchased at an early opened shop. Willi felt
a certain envy of these two, of the old man watering
his little garden, of the woman who was bringing
home milk to her husband and children. He knew
that these two were happier than he. The carriage
passed a high, bleak building, where a soldier walked
up and down; he saluted the Lieutenant, who acknowl-
edged the salute more politely than it was usual for
one of his class to greet a common man from the ranks.
The Consul looked long at this building, with an
expression that was at once contemptuous and full of
memories. This gave Willi something to think about.
But how could it help him, at this particular moment,
that in all probability the Consul's past had not been
without stain? Gambling debts were gambling debts,
and even a convicted criminal had the right to insist
upon payment. Time was passing; the horses were
going faster and faster, and in an hour, in half an

hour, they would be in Vienna. And what to do then?

"And such creatures as, for example, your Lieutenant Greising, are permitted to go about at liberty!"
the Consul said, as if in completion of a sequence of
unuttered thoughts.

So I was right, Willi reflected. The man has been
in prison! But at this moment, it does not matter.
The Consul's remark implied a manifest insult to an
absent comrade. Was that simply to be passed over,
as though he had not heard it, or as though he even
agreed that the implication was just?

"I must beg you, Consul, to leave my comrade Greising out of the discussion!"

For this, the Consul had only a deprecatory gesture. "It's quite remarkable," he said, "how these gentlemen who are so severe in their professional honor,
allow a man to remain in their midst who, with complete consciousness of what he does, endangers the
health of another person; for example, a stupid, inexperienced girl, and thus sickens the creature, possibly kills her—"

"It is not known to us," Willi replied hoarsely. "In
any case, it is not known to me."

"But, Lieutenant," the Consul said, "I had absolutely no intention of reproaching you. You personally
are not responsible for these things, and it is not in
your power to alter them."

Willi sought vainly for a reply. He reflected whether
he was not in duty bound to report the observations
of the Consul to his comrade—or ought he not, perhaps, talk the matter over thoroughly with Army
Doctor Tugut? Or perhaps ask Lieutenant Wimmer
for advice! But what had all this to do with him? His
exigent concern was for himself, himself alone. His

particular case—his career—his life! There, in the first
beams of the sun, the monument of the Weaver at
the Cross stood forth. And still he had not spoken a
single word that was calculated to procure him an ex-
tension, even a short respite. Even as these thoughts
flashed through his mind, he felt his companion's hand
lightly touching his sleeve.

"I beg your pardon, Lieutenant," said the Consul.
"Let us drop the subject! As a matter of fact, it ought
not to trouble me if Lieutenant Greising, or anybody
else, for that matter—all the more so, since I shall
hardly have the pleasure of again sitting at the same
table with these gentlemen."

Willi started.

"Just what do you mean, Consul?"

"I am leaving the country," the Consul answered
calmly.

"So soon?"

"Yes, the day after tomorrow—more precisely, tomorrow—Tuesday!"

"Shall you be gone long, Consul?"

"Rather! From three to—thirty years."

The National Highway was already quite crowded
with trucks and hucksters' wagons. Willi, whose head
was bowed, saw the golden buttons of his cape glisten
in the rays of the rising sun.

"Is this journey of yours the result of a recent decision?" he asked.

"Oh, not at all, Lieutenant! It was decided long
ago. I am leaving for America. For the present, I am
not going to Ecuador, but rather to Baltimore, where
my family lives and where I also have a business. I
haven't been there for eight years, and have not been
able to supervise it personally."

So he has a family! Willi thought to himself. And how about Fräulein Rihoschek? Does she know that he is leaving? But what concern is that of mine! It's high time. I'm choking! And, involuntarily, he put his hand up to his throat.

"It is really most unfortunate," he said helplessly, "that you intend to leave tomorrow. For, you know, I was really expecting with some certainty"—he assumed a lighter, somewhat jocular tone—"that you would allow me the opportunity of a revenge next Sunday."

The Consul shrugged his shoulders, as though such a possibility were entirely out of the question. What shall I do now? Willi wondered. What shall I do? Shall I—beg him? Why should he be so insistent about a few thousand gulden? He has a family in America —and Fräulein Rihoschek! He has a business over there. What can these few thousand gulden mean to him? And to me, they are a matter of life and death!

They rode under the viaduct into the city. A train was just puffing out of the south station. There are people riding to Baden, Willi reflected, and further —to Klagenfurt, to Trieste—and from thence, perhaps, over the sea to another hemisphere . . . and he envied all of them.

"Where shall I take you, Lieutenant?"

"Oh, please," Willi replied, "don't put yourself to any trouble! Drop me wherever it happens to be convenient for you. I live in the Alser Barracks."

"I will take you to the door, Lieutenant." He gave the coachman the necessary instructions.

"Thank you very much, Consul. It is really not necessary—"

The houses were all asleep. The street car tracks,

still untouched by the day's traffic, ran along, smooth and gleaming, at their side. The Consul looked at his watch.

"We have made good time—an hour and ten minutes! Are you marching today, Lieutenant?"

"No," Willi replied, "Today I am to give classroom instruction."

"Well, in that case, you will be able to lie down for a while."

"So I shall, Consul, but I think I will take the day off. I shall report myself sick."

The Consul nodded his head, saying nothing.

"So you are leaving on Wednesday?"

"No, Lieutenant," the Consul replied, emphasizing every word, "tomorrow—Tuesday evening!"

"Consul, I must make a frank confession to you. It is extremely painful to me, but I am very much afraid that it will be wholly impossible for me, in such a short time—before tomorrow, at noon . . ." The Consul remained silent. He did not seem to be listening. "If you would be so kind as to give me a respite?" The Consul shook his head. "Oh, nothing very long," Willi continued, "and I might give you a confirmation or a promissory note, and I would engage upon my word of honor to find a way to settle it within two weeks . . ." The Consul still shook his head, mechanically, without any emotion. "Consul," Willi began again, and his voice, against his will, was pleading, "Consul, my uncle, Robert Wilram—perhaps you have heard of him?" The other continued to shake his head firmly. "You understand, I am not absolutely certain that my uncle, upon whom I can otherwise positively rely, will have this sum immediately at hand. But, of course, within a few days. . . .

He is a rich man, my mother's only brother—a retired
man, living on his income." And suddenly, with a
queer catch in his voice which sounded like a laugh,
he added: "It is really disastrous that you are going
so far away as America, and so soon!"

"My destination, Lieutenant," the Consul replied
calmly, "is a matter of absolutely no concern to you.
It is common knowledge that debts of honor are to
be paid within twenty-four hours!"

"I am aware of that, Consul, I am aware of that!
Still, it happens now and then—among my comrades,
I know many who, in a similar position. . . . It is entirely subject to your choice, Consul, whether you
are willing to content yourself with a promissory note,
or my word of honor, until—until next Sunday, at
least."

"I shall not be satisfied, Lieutenant. Tomorrow,
Tuesday, at noon—that's the limit of the period . . .
otherwise, I shall report you to the commander of
your regiment!"

The carriage went over the Ring and past the Volksgarten, whose rich, green foliage hung down over the
gilded fence. It was a delightful spring morning.
Hardly a person was as yet to be seen on the street;
only a young and very elegant lady in a tailored suit
was walking rapidly with her little dog, as if fulfilling
a duty. She cast an indifferent glance toward the Consul, who turned round to look at her, in spite of his
wife in America and Fräulein Rihoschek in Baden,
who really belonged more to the actor, Elrief. What
has Elrief to do with me, Willi said to himself, and
why should I worry about Fräulein Rihoschek? Perhaps—who knows?—if I had been nicer to her, perhaps she would have put in a good word for me! And

for a moment, he seriously considered whether he ought not to ride back to Baden at once, to beg for her intercession. Intercession with the Consul? She would laugh at the idea. She knew the Consul too well; she must undoubtedly so know him. . . . And the sole possibility of deliverance was Uncle Robert. That much was certain. Nothing else was left beyond this, save a bullet in his temple. One was obliged to perceive that much very clearly.

A measured sound, like the approaching steps of a marching body of men, struck his ear. Was the 89th drilling today? On the Bisamberg? It would have been painful for him at that moment to be in a carriage and to meet his comrades at the head of their company. But it was not a military troop that was marching along; it was a group of boys, evidently school boys, who were going with their teacher on an outing. The teacher, a pale young man, looked with instinctive respect at the two gentlemen who were passing him in a carriage at this early hour. Willi had never fancied that he would live to know the moment when he would consider a poor school teacher as a being worthy of envy. Then the fiacre overtook the first street car, in which a couple of men in working clothes, and an old woman, were the only passengers. A street cleaning spray came towards them, on the top of which a wild looking fellow, with rolled-up sleeves, swung the hose like a rubber band. Two nuns, with lowered eyes, crossed the street in the direction of the Votive Church, which pointed its slender, light gray steeples to the sky. On a bench, under a tree covered with white blossoms, sat a young creature with dusty shoes, her straw hat in her lap, laughing as if after some agreeable experience. A closed

carriage, with drawn curtains, whizzed past. And a
fat old woman with a broom and a polishing cloth
was cleaning the plate-glass windows of a coffee house.

All these people and things, which Willi otherwise
would not have noticed, now assumed a sharp and
almost painful clarity in his wakeful eyes. And the
man at whose side he was sitting had vanished from
his mind. Now he looked at him again with a shy
glance. The Consul was leaning back with closed eyes,
his hat lying on the robe. How gentle, how kind-
hearted he looks! And he—he was driving him to
death! He was actually sleeping—or was he only pretending to be asleep? Don't worry, don't worry, Consul, I shall not importune you any more! You shall
have your money, Tuesday, at twelve o'clock. Or perhaps not! But in no case . . . The carriage stopped
before the gates of the barracks, and the Consul woke
up at once—or pretended to have awakened at that
very moment, and even went so far as to rub his eyes,
with a gesture somewhat exaggerated to dispel a two
and a half minutes' slumber. The guard at the door
saluted. Willi leaped deftly from the carriage, without
touching the running board, and smiled at the Consul. He even did something else; he gave the coachman a tip—not too much, not too little, like a cavalier,
to whom losses or winnings meant nothing.

"Thank you very much, Consul—till we meet
again!"

The Consul extended his hand from the carriage to
Willi, as if he wished to confide to him something that
everybody ought not to hear.

"I advise you, Lieutenant," he observed, in an almost paternal tone, "do not take this situation too
lightly, if you place any value on your officer's com-

mission! Tomorrow, Tuesday, at twelve o'clock!" Then, aloud: "Well, until later, Lieutenant!"

Willi smiled courteously, raised his hand to his cap, and the carriage turned and went off.

9

THE clock in the Alser tower struck a quarter to five. The big gate swung open. A company of the 89th, with eyes right, marched past Willi. Willi saluted several times, gratefully.

"Where are you going, Wieseltier?" he gently inquired of the last cadet.

"Rifle practice, Lieutenant."

Willi nodded, as if in agreement, and stopped for a moment to look at the receding company, although without seeing them. The guard still stood saluting as Willi passed through the gate, which was closed behind him.

He could hear sharp commands from the opposite end of the courtyard. A troop of recruits were practising the various rifle positions under the direction of a Corporal. The court lay in the glare of the sun, bare, except for a few trees scattered here and there. Willi walked along the wall; he looked up to his room, where his orderly had appeared at the window and, looking down, had stiffened for a moment in salute and disappeared. Willi hurried up the steps; he began to remove his clothes in the anteroom, where his orderly was lighting the little grate.

"At your service, Lieutenant! Coffee will soon be ready."

"Good," said Willi; and, going into his room, he closed the door behind him, took off his coat, and threw himself, in his trousers and shoes, on the bed.

I can't possibly reach Uncle Robert before nine o'clock. In any case, I shall ask him at once for twelve thousand, so Bogner will get his thousand, too, unless he has killed himself in the meanwhile. Anyhow, who knows? perhaps he really won at the races, and is even in a position to help me out! Nonsense! Eleven or twelve thousand gulden are not so easily won at the races!

His eyes closed. Nine of spades—ace of diamonds—king of hearts—eight of spades—ace of spades—jack of clubs—four of diamonds—thus the cards danced before him. His orderly brought in the coffee, pushed the table up to the bed, and poured; and Willi drank, reclining on one arm.

"Shall I take off your shoes, Lieutenant?"

Willi shook his head.

"It's no longer worth the trouble."

"Shall I wake you later, Sir?"—and, as Willi looked at him blankly— "Do you wish to report at the Academy at seven?"

Willi shook his head again.

"I am sick; I must go to see the doctor. Report me to the Captain . . . sick. You understand? I will send in the slip later. I have an appointment with an eye specialist at nine o'clock. Please ask the cadet-substitute, Brill, to take my place at the Academy. That is all. But wait!"

"Yes, Lieutenant?"

"At a quarter to eight, you will go over to the Alser Church, and you will tell the gentleman who was here yesterday—yes, Lieutenant von Bogner, who will be waiting there—that he must be so kind as to excuse me—that, unfortunately, I was unable to do anything. Do you understand?"

"Right, Lieutenant!"

"Repeat!"

"The Lieutenant wishes to be excused; the Lieutenant was unable to arrange matters."

"Unfortunately, he was unable to accomplish anything. Wait! If there is still time before this evening or tomorrow morning"—he paused abruptly— "No, nothing more! I was unfortunately unable to accomplish anything, and that is all. Do you understand?"

"Right, Lieutenant."

"And when you come back from the Alser Church, be sure to knock. And now, close the window."

The orderly did as he was instructed, and a sharp command from the court below was cut short in the middle. When Joseph had closed the door behind him, Willi stretched himself out again, and his eyes closed. Ace of diamonds—seven of clubs—king of hearts—eight of diamonds—nine of spades—ten of spades—queen of hearts—damned canaille! Willi reflected. For the queen of hearts was really Fräulein Kessner. If I had not stopped at her table, the whole disaster would not have occurred. Nine of clubs—six of spades—five of spades—king of spades—king of hearts—king of clubs! "Don't take this matter too lightly, Lieutenant!" The devil take him, he will get his money! Then I shall send him two seconds!—It's a pity, but that will not do; he is not of rank! King of hearts—knave of spades—queen of diamonds—nine of diamonds—ace of spades! Thus they danced in procession before him—ace of diamonds—ace of hearts—irrelevantly, incessantly, until his eyes burned beneath their lids. There were certainly in the whole world not so many hands of cards as passed before his vision in this hour!

Some one was knocking. He woke up precipitately, the cards still passing before his open eyes. The orderly was standing before him.

"I wish to report, Lieutenant, that the Lieutenant thanks you many times for your trouble, and sends his respects."

"Is that all? He did not say more than that?"

"No, no, Sir! The Lieutenant turned round and left at once."

"Is that so! He left at once! . . . And you have reported me sick?"

"Right, Lieutenant!"

And, as Willi saw that his orderly was grinning, he asked: "What makes you laugh so stupidly?"

"Excuse me, Sir, it is because of the Captain!"

"Why, what do you mean? What did the Captain say?"

And the orderly explained, still grinning: "The Captain remarked that, if the Lieutenant has to go to an eye doctor, he no doubt ruined his eyes looking at some girl!" And, when Willi did not smile, the orderly, becoming alarmed, added: "I felt that I ought to report what the Captain said!"

"You may go!" said Willi.

While he was preparing himself for the impending expedition, Willi revolved in his mind all manner of phrases, silently practising the tone which he should use, and by which he hoped to move his uncle's heart. He had not seen him for two years. At this moment, he was not able to visualize Wilram's bearing, nor even the lineaments of his countenance. The images which he brought to his mind were those of some one else, with different expressions, different manners, different ways of speaking; and he did not know which of these various images he was to meet. He had always thought of his uncle as a slender, rather fastidiously dressed, youthful man. Even in his boyhood, he had thought of him in that way, although, at that period, twenty-five years seemed to him a mature age. Robert Wilram had come to visit his brother-in-law, at that time still Major Kasda, for only a few days, in the Hungarian town where the latter was stationed on garrison duty. His father and his uncle had not appeared to get on very well together, and Willi retained a somewhat disquieting memory of one particular verbal encounter between these two, which had ended with his mother leaving the room, weeping. His uncle's profession had never come up in conversation, but Willi seemed to remember that he had once held some civil post, which he had given up when he became a widower. He had inherited a small fortune from his deceased wife, and since then, had lived on his income, traveling a great deal about the world. The news of his sister's death had reached him in Italy, and he had not arrived until after the burial; and in Willi's memory, there always remained the picture of his uncle standing at the grave, tearless, but with a desolated, grief-stricken expression, looking down at the still unfaded wreaths. Shortly after that, they both left the little city together—Robert Wilram to return to Vienna, and Willi to his cadet-school in Wiener-Neustadt. From this time on, his uncle had visited him occasionally on Sundays and holidays, taking him to the theatre or to a restaurant. Later, after his father's sudden death, and after Willi had been assigned as a Lieutenant to a Viennese regiment, his uncle, acting upon his own initiative, had allotted him a monthly allowance, which was paid at regular intervals through a bank when Wilram was absent on a journey.

Wilram had come back from one of these journeys, a completely altered man. He had been through a dangerous illness and, although the monthly allowance still came regularly, the personal relationship between the uncle and nephew suffered protracted interruptions, with occasional resumptions, which, in point of fact formed the curious rhythm in the epochs of Robert Wilram's existence. There were periods when he lived a gay and social life, devoting himself entirely to the good things of the world; and then he would take his nephew to restaurants as before, and also to theatres, and to other pleasure resorts of a lighter character, upon which occasions there was usually also present some lively young lady, whom Willi then saw for the first, and indeed for the last, time. Then followed weeks during which his uncle seemed to have withdrawn himself entirely from the world and from people; and if Willi was admitted to his presence, he found a serious, laconic man, prematurely aged, who had wrapped himself in a dark brown dressing-gown resembling a clergyman's cassock, and who looked very much like a soured actor, as he strode up and down in his high-arched rooms in which the light never penetrated, or sat working beneath the electric light at his writing desk. The conversation usually dragged, as if the two were total strangers; upon a single occasion, however, when Willi chanced to mention a comrade of his who had killed himself in consequence of an unfortunate love affair, Robert Wilram had opened a drawer in his desk, and, to Willi's surprise, extracted a large number of manuscript pages, from which he read to his nephew some philosophic ob-

servations concerning death and immortality, and a
number of other disapproving and melancholy remarks concerning women in general, during the
course of which he seemed to have completely forgotten the presence of his nephew, who listened, a little
embarrassed, and more than a little bored. Just as Willi
was vainly endeavoring to stifle a yawn, his uncle
happened to glance up from his papers. His lips curved
into a vacant smile; he folded his papers together, put
them back into the drawer, and immediately began
to speak of other matters, which might be supposed to
be of greater interest to an officer.

But even after this somewhat unfortunate meeting,
there had still occurred a number of endurable evenings in the old manner; there were also some little
walks together, especially on fine holiday afternoons.
But one day, when Willi was to meet his uncle at the
latter's home, he had received a message abruptly
cancelling the appointment and, shortly thereafter, a
letter explaining that Wilram was exceedingly busy
at this time, and must beg Willi to cease his visits
for the present. Soon afterwards, the allowance also
ceased. A polite note, sent as a reminder, was un-
answered. A second received the same fate. To a third,
he received the reply that Robert Wilram was exceedingly sorry to be forced, "on account of fundamental
changes in his situation," to cease further allowances
"even to near relatives." Willi then sought a personal
interview with his uncle. Twice he was not received,
and on a third occasion, he saw his uncle disappearing
through a door, at the moment when he had been told
that he was not at home. The very small inheritance
which had come from his mother, and which had suf-
ficed him for his living expenses, had just been ex-

hausted, but, up to this time, he had not given serious
thought to the future. In his habitual fashion, he had
neglected this detail until, suddenly, from day to day
—yes, even from hour to hour—his difficulties had
increased, and had gradually assumed threatening
proportions.

Willi walked down the dark flight of steps. He was
depressed, but not without hope. In the perpetual
darkness of the spiral staircase, he did not immediately recognize the man who was barring his way.

"Willi!" It was Bogner addressing him.

"You?" What could he want? "Didn't you get my
message? Did not Joseph tell you?"

"I know, I know! I only wanted to say to you—in
case anything turns up—that the examination will not
take place until tomorrow!"

Willi shrugged his shoulders. It really did not interest him very much.

"Postponed, do you understand!"

"That is not difficult to understand!" And he took
another step down.

Bogner would not let him pass. "It is an omen!" he
cried. "It means that I am going to be saved! Do not
be angry, Kasda, that I have come again. I know, of
course, that you had no luck yesterday—"

"You may be sure of that!" Willi exploded. "You
may be sure that I had no luck!" And, with a burst
of laughter, he added: "I lost everything—and a little
more!" He could control himself no longer, as though
he saw in Bogner the one and only cause of his misfortune. "Eleven thousand gulden, man! Eleven thousand gulden!"

"Good God, that is terrible! . . . What are you going to do?" Then he interrupted himself. Their eyes

met, and Bogner's face lit up. "I suppose you will be
compelled to go to your uncle now?"

Willi bit his lips. Pusher! Shameless! he said to
himself, and he was not far from saying it aloud.

"Pardon me!—It is none of my business—I mean,
I ought not to interfere, all the more since I am, to
a certain extent, the cause of it. Of course—! But if
you are going to try it, Kasda—it might just as well
be twelve thousand, instead of eleven thousand! It
can't make much difference to your uncle!"

"You're crazy, Bogner! I have little enough chance
of getting eleven thousand, let alone twelve thousand!"

"But you are going to try anyhow, Kasda!"

"I don't know—"

"Willi—"

"I do not know," he repeated impatiently. "Perhaps
—and then again, perhaps not! . . . Good-bye!" He
thrust him aside, and dashed down the steps.

Twelve or eleven, it was not at all a matter of no
importance! A single thousand might break or make
his chances! And the figures buzzed through his head:
"Eleven, twelve—eleven, twelve—eleven, twelve!
Well, he did not have to decide until he was actually
in his uncle's presence. He would hear the answer
at the proper moment. In any case, it was stupid of him
to have told Bogner the sum, to have even allowed
himself to be detained on the steps. What was wrong
with the fellow? Yes, of course, they had been comrades, but never really friends! And now, was Fate
to bind him and Bogner inextricably together? Nonsense! Eleven, twelve—eleven, twelve! Twelve had a
better sound than eleven; perhaps it would bring him
luck . . . perhaps a miracle would occur—if he asked
for twelve, and not otherwise! And on the whole jour-

ney, from the barracks at Alser, through the city, to
the ancient house in the narrow street behind the
Cathedral of Saint Stephen, he considered whether
he should ask his uncle for eleven or twelve thousand
—as though success, and ultimately his life, depended
upon his choice.

An elderly person, whom he did not know, answered his ring. Willi gave his name. He apologized
for disturbing his uncle. Yes, he was really Herr Wilram's nephew. It was a matter of great urgency, and
he would not take up much time. The woman was at
first undecided; then she withdrew, and came back
surprisingly quickly, with a more friendly expression,
and Willi was admitted at once. He breathed freely ·
again, and deeply.

10

His uncle was standing near one of two high windows. He was not wearing the clerical dressing-gown in which Willi had expected to find him, but had on instead a well-cut, although rather worn, light summer suit, with brown oxfords which had lost their gloss. With a remote and weary gesture, he motioned his nephew to approach.

"Glad to see you, Willi!" he said. "It is nice of you to think of dropping in on your uncle. I had thought that you had completely forgotten me!"

Willi was on the point of replying that he had not been received on his last visits and that his letters had not been answered, but he thought it best to express himself more affably.

"You live such a secluded existence," he said, "that I had no means of knowing if a visit from me would be agreeable to you."

The room was unchanged. There were papers and books on the writing table; the green curtain over the book-case had been half drawn aside, so that the same old leather-bound volumes were visible; the same Persian rug was spread over the divan, and the same embroidered cushions surmounted it. On the wall, there were two yellowed engravings, representing Italian landscapes, and there were family portraits in dull gold frames. His sister's picture stood, as formerly, on the desk, Willi recognized it from the rear, by its shape and the frame.

"Won't you sit down?" Robert Wilram asked.

Willi was standing with his cap in his hand, his sword at his side, stiffly erect, as if he were making an official report. In a voice which did not quite suit his posture, he began: "To tell you the truth, my dear Uncle, I would not have come today either, if my business were not so extremely serious."

"You don't say so!" Wilram remarked, and his manner was friendly, but not particularly sympathetic.

"At least, it is very serious for me! In short, without beating about the bush, I have committed a stupidity, an enormous stupidity. I—I have gambled and lost more money than I possess!"

"Ah, that certainly is a little more serious than stupid!" his uncle observed.

"It was thoughtless," Willi agreed. "Criminally thoughtless! I don't wish to present it as any better than it is. But, remorse aside, my position is as follows: If I have not paid my debt by tomorrow at twelve, I am—I am simply—" He shrugged his shoulders, and stopped like a stubborn child.

Robert Wilram shook his head regretfully, but he made no reply. The silence in the room became at once so unbearable that Willi was forced to speak. In rapid phrases, he told of the occurrences of the preceding day. He had gone to Baden, to visit a sick comrade; there he had met some other officers, old acquaintances, and had permitted himself to be drawn into a game, which had started innocently enough, but which developed, without his having anything to do with it, into a hectic affair. He would rather not reveal the names of those who had taken part, with the exception of the man who had become his creditor, a wholesale merchant, a South American Consul, a

certain Herr Schnabel, who was unfortunately leaving at once for a long stay in America, and who had
threatened to report him to the commander of his
regiment, in case the sum were not immediately paid.
"You know what that means, Uncle!" Willi concluded, and he sank exhausted on the divan.

Still his uncle did not look at him, but asked, in the
same friendly voice: "How large is the sum in question?"

Willi hesitated again. First, he thought of adding
on the thousand for Bogner, and then he was suddenly convinced that this very addition might interfere with the outcome. So he asked only for the sum
for which he himself was responsible.

"Eleven thousand gulden!" Robert Wilram repeated, shaking his head; and it sounded almost as if
there was a tone of admiration in his voice.

"I know," Willi answered quickly, "it is a small
fortune! And I do not seek to excuse myself. It was
an act of unspeakable frivolity. I think it was the
first, and I can assure you with certainty that it will
be the last in my life. I can do no more than swear
to you, Uncle, that I shall never again touch a card,
as long as I live—that I shall exert myself, by a severe
and scrupulous manner of living, to prove to you my
eternal gratitude, I am even prepared—I swear it by
all that I hold sacred—to forego all the claims which
our relationship may have allowed to become established—for ever!—if only this time, just this once,
Uncle—"

Robert Wilram had shown no emotion up to this
point, but now he seemed to be affected to a certain
degree. At first, he had raised one hand, as if to ward
off his nephew's appeals; now he raised the other

hand as well, as if he could silence him by this extremely expressive gesture; and, in a voice pitched
unusually high, now almost mounting to shrillness,
he interrupted him:

"I am very sorry! I am genuinely distressed, but,
with the best intentions in the world, I cannot help
you!" And, as Willi opened his mouth to reply, he
added: "Absolutely, I am powerless to help you! It is
useless to say anything more, so spare yourself the
trouble!" And he turned toward the window.

At first, Willi was stricken, but upon consideration,
he realized that he could not actually have expected
to win over his uncle at the very first attack. And so
he began again: "I am not deceiving myself, Uncle.
I know that my request is an effrontery, a bit of un-
surpassed impudence. And I should certainly never
have dared to approach you, if there were even the
slightest chance of getting the money in any other
way. You must put yourself in my place, Uncle! Everything is at stake; not only my position as an officer!
What should I do? How should I begin now? I have
never studied anything; I don't know anything else.
And I can't just go on living as a cashiered officer!
Why, only yesterday, I chanced to meet a former comrade who, like myself— No, no! I would rather shoot
myself! Don't be angry with me, Uncle. You must
remember, Uncle, that my father was an officer; that
my grandfather was a Lieutenant Field-Marshal when
he died! For God's sake, I can't end it all in this way!
That would be too enormous a punishment for a
foolish prank! I am not a hardened gambler. You
know that. I have never gotten into debt. Not even
in the last year, when I often had great difficulty in
getting through. And I never allow myself to be

tempted, although I might do so very often. Of course, it is quite a large sum! I don't believe I could get such an amount from a usurer. And what would happen if I could? In half a year, I should owe twice as much; at the end of a year, ten times—and—"

"Enough, Willi!" Wilram interrupted him in a still shriller voice. "That is enough! I can't help you! I wish I could, but I cannot! Don't you understand? I myself have nothing! I haven't even a hundred gulden in all, as I stand here before you! There, there! . . . " He pulled out, one after another, the drawers of the dressing table, as if these were witnesses to the truth of his words, since there were no notes or coins to be seen, but only papers and boxes and linen, of every description. Then he tossed his purse on the table. "You can look for yourself, Willi, and if you can find more than a hundred gulden, then you may hold me responsible for whatever you wish!" And he sank suddenly into the desk chair and let his arms fall on the surface of the table, so heavily that some sheets of paper fluttered to the ground.

Willi picked them up carefully, and then he looked round the room, as if he thought that he might discover some change which would help him to understand the inconceivably altered circumstances of his uncle. But everything was just as it had been two or three years before. And he asked himself if conditions were really as his uncle had represented them. Was not this extraordinary old man, who had so suddenly left him stranded two years earlier, capable of prevarication, of enacting a comedy fabricated for the purpose of rendering his refusal realistic and of securing himself against the continued importunities of his nephew?

Was all that he claimed possible? How could one who, as he himself stated, possessed nothing, live in such a well-ordered house, in the central part of the city, and keep a housekeeper? The beautiful leather bindings still filled the book-cases; the pictures framed in dull gold still hung on the walls—and the owner of all these treasures had meanwhile become a beggar? What had he done with all his fortune, in the past two or three years? Willi did not believe him, and he had not the slightest reason to believe him, and still less cause to confess himself beaten, since, in any case, he had nothing more to lose. Consequently, he determined to make a last attempt, which did not turn out to be as bold as he had planned; for, to his own surprise and shame, he suddenly found himself standing before his Uncle Robert, with clasped hands, and pleading: "It is a matter of my life. My life is at stake. I beg you. I—" His voice failed him and, following a sudden inspiration, he grasped the photograph of his mother and held it before his uncle, as if he were adjuring him on her behalf. The latter, however, merely wrinkled his brow, gently removed the picture from his hand, and calmly put it back in its place.

"Your mother has nothing to do with the case," he remarked, in a low, but by no means angry voice. "She cannot help you any more than I can. If I did not really wish to help, you, Willi, I should not need any excuses. I do not recognize any duties, especially in such a situation as this. And, in my opinion, one can still be a very honorable man—even in civilian life! Honor is lost in other ways. You have not reached the point where you can understand that. Therefore, I tell you again, if I had the money, you may be cer-

tain that I would give it to you. But I have nothing.
I have nothing at all! I no longer possess a fortune. I
have only an annuity. Yes, on the first and the fifteenth
of every month, I get exactly so much, and today"—
he pointed to the purse with a lugubrious smile—
"today is the twenty-seventh!" Then, observing in
Willi's eyes a sudden gleam of hope, he immediately
added: "And you fancy that I could make a loan on
the strength of my annuity? But, my dear Willi, such
an arrangement is entirely dependent upon the circumstances under which one has procured his annuity!"

"Perhaps, Uncle, perhaps it might still be possible!
Perhaps we two together—"

Robert Wilram interrupted him furiously. "Nothing
is possible! Absolutely nothing!" And, as though in
the deepest despair: "I can't help you! Believe me, I
cannot!"—and he turned away.

Willi reflected briefly. Then he spoke. "Well, there
is nothing to be done, then, but to beg your pardon
for having thus—good-bye!"

He had already reached the door when Robert's
voice stopped him. "Willi, come here! I don't want you
to judge me harshly. I must explain to you. You must
understand that I have turned over my entire fortune,
or rather, what remained of it, to my wife!"

"You are married!" Willi cried in astonishment, and
a new hope rose in his eyes. "Then, if your wife has
the money, a way out ought certainly to be found. I
mean, if you were to tell your wife that it is a
matter—"

Robert Wilram interrupted him with an impatient
gesture. "I shall tell her nothing. Don't urge me any
further. It would be useless!" He was silent.

But Willi, unwilling to relinquish this last hope so quickly, sought to press the subject. "I suppose," he said, "your wife does not live in Vienna?"

"Oh, yes, she lives in Vienna, but not with me, as you may perceive." Wilram strode up and down the room, and then, with a bitter laugh, he said: "Yes, I have lost more than a sword belt, and you see that I am still alive! Yes, Willi—" He stopped suddenly, and then began again: "A year and a half ago, I turned over my entire fortune to her, of my own free will. And I did it really as much for my own sake as for hers . . . for I am not very domestic nor economical, and she— she is very thrifty, one must admit that, and very business-like, and she has invested the money most wisely. Better than I had ever managed it. She invested it in some kind of enterprise—I have not been apprised of the exact circumstances—I would not understand it anyhow! And the income which I receive amounts to twelve and one-half percent. That is not so meagre, and I have no right to complain . . . twelve and one-half percent. And not a kreuzer more! And every attempt that I made in the beginning to get an occasional advance was in vain. After the second attempt, I very wisely gave up trying. For I subsequently was not allowed to see her for six weeks, and she swore that I should never see her again, if I ever came to her with any such requests. And I have never cared to take that risk. I need her very badly, Willi; I can't exist without her! Every week I see her. She comes to me once a week. Yes, she holds to our agreement! She is really the most punctual creature in the world. She has never failed to come, and the money has always come promptly on the first and the fifteenth.

And in the summer, every year, we go together to the country for two weeks. That is also in our contract. And the rest of the time is her own."

"And you yourself, Uncle, do you never visit her?" Willi asked, somewhat confused.

"Why, of course, Willi! Every Christmas day, every Easter Sunday, and every Whitmonday! That comes on the eighth of June, this year."

"Pardon me, Uncle, but what if it should occur to you to go to visit her on some other day? Why, after all, you are her husband, and who knows but that it might rather flatter her, if sometimes—"

"I dare not risk it!" Robert Wilram interrupted. "Once—since I have told you so much, I may as well tell you this!—well, once I walked up and down in front of her house, in the evening, for two hours—"

"And what happened?"

"She did not show herself. But the next day, I received a note from her which contained only these words, that I should never in her life see her again, if I ever again took a notion of promenading up and down before her house. Yes, Willi, that is the way it is! And I know that if my own life depended on it, she would see me die before she would pay me even a tenth of what you ask, before it became due. You stand a much better chance of persuading the Consul to have clemency than I have of persuading my wife."

"And—was she always that way?" Willi asked.

"That has nothing to do with the matter," Robert Wilram replied impatiently. "Even if I had foreseen everything, it would not have helped matters. I was doomed from the moment I laid my eyes on her; at least from our first night on—and that was our wedding night!"

"Of course!" Willi said, as if to himself.

Robert Wilram burst into laughter. "Oh, you imagine that she is a young lady from a good, respectable home? Far from it, my dear Willi! She was a prostitute. And who knows if she is not one still—for others!"

Willi felt called upon to express his doubt through some gesture; and he really entertained a doubt, for after his uncle's story, it was impossible to imagine this prodigious woman as a young and charming creature. Throughout his uncle's recital, he had thought of her as a spare, yellow, inelegantly dressed, elderly person, with a sharp nose, and he wondered hastily if his uncle were not inclined to revenge himself for her shameful treatment of him by calling her undeserved names. But Robert Wilram cut short his thoughts by continuing. "Well, prostitute is perhaps a little too severe—in those days, she was really a flower girl. I met her at Hornig's. I saw her there, for the first time, four or five years ago. You were with me. You might perhaps recall her." And, encountering Willi's questioning look, he continued: "We were there among a large company. It was a banquet for the singer, Kriebaum. She wore a bright red dress, and she had wild, blonde hair, and a blue ribbon round her neck." And he added, with a kind of suppressed joy: "She looked quite different. She was able to take her pick of men then. Unfortunately, I never had any luck with her. In other words, I was not worth her trouble, on account of my age. And then it happened, just as it always happens when an old fool goes mad over a young girl. So, two and a half years ago, I married Fräulein Leopoldine Lebus."

So her name was Lebus, Willi thought. For Willi at once remembered, although he had long since forgot-

ten the episode, that this was none other than his own
Leopoldine. He was certain of it, as soon as his uncle
mentioned Hornig's, the red dress, and the wild,
blonde hair. Naturally, he did not tell his uncle how
that evening at Hornig's had ended. For, although his
uncle cherished no illusions concerning Leopoldine's
past life, it would doubtless have pained him a great
deal to have learned that, after he had accompanied
his uncle home, Willi had secretly met Leopoldine
again and stayed with her until the next morning. So
to prevent this, he pretended that he could not quite
remember the occasion; and he remarked, as if thereby
to console his uncle, that such wild blondes sometimes made very fine wives and housekeepers, whereas,
on the contrary, girls with excellent reputations and
coming from good families often gave their husbands
terrible surprises. He had observed an example in the
case of a certain baroness, who had married a comrade of his. She was a young lady from one of the
finest aristocratic houses, and another of his comrades
had been presented to her, not two years after the marriage, in a "salon" where "respectable women" were
to be had at stipulated prices. The unmarried comrade
had felt himself obliged to reveal this circumstance to
the husband. The result—a court of honor, a duel, the
severe wounding of the husband, the suicide of the
wife. Uncle Robert must have read about it in the
papers, there had been so much talk about the matter.
Willi spoke with animation, as if this affair interested
him more than his own, and Robert Wilram began to
look at him more amiably. Willi was thinking rapidly,
and he had decided upon a sudden, bold coup; and,
although his uncle could not possibly suspect it, he
judged it wiser to lower his voice and to abandon the

subject which did not rightly belong to the situation before him. And, without transition, he declared that, after the revelations which his uncle had made, he would certainly not urge him further, and he even allowed his uncle to believe that it was better to attempt to persuade Consul Schnabel than the former Fräulein Leopoldine Lebus. Moreover, it was not at all inconceivable that Lieutenant Hoechster, who had inherited some money, and a certain Army Doctor, who had taken part in the game, would co-operate to help him out of his dreadful situation. He ought to go to see Hoechster at once. He was on duty at the barracks today.

Willi looked at his watch. His feet were itching to depart, and, suddenly declaring that there was no time to be lost, he shook hands with his uncle, tightened his sword belt, and left.

II

THE first thing to be done was to discover Leopoldine's address, and that without loss of time. Willi went directly to the registration office. That they might refuse his request, he could not at the moment believe, especially if he were to convince them that his life depended upon it. Her image, which had not come to his mind in all these years, suddenly rose clear and distinct before him, together with the memory of all the other events of that evening. Again he saw her blonde head lying on the rough linen pillowcase, through which the red pillow beneath shimmered like a blush. He remembered her pale, childlike face, striped by the split rays of the morning sun that pierced the latticed window, saw again her arm stretching out from beneath the covers to bid him good-bye, and recalled a gold ring with a semi-precious stone, and a slender silver bracelet. She had pleased him so well that he was firmly decided, when he had left her, that he should see her again. It happened, however, that at that time another woman had previous claims on him, one who, being kept by a banker, never cost him a kreuzer— which, in his position, was a point in her favor which was not to be lightly considered; and thus it chanced that he had never gone to Hornig's again, and had never made use of the address of Leopoldine's married sister, with whom she lived, and where he might have written to her. Thus, he had never seen her again, after that single night. Still, however vastly her life may

86

have changed since that time, she could not possibly
have so greatly altered that she would stand by and
see happen—what had to happen, should she refuse
his so easily satisfied plea.

He was obliged to wait an hour at the registration
office before they gave him her address on a slip of
paper. Then he took a closed carriage to the corner of
the street where Leopoldine lived, and got out.

It was a new house, four stories high, of a not very
prepossessing appearance, situated directly opposite a
lumber yard. On the second floor, a neatly garbed maid
opened the door for him. At his question, whether
Frau Wilram was at home, she looked at him hesitatingly, whereupon he handed her his visiting card—
Wilhelm Kasda, Lieutenant in the 89th Imperial and
Royal Regiment of Infantry, Alser Barracks. The maid
came back at once with the answer that Frau Wilram
was very busy—what did the Lieutenant desire? And
then only did it occur to him that Leopoldine did not
know his last name. He was wondering whether he
ought to present himself simply as an old friend, or
jocularly as a cousin of Herr von Hornig, when the
door opened and an old, poorly dressed man with a
black brief case emerged and walked toward the outer
door. Then a woman's voice called out: "Herr Krassny!" but the latter did not seem to hear, for he was already descending the steps. Then the lady herself came
into the hall and called again to Herr Krassny, so that
this time he turned round. Leopoldine had already
noticed the Lieutenant, and had recognized him at once,
as her glance and her smile disclosed. She was not at all
the same creature as his mind's eye had recalled. She
was better poised and of a fuller figure; she even appeared to be taller, and she wore her hair in a flat,

severe coiffure. And—this was the most surprising thing of all—a golden pince-nez surmounted the piquancy of her tiny nose.

"How do you do, Lieutenant?" she said, and for the first time he noticed that her features were really quite unchanged. "Please go right in. I'll be ready in a moment." She pointed to the door whence she had come, turned to Herr Krassny, and seemed to be admonishing him very particularly with regard to some commission, but in a voice so low that Willi could not understand what she said. Meanwhile, Willi entered a large, light room, in the centre of which stood a long table with pens and ink, pencils, a ruler, and ledgers; along the walls, to the right and to the left, were two high filing cabinets; on the rear wall, over a table covered with newspapers and prospectuses, hung a huge map of Europe: and Willi was unconsciously reminded of a traveler's agency in a provincial city, where he had once transacted some business. And a moment later, he remembered the poor hotel room, with its dilapidated lattice and the worn pillowcase—and he had a strange sensation, as if he were dreaming.

Leopoldine entered, closing the door behind her. She took off her eye-glasses and toyed with them for a moment; then she extended her hand to the Lieutenant, in a friendly enough manner, but with a complete absence of enthusiasm. He bent over her hand, as if he were about to kiss it, but she withdrew it at once.

"Won't you sit down, Lieutenant? To what do I owe this pleasure?" She pointed to a comfortable armchair, while she herself took her apparently customary place in a straight-backed chair opposite the long table with the ledgers. Willi had the impression that he was in the office of a lawyer or a physician. "What can I do for you?" she asked, and her voice, which was almost impatient, did not sound very encouraging.

"In the first place," Willi began, clearing his throat in embarrassment, "I must say it was not my uncle who gave me your address!"

Leopoldine looked up in astonishment.

"Your uncle?"

"My uncle, Robert Wilram!" Willi replied, with emphasis.

"Oh, of course!" She smiled and looked down.

"He knows absolutely nothing of this visit," Willi continued rapidly. "I want to make that very plain." And, at her astonished glance, he added: "I really had not seen him for a very long time, but that was not my fault. Only today, in the course of our conversation, he revealed to me the fact that, in the meanwhile, he had —married."

Leopoldine nodded her head. "A cigarette, Lieutenant?" She indicated an open box. He took a cigarette; she struck him a match, and also lit one for herself. "Very well! And may I now finally know to what circumstance I am indebted for the pleasure of this visit?"

"It has to do with the same business which led me to visit my uncle. A rather unpleasant affair, as I am sorry I have to admit at once!" And he continued, as her expression grew severe: "I don't wish to take up too much of your time. So, without further preliminaries, let me say that I should like to have a certain sum advanced to me, for a period of three months!"

Her expression at once became surprisingly amiable. "Your confidence is extremely flattering, Lieutenant!" —and she brushed the ashes off her cigarette—"although I really can't imagine why you should honor me in this way! However, may I ask what the amount

would be?" And she drummed lightly upon the table
with the edge of her pince-nez.

"Eleven thousand gulden, Madam!" He was sorry
he had not said twelve. He was about to correct himself, when it suddenly occurred to him that the Consul
would be satisfied with ten thousand, and in that case,
he would have enough with eleven.

"Ah!" Leopoldine exclaimed. "Eleven thousand!
Eleven thousand! That really is quite a considerable
sum!" Her tongue played against her teeth. "And what
security can you offer me, Lieutenant?"

"I am an officer, Madam!"

She smiled, almost gently. "I beg your pardon, Lieutenant, but, in business practice, that is hardly sufficient as security. Who would be willing to answer
for you?" Willi remained silent and gazed at his shoes.
A curt refusal could not have embarrassed him more
than this cold politeness.

"And I beg *your* pardon, Madam!" he replied. "I
have not, I admit, sufficiently considered the formal
side of the situation. As it happens, I am in a desperate
position. It concerns a debt of honor, which must by
all means be settled tomorrow: for otherwise, my
honor shall be forfeited, and in addition—that which,
among us officers, must not be kept when honor has
been lost!" And, fancying that he saw a gleam of
sympathy in her eyes, he related, just as he had related
to his uncle an hour before, but using more elegant
and lively phrases, the story of the preceding night.
She listened to him with visibly increasing signs of
sympathy, even of pity; and when he had ended, she
asked, with promise shining in her eyes: "And I—I,
Willi! Am I the only person on earth to whom you can
go in this emergency?"

These words, and especially her use of the familiar form, encouraged him. Already he believed himself saved. "Would I be here, if it were otherwise?" he asked. "I have really no one else!"

She shook her head sympathetically. "That makes it all the more painful," she replied—slowly, she extinguished her glowing cigarette—"for I am really not able to help you. My money is invested in various enterprises. I never have access to large sums of cash. I am really very sorry!" And she rose from her chair, as if to bring the interview to an end. Willi, terribly frightened, remained seated, and hesitatingly, clumsily, almost stutteringly, he suggested that there might possibly be some hope of securing a loan from some bank, or that some credit might be at her disposal in view of the excellent condition of her commercial enterprises. Her lips curved ironically, and she smiled indulgently at his ingenuousness.

"You imagine that these things are much more simple than they are," she said, "and apparently you take it quite for granted that I should undertake, in your interests, a financial transaction which I should never think of resorting to in my own! And, in addition to that, without any security! Your assurance astounds me!" These last words were spoken in a tone so cordial, even so coquettish, that it seemed to Willi that in her heart she was already prepared to yield, and was only waiting for a beseeching word upon his part. He thought that he had found it, and exclaimed: "Madam!—Leopoldine!—My existence, my life is at stake!"

She started, and, fearing that he had ventured too far, he added softly: "I beg your pardon!"

Her eyes became impenetrable, and, after a short

silence, she remarked shortly: "In any case, I can't make a decision until I have consulted my lawyer." Then, as his eye gleamed with resurrected hope, she made an evasive gesture: "I had an appointment with him anyhow—for today, at five o'clock, in his office. I will see what can be done. However, I should advise you not to depend on it at all. For I have no intention of making it a question of vital importance!" And, with a sudden hardness, she added: "I don't really know why I should!" But then she smiled again, and gave him her hand. And this time she even permitted him to kiss it.

"When may I come for my answer?"

She seemed to be considering for a moment. "Where do you live?" she asked.

"Alser Barracks," he answered promptly. "Officers' wing, third floor, room four!"

She smiled vaguely; then she said, slowly: "At seven, at half-past seven, at the latest, I shall know whether or not I shall be able . . ." She reflected again for a moment, and then finished decisively: "I shall send you my answer between seven and eight, by a person whom I can trust." She opened the door for him, and accompanied him into the hall. "Good-bye, Lieutenant!"

"Till we meet again!" he amended, somewhat taken aback. Her expression remained cold and distant. And when the maid opened the door to the staircase for Willi, Frau Leopoldine Wilram had already disappeared into her room.

12

DURING the short time that Willi had remained with
Leopoldine, he had traversed so many changing emotions of despair, of hope, of security, of renewed disappointment, that he felt, as he descended the staircase,
as if he had lost his mind. But, when he had come again
into the open air, his brain cleared, and now it seemed
to him, upon reflection, that, on the whole, his condition
was not unfavorable. It was certain that, if she but
wished to do so, Leopoldine was perfectly able to
procure the money for him. Her entire attitude had
made it clear to him that it was in her power to influence her attorney as she pleased. And in particular,
the feeling that there was still something remaining
in her heart which pleaded for him, so powerfully
intoxicated Willi that in his mind he jumped the inter-
vening interval, and contemplated himself suddenly
as the husband of the widow, Frau Leopoldine Wilram, now Frau Major Kasda.

But this dream-picture soon faded as he walked
aimlessly in the midday heat through the slightly
crowded streets, in the direction of the Ring. He remembered again the disagreeable office room in which
she had received him, and her aspect, which for a
while had been graced by a certain womanly spirit,
but which had then taken on the hard, almost severe
expression which, from time to time, had intimidated
him. There were still a great many hours of uncer-
tainty before him; and no matter what the result was

to be, these had to be passed in some manner. He conceived the fancy of having a good time, even if it were to be his last. Precisely because it was to be his last! He determined to have luncheon in an aristocratic hotel restaurant, where he had gone occasionally with his uncle. He selected a table in a cool, quiet corner, ordered an excellent meal, drank a bottle of dry, sweet Hungarian wine, and soon found himself in such a placid mood that even the thought of his lamentable situation could not disturb it. He sat for a long time, now the solitary guest, smoking a good cigar in the corner of a velvet couch, and felt half giddy, half sleepy. When the waiter offered him imported Egyptian cigarettes, he purchased a whole box at once. What did it matter? At the worst, his orderly would inherit them.

When he passed again into the street, his mood was no different than if he had been involved in a somewhat serious, but in the main rather interesting adventure; as if he were anticipating a duel. And he remembered half a night which he had passed, two years before, with a comrade who was to fight with pistols the next morning. Earlier in the evening, they had enjoyed the company of a couple of young ladies; then, when they were alone, they had had a serious and somewhat philosophical discussion. Yes, his mood then must have been the same. And since that affair had turned out well, it seemed to Willi a favorable omen.

He sauntered through the Ring—a young, not overly elegant officer, but of good, slender build, passably handsome, and certainly of a pleasing appearance to the young ladies of all classes who passed him, and whose eyes he watched. In front of a coffee house, at a table in the open, he drank Mocha, smoked his cigarettes, and turned the pages of a few illustrated journals, surveying the passers-by, but without actually noticing them. Then, at first gradually, in spite of himself, but of necessity, he awoke to a clear consciousness of actuality. It was five o'clock. Steadily, even if all too slowly, the hours of the afternoon were passing; now undoubtedly the wisest thing to do was to go home and take a good rest, as far as such a thing might be possible. He took the horse-car, descended before his barracks, and, without encountering any unwelcome acquaintance, reached his quarters on the far side of the court. Joseph was in the anteroom, occupied with the Lieutenant's wardrobe, and reported that nothing had occurred, save that Herr von Bogner had been there, shortly before noon, and had left his visiting card. "What do I want with his card?" Willi observed crossly. The card was lying on the table; Bogner had written upon it his private address: Number 20, Piaristengasse. Not far away! Willi reflected. But what does it matter to me, whether he lives near or far, the imbecile! Willi was on the point of tearing up the card, when he changed his mind and tossed it carelessly on the dresser. He turned to his servant: In the evening, between seven and eight, some one would inquire for him; a gentleman, perhaps a gentleman with a lady, perhaps a lady, unaccompanied. "Do you understand?"

"Certainly, Lieutenant."

Willi closed the door, stretched himself upon the divan—which was a little too short, so that his feet hung over the arm—and sank into slumber as though into an abyss.

13

It was already growing dark when the indistinct murmur of a voice aroused him. He opened his eyes and perceived, standing before him, a young lady in a blue and white polka-dot dress. His eyes heavy with sleep, he rose, and as he did so, he saw that his orderly was standing behind the young lady, looking guilty and frightened.

"I must apologize, Lieutenant," he heard Leopoldine's voice say, "for not allowing myself to be announced, but I wished rather to wait until you awakened of your own accord!"

How long has she been here already, Willi wondered, and what am I to assume from her voice? And how different she looks than she did this afternoon! She has surely brought the money! He dismissed the orderly, who disappeared at once. Then, turning to Leopoldine, he said: "Welcome, Madam! Make yourself comfortable. I am very happy to see you! Please, Madam—" And he invited her to be seated.

She glanced round the room with bright, almost happy eyes, and seemed to like the place. In her hand, she was holding a white and blue striped parasol, which perfectly suited her blue and white polka-dot foulard dress. She wore a straw hat, not of the fashionable wide-brimmed style, but of a Florentine type, with long, drooping, artificial cherries.

"Your place is quite attractive, Lieutenant," she said, and the cherries swung against her ear. "I never im-

agined that a room in barracks could be so comfortable
and neat!"

"They are not all the same," Willi remarked, with
some satisfaction.

"In general, I suppose it depends on the occupant!"
she added, with a smile.

Willi, embarrassed and happy, set the books on the
table in order, closed the door of a small cabinet, and
offered Leopoldine cigarettes from the box which he
had purchased at the hotel, She declined, and sat down
in the corner of the divan. She looks marvelous! Willi
exclaimed to himself. Actually like a lady from a good,
respectable family! She reminds one as little of the
business woman of this morning as she does of the
wild blonde of former times. But where is she carrying
the eleven thousand gulden? As if she had surmised
his thought, she looked at him smilingly, with an arch
expression, and asked an apparently irrelevant question:

"How do you ordinarily live, Lieutenant?"

Then, as Willi hesitated over the proper answer to
her entirely too general question, she began to inquire
in detail, whether his service was easy or difficult,
whether he was soon to be advanced, what were his relations with his superiors, and if he often made excursions into the surrounding country, as, for example,
that of the preceding Sunday. Willi replied that his
service was sometimes this way and sometimes that
way; that his superiors were in general quite pleasant,
especially Lieutenant-Colonel Wositzky, who was
really quite nice to him; that he could hardly expect a
promotion before three years; that he had, of course,
very little time for excursions, as Madam could imagine,
except on Sundays—and at that, he sighed. Thereupon,

Leopoldine, glancing up at him with an infinite cordial-
ity—for he was still standing on the far side of the table
—remarked that she hoped that he knew better ways of
spending his evenings than in gambling. And how
easily she might have added: And while I am on that
subject, Lieutenant, let me not forget that I have here
the little matter which we spoke about this morning!
—But no, not a word, not a motion, to that purpose!
She still looked at him smilingly, approvingly, and
there was nothing for him to do but to carry on the
conversation as well as he could. So he told her of the
hospitable Kessner family and of the beautiful villa
in which they lived, of the stupid actor, Elrief, of the
painted Fräulein Rihoschek, and of the night ride to
Vienna in a fiacre.

"I hope you were in good company?" she hazarded.

Oh, not at all; he had gone home with one of his
partners! Then she asked, in a teasing voice, whether
Fräulein Kessner was blonde or dark. He really could
not say with certainty, he replied. And his voice intentionally revealed that, in his life, no affairs of the heart
held any great significance.

"On the whole, Madam, I think you must imagine
my life to be quite different than it actually is!"

Sympathetically, her lips half opened, she looked up
to him.

"If one were not so utterly alone," he added, "such
fatal occurrences could not come about!"

She glanced up again with innocent, questioning
eyes, as though she did not quite understand him. Then
she nodded gravely. But even now she did not make
use of the opportunity; and, instead of speaking of the
money, which of course she had brought with her—
or still more simply, putting the bills on the table with-

out unnecessary words—she remarked: "To stand alone, and to be alone, are two different things!"

"That is too true!" he exclaimed.

And since she nodded understandingly, and since he grew more anxious each time the conversation lagged, he determined to ask her how she had got on all this time, and whether she had had many pleasant experiences. He avoided mentioning the old man whom she had married, and who was his uncle, just as he left out of his conversation any reference to Hornig's and above all, to a certain hotel room, with a dilapidated lattice and a worn pillow with a ruddy shimmer. It was a conversation between a not particularly adroit Lieutenant and a pretty young woman of the middle-class, both of whom knew various things about the other—quite deceptive things—but both of whom had his own reasons for preferring not to touch those subjects, even if the reasons were only to avoid endangering a mood which was not without its charm, and even its promise. Leopoldine had taken off her Florentine hat and laid it upon the table. She still wore the close coiffure of the morning, but she had allowed a few locks of hair to escape and fall in curls upon her temples; and, very remotely, they recalled a former tousled head.

The darkness mounted. Willi was considering whether he ought to light the lamp, which stood in the niche of the white tile stove, when at this moment, he noticed that Leopoldine had taken up her hat again. At first, this did not convey any particular meaning to him, for she had meanwhile begun to tell of an excursion which she had made, the year before, through Mödling, Lilienfeld and Heiligenkreuz, to Baden; but suddenly she put on her Florentine hat, pinned it, and, with a reserved smile, remarked that it was time for her to go. Willi also smiled; but it was an uncertain, almost frightened smile which trembled on his lips. Was she making sport of him? Or did it merely please her to arouse his anxiety, his fear, in order to make him happy at the last moment with the information that she had brought the money with her? Or perhaps she had come with the purpose of excusing herself, of saying that it had not been possible for her to secure the desired sum in cash? And she was simply not able to find the proper words to tell him? In any case, it was unmistakable that she was in earnest about leaving; and in his helplessness, nothing remained to him but to maintain the attitude of a gallant young man who had received a pleasant visit from a young and beautiful woman, and who now found it utterly impossible to let her go at the most interesting moment of their conversation.

"Why do you wish to leave so soon?" he asked, in the voice of a disappointed lover. Then, more urgently: "You don't really wish to leave now, Leopoldine?"

"It is late," she replied. And she added, lightly: "And you doubtless have some better occupation on such a beautiful summer evening!"

He breathed deeply, for she had suddenly begun to speak to him again in the familiar form, and it became difficult for him to keep from betraying his newly mounting hopes. No, he had planned nothing at all, he said; and he had rarely been able to speak with such certainty and with such a clear conscience. She pleaded the formalities, keeping on her hat, and, crossing to the open window, she gazed down with sudden interest into the courtyard below. There was not much to see: there, on the far side, in front of the canteen, soldiers were sitting round a long table; an officer's servant, with a package under his arm, was hurrying across the court; another was pushing a wheelbarrow with a cask of beer toward the canteen; two officers, engrossed in conversation, were walking toward the gate. Willi was standing at Leopoldine's side, somewhat in back of her. Her blue and white polka-dot foulard dress swished lightly; her left arm hung down limply, and at first her hand remained unmoving as his hand touched it, but gradually her fingers slipped between his. From the barracks across the way, through the open window, a trumpet was sounding a melancholy scale. Silence.

"It is rather sad here!" Leopoldine observed at last.

"Do you think so?"

And, as she nodded, he said: "But there is no need for it to be sad!"

Slowly, she turned her head toward him. He had expected to see a smile on her lips, but all that he saw was a delicate, almost unhappy tremor at her lips. Then, abruptly, she turned. "But now it is really high time that I should go!" she exclaimed. "Mary will be waiting for me at table."

"Have you never let Mary wait?" And, since she looked at him smilingly at this last remark, he became bolder and asked her if she would not give him the pleasure of dining this evening in her company. He would send his orderly over to Riedhof's, and she would certainly be home before ten o'clock. Her remonstrances seemed so little in earnest that, without further ado, Willi ran to the anteroom and quickly gave his orderly the necessary instructions. Then he returned at once to Leopoldine.

Although she was still standing at the window, she had just given her Florentine hat a lively swing, so that

it flew over the table and dropped upon the bed; and
from this moment on, she seemed to be another person.
She stroked Willi's smooth head and laughed. He
seized her round the waist and drew her down upon
the divan. But when he wished to kiss her, she turned
away so abruptly that he did not venture any further
attempts, but instead asked her how she usually passed
her evenings. She looked at him seriously.

"I have so much to do the whole day long," she said,
"that I am only too glad to be able to rest at night. I
see no one!"

Willi confessed that he could not form any but the
vaguest of notions of what her business was really like,
and that it puzzled him how she could have entered
upon such a career at all. She evaded his questions. He
really could not understand such matters. But Willi
would not be so easily satisfied; she must at least tell
him something of her life—not everything, of course,
for that he could not expect, but he would so much
like to know, just in general, what had happened since
that day when—he had seen her for the last time. Other
questions rose to his lips, and his uncle's name as well;
but some impulse restrained him, and he did not give
them utterance. Without preliminaries, too hastily, he
asked her if she were happy.

She looked down. "I think so," she answered softly.
"In the first place, I am a free individual; that is what
I always wanted to be, more than anything else. I am
independent, like—a man!"

"Fortunately, that is the only thing about you which
suggests a man," Willi said. He moved closer to her and
began to caress her. She allowed him to continue, as
if her mind were far away. When the outside door
opened, she drew away from him quickly and, rising,

took the lamp out of its niche and lit it. Joseph entered
with the meal. Leopoldine glanced at what he had
brought, and nodded with satisfaction. "The Lieutenant has apparently had experience!" she remarked,
smiling. Then she and Joseph together set the table,
and, as she would not permit Willi to help, he remained
sitting on the divan, "like a pasha," as he remarked,
smoking a cigarette. When everything was ready and
the hors d'œuvres were served, Joseph was dismissed
for the night. Before he left, Leopoldine handed him
such a liberal tip that he was utterly taken aback with
surprise, and saluted her as if she were a general.

"Your health!" said Willi, and their glasses touched.
When they had both drunk, she put aside her glass and
pressed her lips passionately against Willi's mouth. And
as he became more impetuous, she pushed him away,
laughing. "First, let us eat!" she cried, and changed
the dishes.

She ate as healthy creatures are accustomed to eat
when, having finished their day's work, they indulge
themselves in the freedom of accomplished tasks. She
ate, with strong, white teeth, but still very delicately
and correctly, in the manner of ladies who have now
and then eaten in aristocratic restaurants with gentlemen of standing. The bottle of wine was soon emptied,
and it was a good thing that the Lieutenant then recol-
lected that he still had half a bottle of French cognac,
left over from God knows what event. After the second
glass, Leopoldine appeared to become drowsy. She
leaned back in a corner of the divan, and, as Willi bent
over her, kissing her eyes, her lips, her neck, she whispered his name, surrendering as if in a dream.

14

Day was breaking when Willi awoke, and a cool morning wind was blowing in through the window. But Leopoldine was standing in the middle of the room, completely dressed, her Florentine hat on her head, her parasol in her hand. Willi's first thought was; Good God, how soundly I must have slept! and his second: Where is the money? There she stood, with her hat and parasol, evidently prepared to leave the room within the next minute. She nodded her head in a morning greeting. He stretched out his arms toward her, as if in longing. She approached, sat down on the edge of the bed, and gazed at him with a friendly but severe countenance. He wanted to embrace her, to draw her to him, but she pointed to her hat and to the parasol which she held in her hand as if it were a weapon, and shook her head. "No more nonsense!" she said, and attempted to arise. But he restrained her.

"You don't intend to go?" he asked, and his voice was almost tearful.

"Certainly!" she replied, and passed her hand over his hair in a sisterly caress. "I would like to get a few hours of rest. I have an important conference at nine o'clock."

It suddenly occurred to Willi that this might be a conference—what a sound that word had!—to discuss his affair; the consultation with the lawyer, which she probably had not had the time to take care of yesterday. In his impatience, he asked her at once.

"A conference with your lawyer?"

"No," she replied with ease, "I am awaiting a business friend from Prague."

She bent over him, pushed his little mustache away from his lips, and gave him a hasty kiss. "Good-bye!" she whispered, and arose. In the next moment she might be outside the door! Willi's heart stood still. She wanted to go? She wanted to go, just like that! But a new hope awoke within him. Perhaps she had discreetly put the money somewhere! Timidly, his eyes wandered round the room—from the table to the niche in the stove. Perhaps she had hidden it under the pillow while he was sleeping! Instinctively, his hand sought the place. Nothing! Or perhaps she had put it in his wallet, which was lying near his watch! If he could only look! And all the while, he could feel, he knew, he could see, how she was following his movements, with derision, with malice. Their eyes met, for the merest fraction of a second. He turned his eyes away, as if he had been detected in some unworthy act. Her hand was already on the door-knob. He wanted to call out her name, but his voice would not come, as in a nightmare one cannot speak. He had an impulse to leap out of bed, to throw himself at her, to hold her back; yes, he was ready to run after her on the steps, in his night-shirt—exactly—he could see the picture in his mind—as he had once seen a prostitute run after a man in a provincial bordello, many years ago, because he had not paid her love-price. . . . But Leopoldine, as if she had heard her name, which he had not spoken aloud, kept one hand on the knob and, with the other, felt in the pocket of her dress.

"I had almost forgotten!" she said casually, and drawing near again, she put a bill on the table. "There!" she said—and was already back at the door.

With a single, spasmodic movement, Willi was sitting on the edge of the bed, staring at the bill. It was only a single bill, a thousand gulden bill—there were no higher denominations; it could not be more than a thousand!

"Leopoldine!" he cried, in a strange, unnatural voice. But when she turned round at his call, her hand still on the knob, and looked at him with a surprised and frigid glance, he was covered with deep, anguished shame, such as never before in his life he had experienced. But now it was too late; he had to go on, no matter where it led him, no matter how black the ignominy. And his lips cried uncontrollably:

"But that is too little, Leopoldine! I did not ask for a thousand! Perhaps you misunderstood me yesterday. I asked for eleven thousand!" And, involuntarily, beneath the gaze of her cold eyes, he pulled the covers over his naked legs.

She stared at him as though she had not quite understood him; then she nodded her head several times, as if it were all clear to her now. "Oh, yes," she said, "you thought . . ."—and she inclined her head contemptuously towards the bill—"That has nothing to do with your request. The thousand gulden are not a loan; they belong to you—for last night!" And between her half open lips, her moist tongue played with her sparkling teeth.

The cover slipped from Willi's legs. He stood erect. The blood mounted to his head and burned in his eyes. She looked at him calmly, curiously. And, as he was unable to utter a word, she asked: "But that is not too little? What did you expect? A thousand gulden! You gave me only ten! Do you still remember?" He advanced a few steps towards her. Leopoldine remained calmly standing at the door. With a sudden movement, he seized the bill, crumpling it in his trembling fingers, as if he were about to throw it at her feet. Then she released the knob, stepped up to him, and looked straight into his eyes.

"That was not to be taken as a reproach," she said. "I had no right to expect more at that time. Ten gulden —was plenty. In fact, too much!" Her eyes held his. "To speak accurately, it was precisely ten gulden too much!"

He stared at her, then looked away, beginning to understand.

"I could not know that!" he said, in a low voice.

"You might have seen it!" she answered. "It was not so difficult to see!"

He looked at her again; and now he was aware of a strange radiance in the depths of her eyes—the same childish and beautiful radiance that he remembered having seen in her eyes on that night long past, so many years ago. And now all his memories were revived—and he recalled not only the pleasure which she had given him, as others before had given him pleasure, and many others since, and the caressing words she had spoken, just as others had spoken them, but also the wonderful surrender, such as he had never experienced since, with which she had put her slender, childish arms about him and had said, in accents that now sounded again across the years: "Don't leave me alone! I love you!"—words, words such as he had never heard from any other. He had forgotten all this. Now he remembered it again. And now—he knew! that what she had done today was just what he had done then. Undisturbed, thoughtlessly, while she still slumbered in sweet lassitude, he had arisen from her side, and reflected hastily if a smaller bill would not do, and then nobly put down a ten gulden bill on her table. Then, feeling the anxious look of the slowly awakening girl, still drunk with sleep, he had run quickly away to snatch a few hours of rest in the barracks. And in the morning, even before he had gone to his duties, he had forgotten the little flower girl from Hornig's.

Meanwhile, however, while this dim light became so surprisingly alive, the childish, beautiful radiance had gradually faded from Leopoldine's eyes. Now she stared at him with cold gray, distant eyes; and, as the picture of that night vanished from his mind, anger, aversion, and exasperation arose in its place. What did she think she was doing? How could she presume so far, as if she really believed that he had actually offered himself to her for money? How dared she treat him like a gigolo, who sold his favors? And she had the effrontery to add to such an unheard-of insult the most insolent disdain, by bargaining for a lower price than the one which had been set—like a lover who has been displeased at his mistress's incapacity! Perhaps she doubted that he would have thrown the entire eleven thousand back at her, if she had dared to offer it to him as the wage of love!

But even as the foul word, which was due her, was finding its way to his lips; as he lifted his fist, as if to crush beneath it the miserable creature before him, the word failed him, his hand sank slowly to his side. For he suddenly became aware—perhaps he had suspected it all the while?—that he had been prepared to sell himself. And not alone to her, but to any other, to any one at all, who might have offered him the sum which could save him; and thus, in the cruel and treacherous

wrong which had been added to his store of misery
by an evil woman, he began to see, in the depths of
his soul, despite himself, a hidden, inescapable justice,
which had ensnarled him, not only in this sorry adventure, but in the very essence of his life.

He looked up; he looked round the room; he felt as
if he were awakening from a confused dream. Leopoldine had gone. He had not yet opened his mouth—
and already she was gone. He could not understand
how she had contrived to leave the room so suddenly—
without his having seen. He felt the crumpled bill in
his still taut fingers. Dashing to the window, he threw it
wide open, as if he wished to fling the thousand gulden
after her. There she was! He would have called after
her, but she was already far away. She was walking
along the wall, her step lilting and joyous, with her
parasol in her hand and her Florentine hat—walking
along, as if she had come from some night of love, as
no doubt she had come from hundreds of others. She
was at the gate. The guard saluted her, as if she were a
person of rank, and then she disappeared.

Willi shut the window and stepped back into the
room. He noticed the disturbed bed, the remnants of
the meal on the table, the empty glasses and bottles.
Involuntarily, his hand opened, and the bill fell. He
caught a glimpse of himself in the mirror above the
dresser—his tangled hair, the dark rings under his eyes
—and he shuddered. It annoyed him unspeakably that
he was still in his night-shirt. He took down his overcoat from the hook, pulled it on, buttoned it, and turned
up the collar. He strode aimlessly up and down the
room several times. Suddenly he stood, as if rooted,
before the dresser. In the middle drawer, between the
handkerchiefs, he knew his revolver lay. Well, he had

got that far, at least! As far as the other, who had perhaps already gone beyond it. Or was Bogner still waiting for a miracle? At any rate, he, Willi, had done his share, and even more. And at this moment, it veritably seemed to him that he had sat down at the card table for Bogner's sake alone, and that he had tempted fate so very long for Bogner's sake alone, until he had himself become a victim.

The bill still lay on a dish among the half-consumed pastry, just as it had dropped from his hand a moment before, and it did not even look particularly crumpled. It had begun to unfold itself; it would not be long before it would be smooth, as smooth as any other cleaner paper, and no one would be able to tell that it was nothing better than the wages of sin—shame-money! Well, whatever the circumstances, it belonged to him—to his estate, so to speak. He smiled bitterly. He might bequeath it to whomever he wished—and he should leave it to the one who had the best right to it. Bogner, more than any other! He burst into laughter. Excellent! That matter would be taken care of, in any case! It was to be hoped that Bogner had not killed himself too early. The miracle had actually happened —for him! All that he had had to do was to wait for it.

But where was Joseph? He knew that there was an expedition scheduled for today. Willi should have been ready at three o'clock to join it. It was now half-past four. The regiment had long since gone. But he had not heard it, his sleep had been so deep. He opened the door to the anteroom. His orderly was sitting there on a stool, near the little iron stove. Joseph stood at attention.

"I wish to report, Sir, that I have reported the Lieutenant ill."

"Ill? Who told you to do that? . . . Oh, yes—of course!"—Leopoldine!—She might just as well have given the order to report him dead; it would have been simpler. "Very well! Get me a cup of coffee," he said, and closed the door.

Where could that visiting card be? He searched through all the drawers, on the floor, in all the corners, as though his own life depended on it. In vain! He could not find it. It was not to be! Bogner was simply condemned to ill-luck; their fates were inextricably bound. Suddenly, he saw a white something glistening in the niche. There was the card, with the address on it: Number 20, Piaristengasse—quite nearby! And what if it had been further! So this Bogner had luck, after all! Suppose he had been unable to find the card!

He took the bill, examined it without really seeing it, folded it, inserted it into a sheet of paper, reflected for a moment whether he ought not to write a few explanatory words, then shrugged his shoulders. "To what end?" he murmured. He wrote the address on the envelope: "Herr Oberleutnant Otto von Bogner." Oberleutnant! To be sure! He gave the fellow back his old commission, upon his own authority. One always remained an officer, no matter what one did—or, at any rate, one became an officer again, when one had paid one's debts!

He called his orderly and gave him the letter to deliver. "And quickly!"

"Any answer, Lieutenant?"

"No. See to it that you give it to him personally, and —no answer! And whatever happens, don't wake me up when you return. . . . Let me sleep until I wake up by myself."

"Very good, Sir!"

Joseph clicked his heels, turned smartly about, and hastened off. On the steps, he could hear the sound of the key being turned in the door.

15

THREE hours later, there was a ring at the hall door. Joseph, who had returned long since and had fallen asleep, awoke with a start and opened. There stood Bogner—the gentleman to whom, three hours earlier, he had delivered the letter with which his master had dispatched him.

"Is the Lieutenant at home?"

"I am sorry, but the Lieutenant is still sleeping."

Bogner looked at his watch. Immediately after the accountants had examined his books, he had taken an hour off, in his anxiety to render thanks to his savior. He paced up and down the small anteroom. "Has he no duties today?"

"The Lieutenant is ill."

The Army Doctor, Tugut, suddenly appeared in the door, which was still open. "Does Lieutenant Kasda live here?" he demanded.

"Yes, Sir."

"May I speak with him?"

"I beg to report, Sir, that the Lieutenant is sleeping now. He is ill."

"Please announce me. Army Doctor Tugut!"

"I beg to report, Sir, that the Lieutenant gave orders that he was not to be disturbed!"

"It is an urgent matter. Go and awaken the Lieutenant. I will be responsible."

As Joseph, with some hesitation, knocked at the door, Tugut looked suspiciously at the civilian who was standing there. Bogner presented himself. The Army Doctor had heard the name before, and knew of the painful scandal connected with it. But of this he gave no sign, and presented himself in return. They did not shake hands.

There was no response from Lieutenant Kasda. Joseph knocked more loudly, put his ear to the door, shrugged his shoulders, and said, as if to quiet his own fears: "The Lieutenant is always a sound sleeper!"

Bogner and Tugut glanced at one another, and one of the barriers between them was broken. Then the Army Doctor stepped up to the door and called out Kasda's name. There was no answer. "Strange!" Tugut muttered, his brow wrinkling, and he twisted the knob in vain.

Joseph stood with pale face and eyes wide open.

"Go fetch the regimental locksmith, quickly!" Tugut commanded.

"Yes, Sir!"

Bogner and Tugut were alone.

"Incomprehensible!" Bogner observed.

"You know about it, Herr von Bogner?" Tugut demanded.

"You mean, do I know of his gambling losses?" And, as Tugut nodded: "Yes, of course."

"I wanted to learn how the affair stood," Tugut began hesitatingly; "whether he had succeeded in obtaining the money. Perhaps you know, Herr von Bogner?"

"I know nothing," Bogner replied.

Tugut went to the door again, shook it, and called out Kasda's name. No answer.

Bogner, who had been watching through the window, announced: "Here comes Joseph with the locksmith!"

"You were his comrade?" Tugut asked.

Bogner answered, out of the corner of his mouth: "I am the one you are thinking of!"

Tugut paid no attention to the remark. "It sometimes happens that, after great excitement . . ." He began again—"I rather suspect that he had no sleep this past night, either."

"Yesterday at noon," Bogner observed, with assurance, "he certainly did not have the money, as yet—"

Tugut looked at Bogner in a way that the latter interpreted as questioning whether perhaps he, Bogner, had not brought the money. So Bogner said, as if in answer to this unspoken question: "Nor, unfortunately, did I succeed in getting the money!"

Joseph appeared, accompanied by the locksmith, a young man in the uniform of the regiment, stocky and red-cheeked, carrying the necessary implements. Tugut knocked once more at the door, violently—a last attempt. They all stood by, holding their breath. There was no sound.

"Very well, then." Tugut turned to the locksmith with a gesture of command, and the latter set to work immediately. His task did not take long. In a few seconds, the door was opened. Lieutenant Willi Kasda, in his overcoat, with his collar raised, was reclining in the corner of the black leather divan, his eyes half closed, his head upon his breast, his right arm relaxed and hanging over the side of the couch, the revolver lying on the floor. From his temple, a narrow stream of dark red blood had trickled over his cheek, disappearing between his neck and the collar of his coat. Prepared as they all were, they were nevertheless deeply moved by the spectacle. The Army Doctor drew near, lifted the drooping arm, let it go, and it dropped once

more over the side. Then Tugut unbuttoned Kasda's
coat. The crumpled shirt beneath was open wide. Mechanically, Bogner stooped to pick up the revolver.
"Halt!" Tugut exclaimed, his ear on the naked breast
of the dead man. "Everything must remain as it is!"
Joseph and the locksmith still stood motionless at the
open door. The locksmith shrugged his shoulders and
looked at Joseph with a half deprecatory, half frightened glance, as if he felt himself responsible for the
sight which had appeared behind the door which he
had violated.

Steps were heard below—at first slow, then increasingly rapid, until they ceased. Bogner turned at once.
An old man appeared near the leaning door, dressed
in a light and somewhat worn summer suit, with something of the manner of a soured actor about him.
Hesitatingly, he looked about.

"Herr Wilram!" Bogner exclaimed. "His uncle!" he
whispered to the Army Doctor, who had straightened
up from his examination of the body.

But Robert Wilram did not at once grasp what had
happened. He saw his nephew lying in the corner of
the divan, with his limp arm hanging down, and he
made a step forward, as if to go to him. He no doubt
suspected that something terrible had taken place, but
he refused to credit it. The Army Doctor held him
back.

"A most lamentable thing has happened! But there
is nothing more that can be done." And as the other
stared at him, unable to understand, he continued:
"My name is Tugut. I am an Army Doctor. Death
must have occurred several hours ago."

Robert Wilram—his behavior struck everybody as
being extremely peculiar—suddenly pulled an envelope

out of his pocket and waved it in the air. "But I have got it here, Willi!" he cried. "Here is the money, Willi! Here is the money, Willi!" he continued, as if he actually imagined that he could thus bring back the life which had departed. "She gave it to me this morning! The whole eleven thousand! Here they are!" And he turned round to the others, as though calling them to witness this portentous fact. "This is the entire amount, Gentlemen—eleven thousand gulden!"—as though, now that they knew that he had brought the money, they would at least make some attempt to revive the dead man.

"It is too late, unfortunately!" the Army Doctor said gently. He turned to Bogner. "I am going to make my report." Then he commanded: "The body is to remain as it is!" And, turning to the orderly, he added severely: "You will be responsible! See to it that everything remains as it is!" And before he left, he turned round once more and shook hands with Bogner.

Bogner wondered: Where did he get that thousand for me? He noticed the table, the glasses, the dishes, and the empty bottles. Two glasses. . . . Did he have a woman with him, then, his last night?

Joseph crossed to the divan, near the body of his dead master. He stood stiffly erect, like a guard. Nevertheless, he did not forbid Robert Wilram, when the latter suddenly went up to the body, with the envelope still in his clasped hand, and pleaded: "Willi!" He shook his head in despair. Then he sank to his knees before his dead nephew; and so near was he to the naked breast that he detected a strangely familiar perfume wafted in his direction from the crumpled shirt. He inhaled it deeply, and looked up into the dead man's face, as though he were tempted to ask him a question.

From the court below came the rhythmical beat of the returning regiment, marching in order. Bogner was anxious to make his departure before some of his former comrades entered the room, as they were likely to do. In any case, his presence was superfluous. He cast a farewell glance at the body, which was reclining stiffly in the corner of the divan; and, followed by the locksmith, he hastened down the steps. He waited before the gate until the regiment had passed; then, pressing close to the wall, he crept away.

Robert Wilram still remained on his knees before his dead nephew. He looked round the room and, for the first time, noticed the table and observed the remains of the meal—the plates, the bottles, the glasses. In one of them there was still a moist, golden-yellow shimmer. He asked the servant: "Did the Lieutenant entertain last night?"

There were steps outside. Confused voices. Robert Wilram rose.

"Yes, Sir," Joseph replied, still standing erect, like a guard. "Until late at night . . . a gentleman, an old comrade. . . ."

And the unreasonable thought which had suddenly come to the old man, vanished.

The voices and the steps came nearer.

Joseph stood more stiffly erect than ever. The committee entered the room.

FRÄULEIN ELSE

Translated from the German by
ROBERT A. SIMON

TRANSLATOR'S NOTE

The word "Filou," which occurs frequently in this novel, is, originally, French argot, and cannot be translated literally. It has been carried into German, and it may mean anything from "flirt" to "roué," depending on the inflection of the voice. When the first syllable is accented, as in French, the word carries a playful implication; when the second is stressed, as in German, the expression is one of contempt. "Filou," as employed by Fräulein Else, may be approximated by the slang term of "sheik," but as the word has no English equivalent, no attempt has been made to supply one.

Similarly, a few colloquialisms, such as "gnädige Frau," and the greeting "Küss die Hand" are also retained in the original.

"So you really don't want to play any more, Else?" —
"No, Paul, I really can't play any more. Adieu. — Auf
Wiedersehen, gnädige Frau." — "Oh, Else, why don't
you call me Frau Cissy—or better yet, just plain Cissy?"
— "Auf Wiedersehen, Frau Cissy" — "But tell me, why
are you going already? Dinner won't be ready for at
least two hours." — "Please go ahead, Frau Cissy, and
finish at singles with Paul. Really, it's no fun playing
with me today." — "Leave her alone, dear lady. She's
in one of her moods today. — As a matter of fact, Else,
being moody is most becoming to you. — And as for the
red sweater you're wearing—that's even more so." —
"Well, Paul, I do hope you'll find me sweeter tempered
in blue. Adieu."

That was rather a good exit. Here's hoping Paul and
Cissy don't think me jealous. — I'll swear there's something between the two, but nothing in the world
worries me less. — I think I'll turn around again and
wave to them. Wave to them and smile. Now, don't
I look gracious? — Oh, Heavens, they're playing again.
As a matter of fact, I play a much better game than
Cissy; and Paul really isn't exactly a champion. — But
he *is* handsome with his open collar and that naughty
look. If only he weren't so affected. Don't worry, Aunt
Emma, so far as I am concerned. . . .

What a perfectly wonderful evening! This would
have been the right sort of weather for a trip to the
Rosetta Camp. How gorgeously the Cimone towers
up into the sky! — We should have started at five

o'clock in the morning. Of course, I would have felt
miserable, as usual, when we began—but that feeling
soon wears off. — There's nothing more divine than
wandering through the gray of the morning. — That
one-eyed American at the Rosetta looked like a prize-
fighter. Perhaps someone knocked his eye out in a
fight. I'd rather like to be married in America, but not
to an American; or perhaps it would be pleasant to
marry an American, and then live in Europe. A villa
on the Riviera with marble steps going into the sea.
How long is it since we were in Mentone? It must be
seven or eight years. I was thirteen or fourteen at the
time. Ah, yes, those were the days when we were in
better circumstances. — It really was silly to postpone
the outing. We'd have been back by now. — At four
o'clock, as I was going out to play tennis, the special
delivery letter about which Mother telegraphed hadn't
arrived. Perhaps it's here now. I might just as well have
played another set. — Why are those two young people
greeting me? I don't know them. They've been living
here at the hotel since yesterday and have been taking
their meals at the left side in the dining room, where
the Dutchmen used to sit. Did I nod back ungraciously
or haughtily? I didn't mean to act that way. What did
Fred call me on the way home from "Coriolanus"?
High-spirited. No, disdainful. You're disdainful, not
high-spirited, Else. — Those are nice words. He's always finding nice words. — Why am I walking so
slowly? Can it be that I'm afraid of the news in
Mother's letter? Well, I can't expect anything very
pleasant. Why a special delivery letter? Perhaps she
wants me home again. Ah me, what a life—in spite
of the silk stockings and the silk sweater. I have three
pair—I, the poor relative, invited out by her rich aunt.

I'm sure she's already sorry she invited me. Dear Auntie, shall I put it in writing for you that I don't love Paul—even in my dreams? Oh, Lord, I don't dream about anybody. I'm not in love and I never have been. I wasn't even in love with Albert, though I may have imagined so for days and days. I think that I just can't fall in love with anyone. That's really remarkable, for I'm certainly a sensualist. But still, I'm proud and haughty. Thank Heaven for that! The first time I really was in love was when I was thirteen. I was in love with Van Dyck and still more in love with the Abbé des Grieux and also with Renard. And at the Wörthersee when I was sixteen years old. — Well, no, that really wasn't anything. Oh, why am I reminiscing about all these things? I'm not writing my memoirs. I don't even keep a diary like Bertha. Fred rather attracts me—nothing more. Perhaps, if he had a little more swank. There; I have it. I'm a snob. Father knows it and always laughs at me. Oh, dear Father, you worry me a great deal. I wonder whether he has ever deceived Mother. *Has* he? Of course, he has. Often. Mother's rather stupid. She really knows nothing about me at all. Neither do other people. As for Fred—well, yes, but only very slightly. — Perfectly heavenly evening. The hotel's all gayly bedecked. One gets the impression of many prosperous care-free people. Me, for instance. Ha ha. It's too bad, because I really was born for a care-free life. It might have been so wonderful. It's a pity. — Now there's a red glow over the Cimone. Paul might look at it and call it an Alpine glow. As a matter of fact, that's far from an Alpine glow. It's beautiful enough to make you weep. Oh, why does one ever have to return to the city!

"*Good evening, Fräulein Else.*" — "Küss' die Hand,
gnädige Frau." — "*Back from tennis?*" — She can see
I'm back from tennis. Why does she ask me? "Yes,
indeed, we played almost three hours. Are you taking
a walk?" — "*Yes, the usual evening constitutional
down the lane. There's such a beautiful path between
the two meadows, but during the daytime it's almost
too sunny.*" — "Yes, the meadows here are gorgeous,
especially so from my window by moonlight." —

"*Good evening, Fräulein Else.*" — "Küss' die Hand,
gnädige Frau." — "Good evening, Herr von Dorsday." — "*Back from tennis, Fräulein Else?*" — "How
observant you are, Herr von Dorsday," — "*Please don't
make fun of me, Else.*" — Why doesn't he call me
"Fräulein Else"? — "*Anyone who looks so beautiful
with a tennis racket is justified in carrying it for
decorative purposes.*" — The ass! I just won't answer
that at all. — "We were playing all afternoon. There
were only three of us, Paul, Frau Mohr and myself."
— "*I was a ranking tennis player in my day.*" — "And
aren't you any longer?" — "*No, I'm too old for that
now.*" — "Old? Why, in Marienlyst there was a Swede
who was sixty-five years old. He played every evening
from six to eight, and the year before that he played
through a whole tournament." — "*Well, I'm neither
sixty-five as yet, thank Heaven, nor, unfortunately, a
Swede.*" — Why unfortunately? I suppose he thinks
that's funny. The best thing for me to do is to laugh
politely and just leave. "Küss' die Hand, gnädige Frau.
Adieu, Herr von Dorsday." What a deep bow he makes
and what calves' eyes! I wonder whether I insulted
him by referring to the sixty-five-year-old Swede. That
doesn't matter. Frau Winawer must lead an unhappy
life. She's fifty, at least. Those tear sacs of hers—as

though she had wept a great deal in her day. How terrible it must be to be so old! Dorsday is walking over toward her. There he is walking along at her side. He still looks rather well with his grayish Van Dyke beard. But I can't feel at all attracted to him. He's only a social climber. What good does your first-class tailor do you, Herr von Dorsday? — Dorsday, rather. I'm sure your name used to be something else. — Here comes that sweet young girl of Cissy's with her Fräulein. — "God bless you, Fritzi. Bon soir, mademoiselle. Vous allez bien?" — *"Merci, Mademoiselle. Et vous?"* — "Well, Fritzi, I see you're carrying an Alpine stick. Are you going to climb to the top of the Cimone?" — *"No, I'm not allowed to climb as high as that."* — "Perhaps you'll be allowed to next year. Good-bye, Fritzi. A bientôt, Mademoiselle." — *"Bon soir, Mademoiselle."*

A most attractive person. I wonder why she ever became a nurse girl—and why did she ever work for Cissy? It must be a mean life. Oh, Heavens, just to think that the same thing might happen to me! But of course it wouldn't, for I'm very accomplished. — Accomplished? — What a priceless evening! "The air is like champagne." That's what Dr. Waldberg said yesterday. And the day before yesterday somebody else said it. — I wonder why people will stay indoors in wonderful weather like this. I just can't understand it. Or is everyone waiting for a special delivery letter? The porter has just seen me. If there had been a special delivery letter he would have brought it to me immediately. Well, thank God, there's none there. I'll lie down a while before dinner. Why does Cissy say "dîner"? That's a stupid affectation. They're just like one another, Cissy and Paul. — Oh, I wish the letter

were here already. It'll probably show up at "dîner,"
and if it doesn't show up then I'll have a restless night.
I slept so miserably last night. I'll take my veronal
today. But I'll get used to that. No, my dear Fred, you
mustn't worry about me. In my thoughts I'm always
with you. — One ought to try everything, even hashish.
I think that Ensign Brandel brought some with him
from China. Is hashish drunk or smoked? It's supposed
to give you marvelous visions. Brandel invited me to
drink—or smoke—hashish with him. — Rather impertinent on his part—but he *is* handsome.

   "Please, a letter for you, Fräulein." — So it's the
porter. — I'm turning toward him quite casually. Perhaps it's only a letter from Caroline, or from Bertha, or
Fred or Miss Jackson. "Many thanks." It's a special
delivery letter from Mother. Why didn't he tell me
immediately that it was a special delivery letter? "I
see it's a special delivery letter." I shan't open it until
I get to my room and then I'll read it all by myself. —
There goes the Marchesa. Doesn't the dusk make her
look young! I'm sure she's forty-five. I wonder where
I'll be at forty-five. Possibly dead. — I hope so. She's
smiling at me just as pleasantly as always. I'll pass by,
nodding a little, and show her that the smile of a
Marchesa doesn't make too much of an impression on
me. — *"Buona sera."* — She bids me buona sera. Well,
now I really must bow slightly. I wonder whether I
bowed too deeply. She really is ever so much older.
What a wonderful walk she has! I wonder if she's
divorced. My walk is beautiful, too, but—I'm aware of
it. That's the difference. — An Italian might be dangerous for me. It's a pity that the good-looking dark one
with the Roman head left so soon. Paul said he looked
like a Filou. My goodness, I've nothing against Filous!

In fact, quite the opposite. — So, here I am at Number
Seventy-seven. Seventy-seven really is a lucky number.
Beautiful room. The pine wood is lovely. — Now we
have a real Alpine glow. Even so, I shan't admit it to
Paul. Paul's really rather shy. He's a doctor and a
woman's specialist as well. Perhaps he's shy for that
very reason. The day before yesterday when we were
walking in the forest we were so far away from everyone that he might have been a bit more forward, only
it would have done him no good. As for being forward, no one ever has tried it with me. Oh, possibly
when we were swimming three years ago in the
Wörthersee. But, *forward*: no, he was just plain indecent—handsome as he was. He was a real Apollo
Belvedere, though I didn't realize it at the time. But
still I was only sixteen. There's my heavenly meadow.
My—! Oh, I wish I could carry you back with me to
Vienna. What beautiful mist! Is it really autumn? Of
course it is. Today's the third of September and we are
high up in the mountains.

Well now, Fräulein Else, will you finally make up
your mind to read that letter? It doesn't necessarily
concern Father. Couldn't it possibly contain some news
about my brother? Perhaps he's engaged to one of
his old flames. Perhaps to a chorus girl or a shop girl.
Oh, no, he'd be too clever to do that. I really know
nothing about him at all. When I was sixteen and he
twenty-one he confided a great many of his affairs to
me, especially as they concerned a certain Lotte; but
all of a sudden he stopped. Lotte must have done something to him. And since then he's confided no more. —
Well, here I've opened the letter without even noticing
it. I'll sit down on the window sill and read it. I must
take care that I don't fall out. According to advices

from San Martino, a lamentable accident happened at
the Hotel Fratazza. Fräulein Else T., a beautiful
nineteen-year-old girl, daughter of the well-known
lawyer . . . Of course, they'll say that I committed
suicide over an unhappy love affair, or worse. Unhappy
love affair? I should say not.

"My dear child" — I'll look at the end first. — "So
again, do not be angry with us, my dear, good child,
and be a thousand times —" — For Heaven's sake,
they haven't killed themselves! ! No; in that case
there'd be a telegram from Rudi. — "My dear child,
you can believe me how sorry we are that into your
pleasant weeks of vacation"—as though I didn't always have a vacation, unfortunately—"we must intrude with such unpleasant news." — Mother has a
fearful style. — "But after mature consideration nothing else remains for me. Briefly and to the point, Father's situation has become acute. I don't know what
to think or do." — Why so many words? — "It involves
a comparatively ridiculous sum—thirty thousand gulden,"—ridiculous?—"which must be obtained in three
days, else all is lost." — For Heaven's sake, what does
that mean? — "Think of it, my dear child, the Baron
Höning"—who, the district attorney?—"summoned
Father to his office today. You know, of course, how the
Baron respects Father. Yes, even loves him. A few
years ago, when matters also hung by a hair, he spoke
personally to the chief creditors and put affairs in
shape at the last moment. But this time nothing can
be done if the money is not forthcoming. Besides the
fact that we shall be ruined, there will be a scandal, the
like of which there has never been. Think of it. A
lawyer, a famous lawyer—who—no, I cannot write
it down. I fight constantly against tears. You know,

child, for you are intelligent, we have been, God help
us, several times in similar situations and the family
has always helped us out. Last time, one hundred
twenty thousand were involved. But that time Father
had to sign an agreement that he never would approach
our relatives again, especially Uncle Bernhard." — Well,
go on, go on. What's the point? What can I do about
it? — "The only one of whom I could think as a last
resort would be Uncle Victor, but he, unfortunately,
is on a journey to the North Cape or Scotland"—yes,
he's well off, the nasty fellow—"and he is absolutely
unreachable, at least for the time being. Among Father's colleagues, especially, Dr. Sch., who frequently
has helped out Father"—good Lord, how do we stand
there?—"is no longer to be thought of, now that he
has married again." — Well, what then? What do you
want me to do? — "And now a letter has come, my
dear child, in which you mention among others, Dorsday, who is also staying in Fratazza, and that seems
like a stroke of Fate. You know how often Dorsday
came to visit us in former years." — Well, not so
often. — "It is sheer accident that we have seen him
less frequently in the last two or three years; he is
supposed to be deeply entangled—between you and
me, nothing very fine." — Why "between you and
me"? — "At the Residenzklub Father plays whist with
him every Thursday and in the past winter he saved
him a pretty piece of money in an action against another art dealer. Furthermore, why should you not
know it? He came to your father's assistance before."
— I thought so. — "That time only a mere bagatelle
was involved—eight thousand gulden—but after all,
thirty isn't a great sum for Dorsday. So I wondered
whether you could not do us a favor and speak to

Dorsday." — What? — "He always liked you particularly." — Never noticed it. He stroked my cheeks when I was twelve or thirteen years old. "Quite a young lady already." — "And as Father, luckily, has not approached him again since the eight thousand, he probably will also not decline this favor. He is supposed to have made eighty thousand a few days ago on a Rubens which he sold to America. Naturally, you may not mention this." — Do you think I'm a goose, Mother? — "But otherwise you can talk to him quite frankly. You might also mention, if occasion arises, that Baron Höning has summoned Father, and that with thirty thousand the worst will be averted, not only for the time being, but, God willing, forever"—do you really believe that, Mother?—"for the Erbesheimer case, which seems to be brilliantly promising, will surely bring Father a hundred thousand. But, of course, he cannot demand anything from Erbesheimer in this instance. So I beg of you, my child, speak to Dorsday. I assure you there is no harm in it. Father could simply have telegraphed him—we discussed it seriously—but it is something quite different, my child, when one speaks face to face with a person. The money must be here on the fifth, at noon. Dr. F." —Who is Dr. F.? Oh, yes, Fiala.—"is implacable. Of course, there is also personal ill-feeling in the matter, but as, unfortunately, it concerns trust funds"— for Heaven's sake, Father, what have you done?— "we can do nothing. And if the money is not in Fiala's hands by twelve noon on the fifth, he will ask an order of arrest. Baron Höning will restrain him that long. So Dorsday would have to transfer the amount by telegraph through his bank to Dr. F. Then we are saved. Otherwise, God knows what will happen. Believe me, you will not reproach yourself in the least, my dear child. Father was doubtful at first. He even made efforts in two directions, but he came home quite in despair,"—can Father ever be in despair?—"perhaps not so much because of the money, but because people have acted so shamefully toward him. One of them was once Father's best friend. You can imagine whom I mean."—I can imagine nothing at all. Father has had so many best friends and actually none at all. Possibly Warnsdorf? — "Father came home at one o'clock and now it is four o'clock in the morning. He is sleeping at last, thank God." — It might be best for him if he never woke up. — "As soon as possible I shall post this letter myself, special delivery, so that you will receive it on the morning of the third." — How did Mother think that possible? She never knows her way about in these things. — "So speak at once with Dorsday, I beseech you, and telegraph at once how it came out. Do not, for God's sake, let Aunt Emma notice anything. It is sad enough that in a case like this one cannot turn to one's only sister, but one might just as well speak to a stone. My dear, dear child, I am so sorry that you must live through such things in your youth, but believe me, Father is only in the smallest way at fault." — Who then, Mother? — "Now we hope to God that the Erbesheimer case will, in every respect, mark a change in our affairs. Only, we shall have to survive these few weeks. It would surely be irony if a catastrophe occurred over the thirty thousand gulden." — She doesn't mean seriously that Father will commit— But would not the other be even worse? — "Now I close, my child. I hope that in any circumstance" — in any circumstance? — "you will be able to remain in San Martino at least until the

ninth or tenth. You must not return, in any case, for
our sake. Remember me to your aunt—continue to be
nice to her. So again, do not be angry with us, my
dear good child, and be a thousand times" — Yes, I
know that already.

So, I am to solicit Herr von Dorsday. . . . Idiotic.
What does Mother take me for? Why didn't Father
simply board a train and come up here immediately? —
He would have arrived at the same time as the special
delivery letter. But perhaps they might have caught
him at the station—that *would* have been terrible. I'm
sure no one will help us out with thirty thousand
gulden. Always the same story for the last seven years.
No, even longer than that. Who would believe it to
look at me? No one would believe it to look either at
Father or at me, and yet everybody knows it. It's a
miracle that we still can keep our heads up. One becomes used to things quickly. As a matter of fact, we're
living quite well. Mother's really an artist. It seems inconceivable that we had a dinner for fourteen people
last New Year's—but the two pair of party gloves I
had—oh, they were a sad affair. And when Rudi
wanted three hundred gulden recently, Mother almost
wept. But Father's always good-natured. Always? No,
not always. When we heard "Figaro" recently, a look
came over his face suddenly that really frightened me.
— In a moment he seemed to become an altogether different man. — But after the opera we dined at the
Grand Hotel and then he was just as brilliant as ever.

And now I'm holding the letter in my hand. The
letter's altogether idiotic. I'm to speak to Dorsday. I'd
just die of shame. — Shame? Why, what have I to be
ashamed of? I'm not to blame. — If I only could speak
to Aunt Emma. But that's nonsense. She probably

hasn't as much money as all that to give away. And
Uncle is nothing more than a miser. O God, why
haven't I any money? Why haven't I ever earned anything? Why didn't I ever study? Oh, I've learned
something. No one can say that I'm altogether unac-
complished. I play the piano; I can speak French,
English and a little Italian; I've attended lectures. —
Haha! And even if I had done more worth-while
things than that, what good would they do me now?
Certainly I couldn't have saved thirty thousand gulden
by this time. —

The Alpine glow has died out. The evening's no
longer wonderful. The surroundings seem sad. No,
not the surroundings, but life itself is sad, and here
I'm sitting quietly on the window sill, and Father is to
be locked up. No, never, never! It mustn't be! I'll save
him! Yes, Father, I'll save you! It's very simple. Just
a few nonchalant words in my best manner. — Haha.
I'll treat Herr Dorsday as if it were an honor for him
to lend us money. And it *is* an honor. — Herr von
Dorsday, possibly you have a few moments' time for
me. I've just received a letter from Mother. She's
temporarily embarrassed—rather, Father — "Why, certainly, my dear lady, with the greatest of pleasure.
How much is involved?" — I wish he didn't have
this revolting effect on me. And the manner he has
of looking at me! No, Herr Dorsday, I'm not taken in
by your elegant manner and your monocle and your air
of nobility. You might just as well be an old-clothes man
as an art dealer. — But, Else, Else, what makes you say
a thing like that? — Oh, I can permit myself a remark
of this sort. Nobody notices it in me. I'm even a blonde,
a strawberry blonde, and Rudi looks absolutely like an
aristocrat. Of course, one can notice it easily in Mother,

especially in her speech, but not at all in Father. Really they ought to notice it in me. More than that—let them notice it. I don't deny it and certainly Rudi doesn't. Quite the contrary. I wonder what Rudi would do if Father were put in jail. Would he shoot himself? What nonsense! Shooting and jail—all these things don't happen. They just appear in the newspapers. —

The air is like champagne. In an hour we'll have dinner—"dîner." I just can't bear Cissy. She doesn't care the least bit about her little girl. What shall I wear? The blue or the black one? Black seems to be the right color for today. Too décolleté? *Toilette de circonstance,* as they say in French novels. At all events, I must look seductive when I interview Dorsday. After the dîner, I'll act nonchalantly. He'll stare his eyes out. Odious fellow. I hate him. I hate all people. Must it be Dorsday? Is Dorsday really the only person in the whole world who has thirty thousand gulden? Suppose I tell Paul about it. If he told Aunt that he had gambling debts he'd certainly be able to get the money. —

It's almost dark now. Night. Deathly night. Oh, I wish I were dead. — It just can't be true. Couldn't I go down right now and speak to Dorsday before dinner? Oh, how terrible! — Paul, if you give me thirty thousand you may have anything of me that your heart desires. No, that speech also comes out of a novel. The noble daughter sells herself for the sake of her beloved father and ends up by finding great joy in it. Oh, that's terrible. No, Paul, you can't have me even for thirty thousand. But for a million? — Or for a palace, or for a pearl necklace? If I marry some day I'll probably do it cheaper. Is it actually so bad?

Fanny really sold herself. She told me that her husband makes her shudder. How would you like it, Father, if I auctioned myself off this evening just to save you from prison? It would make a sensation — ! I have fever, I'm sure of it. Perhaps it's the air, like champagne. — If Fred were only here he could advise me. I need no advice. There's no advice to give. I'll talk to Herr Dorsday of Eperies and I'll appeal to him, I, the haughty, the aristocrat, the Marchesa, the beggarmaid, the embezzler's daughter. How have I come to this? No one is a better climber than I am; no one has so much spunk. I'm a sporting girl. I should have been born in England, or else been a Countess.

There are my clothes hanging in the closet. I wonder whether the green felt has already been paid for, Mother. Only one installment, I think. I'll wear the black one. They all stared at me yesterday, even the pale little man with the golden pince-nez. I don't look exactly beautiful today but I do look interesting. I should have gone on the stage. Bertha already has had three lovers and no one thinks less of her for it. In Düsseldorf it was the manager. In Hamburg she lived with a married man at the Atlantic Hotel—rooms with bath. I'm sure she's proud of it. They're all stupid. I'll have a hundred lovers, a thousand; why not? Is the décolleté deep enough? If I were married it could be even deeper. — How fortunate, Herr von Dorsday, that I meet you here. I've just received a letter from Vienna . . . I'll take the letter with me in case of emergency. Shall I ring for the maid? No, I'll dress myself alone. I need no one to help me with the black gown. If I were rich I'd never travel without a personal maid.

I'd better turn on the light. It's getting cool, so I'll

close the window. — It won't be necessary to pull down the shade. Nobody's standing over there on the hill with a telescope, — Herr von Dorsday, I've just received a letter. — Oh, perhaps it'll be better to do it all after dinner when both of us will be in a lighter mood. It might do me good to drink a glass of wine first. On the other hand, dinner would prove very much more appetizing if I finished the whole business beforehand. — All these wonderful dishes: Pudding à la merveille, fromage et fruits divers. Yes, but what if Herr von Dorsday shoudl say No? — And suppose he grew impertinent. Oh, no, nothing like that could happen. No one ever has been impertinent with me. Of course, Brandel, the young marine lieutenant, went a little too far, but he was so good-natured about it all. — I am getting thin again. That's becoming to me. — Darkness is peering in again—peering in like a ghost—like a hundred ghosts. Ghosts are rising up out of the meadow. How far away is Vienna? How long ago did I leave it? Oh, I feel so all alone! When will I marry? Who would marry the daughter of an embezzler? — Herr von Dorsday, I've just received a letter. — "Oh, Fräulein Else, pray don't waste your breath talking to me about it. Just yesterday I sold a Rembrandt. Pray, Fräulein Else, don't shame me by mentioning it." And now he's tearing a page out of his check book and signing it with his golden fountain pen; and tomorrow morning I'll take the train to Vienna. Oh, yes, I'll do that in any case, check or no check. I can't stay here any longer. I can't, and I won't. I'm living here as a smart, elegant young woman, while Father is back there in Vienna with one foot in the grave—or rather in jail. — Well, so this is the last pair of silk stockings. But nobody can notice the little rip

under the knee. No one? Who can tell? Don't be
frivolous, Else. — Bertha's nothing but a hussy. But
is Christine even the least bit better? Her future husband has a pleasant prospect ahead of him. I'm sure
Mother was always a faithful wife. But I'll never be
faithful. I'm haughty, but I'll never be faithful. Filous
attract me too much. I am sure that the Marchesa is
in love with a Filou. If Fred knew me as I really am,
his veneration for me would disappear at once. —
"Everything would have been possible for you, Fräulein. You could have been a pianist, or a bookkeeper,
or an actress. There is no end of possibilities in you,
but you have always been too well off." Too well off.
Haha. Fred overestimates me. As a matter of fact, I've
no talent at all. — Who knows, I might have gone as
far by this time as Bertha, but I lack energy. A young
woman of good family. — Haha, good family! And
the father embezzles trust funds. Why did you do
this to me, Father? If only you had something to
show for it—but gambling on the exchange! Is the
effort worth it? And the thirty thousand won't help
you, either. It might for three months. But in the end
you'd be ruined. A year and a half ago you were almost in the same position as you are now. Help came
then, but some time help won't come, and then what
will happen to us? Rudi'll go to the Vanderhulst bank
in Rotterdam, but what'll become of me? A wealthy
husband. Oh, if I could only concentrate on that!
Today I'm really beautiful. It's probably because I'm
excited. For whom am I beautiful today? Was I happier while Fred was here? Oh, Fred isn't really the
right man for me. He isn't a Filou, but I'd marry him
if he had money. And then, no doubt, a Filou would
come along—and the fun would begin. — Herr von

Dorsday, wouldn't you like to be a Filou? — At a
distance you sometimes look like one. Just like a dis-
sipated vicomte, like a Don Juan—with your stupid
monocle and your white flannel suit. But, really, you
aren't a Filou at all. — Have I everything? Am I
ready for dinner? — But what is there to do for a
whole hour in case I don't meet Dorsday? What if
he's walking with Frau Winawer? She really isn't unhappy at all. She doesn't need thirty thousand gulden.
Well, then I'll sit down in the hall, look magnificent
in a fauteuil, skim over the Illustrated News and the
Vie Parisienne, cross my legs, — no one will notice the
rip under the knee. Perhaps a millionaire has just arrived. — I'll take along the white shawl. It's becoming
to me. I'll throw it carelessly over my gorgeous
shoulders. For whom have I gorgeous shoulders? I
could make a man happy, if the right man for me only
existed. But I'll not have children. I'm not maternal.
Marie Weil is maternal. So is Mother. Aunt Irene is
maternal. I have a noble brow and a beautiful figure. —
"If I only were permitted to paint you as I want to,
Fräulein Else." — Yes, that would please you. I don't
even remember his name. I know that it wasn't Titian;
therefore, it was just plain impertinence. — I've just
received a letter, Herr von Dorsday. — I need a bit
more powder on my throat and neck, a drop of Ver-
veine in my handkerchief. So; I'll lock the cabinet, open
the windows. Oh, it's too marvelous for tears! I'm
nervous. Hasn't one the right to be nervous under circumstances like these? I'll put the box with the veronal
in it under my chemises. I need new chemises too.
That'll be another nuisance. Oh, Lord!

It's uncanny, that enormous Cimone, as if it were
ready to fall down on me. Not a star yet in the sky.

The air is like champagne! And the perfume from the meadows! I'll live in the country. I'll marry a landowner and have children. Possibly the only man with whom I might have been happy was Dr. Froriep. What wonderful evenings those two were—first at Kniep and then at the Artists' Ball. Why did he disappear so suddenly? Perhaps because of Father. Yes; that's probably it. I'll blow a kiss up into the air before I go downstairs to that rabble. But to whom shall I send my greeting? I'm all alone. No one can imagine how terribly alone I am. Good evening, my lover! Who? Good evening, my bridegroom! Who? Good evening, my friend! Who? — Fred? — Hardly. I'll keep the window open even if it is growing cool. I'll turn on the light. So. — Yes, that's right. Here's the letter. I'll take it with me to be prepared for any emergency. I'll keep the book there on the table. No matter what happens I'll read further tonight in "Notre Cœur." Good evening, lovely lady of the looking-glass. Think well of me. Farewell. . . .

Well, why do I lock the door? Nothing will be stolen here. I wonder whether Cissy leaves her door open at night, or does she open it only after he knocks? I wonder whether it's quite safe. Oh, certainly it is. — The stairs are altogether empty. They always are at this time. My steps are echoing. I've been here three weeks now. I left Gmunden on the twelfth of August. Gmunden was a bore. I wonder where Father got the money to send Mother and me to the country. And even Rudi traveled for four weeks. God knows where he traveled. He didn't write twice during the whole time. I just can't understand our way of living. Mother no longer has any jewelry. — I wonder why Fred was in Gmunden for only two days. I'm sure he has a mistress there, though it doesn't seem possible. Nothing seems possible. He hasn't written to me for a whole week. He writes lovely letters. — Who's that sitting over there at the little table? No, it isn't Dorsday. Thank God for that. It would be impossible to talk to him now before dinner. — Why is the porter looking at me so curiously? I wonder whether he read Mother's special delivery letter. Am I going crazy? I must give him a tip soon again. — The blonde over there is already dressed for dinner. How can anybody be as fat as that? — I'll go out in front of the hotel and stroll up and down a bit, or shall I go into the music room? Isn't someone playing there? It sounds like a Beethoven Sonata. How can anyone play a Beethoven Sonata in this place? I've neglected my piano playing. As soon as I return to Vienna I'll practice regularly again. In fact, I'll start an entirely new life. We all must do that. Nothing like this must ever happen again. I'll talk to Father in all seriousness—if there's still time for it. There'll be time. There certainly will. Why haven't I done it already? Everything at home is settled in a jesting manner and yet none of us is really gay at heart. Each is really afraid of the other and each is all alone, by himself. Mother's alone just because she isn't bright enough and doesn't know anything about anyone. She knows nothing about me, nor about Rudi, nor about Father. But she doesn't know that she doesn't know and neither does Rudi. He's really a good, handsome fellow, but he gave promise for more when he was twenty-one. It'll do him good to go to Holland, but where shall I go? I'd like to travel and do just exactly as I please. If Father runs away to America I'll go with him. I feel all confused. . . . The porter probably thinks me insane—the way I sit here on the bench, staring into space. I'll light a cigarette. Where's my cigarette case? Upstairs. But where, upstairs? I put the veronal in with the underwear but where did I put the cigarette case? Here come Cissy and Paul. She's evidently decided she must get dressed for dinner, otherwise they would have kept on playing in the dark. — They don't see me. I wonder what he's saying to her. Why does she laugh so inanely? It would be amusing to write an anonymous letter to her husband in Vienna. Would I do such a thing? Never. But, who knows? They've just seen me. I'm bowing to them. She's piqued that I'm looking so well. She certainly seems embarrassed.

"Dressed for dinner so soon, Else?" — Why "dinner" this time, instead of "dîner"? She's never consistent. — "As you notice, Frau Cissy." — *"You really look ravishing, Else. It would give me the greatest pleasure to make love to you."* — "Don't trouble to, Paul. I'd rather have a cigarette." — *"With pleasure."* — "Thank you. How did your singles match come out?" — *"Frau Cissy beat me three times in succession."—"He was absent-minded. By the way, Else, do you know that the Crown Prince of Greece is expected here tomorrow?"* — What's the Crown Prince of Greece to me? "Oh, really!" — Heavens! There's Dorsday with Frau Winawer. They're bowing to me. Now they're going on. I returned the bow too politely. Not as I usually do. Oh, what a strange person I am! — *"Can't you light your cigarette, Else?"* — "Oh, give me another match, please. Thank you." — *"Your shawl is very pretty, Else. It looks perfectly marvelous with the black dress. And now I must change my clothes."* — I'd rather she stayed. I'm afraid of Dorsday. — *"And I've ordered the hairdresser for seven o'clock. She's excellent—spends*

the winter in Milan. Well, adieu, Else, adieu, Paul." —
"*Küss' de Hand, gnädige Frau.*" — "Adieu, Frau
Cissy." — She's gone. I'm glad that Paul, at least, is
staying — "*May I sit with you a moment, Else, or am
I intruding on your reveries?*" — "Why on my reveries?
Perhaps on my realities." That really means nothing.
I'd rather he left me. I *must* speak to Dorsday. There
he is, still standing with the unhappy Frau Winawer.
He's bored. I can see it. He'd like to come over to
me. — "*Then there are realities on which I may not
intrude?*" — What is he saying? He can go to the
devil! Why do I smile at him so coquettishly? I don't
mean it for him at all. Dorsday's leering at me. Where
am I? Where am I? — "*What's the matter with you
today, Else?*" — "What do you think is the matter?" —
"*You're secretive, devilish, misleading.*" — "Don't talk
nonsense, Paul." — "*One could go mad looking at
you.*" — What is he thinking of? What sort of nonsense is he talking? He's good-looking. The cigarette
smoke catches in his hair. But I can't make use of him
now. — "*You're looking past me in such a peculiar
way. Why, Else?*" — I won't answer. I can't make
use of him now. I'll look as disagreeable as possible.
No conversation now. — "*Your thoughts are somewhere else.*" — "That's quite possible." He's nothing
to me. Does Dorsday know that I'm waiting for him?
I don't see him but I know that he's looking at me. —
"*Well then—good-bye, Else.*" — Thank God! He's
kissing my hand. He's never done that. "Adieu, Paul."
Where did I acquire that melting voice? He's leaving
—the fraud! Probably he has to arrange details about
tonight with Cissy. I wish him great joy. I'll draw the
shawl about my shoulders and rise and go out in front
of the hotel. Probably it'll be a trifle cool now. Too

bad that my coat—ah, I hung it in the porter's office this morning. I can feel Dorsday's gaze on my back, piercing through the shawl. Frau Winawer is going up to her room now. How do I know that? Telepathy. "I beg your pardon, Mr. Porter." — *"Fräulein wishes her coat?"* — "Yes, please." — *"The evenings are beginning to be cool. It comes on suddenly here."* — "Thank you." Ought I really to go in front of the hotel? Surely. Why not? At least to the door. Now they're passing by, one after the other. The gentleman with the golden pince-nez; the tall, blond one with the green vest; they all look at me. The little Geneva girl is pretty. No; she's from Lausanne. It really isn't so cool.

"Good evening, Fräulein Else." — Heavens! It's Dorsday. I won't mention Father. Not a word. Only after dinner. Or, I'll go to Vienna tomorrow. I'll go to Dr. Fiala myself. Why didn't I think of that immediately? I'm turning about, looking as though I didn't know who was standing behind me. — "Ah, Herr von Dorsday." — *"Would you still like to take a little stroll, Fräulein Else?"* — "Well, not exactly a stroll. Just a few turns before dinner." — *"We have almost half an hour."* — "Really." It really isn't so cool. The mountains are blue. It would be jolly if he suddenly proposed to me. — *"There surely isn't a prettier spot in the world than this."* — "You find it so, Herr von Dorsday? But please don't tell me that the air is like champagne." — *"No, Fräulein Else. I only say that when we reach two thousand meters. And here we are hardly sixteen hundred and fifty above sea level."* — "Does that make such a difference?" — *"Certainly. Were you ever in the Engadin?"* — "No, never. Is the air there really like champagne?" — *"One might*

almost say so. But champagne is not my favorite beverage. I prefer this vicinity for its wonderful forests." How tiresome he is! Doesn't he realize it? He obviously doesn't know what to say to me? It would be simpler with a married woman. A slightly indecent remark and the conversation is well under way. — *"Will you stay a while here in San Martino, Fräulein Else?"* Idiotic. Why do I look at him so coquettishly? He's already smiling knowingly. Oh, how stupid men are! "That depends partly on my aunt." That isn't really true. I could go alone to Vienna. "Probably until the tenth." — *"Your mother is still in Gmunden?"* — "No, Herr von Dorsday. She's been back in Vienna for three weeks. Father is also in Vienna. This year he's taken a vacation of less than a week. I believe the Erbesheimer case is making a lot of work for him." — *"I can imagine that. But your father is probably the only one who can save Erbesheimer. Success is already indicated by the fact that it has become a civil action."* — That's good. That's good. "I'm pleased to hear that you have so favorable a premonition." — *"Premonition? How so?"* — "That Father is to win the case for Erbesheimer." — *"I shouldn't assert that too confidently."* — How? Is he retreating? That won't do him any good. "Oh, I believe in premonitions and fancies. Think of it, Herr von Dorsday, just today I received a letter from home." That was not so good. He looks rather astonished. But go on. Don't hesitate. He's a good old friend of Father's. Go on. Go on. Now or never! "Herr von Dorsday, you just spoke so well of Father that it would be downright wrong if I weren't completely honest with you." What calves' eyes he is making at me! Oh, dear, he notices something. Go on. "For there was talk of you in that letter,

Herr von Dorsday. It is, in fact, a letter from Mother."
— *"So."* — "Really a very sad letter. You know our
circumstances, Herr von Dorsday." — For Heaven's
sake, I really have tears in my voice. Go on. Go on.
There's no retreat now. Thank God! "To be short and
to the point, Herr von Dorsday, we are once more in
—in the usual situation." — Now he'd like to disappear. "It involves—a small amount. Really only a
bagatelle, Herr von Dorsday. And yet, so Mother
writes, everything depends on it." I ramble on as stupidly as a cow. — *"Please calm yourself, Fräulein
Else."* — He said that nicely. But he needn't pat my
arm on that account. — *"What, then, really is the
trouble, Fräulein Else? What is in that sad letter from
Mother?"* — "Herr von Dorsday, Father"— My knees
are trembling. — "Mother writes that Father" — *"But
for goodness' sake, Else, what's wrong? Wouldn't you
rather—here's a bench. May I put your coat about
you? It's rather cool."* — "Thanks, Herr von Dorsday.
Oh, it's nothing. Nothing special." So—suddenly I'm
sitting on the bench. Who's the lady coming this way?
I don't know her at all. If only I didn't have to say
more. How he stares at me! How could you ask this
of me, Father? That wasn't right of you, Father. But
now it's happened. I should have waited until after
dinner. — *"Well, Fräulein Else."* — His monocle's
dangling. That looks silly. Shall I answer him? I must.
Quickly now, and have it over with. After all, what
could happen to me? He's a friend of Father's. "Oh,
Lord, Herr von Dorsday, after all, you're an old friend
of our family." I said that very well. "And probably you
won't be surprised when I tell you that Father is once
again in a very dangerous position." How remarkable
my voice sounds! Is it I speaking? Am I perhaps

dreaming? I certainly must have an entirely different
voice than usual. — *"It certainly does not surprise me
completely. You are right about that, dear Fräulein
Else—even though I regret it deeply."* — Why do I
look at him so pleadingly? Smile. Smile. It will work.
— *"I feel most friendly towards your Father—towards
all of you."* — He oughtn't to look at me that way. It's
indecent. I'll speak differently and stop smiling. I
must act more worldly. "Well, Herr von Dorsday, now
you will have an opportunity to demonstrate your
friendship for my father." Thank Heavens, I have my
old voice again. "It seems, Herr von Dorsday, that
among all our friends and relations—most of them are
not yet back in Vienna—otherwise Mother probably
wouldn't have hit on the idea. — The other day in a
letter to Mother, I casually mentioned your presence
here in San Martino—among others, of course." — *"I
took it for granted, Fräulein Else, that I wasn't the
exclusive theme of your correspondence with Mother."*
— Why does he press his knee against mine? Oh, I'll
put up with it! What's the difference, once you've
sunk so low? — "The matter's simply this: It's Dr.
Fiala who seems to be causing particular trouble for
Father this time." — *"Oh, Dr. Fiala."* — He evidently
knows what kind of person Fiala is. "Yes, Dr. Fiala.
And the sum involved is due on the fifth—that is, the
day after tomorrow—at twelve noon—or rather, it
must be in his hands, for if it isn't, Baron Höning—
yes, think of it, the Baron summoned Father to him
privately. He likes him so much." Oh, why am I
speaking of Höning? That wasn't necessary. — *"You
mean, Else, that otherwise an arrest would be inevi-
table?"* — Why does he put it so severely? I won't answer. I'll merely nod. — *"Hm. That is really—bad.*

*That is truly very—this greatly gifted, brilliant man.
— And how much is really involved, Fräulein Else?"*
— Why does he smile? He finds it "bad," and he
smiles. What does his smile mean? Is the amount of
no consequence to him? And if he says No! I'll do
away with myself if he says No! So—I'm to name the
sum. "What, Herr von Dorsday? Haven't I told you
the amount? One million." Why did I say that? This
is no time for joking! But then, when I tell him how
much less it really is, he'll be pleased. How he'll open
his eyes! Does he really think it possible that Father
could be involved in a million — "Pardon me, Herr
von Dorsday, for joking at a time like this. I can assure you that I'm not gay at heart." Yes, yes, press your
knee against mine. You may take that liberty. "Of
course, a million isn't involved. All in all, the amount
runs to thirty thousand gulden, Herr von Dorsday,
which must be in the hands of Dr. Fiala by noon of
the day after tomorrow. Yes. Mother writes that
Father made every possible effort, but, as I said, the
relatives we sought were not in Vienna." — Oh, Lord,
how I've debased myself! "Otherwise, Father naturally
wouldn't have thought of turning to you, Herr von
Dorsday. Much less, ask me—" Why is he silent? Why
doesn't he say Yes? Where's the check book? And the
fountain pen? For Heaven's sake, he isn't going to
say No! Shall I go down on my knees before him?
Oh, God! Oh, God! —

"On the fifth, you say, Fräulein Else?" — Thank
God! At least he's saying something. "Yes indeed. At
noon of the day after tomorrow, Herr von Dorsday.
Therefore, it'll be necessary to—I don't believe it could
be done so late by letter." — *"Of course not, Fräulein
Else. We'll have to telegraph."* — "We"—that's good.

That's very good. — *"Well, that would be the least of it. How much did you say, Else?"* — He's heard me say it. Why does he torture me? "Thirty thousand, Herr von Dorsday. Really an absurdly small amount." Why did I say that? How stupid! But he's smiling. Stupid girl, he thinks. He's smiling quite amiably. Father is saved. He'd as soon lend me fifty thousand and then we could get ourselves all kinds of things. New chemises for me. How selfish I am! One gets that way — *"Not quite so absurd, my dear child—"* Why does he say "dear child"? Is it a good sign or not? *"—as you imagine. Even thirty thousand gulden have to be earned."* — "Pardon me, Herr von Dorsday. I didn't mean it that way. I thought only how sad it was that Father—because of such a small amount—" Oh, Lord, I'm bungling it again! "You can't imagine, Herr von Dorsday, even if you have some knowledge of our circumstances, how terrible it is for me, and more especially for Mother." — He's putting a foot on the bench. Is that supposed to be good form, or what? — *"Oh, I can imagine it easily, dear Else."* — How his voice sounds! Altogether different. Remarkable. — *"And I've often thought: a pity about this brilliant man."* — Why does he say "a pity." Won't he give the money? No; he's merely generalizing. Why doesn't he say "Yes" once and for all—or does he take that for granted? How he stares at me! Why doesn't he say more? Oh, because the two Hungarian ladies are passing by. At least he's resumed a decent attitude now. The foot's no longer on the bench. The cravat's too bright for an elderly gentleman. Does his mistress select them for him? Nothing very fine, "between you and me," Mother writes. Thirty thousand gulden. But I'm smiling at him. Why am I smiling? Oh, I'm so cowardly! — *"If one really could take it for granted that something might be done with this amount. But —you're a clever creature, Else. What would thirty thousand gulden be? A drop in the bucket."* — Oh, Heavens! Doesn't he want to give the money? I mustn't look so frightened. Everything depends on this. Now I must say something intelligent and convincing. "Oh, no, Herr von Dorsday, this time it would be no mere drop in the bucket. The Erbesheimer case is at hand. Don't forget that, Herr von Dorsday, and today it's as good as won. And Father has other cases, too. Furthermore, I intend—you mustn't laugh, Herr von Dorsday—to talk very seriously to Father. He takes me seriously. I may say that if there's one person who can influence him, it is—" *"You certainly are a delightful creature, Fräulein Else."* — His voice has that ring again. How disagreeable it is when men begin to "ring" this way. I don't like it in Fred, either. — *"A delightful creature, upon my word."* — Why does he say "upon my word"? It's banal. It sounds like a small-town theatre. — *"But gladly as I would share your optimism—once the cart has gone astray."* — "Not this time, Herr von Dorsday. If I didn't believe completely in Father, if I weren't completely convinced that these thirty thousand gulden—" I don't know what to say now. I can't exactly beg. He's thinking it over. Obviously. Perhaps he doesn't know Fiala's address. Nonsense. The situation is impossible. I sit here like a poor sinner. He stands before me and puts his monocle into his eye and says nothing. I'll leave now. That'll be best. I won't be treated this way. Father may kill himself. I'll kill myself, too. It's a shameless life. It would be best to jump from that cliff and have it over with. It would serve everyone

right. I'll go. — *"Fräulein Else."* —"Pardon me, Herr
von Dorsday, for bothering you at all. Everything considered, I can readily understand your inclination to
refuse." So. I'm through. — *"Stay, Fräulein Else."* —
Stay? Why should I stay? He'll give the money. Yes,
of course. He must. But I won't sit down again. I'll
remain standing as though I were going in half a
second. I'm a little taller than he is. — *"You haven't
waited for my answer, Else. Once before—pardon me,
Else, for referring to it in this connection—"* He
needn't say "Else" so often — *"I've been in a position
to help your father out of a difficulty. To be sure, that
was an—even more absurd sum than the present one
—and I didn't flatter myself with the hope of ever seeing the money again. So there really seems to be no
reason for refusing my assistance this time—and especially when a young girl like you, Else, comes in person as an intermediary."* — What is he driving at?
His voice "rings" no longer. Or it has a different
"ring." How he stares at me! He'd better be careful!
— *"And so, Else, I'm prepared—Dr. Fiala shall have
thirty thousand gulden at noon of the day after tomorrow, on one condition."* — He shouldn't say more.
He's said quite enough. "Herr von Dorsday, I, I personally will guarantee that my father will return this
sum as soon as he receives his fee from Erbesheimer.
So far, Erbesheimer has paid nothing. Not even a re-
tainer. Mother herself wrote that to me." — *"Let it
be, Else. One never should undertake a guarantee for
another. Not even for one's self."* — What does he
want? His voice "rings" again. Never has anyone
stared at me so! I suspect his intentions. He'd better
be careful! — *"Could I have thought it possible an
hour ago that I'd ever be in a position to dictate terms!*

*And now I'm doing it. Yes, Else, after all, I'm only
human and it isn't my fault that you're so beautiful,
Else."* — What does he want? What does he want? —
*"Perhaps I might have asked of you today or tomor-
row what I ask of you now. Even if you hadn't sought
a million—I beg your pardon, thirty thousand—gulden
from me. But really, if things had been otherwise, you
hardly would have given me this opportunity to speak
with you alone."* — "Oh, I really have taken up too
much of your time already, Herr von Dorsday." —
That was well said. Fred would have been satisfied
with it. What's this? Is he reaching for my hand?
What's the matter with him? — *"Haven't you been
aware of it for a long time, Else?"* — He should let
go of my hand. Now, thank Heaven, he's let go of it.
Not so close. Not so close. — *"You wouldn't be a
woman, Else, if you didn't notice it. Je vous désire."*
— He didn't have to say that in French, the noble
Vicomte. — *"Must I say more?"* — "You've said
quite enough, Herr von Dorsday." I'm still standing
here. Why? I'll leave. I'll leave without a word.
— *"Else, Else."* — Now he's next to me again. —
*"Forgive me, Else. I too have only been joking,
just as you did a little while ago, about the million. My demand, too, shall not be so exorbitant—as
you may have feared. So that the lesser demand will,
perhaps, be a pleasant surprise. Please stay, Else."* —
And I actually remain here! Why? Here we are, facing each other. Shouldn't I simply have slapped his
face? Wouldn't there still be time for that now? The
two Englishmen are passing. This would be the very
minute. Right now. Why didn't I do it? I'm cowardly.
I'm broken. I'm humiliated. What will he want now
in place of the million? A kiss, perhaps. That might

be considered. A million is to thirty thousand as—there are some funny comparisons. — *"If you really need a million some day, Else, you may be certain that I'll see to it, although I'm not a rich man. But this time I shall be reasonable, as you are. And this time I wish nothing more, Else, than—to see you."* — Is he crazy? He sees me. — Oh, he means it *that* way! Why don't I slap his face? The rotter! Have I turned red or pale? You want to see me naked? Many would like that! I'm beautiful when I'm naked. Why don't I slap his face? It's enormous. Why so close, you rotter? I don't want your breath on my cheeks. Why don't I just leave him? Are his eyes holding me? We glare at each other like deadly enemies. I'd like to call him a rotter to his face, but I can't. Or don't I want to? — *"You look at me as though I were crazy, Else. Perhaps I am slightly so. For there's a magic in you, Else, that you yourself can't realize. You must understand, Else, that my request implies no insult. Yes—request, I say. Though to you it may seem dangerously like coercion. But I'm no coercionist. I'm only a man who has had many experiences—among others, this: that everything in the world has its price, and that anyone who gives away his money when he might receive a return for it is a consummate fool. And—parting with what I wish to buy this time, Else, much as it is, will not make you poorer. And that the transaction will remain a secret between you and me, Else—that I swear to you by—by all the charms whose revelation will make me happy."* — Where did he learn to talk like that? It sounds like a book. — *"And I swear to you that I will never take any unfair advantage of the situation created by our agreement. I ask of you only to be allowed to stand for a quarter of an hour in con-*

*temptation of your beauty. My room is on the same
floor as yours, Else. Number Sixty-five. Easy to remember. The Swedish tennis player you mentioned
today—wasn't he just sixty-five years old?"* — He's
crazy. Why do I let him go on? I'm paralyzed. — *"But
if for any reason you don't care to visit me in room
Number Sixty-five, Else, then I suggest a little stroll
after dinner. There's a clearing in the woods. I discovered it by chance the other day. Hardly five minutes from our hotel. — It will be a wonderful summer
night, almost warm, and the starlight will clothe you
divinely."* — He speaks as he would to a slave. I feel
like spitting in his face. — *"You need not answer immediately, Else. Think it over. After dinner, you may
render your decision."* — Why does he say "render"?
What a stupid word: "render." — *"Think it over
calmly. Perhaps you'll come to the conclusion that
I'm not merely driving a bargain with you."* — What
else, you whining rotter! — *"Perhaps you'll suspect
that a man is speaking to you, a man who is rather
lonesome and not particularly happy, and who, perhaps, deserves a little sympathy."* — Affected rotter!
He speaks like a poor actor. His manicured fingers
look like claws. No! No! I won't! Why don't I tell him
so? Kill yourself, Father. What is he doing with my
hand? My arm's quite limp. He draws my hand to
his lips. Hot lips. Augh! My hand's cold. I'd like to
knock his hat off. Ha, how funny that would be! Had
your fill of kissing, you rotter? — The arc lamps in
front of the hotel are already lighted. Two windows
are open in the third story. The one in which the curtain is stirring is mine. Something's shining on the
cabinet. There's nothing on it. Only a brass ornament.
— *"So, auf Wiedersehen, Else."* — I don't answer. I

stand here motionless. He looks into my eyes. My
face is blank. He knows nothing. He doesn't know
whether I'll come or not. Neither do I. I only know
that everything's over. I'm half dead. There he goes.
A little bent. Rotter! He senses that I'm staring after
him. Whom is he greeting? Two ladies. He bows as if
he were a Count. Paul ought to challenge him and
shoot him. Or Rudi. What does he think anyway?
Brazen fellow! Never, never! There's nothing left to
do, Father. You'll have to kill yourself. — The couple
obviously is returning from a trip. Both handsome, he
and she. Have they time to change their clothes before
dinner? They're surely on their honeymoon—or perhaps they aren't married at all. I'll never go on a honeymoon. Thirty thousand gulden. No, no, no. Aren't
there thirty thousand gulden somewhere in the world?
I'll go to see Fiala. Mercy, mercy, Dr. Fiala. With
pleasure, my dear young lady. And there's my bedroom. — Please, Paul, do me a favor. Ask your Father
for thirty thousand gulden. Tell him you have gambling debts. That otherwise you must shoot yourself.
"Gladly, my dear cousin. My room is Number So-
and-so, and I'll expect you at midnight." Oh, Herr
von Dorsay, how modest you are. For the time being,
at least. Now he's dressing, putting on a smoking
jacket. Now we each go our own way. The meadow
by moonlight or Room Number Sixty-five. Will he
wear his smoking jacket when he's in the woods with
me?

There's still time before dinner. A little walk. Let's
think it over calmly. I'm a lonesome old man—ha, ha!
Heavenly air, like champagne. It's no longer cool. —
Thirty thousand . . . thirty thousand. . . . I must
look very pretty in this wide landscape. Too bad there

aren't more people in the clearing. Obviously I'm attractive to the gentleman out there near the edge of
the wood. Oh, my dear sir, I'm even more beautiful
naked, and the price is laughable. Thirty thousand
gulden. Perhaps you'll bring your friends with you.
Then it'll be cheaper for each one. Let's hope you have
many handsome friends, handsomer and younger than
Herr von Dorsday. Do you know Herr von Dorsday?
He's a rotter. Vile rotter. . . .

Oh, I must think it over. . . . A human life is at
stake. Father's life. But no—he won't kill himself. He'd
rather be imprisoned. Three years at hard labor—or
five. He's been living in terror of this for five or ten
years. . . . Trust funds. . . . And Mother, too. And
even I. — For whom will I have to strip next time? Or
shall we make permanent arrangements with Herr
von Dorsday for simplicity's sake? His present mistress is nothing very fine. "Just between you and me."
He'd certainly prefer me. I'm not at all sure that I'm
so much finer. Don't take on airs, Fräulein Else. I
could tell tales about you. . . . A certain dream, for
instance, that you've had three times now—and that
you haven't even told to your friend Bertha. And she's
going through something. And what was that affair
a little while ago in Gmunden? Six o'clock in the
morning, on the balcony, my proud Fräulein Else.
Perhaps you didn't notice the two young people in a
boat who were staring at you. Of course they couldn't
identify my face at that distance, but they couldn't help
noticing that I was in negligee. And it made me happy.
Oh, more than happy. It was intoxicating. I drew my
hands across my hips and acted as though I didn't
know that anyone saw me—and the boat didn't move
from the spot. Yes—I'm like that. Indeed I am. I'm a

hussy. They all know it. Even Paul knows it. Of
course, he's a woman's specialist; and the marine lieutenant knew it too, and so did the painter. Only Fred
doesn't know it, the stupid fellow. For he loves me.
But I'd rather not be naked in front of him. Never,
never! I wouldn't like it at all. I'd be ashamed. But for
the Filou with the Roman head—how gladly! Even
if I had to die the next minute. But I wouldn't have to
die the next minute. One can go through all sorts of
experiences. Bertha has gone through more.

No, no, I won't! I'll go to anyone else—but not to
him. To Paul, for all I care. Or I'll pick somebody for
myself this evening, at dinner. It's all the same. But I
can't tell everyone that I want thirty thousand gulden
in return. That would be like a woman from the
Kärntnerstrasse. No; I won't sell myself. Never. I'll
never sell myself. Yes; if once I find the right man, I'll
give myself. But I'll not sell myself. I'll be a wanton,
not a prostitute. You miscalculated, Herr von Dorsday. And so did Father. Yes, he miscalculated. He
should have foreseen it. He knows people. He knows
Herr von Dorsday. He could have known that Herr
von Dorsday wouldn't give something for nothing.
— Otherwise, he could have telegraphed, or come
here himself. But this way it was easier and safer,
wasn't it, Father? If a man has a pretty daughter, why
must he be marched off to prison? And Mother, stupid as ever, sits down and writes the letter. Father
didn't trust himself to do it. If he had written, I should
have noticed something peculiar immediately. But you
won't succeed. No; you've counted too definitely on
my childish affection, Father. You assumed too certainly that I'd rather undergo any indignity than let
you suffer the consequences of your criminal frivolity.

Certainly you're a genius. Herr von Dorsday says it.
Everybody says it. But how does that help me? Fiala's
a nobody, but he doesn't embezzle trust funds. Even
Waldheim isn't to be mentioned in the same breath
with you. . . . Who said that? Dr. Froriep. "Your
father is a genius." And I've only heard him speak
once! Last year at the assizes—for the first and last
time. It was glorious. Tears ran down my cheeks. And
the poor wretch he defended was acquitted. Perhaps
he wasn't such a poor wretch. In any case, he only stole
something. He didn't embezzle trust funds to play
baccarat and speculate on the exchange. Now Father
himself will be tried before the jury. It will be in all
the papers. Second day of the trial, third day of the
trial. The attorney for the defense arose to reply.
Who will defend him? Not a genius this time. Nothing will help him. Unanimous verdict of guilty. Sen-
tenced to five years. Stones, striped clothes, cropped
hair. Visitors permitted once a month. I go there with
Mother, third class. For we have no more money. No
one lends us anything. A little home in Lerchenfelder-
strasse, like the one in which I saw our seamstress ten
years ago. We bring him something to eat. From
where? For we have nothing ourselves. Uncle Victor
will allow us an income. Three hundred gulden a
month. Rudi will be in Holland with Vanderhulst—
if they still think of him. A convict's children. Novel
by Temme, in three volumes. Father receives us in the
striped suit of the criminal. He doesn't look angry—
merely sad. After all, he never can look angry. — Else,
if you had gotten me the money that time—that's what
he'll think, but he'll say nothing. He won't have the
heart to reproach me. He's endlessly kind, but he's
careless. His weakness is the love for gambling. He

can't help it. It's a sort of insanity. Perhaps they'll dis-
charge him because he's insane. And he didn't give
enough thought to the letter. Perhaps it never occurred to him that Dorsday would take advantage of
the situation and demand such an indignity of me.
He's a good friend of the family. Once before, he
loaned Father eight thousand gulden. Why should
one suspect a man like that? Father certainly tried
everything else first. What he must have suffered when
he had Mother write this letter! He went from Wars-
dorf to Burin, from Burin to Wertheimstein, and God
knows to whom next. He certainly went to Uncle Carl,
too; and they've all left him in his trouble. All the so-
called friends. And now Dorsday is his hope, his last
hope, and if the money doesn't arrive he'll kill himself. Of course he'll kill himself. He surely won't let
them put him in prison. Examination, trial, assizes,
jail, convict's clothes. No, no! When the summons
comes, he'll shoot or hang himself. He'll hang himself.
He'll hang himself from the window bars. They'll
send word to us from the house across the way. The
locksmith will have to open the door and I'll have
been at fault. And now he's sitting with Mother smoking a Havana cigar in the very room in which he'll
hang himself the day after tomorrow. Where does he
keep on getting all the Havana cigars? I can hear him
speaking as he quiets Mother. Depend on it, Dorsday will supply the money. Remember I saved him a
great sum this winter through my intervention. And
now comes the Erbesheimer case . . . — Surely. — I
hear him speaking. Telepathy! Remarkable. I also see
Fred this very moment. He's passing the casino in the
city park with a girl. She's wearing a light blue waist
and light shoes and she's a little hoarse. I'm sure of all

of it. When I go to Vienna I'll ask Fred whether he was in the city park with his sweetheart on the third of September between seven and eight o'clock.

What next? What's to be done? It's almost completely dark. Now nice and quiet. No one near or far. They're already at dinner. Telepathy? No; that isn't telepathy. Because I heard the gong a little while ago. ‚ Where's Else? Paul will think. He'll notice it if I'm not there for the first course. They'll send up for me. What's wrong with Else? She's always so punctual. The two men at the window will think, Where's that pretty girl with the reddish blonde hair today? And Herr von Dorsday will be frightened. He certainly is cowardly. Calm yourself, Herr von Dorsday, nothing will happen to you. I despise you far too much. If I wished it, you'd be a dead man tomorrow night. — I'm convinced that Paul would challenge you if I told him the story. I make you a present of your life, Herr von Dorsday.

How tremendously broad the meadow is, and how terribly dark the mountains. Hardly any stars are out. Yes, a few—three, four—there'll soon be more. And it's so quiet in the wood behind me. It's pleasant to sit here on the bench, at the edge of the wood. The hotel's so distant, so distant, and the lights are like the lights of fairyland. And what rotters live in it! Oh, no—people, poor people; I pity them all. I even pity the Marchesa—I don't know why—and Frau Winawer and the nurse of Cissy's little girl. She doesn't eat at the table d'hôte. She has her dinner earlier, with Fritzi. What's this about Else? asks Cissy. What? Isn't she in her room? They're all worried about me. I can feel they are. Only I don't worry about myself. Yes, here I am in Martino di Castrozza, sitting on a bench at the edge of the wood, and the air is like champagne, and it seems to me that I'm crying. Yes, and why am I crying? There's no reason for crying. My nerves are getting the better of me. I must control myself. I mustn't let myself go to pieces this way. But crying isn't at all unpleasant. Crying's always good for me. When I visited our old French nurse in the hospital —the one who died later—I also cried. At Grandmother's funeral, when Bertha left for Nuremburg, and when Agatha's baby died, and when we saw "Camille"—I cried then, too. Who'll cry when I'm dead? Oh, how beautiful it would be to be dead! I lie on a bier in the salon, with candles burning. Long candles. Twelve long candles. The hearse is already downstairs. People are standing at the gate. How old was she? Only nineteen. Really only nineteen? — Think of it, her father in jail. Why did she kill herself? Because she loved a Filou in vain. But what are you talking about? She was to have had a child. No; she fell from the Cimone. It's supposed to have been an accident. Good day, Herr von Dorsday. You too pay your last respects to little Else. Little Else, the old woman says. — Why? Certainly; I must pay my last respects. Wasn't I the first one to disgrace her? Oh, it was worth the trouble, Frau Winawer. I've never seen such a beautiful body. It cost me only thirty million. A Rubens costs three times as much. She poisoned herself with hashish. She merely longed for beautiful visions, but she took too much and never awoke. Why is Herr von Dorsday wearing a red monocle? At whom is he waving that handkerchief? Mother comes down the steps and kisses his hand. Terrible, terrible. Now they whisper to each other. I can't understand a word, because I'm on a bier. The

crown of violets about my brow came from Paul. The
ribbons stream to the floor. No one trusts himself in
the room. I'd rather get up and look out of the window.
What a great, blue sea! A hundred ships with yellow
sails. The waves glisten. So much sunlight. Regatta.
The men are wearing life preservers. The ladies are
in bathing suits. That's indecent. They think I'm
naked. How stupid they are! I'm wearing deep mourning, because I'm dead. I'll prove it to you. I'll lay myself on the bier again. Where is it now? It's gone.
They've taken it away. They've embezzled it. That's
why Father's in jail. And they've pardoned him after
three years. The jailers all were bribed by Fiala. Now
I'll go to the cemetery on foot. That'll save Mother the
funeral expenses. We must economize. I'm going so
quickly that no one follows me. Oh, how fast I can
go! They're all still standing in the streets, marveling.
How dare they stare so at one who's dead? This is oppressive. I'd rather go across the field. It's all blue with
forget-me-nots and violets. The marine officers stand
with swords at present-arms. Good morning, gentlemen. Open the gate. Open the gate, Sir Matador. Don't
you recognize me? I'm the girl that just died. . . .
Therefore, you mustn't kiss my hand. Where's my
grave? Is that embezzled too? Thank God, it's not the
cemetery at all. It's the park in Mentone. Father'll be
glad that I'm not buried. I'm not afraid of snakes. If
only my foot isn't bitten by one. Oh, dear!

What's happened? Where am I? Have I been
asleep? Yes; I've been asleep. I must have been dreaming. My feet are so cold. My right foot's cold. Why?
There's a little rip in the stocking, across the ankle.
Why am I still sitting in the woods. They must have
rung for dinner long ago. "Dîner."

Oh, Lord, where was I? I was so far away! What
was I dreaming? I think I was dead. And I had no
sorrows and didn't have to rack my brains. Thirty
thousand, thirty thousand . . . I haven't got them
yet. I must earn them first. And here I'm sitting alone
on the edge of the wood. The lights from the hotel
are shining all the way over here. I must return. It's
terrible that I must return. There's no more time to
be lost. Herr von Dorsday waits for my decision. Decision. Decision! No. No, Herr von Dorsday, once
for all, No. You've been joking, of course, Herr von
Dorsday. Yes; I'll say that to him. Oh, that's excellent! Your joke wasn't very delicate, Herr von Dorsday, but I'll forgive you. I'll telegraph Father in the
morning, Herr von Dorsday, that the money will be
in Dr. Fiala's hands punctually. Wonderful. I'll say
that to him. There'll be nothing left for him to do;
he'll have to send the money. Have to? Does he have
to? And why does he have to? And if he did, he'd
even the score in some way. He'd arrange it so that
the money arrived too late. Or he'd send the money
and tell everybody that he'd had me. But he won't
send the money at all. No, Fräulein Else, that wasn't
our bargain. Telegraph your Father what you please,
I'll not send the money. You shan't believe, Fräulein Else, that I allow myself to be outwitted by a
mere girl—I, the Vicomte of Eperies.

I must walk carefully. The road's quite dark.
Strangely enough, I feel better than I did. Nothing at
all has changed and I feel better. What could I have
been dreaming about? About a matador? What sort
of matador was he? It's farther to the hotel than I
thought. Surely they're still at dinner. I'll sit down
quietly at the table. I'll tell them that I've had a sick

headache and let them serve me later. Herr von Dorsday eventually will come to his senses and say that
the whole affair was only a joke. Forgive me, Fräulein Else, forgive me for my bad joke. I've already
telegraphed to my bank. But he won't say it. He hasn't
telegraphed. Everything is as it was before. He's waiting. Herr von Dorsday is waiting. No! I don't want
to see him. I can't see him any more. I don't want to
see anyone any more. I don't want to return to the
hotel; I don't want to return home; I don't want to
return to Vienna; I don't want to go to anybody; to
anyone at all; not to Father and not to Mother; not
to Rudi and not to Fred; not to Bertha and not to
Aunt Irene. She's still the best of them. She'd understand everything. But I'll have nothing more to do
with her or with anybody else. If I were a magician,
I'd be in some other part of the world. On some gorgeous ship in the Mediterranean, but not alone. With
Paul, perhaps. Yes, I could imagine that very easily.
Or I could be living in a villa by the sea, and we
would be lying on the marble steps that lead into the
water, and he'd be holding me close in his arms and
biting my lips, as Albert did at the piano two years
ago. The bounder! No. I'd like to lie alone by the
sea on the marble steps and wait, and at last a man
would come, or several men, and I'd choose one, and
the others whom I'd reject would throw themselves
despairingly into the sea. Or they'd have to be patient, until the next day. Oh, what a marvelous life
that would be! Why have I my glorious shoulders
and my beautiful slender legs, and for what reason,
after all, do I exist? And it would serve them right,
all of them. They've brought me up only to sell myself one way or another. They wouldn't hear of act-

ing. They laughed at me. It would have served them altogether right if last year I had married Wilomitzer, the stage director, who's almost fifty. If only they hadn't suggested things to me. Father, to be sure, seemed embarrassed. But Mother dropped some very plain hints.

How huge the hotel is! Like a monstrous, shining magic city. Everything's gigantic. The mountains, too. Terrifyingly so. They've never been so black. The moon hasn't risen yet. It'll rise only for the performance, for the great performance on the meadow, when Herr von Dorsday bids his slave dance naked. What's Herr von Dorsday to me? Well, Mademoiselle Else, what pretentious nonsense you are talking! You were prepared to be the mistress of strange men, of one after the other. And the trifle which Herr von Dorsday asks horrifies you. You're prepared to sell yourself for a string of pearls, for beautiful clothes, for a villa by the sea, and the life of your father isn't worth as much as that? That would have been just the right start. That would have been the correct preface to everything else. You were guilty, I could say. You brought me to it. You're all to blame that I've become what I am. Not merely Father and Mother. Rudi's to blame, too, and Fred, and everybody; yes, everybody because no one has troubled himself about me. A little caress when you look pretty, a little anxiety when you have fever; they send you to school and you take lessons in piano and French at home; in the summer you go to the country and on your birthday you get presents; and they talk about all sorts of things at dinner. But what I feel—the things stirring and trembling in me—have you ever thought of that? Sometimes I could see something of the sort in Father's eyes, but it passed quickly. The next moment he was wrapped up again in his practice and his troubles and his speculations. — And probably some common woman. Furtively. "Nothing very fine, between you and me." And I'd be alone again. Well, what would you do, Father? What would you do if I weren't here?

I'm standing here. Yes, here I'm standing in front of the hotel. — It'll be terrible to go in and see all the people, Herr von Dorsday, my Aunt, Cissy. How pleasant it was a little while ago on the bench—when I was already dead. Matador. — If only I could remember what it was. — It was a regatta. — Right. — And I was watching it from the window. But who was the matador? — Oh, if only I weren't so tired, so terribly tired. And now, I'm to sit up until midnight and then slip quietly into Herr von Dorsday's room? Perhaps I'll meet Cissy in the hall. Does she wear anything under her kimono when she goes to him? It's so difficult for a beginner! Oughtn't I to ask Cissy for advice? Of course, I mustn't tell her that it's Dorsday. I'd rather have her understand that I have a nightly rendezvous with one of the handsome young men in the hotel. For instance, the tall blond man with glowing eyes. But he's no longer here. He disappeared suddenly. I never even thought of him until this very minute. But unfortunately it's not the tall blond man with glowing eyes and it's not Paul. It's Herr von Dorsday. How shall I manage it? What shall I say to him? Just "Yes." And yet I can't visit Herr von Dorsday in his room. Of course he has all kinds of magnificent scent bottles on his washstand, and the room always smells of French perfume. No—not for anything in the world—I won't go to see him. It'll be better in

the open. The sky's so high and the meadow's so wide.
I mustn't think of Herr Dorsday at all. I mustn't even
look at him. And if he dares to touch me, I'll kick
him with my naked feet. Oh, if it only were somebody else. Anybody else. He could have everything
he wanted tonight. But not Dorsday. Not Dorsday!
Not Dorsday! How his eyes will stab and drill their
way into me. He'll stand there with his monocle and
leer. But no; he won't leer. He'll look dignified. Aristocratic. For he's used to such things. How many has
he seen—so? A hundred, or a thousand—but was there
one among them like me? No; certainly not. I'll tell
him he's not the first to see me this way. I'll tell him
I have a lover—but only after the thirty thousand
gulden have been sent to Fiala. Then I'll tell him that
he's a fool. That he could have had me, as well, for
the same amount. — That I've already had ten lovers
—twenty—a hundred. — But he won't believe that of
me. — And if he believed it, how would it help me?
— If only I could spoil his pleasure somehow. If only
someone else were present. Why not? He didn't stipu-
late that he had to be alone with me. Oh, Herr von
Dorsday, I'm so afraid of you. Won't you please do
me the favor of bringing some mutual acquaintance
with you? Oh, that's not at all contrary to our agreement, Herr von Dorsday. If I felt like it, I could invite the whole hotel and you'd still be bound to send
the thirty thousand gulden. But I'll be content if my
Cousin Paul comes. Or would you prefer somebody
else? The tall blond man unfortunately isn't here
now. And the Filou with the Roman head, unfortunately, has gone, too. But I'll find another, easily.
You fear a scandal. That's out of the question. Scandal has nothing to do with it. Nothing matters to one

who has gone as far as I have. Today's just the beginning. Or, do you think perhaps that I'll go home
from this adventure, a decent girl of good family?
No—neither good family nor decent young girl. That
matter would be settled, once for all. Hereafter, I'll
stand on my own feet. I have beautiful legs, as you
and the other participants in the festival will soon
have occasion to observe. So the matter's arranged,
Herr von Dorsday. At ten o'clock, while everybody's
still in the salon, we'll wander in the moonlight across
the meadow, through the woods to your famous
clearing. At all events, you'll have to bring the telegram to the bank with you. For it's my privilege to
demand a guarantee from a rascal like you. And at
midnight, you may return home, and I'll stay with
my cousin, or possibly with somebody else, in the
moonlit meadow. You've no objection to that, Herr
von Dorsday? You can't have. And if I should be
found dead tomorrow morning, don't be surprised. In
that event, Paul will send the telegram. I'll have seen
to that. But don't think, for Heaven's sake, that you,
you miserable scoundrel, have driven me to my death.
I've known for a long time that I'd end up this way.
Just ask my friend, Fred, if I haven't mentioned it to
him time and again. Fred. I mean Herr Friedrich
Wenkheim. Incidentally, the only decent person I ever
knew in my life. The only one I could have loved—
if he hadn't been such a decent person. Yes, I'm a very
corrupt creature. I wasn't meant for domesticity and I
haven't any talents. As it is, it might be best for our
family if it died out. Some catastrophe will overtake
Rudi. Some Dutch chorus girl will get him into debt
and then he'll defraud Vanderhulst. It runs in the
family. My father's youngest brother shot himself

when he was fifteen years old. No one knows why. I
didn't know him. Ask them to show you his photograph, Herr von Dorsday. We have it in an album.
. . . I'm supposed to look like him. Nobody knows
why he killed himself. And nobody will know why
I did. In any case, not on account of you, Herr von
Dorsday. I'll not do you that honor. At nineteen or
twenty-one—it's all the same. Or shall I become a
nurse girl or a telephone operator or marry Herr Wilomitzer or let you keep me? It's all equally disgusting,
and I'll not go to the meadow with you at all. No; all
of that's too tiring and too stupid and too disagreeable.
When I'm dead, will you be so good as to send a few
thousand gulden to Father, because it certainly would
be sad if he were to be arrested on the very day that
my body was taken to Vienna. But I'll leave a letter,
with this testament: Herr von Dorsday has the right
to see my body, my beautiful, naked corpse. So you
can't complain, Herr von Dorsday, that I made false
promises. You're getting something for your money.
Our contract doesn't specify that I must be alive when
you see me. Oh, no. There's nothing to that effect. So
—a view of my corpse I bequeath to the art dealer,
Dorsday, and to Herr Fred Wenkheim I bequeath my
diary up to my seventeenth year—that's as far as I
wrote it—and to Cissy's Fräulein I bequeath the five
twenty-franc pieces which I brought from Switzer-
land years ago. They're in the desk, next to the letters.
And to Bertha I bequeath my black evening gown.
And to Agatha my books. And to my Cousin Paul
I bequeath a kiss on my pale lips. And to Cissy—I bequeath my tennis racket—because I'm generous. And
I'm to be buried here in San Martino di Castrozza, in
the pretty little cemetery. I don't want to go home.

Even when I'm dead I don't want to return. And Father and Mother mustn't grieve. I'm better off than they are. And I forgive them. I'm not to be pitied. — Haha, what a funny will! Really, I'm touched to think that by this time tomorrow, while the rest are at dinner, I'll be dead. — Aunt Emma, of course, won't go down to dinner, and neither will Paul. They'll have their meals served in their rooms. I'm curious to know how Cissy will act. Only, I won't know, unfortunately. I'll know nothing more. Or perhaps you know everything so long as you're not buried. And, after all, I'm only making believe I'm dead. And if Herr von Dorsday approaches my corpse, I'll wake up and open my eyes and he'll be so frightened that he'll drop his monocle.

But, unfortunately, none of it's true. I'll be neither make-believe nor really dead. I won't kill myself at all. I'm too much of a coward. I may be a brave mountain-climber, but even so, I'm a coward. And perhaps I haven't even enough veronal. How many powders are needed? Six, I believe. But ten are more certain. I think I still have ten. Yes, that'll be enough.

I wonder how many times I've actually walked around the hotel. And what next? I'm standing in front of the door. Nobody's in the salon. Of course— they're all at dinner. The salon is seldom entirely deserted. There's a hat on the settee. A tourist's hat. Very smart. Pretty chamois tufts. There's an old gentleman in the fauteuil. Probably hasn't any appetite. Reading the paper. He's well off. He hasn't any worries. While he is reading his paper quietly, I must rack my brains to get thirty thousand gulden for Father. But no. I know how. After all, it's so terribly simple. What am I after? What am I doing here in

the salon? Soon they'll all be coming in from dinner.
What shall I do? Herr von Dorsday's certainly on
pins and needles. Where is she, he's thinking. Has she
killed herself, or is she hiring somebody to kill me, or
is she stirring up her Cousin Paul against me? Have
no fear, Herr von Dorsday, I'm not so dangerous.
I'm a little hussy, nothing more. You'll be rewarded
for your anxiety. Twelve o'clock, Room Sixty-five.
It'll be too cool for me in the meadow and from your
room, Herr von Dorsday, I'll go straight to my Cousin
Paul. You certainly don't object to that, Herr von
Dorsday?

"*Else! Else!*"

How? What? That's Paul's voice. Is dinner already
over?

"*Else!*" — "Oh, Paul. Why, what's the matter,
Paul?" I'll act innocent. — "*Where've you been hiding yourself, Else?*" — "Where do you suppose I've
been hiding? I've been taking a walk." — "*Right now
—during dinner?*" — "Well, why not? After all, it's
the best time for it." I'm talking nonsense. — "*Mother's
been imagining all sorts of things. I went to your door.
I knocked.*" — "Never heard you." — "*Please be serious, Else. How can you make us so uneasy? You
could at least have informed Mother that you weren't
coming down for dinner.*" — "You're quite right,
Paul. But you've no idea what a headache I had." I
said that quite disarmingly. Oh, what a hussy I am! —
"*Is it somewhat better now?*" — "I couldn't really say
that." "*Before everything else, Mother—*" "Stop, Paul;
not yet. Make my apologies to my aunt. I want to go
to my room for a few minutes to primp up. Then I'll
come right down and have a little something to eat."
— "*You're so pale, Else. Shall I send Mother up to*

you?" — "Don't make so much fuss about me, Paul, and don't look at me that way. Haven't you ever seen a woman with a headache? Of course I'll come down. In ten minutes, at the latest. Good-bye, Paul." — *"Good-bye, Else."* — Thank Heaven, he's gone. Stupid boy—but dear. What does the porter want of me? What—a telegram? "Thank you. When did the message arrive?" — *"Fifteen minutes ago, Fräulein."* — Why does he look at me so—pityingly? For Heaven's sake, what can be in this message? I'll wait until I'm upstairs before opening it. Otherwise, I might faint. After all, Father has—if Father's dead, then everything's all right. Then I needn't go with Herr von Dorsday to the meadow. . . . Oh, what a wicked soul I am! Dear God, please let there be nothing bad in the message. Dear God, please let Father live. Have him arrested, for all I care, but not dead. If there's no bad news in it, I'll offer up a sacrifice. I'll become a nurse. I'll take a position in an office. Don't die, Father. I'll do everything you ask. . . .

Thank Heaven, I'm upstairs. Turn on the light. Turn on the light. It's become cool. The window was open too long. Courage. Courage. Oh, perhaps I'll hear that matters have been settled. Perhaps Uncle Bernard is giving the money, and they're wiring me: "Don't ask Dorsday." I'll know immediately. But if I look up at the ceiling I can't read the message. Trala, trala, courage. It's necessary. "Repeat urgently ask Dorsday. Sum not thirty but fifty. Otherwise everything useless. Address remains Fiala." — But fifty. Otherwise everything useless. Trala, trala. Fifty. Address remains Fiala. Fifty. But surely fifty or thirty makes no difference one way or the other. Not even to Herr von Dorsday. The veronal is under the laun-

dry—for any emergency. Why didn't I ask for fifty
thousand in the first place? I thought of it! Otherwise
everything useless. So—I must go downstairs at once.
I can't stay here, sitting on the bed. A little mistake,
Herr von Dorsday. Forgive me. Not thirty, but fifty.
Otherwise everything useless. Address remains Fiala.
— "Do you take me for a fool, Fräulein Else?" Not at
all, Herr Vicomte. Why should I? But for fifty, I'd
certainly have to demand considerably more, Fräulein.
Otherwise everything useless. Address remains Fiala.
As you wish, Herr von Dorsday. Pray command me.
But first of all, write the message to your bank. Other-
wise, I have no guarantee. —

Yes, that's how I'll do it. I'll go to his room. Only
after he's written out the message before my eyes—
then I'll disrobe. I'll hold the message in my hand.
Oh, how disgusting! And where shall I lay my
clothes? No, no! I'll undress here and put on my
big black coat, which will cover me completely. That'll
be the most comfortable way. For both parties. Address remains Fiala. My teeth are chattering. The
window's still open. Closed. In the clearing? I could
have died there. Rotter! Fifty thousand. He can't say
No. Room Number Sixty-five. But before that, I'll
tell Paul to wait in his room for me. Then from
Dorsday I'll go direct to Paul and tell him everything. And then Paul shall box his ears. Yes—this very
evening. It'll be a rich program. And then comes the
veronal. No—why the veronal? Why die? Not a bit
of it. Be merry, be merry. Life's only beginning now.
You'll have your share of it. You'll be proud of your
little daughter. I'll be a wanton such as the world
has never seen. Address remains Fiala. You shall have
your fifty thousand gulden, Father, but with the next

money I earn I'll buy myself nightgowns, with lace, quite transparent, and expensive silk stockings. One lives only once. Light. I'll light the lamp over the mirror. How beautiful my blondish red hair is, and my shoulders: and my eyes aren't bad, either. Oh, how big they are. It would be a pity. There's still time for veronal. — But I must go down. Way down. Herr von Dorsday is waiting and he doesn't even know that meanwhile it's become fifty thousand. Yes, I've gone up in price, Herr von Dorsday. I must show him the telegram. Otherwise he really won't believe me, and he'll think I'm making a profit out of the transaction. I'll send the telegram to his room and write something to go with it. To my great regret, it has become fifty thousand, Herr von Dorsday, but that's surely all the same to you. And I am convinced that your suggestions for payment were not meant seriously at all. For you are a Vicomte and a gentleman. Tomorrow morning you'll send the fifty thousand—my Father's life depends on it—to Fiala without delay. I count on it. — "Why, of course, my dear young lady. I'll send a hundred thousand immediately to cover any further contingencies. I shan't ask a guarantee and I'll pledge myself furthermore from this day on to look after the welfare of your whole family, to pay the market debts of your father and to make good all embezzled trust funds." Address remains Fiala. Hahaha! Yes, just like the Vicomte of Eperies. But that's all nonsense. What can I do now? Something must be done. I must do something. I must do everything that Herr von Dorsday asks so that Father may have the money tomorrow—so that he won't be arrested; that he won't kill himself. And I'll do it, too. Yes, I'll do it. Although it's all for nothing. In half a year we'll all be just as far as we are today! In four weeks, in fact! — But then it will make no difference to me. I'll make this one sacrifice—and no more after that. Never, never, never again. Yes, I'll tell Father so as soon as I get to Vienna; then out of the house—anywhere. I'll consult Fred. He's the only one who really cares for me. But I'm not that far yet. I'm not in Vienna. I'm still in Martino di Castrozza. Nothing has happened yet. So now—how? What? There's the telegram. What'll I do with the telegram? I know what I was going to do with it. I must send it to him in his room. But what else? I must write him something to go with it. Yes—but what shall I write him? Expect me at twelve. No, no, no. He'll not have that satisfaction. I won't, I won't, won't, won't. Thank God, I have the powders. That's the only way out. Where are they? For Heaven's sake, they haven't been stolen! No. Here they are. Right here in the box. Are all of them still there? Yes, here they are. One, two, three, four, five, six. I only want to look at them—the precious powders. Looking at them commits me to nothing. And I pour them into the glass, but that commits me to nothing. One, two—but I surely won't kill myself. I wouldn't think of it. Three, four, five,—even five won't really kill anybody. It would be terrible if I didn't have the veronal with me. Then I'd have to jump out of the window, and I wouldn't have the courage for that. But veronal—you go to sleep quietly and never wake up again. No trouble. No pain. You lie in bed. You drink it in one draught. Dream—and all is over. The day before yesterday I took a powder, and a few days ago I even took two. Ssh, don't tell anybody. Today it'll have to be a little more. It's only for emergencies. In case he

revolts me too much. But why should he revolt me?
If he touches me, I'll spit in his face. Very simple.

But how shall I get the letter to him? I can send
the letter to Herr von Dorsday by the chambermaid.
It would be best if I went downstairs and talked with
him and showed him the telegram. In any event, I
must go down. I can't stay up here in my room. I
couldn't stand it for three hours—until the moment
arrives. I must go down, too, for my aunt's sake. Ha,
what's my aunt to me? What are the people to me?
Look, my good people, there's the glass with veronal.
So—now I take it up in my hand. Now I lift it up
to my lips. Yes, at any moment I can be over there
where there are no aunts and no Dorsday and no father
who embezzles trust funds. . . .

But I won't kill myself. That isn't at all necessary.
And I won't visit Herr von Dorsday in his room. I
wouldn't think of it. I'm blessed if for fifty thousand
gulden I'll stand naked in front of an old roué just
to save a good-for-nothing from jail. No, no—not in
any case. How does Herr von Dorsday come into the
picture? Must it be Herr von Dorsday? If one sees
me, others shall see me. Yes! Wonderful idea! Everybody shall see me. The whole world shall see me—
and then comes the veronal. No, not the veronal.
What for? Next will come the villa with the marble
steps and the handsome youths and freedom and the
wide world. Good evening, Fräulein Else, I like you
this way. Haha, down there you'll all think that I've
gone mad. But I've never been sensible. For the first
time in my life I'm really sensible. Everybody, all of
them shall see me! — After that, there's no return.
No return home to Father and Mother or uncles and
aunts. Then I'll no longer be the Fräulein Else who

can be married off to any old Director Wilomitzer. I'll make fools of them all—especially that rotter Dorsday—and come into the world for a second time. . . . Otherwise everything is useless—address remains Fiala. Haha!

No more time to lose. Don't become cowardly again. Off with the dress. Who'll be the first? Will it be you, Cousin Paul? Your luck, that the Roman head isn't here any more. Oh, how beautiful I am! Bertha has a black silk chemise. Refined. I'll be much more refined. Wonderful life. Off with the stockings. They'd be indecent. Naked, altogether naked. How Cissy will envy me. And others, too. But they don't dare. They'd all like to—so much. Take me as an example, all of you. I, the virgin, I dare. I'll laugh myself to death over Dorsday. Here I am, Herr Dorsday. Quick—to the post-office. Fifty thousand. Isn't it worth that much?

Beautiful, I'm beautiful! Look at me, Night! Mountains, look at me! Sky, look at me—how beautiful I am. But you are all blind. What are you to me? The people downstairs have eyes. Shall I loose my hair? No. I'd look like a madwoman. But you shan't think me mad. You're only to think me shameless. Canaille. Where's the telegram? For Heaven's sake, where have I left the telegram? There it is lying peacefully beside the veronal. "Repeat urgently—fifty thousand—otherwise everything useless. Address remains Fiala." Yes, that's the telegram. That's a piece of paper, and there are words on it. Despatched in Vienna at four-thirty. No; I'm not dreaming. It's all true, and at home they're all waiting for fifty thousand gulden, and Herr von Dorsday is waiting, too. Let him wait. There's plenty of time. Oh, how pleasant it is to walk up and down the room, naked. Am I really as beautiful as I look in that mirror? Oh, won't you come closer, pretty Fräulein? I want to kiss your blood-red lips. What a pity that the mirror comes between us. The cold mirror. How well we'd get on together. Isn't that so? We need nobody else. Perhaps there are no other people. There are telegrams and hotels and mountains and railroad stations and woods, but there are no people. We merely dream of them. Only Dr. Fiala exists—and his address. It always remains the same. Oh, I'm not at all mad. I'm only a little excited. That's quite natural when one is about to come into the world for a second time. For the Else that once existed is now dead. Yes, most certainly I'm dead. The veronal isn't necessary. Shouldn't I pour it out? The chambermaid might drink it by mistake. I'll leave a slip of paper there, and write on it: Poison; No—better: Medicine. So that nothing will happen to the chambermaid. I'm so noble!! So. Medicine, underscored twice, and three exclamation points. Now nothing can happen. And if I come upstairs and don't feel that I want to commit suicide, and only want to sleep, then I won't drink the whole glass—only a quarter of it, or perhaps even less. Very simple. Everything's prepared. It would be simplest to run down, as I am—across the hallways and the stairs. But no—I might be stopped before I got downstairs. And I must have assurance that Herr von Dorsday will be present. Otherwise, of course, he won't send the money—the reprobate. — But I still have to write to him. That's the most important of all. Oh, the back of the chair is cold, but agreeable. I'll leave my fountain pen to Fred, when I die. But just now I've something more important to do than die. "Most honored Herr Vicomte—" But be sensible, Else. No salutation. Neither most honored nor most despised. "Your condition, Herr von Dorsday, is fulfilled. — At the moment that you read these lines, Herr von Dorsday, your condition is fulfilled, although perhaps not in the manner you had anticipated." — "My, how well the girl writes," Father would say. — "And so I cannot but hope that you will keep your part of the agreement and send the fifty thousand gulden by telegraph to the given address. Else." — No, not Else. No signature at all. So. My pretty yellow writing paper. A Christmas present. Too bad. So—and now the telegram and letter go into the envelope. — "For Herr von Dorsday," Room Number Sixty-five? Why use the number? I'll just drop the letter at his door as I go by. But I needn't. I needn't do anything. If I felt like it, I could lie in bed now, and sleep, and do no more worrying about anything. Not about Herr von Dorsday, and not about Father. A striped convict's uniform really is very stylish, and many people have killed themselves. After all, everyone must die.

But you needn't do anything for the time being, Father. After all, you have a beautiful grown-up daughter, and address remains Fiala. I'll start a collection. I'll pass the plate. Why should Herr von Dorsday be the only one to contribute? That would be unfair. Everyone according to his means. How much will Paul drop on the plate? How much from the man with the pince-nez? But don't imagine that the fun will last. I'll cover myself again, run upstairs to my room, lock myself in, and, if I feel like it, drink the whole glass at one gulp. But I won't feel like it. It would be pure cowardice. They don't deserve such an honor, the rotters. Ashamed before you? Be-

fore whom am I to be ashamed? It's not at all necessary. Just let me look into your eyes, beautiful Else.
What enormous eyes you have, when one comes near
to you. I wish someone would kiss me on the eyes,
on my blood-red mouth. My coat hardly covers my
ankles. They'll notice that my feet are bare. What of
it? They'll see more! But I'm not committed to it.
I can go back now, before I've been downstairs. I can
turn back on the first floor. In fact, I needn't go down
at all. But I will do it. I look forward to it. Haven't I
longed for something like this all my life?

What am I waiting for? After all, I'm ready. The
performance may begin. But don't forget the letter.
Fred insists my handwriting's aristocratic. Auf Wiedersehen, Else. You're beautiful in that coat. Florentine ladies had themselves painted that way. Their
portraits are hung in galleries and it's considered an
honor. — Nothing's noticeable when I have the coat
about me. Only the feet. My feet. I'll put on my black
patent leather shoes. Then they'll think I'm wearing
flesh-colored stockings. Done. I'll go through the halls
and nobody'll suspect that there's nothing beneath the
coat except me. Just me. And besides I can always
return upstairs. . . . Who's playing piano so won-
derfully down there? Chopin? — Herr von Dorsday
must be rather nervous. Perhaps he's afraid of Paul.
Patience—just patience—everything will take care of
itself. I don't know anything yet, Herr von Dorsday.
I'm in terrible suspense, myself. Put out the light.
Oh, is my room in order? Farewell, veronal. Good-
bye. Farewell, my dearly beloved looking-glass. —
How you shine out in the darkness. Now I'm quite
used to being naked under the coat. Rather pleasant.
Who knows if there aren't many sitting this way in the

hall with no one aware of it? I wonder whether many women don't go to theatre and sit in the loges this way—for fun or for entirely different reasons.

Shall I lock the door? Why? Nothing will be stolen here. And what if there were—I no longer need anything. Finished. . . . Where's Number Sixty-five? There's nobody in the hall. Everybody's still at dinner. Sixty-one. . . . Sixty-two. . . . Such huge mountain-boots in front of the door. There are a pair of trousers hanging on the hook. How indecent. Sixty-four. . . . Sixty-five. . . . That's where he lives, the Vicomte. . . . I'll lean the letter against the door. He can't help seeing it there. Nobody'll steal it. So—there it is. . . . It doesn't matter. . . . I still can do as I please. I've merely made a fool of him. . . . If only I don't meet him on the steps now. Here he comes. . . . No, it isn't he! . . . This one is much handsomer than Herr von Dorsday. Very aristocratic with that small black moustache. When did he arrive? I might stage a little rehearsal—lift the coat a trifle. I'm very much tempted. Just look at me, my dear sir. You have no idea whom you're passing by. Too bad you're so occupied with climbing the stairs just now. Why don't you stay in the hall? You're missing something. Great performance. Why don't you stop me? My fate lies in your hands. If you greet me, I'll go back again. So, please greet me. After all, I'm looking at you so tenderly. . . . He won't greet me. He's gone. He's turning back! I feel it. Call me! Greet me! Save me! Perhaps, my dear sir, you will be responsible for my death. But you'll never realize it. Address remains Fiala. . . .

Where am I? In the hall so soon? How did I get here? So few people and so many strangers. Or is my eyesight bad? Where's Dorsday? He's not here. Is this

a stroke of fate? I'll go back. I'll write a different letter
to Dorsday. I expect you in my room at midnight.
Bring the message to the bank with you. No. He
might regard it as a snare. It might be one, too. I
could have Paul hidden with me, and he could force
him to give up the despatch at the point of a revolver. Blackmail. A couple of criminals. Where's
Dorsday? Dorsday, where are you? Has he perhaps
killed himself in remorse over my death? He'll be
in the card room. Of course. He'll be sitting at the
card table. If he is, I'll signal to him from the doorway with my eyes. He'll get up at once. "Here I am, my
dear young lady." His voice will have that strange
sound to it. "Shall we take a little walk, Herr Dorsday?" "As you please, Fräulein Else." We cross the
virgin path to the woods. We're alone. I open my
coat. The fifty thousand are due. The air's cold. I contract pneumonia and die. . . . Why are those two
ladies looking at me? Do they notice something? Why
am I here? Am I mad? I'll return to my room. I'll
dress quickly. Put on the blue dress, the coat over it
—but open, this time—and nobody'll believe that I had
nothing on before. . . . I can't go back. I won't go
back. Where's Paul? Where's Aunt Emma? Where's
Cissy? Where are they all? No one will notice it.
. . . It can't be noticed. Who's playing so beautifully?
Chopin? No, Schumann.

I flit about in the hall, like a bat. Fifty thousand!
Time flies. I must find this confounded Herr von
Dorsday. No, I must return to my room. . . . I'll
drink some veronal. Only a few drops of it. Then
I'll sleep well. . . . After work well done, sleep is
welcome. . . . But the work hasn't been done. . . .
If the waiter serves that black coffee to the old gentle-

man over there, everything will be all right. And if
he takes it to the young bridal couple in the corner,
everything's lost. What's that? What is he doing?
He's bringing the coffee to the old gentleman. Tri-
umph! Everything's all right. Ha, there go Cissy and
Paul! They're strolling in front of the hotel. They're
chatting quite gaily. He isn't so very wrought up over
my headache. Hypocrite! . . . Cissy's figure isn't as
good as mine. Of course, she's had a child . . . What
are they talking about? If only I could hear them!
Why should their conversation interest me? I might
go out, bid them good evening and then go on, flit
over the meadows, into the woods, step up, climb
up, higher, higher, up to the Cimone, lie down, sleep,
and freeze. Mysterious suicide of young Viennese society woman. Dressed only in her black evening coat,
the beautiful young lady was found dead in an unfre-
quented part of the Cimone della Pala. . . . But perhaps they won't find me. . . . Or perhaps not until
next year. Or even later. Rotted. A skeleton. Better to
remain in these warm halls and not freeze. Well, Herr
von Dorsday, where are you hiding? Am I obliged
to wait? You must find me—not I you. I'll look in the
card room. If he isn't there, he has forfeited his privilege and I'll write to him: You were not to be found,
Herr von Dorsday. You disappeared of your own voli-
tion. This does not release you of your obligation to
forward the money at once. The money. What money?
What's that to me? I don't care whether he sends it
or not. I've no more sympathy for Father, not the least.
I've sympathy for no one. Not even for myself. My
heart is dead. I believe it has stopped beating. Perhaps
I've drunk the veronal already. . . . Why does the
Dutch family stare at me so? It's impossible to notice

anything. The porter also regards me with suspicion. Has another message arrived? Eighty thousand? A hundred thousand? Address remains Fiala. If there were a message, he'd tell me. He looks at me most respectfully. He doesn't know that there's nothing under the coat. Nobody knows it. I'll return to my room. Back, back, back! If I tripped on the stairs—that would be pretty! Three years ago, on the Wörthersee, there was a young woman who went in swimming without clothes, but she left on the same afternoon. Mother says it was an opera singer from Berlin. Schumann? Yes—Carnival. He or she plays very well. The card room is at the right side. Last chance, Herr von Dorsday. If he's there, I'll summon him with my eyes and say to him, "I'll be with you at midnight, you rotter." — No, I'll not call him a rotter. But I'll call him that afterwards. . . . Somebody's following me. I won't look back. No, no. —

"*Else!*" — For Heaven's sake, my aunt! I'd better keep right on walking. "*Else!*" — I must turn around. There's no way out. "Oh, good evening, Aunt." — "*Oh, Else, what's wrong with you? I was just about to go up to you. Paul told me— Oh, how you look!*" "How do I look, Aunt? I'm feeling quite well. I just ate something." She notices something. — "*Else—you have—you have no stockings on!*" — "What did you say? My soul, I have no stockings on! No—!" — "*Aren't you well, Else? Your eyes—you have temperature.*" — "Temperature? I think not. I've just had the worst headache of my life." — "*You must go to bed at once, child; you're deathly pale.*" — "That's on account of the bad light. Everybody looks pale in this hall." She looks at me so strangely. She can't notice anything? Now, I must keep my poise. All's over with Father if I lose my poise. I must say something. "Do you know, Aunt, what happened to me in Vienna a little while ago? I went out walking with one yellow shoe and one black one." Not a word of it's true. I must keep on talking. What'll I say now? "Do you know, Aunt, I sometimes have attacks of absent-mindedness. Mother used to have them, too." Not a word of it's true. — *"In any case, I'll send for the doctor."* — "But please, Aunt! There isn't one in the hotel. They'll have to call one from the next town. He certainly would laugh if he were called because I had no stockings on. Haha." I oughtn't to laugh so loudly. My aunt's face is distorted with fear. The thing's too weird for her. Her eyes are popping out. — *"Tell me, Else, have you by any chance seen Paul?"* — Ah, she's looking for help. Poise. Poise. Everything depends on it. "I think he's walking in front of the hotel with Cissy Mohr, if I'm not mistaken." — *"In front of the hotel? I'll call them both in. We'll all have a little tea. Yes?"* — "Gladly." What a stupid face she makes! I nod at her quite amiably and innocently. She's gone. Now I'll go to my room. No; what'll I do in my room? It's high time. High time. Fifty thousand. Fifty thousand. Why am I hurrying so? Slowly. Slowly. . . . What do I want? What's the man's name? Herr von Dorsday. Funny name. . . . Here's the card room. Green curtain over the door. They see nothing. I'll stand on tiptoe. A game of whist. They play every evening. Two gentlemen are playing chess over there. Herr von Dorsday isn't here. Victory! Saved! But how so? I must look further. I'm condemned to look for Herr von Dorsday till the end of my life. Probably he's looking for me too. We always miss one another. Perhaps he's looking for me up-

stairs. We'll meet on the steps. The Dutch people are
staring at me again. The daughter is very pretty.
The old gentleman has spectacles, spectacles, spectacles. . . . Fifty thousand. That's not so much, fifty
thousand, Herr von Dorsday. Schumann? Yes, Carni-

val. I once studied that myself. She plays well. But
why she? Perhaps it's a he. Perhaps it's a virtuoso. I'll
take one look into the music room.

Yes, there's the door. — Dorsday! I'm falling. Dorsday! He's standing at the window, listening. Is it
really possible? I'm burning up—I'm going insane—
I'm dead—and he's listening to a strange lady playing
piano. Two gentlemen are sitting on the divan. The
blond one just arrived today. I saw him get out of the
carriage. The lady's no longer young. She's been here
for a couple of days. I didn't know that she played
piano so beautifully. She's well off. All people are well

off . . . only I am doomed . . . Dorsday! Dorsday!
Is that really he? He doesn't see me. Now he looks
like a decent person. He's listening. Fifty thousand.
Now or never. Open the door softly. Here I am, Herr
von Dorsday! He doesn't see me. I'll signal to him just
once with my eyes; then I'll raise the coat a little.
That'll be enough. After all, I'm a young girl. A decent young girl. A decent young girl from a good

family. Not a prostitute. . . . I want to go away. I
want to take veronal and sleep. You've made a mistake, Herr von Dorsday. I'm no prostitute. Adieu,
adieu! . . . Oh, he's looking up. Here I am, Herr
von Dorsday. What eyes he's making. His lips tremble. His eyes are burning into my forehead. He doesn't
suspect that there's nothing beneath the coat. Let me
go. Let me go. His eyes are shining. His eyes are
threatening. What do you want of me? You're a rotter. Nobody sees me—except him. They're listening.
So come then, Herr von Dorsday! Don't you notice
anything? There in the fauteuil—great God, in the
fauteuil—there's the Filou! Heaven be praised! He's
here again. He's here again! He was only on a trip
and now he's here again. The Roman head is here
again. My bridegroom, my beloved! But he doesn't see
me. Nor should he see me. What do you want, Herr
von Dorsday? You look at me as though I were your
slave. I'm not your slave. Fifty thousand! Does our
agreement still hold, Herr von Dorsday? I'm ready.
Here I am. I'm quite calm. I'm smiling. You understand my look? His eyes say to me: come! His eyes
say: I want to see you naked. Well, you swine, I *am*
naked. What more do you want? Send the message
. . . immediately. Chills are running up and down my
spine. She's playing on. How wonderful it is to be
naked. Chills are running up and down my spine.

She's playing on. She doesn't realize what's happening
here. Nobody realizes it. No one sees me yet. Filou!

Filou! Here I'm standing naked! Dorsday opens his
eyes wide. At last he believes it. The Filou gets up.
His eyes are glowing. You understand me, beautiful
youth. "Ha, ha." The lady is playing no more. Father
is saved. Fifty thousand! Address remains Fiala! "Ha,
ha, ha!" Who's laughing there? Am I laughing? "Ha,
ha, ha!" What are all those faces around me? "Ha,
ha, ha!" How stupid of me to laugh. "Ha, ha, ha!" I
don't want to laugh—I don't want to. "Ha, ha!" —
"Else!" — Who's calling Else? That's Paul. He must
be behind me. I feel his breath on my bare back. My
ears are ringing. Perhaps I'm already dead. What do
you wish, Herr von Dorsday? Why are you so enormous, and why are you staggering towards me? "Ha,
ha, ha!"

Now what have I done? What have I done? What
have I done? I'm falling. All is over. Why has the
music stopped? An arm is supporting my back. That's
Paul. Where's the Filou? I'm lying here. "Ha, ha,
ha!" The coat's thrown over me and I'm lying here.
The people think me unconscious. No, I'm not unconscious. I'm in all my senses. I'm a hundred times
awake, a thousand times awake. Only, I always have
to laugh. "Ha, ha, ha!" Now you have your wish, Herr
von Dorsday. You must send the money to Father,
immediately. "Haaaaah!" I don't want to cry out and
I always have to cry out. Why must I cry out? —
My eyes are closed. No one can see me. Father is

saved. — *"Else!"* — That's my aunt. — *"Else! Else!"*
— *"A doctor, a doctor!"* — *"Run for the porter!"* —
"What's happened?" — *"It's impossible."* — *"The
poor child."* — What are they talking about there?
What's all this murmuring? I'm no poor child. I'm
happy. The Filou has seen me naked. Oh, I'm so
ashamed! What have I done? Never again will I open
my eyes. — *"Please close the door."* — Why close the
door? What a murmur! A thousand people are crowding around me. They'll think I'm unconscious. I'm not
unconscious. I'm only dreaming. — *"Try to calm
yourself, my dear lady."* — *"Has a doctor been sent
for?"* — *"It's a fainting spell."* — How far away they
all are. They're all speaking from Cimone. — *"We
can't let her lie on the floor."* — *"Here's a shawl."* —
"A blanket." — *"A blanket, or a shawl—it's all the
same."* — *"Quiet, please."* — *"On the divan."* — *"Will
you please close that door!"* — *"Don't be so nervous.
It's already closed."* — *"Else! Else!"* — If my aunt
would only be quiet! — *"Do you hear me, Else?"* —
"Don't you see, Mother, that she's unconscious?" —
Yes, thank God, to you I'm unconscious and I'll remain unconscious. — *"We must take her up to her
room."* — *"What's happened here, for God's sake?"*
— Cissy. How does Cissy happen to be in the meadow?
Ah, but it isn't the meadow. — *"Else!"* — *"Please be
quiet."* — *"Please step back a bit."* — Hands, hands
under me. What do they want? How heavy I am.
Paul's hands. Go away, go away. The Filou's near
me; I can feel it. And Dorsday's gone. They must
look for him. He mayn't kill himself before he has
sent off the fifty thousand. My good people, he owes
me money. Arrest him. — *"Have you any idea from
whom the message was, Paul?"* — *"Good evening, my*

good people." — "Else, do you hear me?" — "Just
let her be, Frau Cissy." — "Oh, Paul." — "The manager says it may be four hours before the doctor arrives." — "She looks as though she were sleeping."
— I'm lying on the divan. Paul is holding my hand.
He is feeling my pulse. Right. After all, he's a physician. — "She's not at all in danger, Mother, An—
attack." — "I won't stay in this hotel a day longer."
— "Please, Mother." — "We'll leave promptly tomorrow morning." — "It will be easier to take her over
the servants' stairway. The stretcher will be here immediately." — Stretcher? Haven't I already been on
a stretcher today? Haven't I already been dead? Do I
have to die again? — "Won't you please see to it, Herr
Director, that the people at least stand clear of the
door?" — "Please don't worry so, Mother." — "It's
terribly inconsiderate of all these people." — Why
are they all whispering? It's like a death chamber. The
stretcher will be here at once. Open the gate, Sir Matador. — "The path is clear." — "The people might at
least have as much consideration as to—" — "Please,
Mother, please calm yourself." — "Please, my dear
lady." — "Won't you look after my mother for a while,
Frau Cissy?" — She's his mistress, but she isn't as
beautiful as I am. What's that again? What's happening there? They're bringing in the stretcher. I can see
it with closed eyes. That's the stretcher for the in-
jured. They laid Dr. Zigmondi on it when he fell off
the Cimone. And now I'm to lie on the same stretcher.
I fell too. "Ha!" No, I won't cry out again. They're
whispering. Who's bending over my head? It smells
like cigarettes. His hand is under my head. Hands
under my back. Hands under my legs. Go away, all
of you. Don't touch me. Shame, shame! What do you

want, anyway? Leave me alone. It was only for Father. — *"Please, carefully, so, slowly." — "The shawl?"*
—*"Yes, thank you, Frau Cissy."* — Why is he thanking her? What has she done for him? What will they
do to me? Oh, how good, how good! I'm shivering,
shivering. I'm shivering all over. They're carrying me,
carrying me. They're carrying me to my grave. —
*"Oh, I'm used to that, Doctor. Heavier people have
already lain on the stretcher. Once last fall, there were
even two." — "Sssh, ssh." — "Perhaps you'd be so good
as to go ahead, Frau Cissy, and see that everything in
Else's room is in order."* — What right has Cissy to
go in my room? The veronal! The veronal! If only
they don't pour it out. If they did that I'd have to
jump out of the window. — *"Thank you very much,
Herr Director, don't bother further." — "I'll take the
liberty of inquiring again later on."* — The steps are
squeaking. The carriers are wearing heavy mountain-
boots. Where are my patent leathers? Back in the
music room. They'll be stolen. I wanted to will them
to Agatha. Fred gets my fountain pen. They're carrying me, they're carrying me. Funeral procession.
Where's Dorsday, the murderer? He's gone away, and
so has the Filou. He has gone away too. He has gone
back to his wanderings. He came back just for a
glimpse of my white body. And now he's gone away
again. He's going on a hazardous path between rocks
and precipices. Farewell, farewell. — I'm shivering,
shivering. Let them carry me upstairs, always further
up, up to the roof, up to the sky. It would be so comfortable there. — *"I've seen it coming all along, Paul."*
— What has Aunt seen coming? — *"For the past few
days I've seen it coming along. She's really not normal. Of course, she must go to an asylum." — "But,*

Mother, this certainly isn't the time to speak of that." — Asylum—? Asylum—?! — *"You don't really imagine, Paul, that I'd return to Vienna in the same compartment with this person. We'd go through some pretty experiences."* — *"Nothing whatsoever will happen to you, Mother. I'll guarantee that you won't have the slightest embarrassment."* — *"How can you guarantee that?"* — No, Aunt, you'll have no embarrassment. Nobody will be embarrassed. Not even Herr von Dorsday. Where are we now? We're standing still. We're on the second floor. I'll just open my eyes for a second. Cissy's standing there in the doorway talking with Paul. — *"Over this way, please. So. Here. Thank you. Move the stretcher very close to the bed."* — They're lifting the stretcher. They're carrying me. It feels good. Now I'm home again. Ah! — *"Thank you. This way. That's right. Please close the door. — If you'd be so good as to help me, Cissy."* — *"Oh, with pleasure, Herr Doctor."* — *"Slowly, please. Here, please, Cissy, take hold of her here. Here at the legs. Carefully, now. And then—Else—? Do you hear me, Else?"* — Why of course I hear you, Paul. I hear everything, but what does that matter to you? It's so wonderful to be unconscious. Oh, go ahead and do as you please. — *"Paul!"* — *"gnädige Frau?"* — *"Do you really think that she's unconscious, Paul dear?"* — Paul dear? She calls him dear! — I've caught you! Dear is what she calls him! — *"Yes, she's altogether unconscious. That's what generally happens after an attack like this."* — *"Paul, I could laugh myself sick when you act so mature in your medical manner."* — I've caught you, you hypocrites! I've caught you. — *"Keep quiet, Cissy."* — *"Why should I keep quiet if she can't hear anything?"* — What's happened? I'm lying naked in bed under the covers. How did they get me here? — *"Well, how is she? Better?"* — That's Aunt. What does she want now? — *"She's still unconscious?"* — She's creeping around the room on tiptoe. She can go to the devil. I won't be taken to an asylum. I'm not insane. — *"Isn't there any way of waking her up?"* — *"She'll soon come to, Mother. She needs nothing right now except rest. So do you, Mother. Don't you want to sleep? There's absolutely no danger. I'll stay here with Frau Cissy and take care of Else through the night."* — *"Yes, indeed, dear lady, I'll be the chaperon, or Else will be, depending on how you look at it."* — Horrible woman. Here I'm lying unconscious and she's joking. — *"And I can definitely depend upon it, Paul, that you'll wake me just as soon as the doctor arrives?"* — *"But, Mother, he won't be here until morning."* — *"She looks as though she is sleeping. Her breathing is regular."* — *"As a matter of fact, Mother, it is a sort of sleep."* — *"I still can't control myself, Paul. Such a scandal!— You'll see, it'll appear in all the papers."* — *"Mother!"* — *"But she can't hear anything if she's unconscious. We're talking very quietly."* — *"In this condition the senses are sometimes unusually acute."* — *"You have such a learned son, gnädige Frau."* — *"Please, Mother, go to bed."* — *"Tomorrow morning we'll leave, no matter what happens. And in Bozen we'll get a nurse for Else."* — What? A nurse? You will be disappointed in that, too. — *"Well, we'll talk about all that tomorrow. Good night, Mother."* — *"I'll have a cup of tea brought up to my room and look in here again in a quarter of an hour."* — *"That's absolutely unnecessary, Mother."* — No, it certainly isn't necessary. You just go to the devil. Where's the veronal? I'll have to wait. They're taking my aunt to the door. No one can see me now. It must be on the night table, that glass of veronal. If I drink it, all will be over. I'll drink it immediately. My aunt is away. Paul and Cissy are standing by the door. Ha, she's kissing him. She's kissing him, and I'm lying naked under the covers. Aren't you two ashamed of yourselves? She's kissing him again. Aren't you two ashamed of yourselves? — *"Do you see, Paul? Now I know that she's uncon-scious. Otherwise she'd jump up at me." — "Won't you please do me a favor, Cissy, and be quiet?" — "But why, Paul? Either she is really unconscious, in which case she can hear and see nothing, or else she's making fools of us. If that's so, it serves her altogether right." — "Someone's knocked." — "I thought so, too." — "I'll open the door softly and see who it is. — Good evening, Herr von Dorsday." — "Excuse me, I just wanted to inquire how Else is."* — Dorsday! Dorsday! Does he really dare? How beastly. Where is he? I hear them whispering in front of the door, Paul and Dorsday. Cissy is standing before the mirror. What are you doing there by the mirror? It's my mirror. Isn't my picture still in it? What are they talking about in front of the door, Paul and Dorsday? I feel Cissy's gaze. She's looking at me through the mirror. What does she want? Why is she coming nearer? Help! Help! I'm calling and no one hears me. What do you want at my bed, Cissy?! Why are you bending over me? Do you want to strangle me? I can't move. — *"Else!"* — What does she want? — *"Else! Do you hear me, Else?"* — I hear, but I can't talk. I'm powerless. I can't talk. — *"Else, you gave us a nice fright down-stairs."* — She talks to me just as though I were awake. What does she want? — *"Do you know what you*

have done, Else? Just think. You came down to the
music room dressed only in your coat and suddenly
you stood there naked before all the people, and then
you fell down unconscious. They say it was an hys-
terical attack. I don't believe a word of it. I also don't
believe that you're unconscious. I'll bet you're hearing
every word of what I'm saying." — Yes, I hear, yes,
yes, yes. But she doesn't hear me. Why not? I can't
move my lips. That's why she can't hear me. I can't
move. What's the matter with me? Am I dead? Do I
seem dead? Am I dreaming? Where's the veronal?
I want to drink my veronal, but I can't stretch out my
arm. Go away, Cissy. Why are you bending over
me? Go away, go away. She'll never know that I
heard her. No one will ever know. I'll never talk to
anyone again. I'll never wake up again. She's going to
the door. She's turning around once more to look at
me. She's opening the door. Dorsday's standing there.
I've just seen him with my eyes closed. No, I really
see him. My eyes are open. The door's ajar. Cissy is
outside. Now they're all whispering. I'm alone. If I
could only move now.

Ha! I can. Yes! I can move my hand. I'm stretching out my finger. I'm stretching out my arm. I'm
opening my eyes wide. I see. I see. There's my glass.
Quick, before they come into the room again. Are
there enough veronal powders in it? I must never
awaken again. What I had to do in the world I've
done. Father is saved. I could never go out among
people again. Paul is peering through the door. He
think's I'm unconscious. He doesn't see that I have
my arm almost extended. Now they're all three standing outside of the room again. The murderers! —
They're all murderers, Dorsday and Cissy and Paul.

Also, Fred is a murderer and Mother is a murderer.
They all murdered me and say nothing about it.
They'll say, "She committed suicide." All of you killed
me. All of you killed me. All of you. All of you. Well,
have I finally reached it? Quick, quick. I must. I
mustn't spill a drop. So, quick. It tastes good. More,
more. It isn't poison at all. Nothing ever tasted so
good. If you only knew how good death tastes! Good
night, my glass. Klirr, klirr! What's that? The glass
is lying on the floor. It's lying down there. Good night.
— *"Else! Else!"* —What do they want? — *"Else!"* —
Are you here again? Good morning. Here I am lying
unconscious with closed eyes. You'll never see my
eyes again. — *"She must have moved, Paul. How else
could the glass have dropped?"* — *"It was an invol-
untary movement. That would have been quite possible."* — *"Well, if she isn't awake."* — *"What's the
matter with you, anyhow, Cissy? Just look at her."* —
I've drunk veronal. I'll die. But everything is just as
it was before. Perhaps it wasn't enough. Paul's holding
my hand. — *"The pulse is quiet. But don't laugh, Cissy.
The poor girl."* — *"I wonder whether you'd call me
a poor girl too if I'd stood naked in the center of the
music room?"* — *"Won't you please keep still, Cissy?"*
— *"Just as you wish, my dear sir. Perhaps I ought to
go away so that I can leave you alone with the naked
lady. But please don't be embarrassed. Just act as
though I weren't here at all."* — I've drunk veronal.
It's good. I'll die. Thank God. — *"Well, now, I'll tell
you what I think. I think that this Herr von Dorsday is in love with the naked lady. He was as excited
as though it were a personal matter with him."* —
Dorsday, Dorsday! Why, that's the— Fifty thousand!
Will he send it off? For God's sake, what will happen

if he doesn't? I must tell him. They must bring him
back. For God's sake, all this might be for nothing.
But I can still be saved. Paul! Cissy! Why don't you
hear me? Don't you know that I'm dying? But I
don't feel anything. I'm just tired. Paul, I'm just tired.
Don't you hear me? I'm tired, Paul. I can't open my
lips. I can't move my tongue, but I'm not dead yet.
That's the veronal. Where are you, anyhow? I'll fall
asleep presently. Then it will be too late. I don't hear
them talking at all. They're talking, and I don't know
it. Their voices buzz so. Oh, Paul, please help me!
My tongue is so heavy. — *"I think, Cissy, that she'll
soon wake up. She looks as though she's trying to
open her eyes. Well, Cissy, what are you doing now?"*
— *"I'm only putting my arms around you. Why
shouldn't I? I know she didn't have any sense of shame
either."* — No, I had no sense of shame. I stood there
naked before all those people. If I could only speak
you would understand. Paul! Paul! I want you to hear
me. I drank veronal, Paul. Ten powders, a hundred.
I didn't want to do it. I was mad. I don't want to die.
Save me, Paul. You're a doctor. Save me! — *"She seems
to be quiet again. Her pulse is fairly regular."* —
Save me, Paul. I implore you. Don't let me die. There
is still time. But I'll soon fall asleep, and you won't
know it. I don't want to die. Please save me. It was
only for Father's sake. Dorsday insisted on it. Paul!
Paul! — *"Look, Cissy, doesn't it seem to you that she's
smiling?"* — *"Well, why shouldn't she smile, Paul,
when you constantly hold her hand so tenderly?"* —
Cissy, Cissy, what did I ever do to you that you are so
cruel? Keep your Paul, but don't let me die. I'm so
young. Mother will grieve. I still want to climb many
mountains. I still want to dance. And some day I'll

marry. I still want to travel. Tomorrow we're going
on a trip up the Cimone. Tomorrow will be a lovely
day. The Filou will come along. I'll invite him humbly.
Run after him, Paul. He's going his hazardous way.
He'll meet Father. Address remains Fiala. Don't forget that. It's only fifty thousand and then everything
will be all right. Look, they're all marching in con-
victs' clothes, and singing. Open the gate, Sir Matador! It's all just a dream. And here comes Fred with
his hoarse lady. And the piano's out under the great,
broad sky. The piano tuner lives in Bartenstein Street,
Mother! Why didn't you write to him, child? You
always forget everything. You ought to practice more
scales, Else. A girl of thirteen ought to be more industrious. Rudi was at a masked ball and he came
home at eight o'clock in the morning. What have you
brought along for me, Father? Thirty thousand dolls.
I'll need a separate house for them. But perhaps they
can go strolling in the garden. Or go with Rudi to the
masked ball. God bless you, Else. Oh, Bertha, are you
back from Naples again? Yes, from Sicily. I want you
to meet my husband, Else. Enchanté, Monsieur. —
"Else, do you hear me, Else? It's I, Paul." — Haha,
Paul. Why are you sitting on the giraffe on the merry-
go-round? — *"Else, Else!"* — Don't ride away from
me. You can't hear me if you ride so fast through the
main street. I want you to save me. I've taken verona-
lica. It's running over my legs, right and left, like ants.
Go and catch Herr von Dorsday. There he goes.
Don't you see him? There he jumps over the pond.
He's killed Father, so run after him. I'll run with you.
They've strapped the stretcher over my back, but I'll
run along. I'm trembling so, but I'll run along. Where
are you, Paul? Fred, where are you? Mother, where

are you? Cissy? Why do you all let me run alone?
I'm afraid being so alone. I'd rather fly. I knew it. I
can fly.

"*Else!*" . . .

"*Else!*" . . .

Where are you? I hear you, but I don't see you.

"*Else!*" . . .

"*Else!*" . . .

"*Else!*" . . .

What's that? A whole chorus? And an organ too?
I'm singing along. What's the song they're all singing? Everybody's singing along. The woods too, and
the mountains, and the stars. Never have I heard anything so beautiful. Never have I seen such a brilliant
night. Give me your hand, Father. We'll fly together.
The world is so beautiful when you can fly. Don't kiss
my hand. I'm your child, Father.

"*Else! Else!*"

They're calling me from so far away. What do you
all want? Don't wake me. Oh, I'm sleeping so well.
Tomorrow morning. I'm dreaming and flying. I'm
flying . . . flying . . . flying . . . sleeping and dreaming . . . and flying . . . not waking . . . early morning . . .

"*El . . .*"

I'm flying . . . I'm dreaming . . . I'm sleeping
. . . I'm drea . . . drea — I'm fly . . .

RHAPSODY

Translated from the German of
TRAUMNOVELLE

by

Otto P. Schinnerer

"Twenty-four brown-skinned slaves rowed the splendid galley which was to bring Prince Amgiad to the palace of the caliph. The prince, wrapped in his purple cloak, lay alone on the deck under the dark-blue, starry sky, and his gaze—"

So far the little girl had read aloud. Then, suddenly, her eyelids drooped. Her parents looked at each other and smiled. Fridolin bent down, kissed her blonde hair and closed the book which was lying on the untidy table. The child looked up as if caught at some mischief.

"It's nine o'clock," her father said, "and time you were in bed." Albertina also bent over her, and as her hand met her husband's on the beloved forehead, they looked at each other with a tender smile not meant for the child. The governess entered and asked the little girl to say good-night. She got up obediently, kissed her father and mother and walked out quietly hand in hand with the young woman. Fridolin and Albertina, left alone under the reddish glow of the hanging-lamp, continued the conversation they had begun before supper.

It dealt with their experiences the night before at the masquerade ball. They had decided to attend it just before the end of the carnival period, as their first one of the season. No sooner had Fridolin entered the ball-room than he was greeted, like a long lost friend, by two women in red dominoes. He had no idea who they were, although they were unusually well informed about many affairs of his student days and interneship. They had invited him into a box with great friendliness, but had left again with the promise that they would soon return without masks. When they did not appear, he became impatient and went down to the ball-room floor hoping to meet them again, but eagerly as he scanned the room, he could not see them anywhere. Instead, however, another woman unexpectedly took his arm. It was his wife. She had just freed herself from the company of a stranger whose blasé manner and apparently Polish accent had at first charmed her. Suddenly he had offended her—frightened her by a rather common and impertinent remark. Fridolin and Albertina were glad to have escaped from a disappointingly commonplace masquerade prank, and soon sat like two lovers, among the other couples, in the buffet, eating oysters and drinking champagne. They chatted gaily, as though they had just made each other's acquaintance, acting a comedy of courting, bashful resistance, seduction and surrender. After driving home quickly through the snowy winter night, they sank into each other's arms and were more blissful in their ardent love than they had been for a long time. The gray of morning awakened them only too soon. Fridolin's profession summoned him to his patients at an early hour, while Albertina would not stay in bed longer because of her duties as housewife and mother. So the ensuing hours passed, soberly and predetermined, in daily routine and work, and the events of the night before, both those at the beginning and at the end, had faded.

But now that the day's work was done—the child

had gone to bed and no disturbance was likely—the shadowy forms of the masquerade, the melancholy stranger and the red dominoes, rose again into reality. And all at once those insignificant events were imbued, magically and painfully, with the deceptive glow of neglected opportunities. Harmless but probing questions, and sly, ambiguous answers were exchanged. Neither failed to notice that the other was not absolutely honest, and so they became slightly vindictive. They exaggerated the degree of attraction that their unknown partners at the ball had exerted upon them while each made fun of the other's tendencies to jealousy and denied his own. Soon, their light conversation about the trifling matters of the night before changed into a more serious discussion of those hidden, scarcely suspected wishes, which can produce dangerous whirlpools even in the serenest and purest soul. They spoke of those mysterious regions of which they were hardly conscious but towards which the incomprehensible wind of fate might some day drive them, even if only in their dreams. For though they were united in thought and feeling, they knew that the preceding day had not been the first time that the spirit of adventure, freedom and danger had beckoned them. Uneasy, and tormenting themselves, each sought with disingenuous curiosity to draw out confessions from the other. Anxiously, they searched within themselves for some indifferent fact, or trifling experience, which might express the inexpressible, and the honest confession of which might relieve them of the strain and the suspicion which were becoming unbearable.

Whether Albertina was more impatient, more honest or more kind-hearted of the two, it was she who first summoned the courage for a frank confession. She asked Fridolin in a rather uncertain voice whether he remembered the young man who—last summer at the sea-shore in Denmark—had been sitting one evening with two other officers at an adjoining table. He had received a telegram during dinner, whereupon he had hastily said "good-bye" to his friends.

Fridolin nodded. "What about him?" he asked.

"I'd already seen him in the morning," she replied, "as he was hurrying up the stairs in the hotel with his yellow hand-bag. He looked at me as he passed, but didn't stop until he had gone a few more steps. Then he turned and our eyes met. He didn't smile; in fact, it seemed to me that he scowled. I suppose I did the same, for I was very much stirred. That whole day I lay on the beach, lost in dreams. Had he called me—I thought—I could not have resisted. I thought I was ready for anything. I had practically resolved to give up you, the child, my future, and at the same time— if you can understand it?—you were dearer to me than ever. That same afternoon—surely you remember— we discussed many things very intimately, among others our common future, and our child. At sunset you and I were sitting on the balcony, when, down below on the beach, he passed without looking up. I was extremely thrilled to see him, but I stroked your forehead and kissed your hair, and my love for you was both sorrowful and compassionate. That evening at dinner I wore a white rose and you yourself said I was very beautiful. Perhaps it wasn't mere chance that the stranger and his friends sat near us. He didn't look at me, but I considered getting up, walking over to him and saying: Here I am, my beloved for whom I have waited—take me. At that moment the telegram was handed to him. He read it, turned pale, whispered a few words to the younger of the two officers—and glancing at me mysteriously he left the room."

"And then?" Fridolin asked dryly when she stopped.

"That is all. I remember that I woke the next morning with a restless anxiety. I don't know whether I was afraid that he had left or that he might still be there. But when he didn't appear at noon, I breathed a sigh of relief. Don't ask any more, Fridolin. I've told you the whole truth. And you, too, had some sort of experience at the sea-shore—I know it."

Fridolin rose, walked up and down the room several times and then said: "You're right." He was standing at the window, his face in shadow and in a hoarse and slightly hostile voice he began: "In the morning, sometimes very early before you got up, I used to stroll along the beach, out beyond the town. Even at that hour the sun was always shining over the sea, bright and strong. Out there on the beach, as you know, were cottages, each one standing like a world in itself. Some had fenced-in gardens, others were surrounded only by the woods. The bathing-huts were separated from the cottages by the road and part of the beach. I hardly ever met people at such an early hour, and bathers were never out. One morning, quite suddenly, I noticed the figure of a woman. She had suddenly appeared on the narrow ledge of a bathing-hut, which rested on piles driven into the sand. She was cautiously advancing, placing one foot before the other, her arms extended backward against the wooden boards. She was quite a young girl, possibly fifteen years old, with loose blonde hair hanging over her shoulders and on one side over her delicate breast. She was looking down into the water and was slowly moving along the wall, her gaze

lowered in the direction of the far corner. All at once
she stopped opposite me and reached far back with her
arms as though trying to secure a firmer hold. Looking up, she suddenly saw me. A tremor passed through
her body, as though she wished to drop into the water
or run. But as she could move only very slowly on the
narrow ledge, she had to stay where she was. She stood
there with a face expressing at first fright, then anger,
and finally embarrassment. All at once, however, she
smiled, smiled marvelously. Her eyes welcomed me,
beckoned to me, and at the same time slightly mocked
me, as she glanced at the strip of water between us.
Then she stretched her young and slender body, glad
of her beauty, and proudly and sweetly stirred by my
obvious admiration. We stood facing each other for
perhaps ten seconds, with half-open lips and dazzled
eyes. Involuntarily I stretched out my arms to her; her
eyes expressed surrender and joy. Then she shook her
head vigorously, took one arm from the wall and commanded me with a gesture to go away. When I didn't
at once obey, her childlike eyes turned on me such a
beseeching look that there was nothing for me to do
but to go, and I went as quickly as possible. I did not
look back once—not because I felt considerate, obedient
or chivalrous, but because in her last glance I sensed
an emotion so intense, so far beyond anything I had
ever experienced, that I was not far from fainting."
And he stopped.

With her eyes cast down and in a monotonous voice,
Albertina asked: "And how often did you see her after
that?"

"What I have told you," Fridolin answered, "happened on the last day of our stay in Denmark. Other-

wise I don't know what might have taken place. You, too, mustn't ask any more, Albertina."

He was still standing at the window, motionless as Albertina arose and walked over to him. There were tears in her eyes and a slight frown on her face. "In the future let's always tell each other such things at once," she said.

He nodded in silence.

"Will you promise me?"

He took her into his arms. "Don't you know that?" he asked. But his voice was still harsh.

She took his hands and looked up at him with misty eyes, in the depths of which he could read her thoughts. She was thinking of his other and more real experiences, those of his young manhood, many of which she knew about. When they were first married he had yielded, all too readily, to her jealous curiosity and had told her (indeed it often seemed to him), had surrendered to her many secrets which he should rather have kept to himself. He knew that she was inevitably reminded of these affairs and he was hardly surprised when she murmured the half-forgotten name of one of his early sweethearts. It sounded to him a little like a reproach, or was it a covert threat?

He raised her hands to his lips.

"You may believe me, even though it sounds trite, that in every woman I thought I loved it was always you I was looking for—I know that better than you can understand it, Albertina."

A dispirited smile passed over her face.

"And suppose before meeting you, I, too, had gone on a search for a mate?" she asked. The look in her eyes changed, becoming cool and impenetrable, and he allowed her hands to slip from his, as though he had caught her lying or committing a breach of faith. She, however, continued:

"Oh, if you men *knew*!" and again was silent.

"If we knew—? What do you mean by that?"

In a strangely harsh voice she replied:

"About what you imagine, my dear."

"Albertina!—then there is something that you've kept from me?"

She nodded, and looked down with a strange smile. Incomprehensible, monstrous doubts crossed his mind.

"I don't quite understand," he said. "You were barely seventeen when we became engaged."

"Past sixteen, yes, Fridolin. But it wasn't my fault that I was a virgin when I became your wife." She looked at him brightly.

"Albertina—!"

But she continued:

"It was a beautiful summer evening at Lake Wörther, just before our engagement, and a very handsome young man stood before my window that overlooked a large and spacious meadow. As we talked I thought to myself—just listen to this—what a charming young man that is—he would only have to say the word—it would have to be the right one, certainly—and I would go out with him into the meadow or the woods—or it would be even more beautiful in a boat on the lake— and I would grant him this night anything he might desire. That is what I thought to myself.—But he didn't say a word, that charming young man. He only kissed my hand tenderly—and next morning he asked me— if I would be his wife. And I said yes."

Fridolin was annoyed and dropped her hand. "And if," he said, "some one else had stood by your window that night and the right word had occurred to him, if it had been, for instance—" He was considering, but she raised her hand protestingly.

"Any other man—no matter who—could have said anything he liked—it would have been useless. And if it hadn't been you standing by the window, then very likely the summer evening wouldn't have been so beautiful." And she smiled at him.

There was a scornful expression about his mouth. "Yes, that's what you say now. Perhaps you even believe it at this moment. But—"

There was a knock on the door. The maid entered and said that the housekeeper from Schreyvogel Strasse had come to fetch the doctor, as the Privy Councilor was very low again. Fridolin went out into the hall, and when the woman told him that the Councilor had had a very serious heart attack, he promised to come at once.

As he was leaving, Albertina asked: "You're going away?" She said it with as much annoyance as if he were deliberately doing her an injustice.

Fridolin replied, with astonishment: "I suppose I've got to."

She sighed regretfully.

"I hope it won't be very serious," said Fridolin. "Up to now three centigrams of morphine have always pulled him through."

The maid brought his fur coat, and absent-mindedly kissing Albertina on her forehead and mouth, as if everything during the last hour had been completely forgotten, he hurried away.

2

WHEN Fridolin reached the street, he unbuttoned his coat. It had suddenly begun to thaw; the snow on the sidewalk was almost gone, and there was a touch of spring in the air. It was less than a quarter of an hour's walk to Schreyvogel Strasse from his home near the General Hospital, and he soon reached the old house. He walked up the dimly lighted winding staircase to the second floor and pulled the bell-rope. But before the old-fashioned bell was heard, he noticed that the door was ajar, and entering through the unlighted foyer into the living room he saw at once that he had come too late. The green-shaded kerosene lamp which was hanging from the low ceiling cast a dim light on the bed-spread under which a lean body lay motionless. Fridolin knew the old man so well that he seemed to see the face plainly, although it was outside the circle of light —the high forehead, the thin and lined cheeks, the snow-white beard and also the strikingly ugly ears with coarse, white hairs. At the foot of the bed sat Marianne, the Councilor's daughter, completely exhausted, her arms hanging limply from her shoulders. An odor of old furniture, medicine, petroleum and cooking pervaded the room, and in addition to that there was a trace of eau de Cologne and scented soap. Fridolin also noticed the indefinite, sweetish scent of this pale girl who was still young and who had been slowly fading for months and years under the stress of severe household duties, nursing and night watches.

When the doctor entered she looked up, but because of the dim light he could not see whether she had blushed, as usual, when he appeared. She started to rise, but he stopped her with a movement of his hand, and so she merely greeted him with a nod, her eyes large and sad. He stepped to the head of the bed and mechanically placed his hands on the forehead of the dead man and on the arms which were lying on the bedspread in loose and open shirt sleeves. His shoulders drooped with a slight expression of regret. He stuck his hands into the pockets of his coat and his eyes wandered about the room until they finally rested on Marianne. Her hair was blonde and thick, but dry; her neck well-formed and slender, although a little wrinkled and rather yellow; and her lips were thin and firmly pressed together.

"Well, my dear Marianne," he said in a slightly embarrassed whisper, "you weren't entirely unprepared for this."

She held out her hand to him. He took it sympathetically and inquired about the particulars of the final, fatal attack. She reported briefly and to the point, and then spoke of her father's last comparatively easy days, during which Fridolin had not seen him. Drawing up a chair, he sat down opposite her, and tried to console her by saying that her father must have suffered very little at the last. He then asked if any of her relatives had been notified. Yes, she said, the housekeeper had already gone to tell her uncle, and very likely Doctor Roediger would soon appear. "My fiancé," she added, and did not look him straight in the eye.

Fridolin simply nodded. During the year he had met Doctor Roediger two or three times in the Councilor's house. The pale young man—an instructor in History

at the University of Vienna—was of an unusually
slender build with a short, blond beard and spectacles,
and had made quite a good impression upon him, without, however, arousing his interest beyond that Marianne would certainly look better, he thought to himself,
if she were his mistress. Her hair would be less dry, her
lips would be fuller and redder. I wonder how old she
is, he reflected. The first time I attended the Councilor,
three or four years ago, she was twenty-three. At that
time her mother was still living and she was more
cheerful than now. She even took singing lessons for a
while. So she is going to marry this instructor! I wonder why? She surely isn't in love with him, and he isn't
likely to have much money either. What kind of a
marriage will it turn out to be? Probably like a thousand others. But it's none of my business. It's quite
possible that I shall never see her again, since there's
nothing more for me to do here. Well, many others that
I cared for have gone the same way.

As these thoughts passed through his mind, Marianne began to speak of her father—with fervor—as if
his death had suddenly made him a more remarkable
person. Then he was really only fifty-four years old?
Well, of course, he had had so many worries and disappointments—his wife always ill—and his son such a
grief! What, she had a brother? Certainly, she had
once told the doctor about him. Her brother was now
living somewhere abroad. A picture that he had
painted when he was fifteen was hanging over there in
Marianne's room. It represented an officer galloping
down a hill. Her father had always pretended not to see
it although it wasn't bad. Oh yes, if he'd had a chance
her brother might have made something of himself.

How excitedly she speaks, Fridolin thought, and

how bright her eyes are! Is it fever? Quite possibly.
She's grown much thinner. Probably has tuberculosis.

She kept up her stream of talk, but it seemed to him
that she didn't quite know what she was saying. It was
twelve years since her brother had left home. In fact,
she had been a child when he disappeared. They had
last heard from him four or five years ago, at Christmas, from a small city in Italy. Strange to say, she had
forgotten the name. She continued like this for a while,
almost incoherently. Suddenly she stopped and sat
there silently, her head resting in her hands. Fridolin
was tired and even more bored. He was anxiously waiting for some one to come, her relatives, or her fiancé.
The silence in the room was oppressive. It seemed to
him that the dead man joined in the silence, deliberately and with malicious joy.

With a side glance at the corpse, he said: "At any
rate, Fräulein Marianne, as things are now, it is fortunate that you won't have to stay in this house very much
longer." And when she raised her head a little, without, however, looking at Fridolin, he continued: "I
suppose your fiancé will soon get a professorship. The
chances for promotion are more favorable in the
Faculty of Philosophy than with us in Medicine." He
was thinking that, years ago, he also had aspired to an
academic career, but because he wanted a comfortable
income, he had finally decided to practice medicine.
Suddenly he felt that compared with this noble Doctor
Roediger, he was the inferior.

"We shall move soon," said Marianne listlessly, "he
has a post at the University of Göttingen."

"Oh," said Fridolin, and was about to congratulate
her but it seemed rather out of place at the moment.
He glanced at the closed window, and without asking

for permission but availing himself of his privilege as a doctor, he opened both casements and let some air in. It had become even warmer and more spring-like, and the breeze seemed to bring with it a slight fragrance of the distant awakening woods. When he turned back into the room, he saw Marianne's eyes fixed upon him with a questioning look. He moved nearer to her and said: "I hope the fresh air will be good for you. It has become quite warm, and last night"—he was about to say: we drove home from the masquerade in a snowstorm, but he quickly changed the sentence and continued: "Last night the snow was still lying on the streets a foot and a half deep."

She hardly heard what he said. Her eyes became moist, large tears streamed down her cheeks and again she buried her face in her hands. In spite of himself, he placed his hand on her head, caressing it. He could feel her body beginning to tremble, and her sobs which were at first very quiet, gradually became louder and finally quite unrestrained. All at once she slipped down from her chair and lay at Fridolin's feet, clasping his knees with her arms and pressing her face against them. Then she looked up to him with large eyes, wild with grief, and whispered ardently: "I don't want to leave here. Even if you never return, if I am never to see you again, I want, at least, to live near you."

He was touched rather than surprised, for he had always known that she either was, or imagined herself to be, in love with him.

"Please—get up, Marianne," he said softly and bending down he gently raised her. Of course, she is hysterical, he remarked to himself and he glanced at her dead father. I wonder if he hears everything, he thought. Perhaps he isn't really dead. Perhaps every one

in the first hours after passing away, is only in a coma.
He put his arms about her in a very hesitating embrace,
and almost against his will he kissed her on the forehead, an act that somehow seemed rather ridiculous.
He had a fleeting recollection of reading a novel years
ago in which a young man, still almost a boy, had been
seduced, in fact, practically raped, by the friend of his
mother at the latter's deathbed. At the same time he
thought of his wife, without knowing why, and he was
conscious of some bitterness and a vague animosity
against the man with the yellow hand-bag on the hotel
stairs in Denmark. He held Marianne closer, but without the slightest emotion. The sight of her lustreless,
dry hair, the indefinite, sweetish scent of her unaired
dress gave him a slight feeling of revulsion. The bell
outside rang again, and feeling he was released, he
hastily kissed Marianne's hand, as if in gratitude, and
went to open the door. Doctor Roediger stood there,
in a dark gray top-coat, an umbrella in his hand and a
serious face, appropriate to the occasion. The two men
greeted each other much more cordially than was
called for by their actual state of acquaintance. Then
they stepped into the room. After an embarrassed look
at the deceased, Roediger expressed his sympathy to
Marianne, while Fridolin went into the adjoining room
to write out the official death-certificate. He turned up
the gas-light over the desk and his eyes fell upon the
picture of the white-uniformed officer, galloping down
hill, with drawn sabre, to meet an invisible enemy. It
hung in a narrow frame of dull gold and rather re-
sembled a modest chromo-lithograph.

With his death-certificate filled out, Fridolin returned to the room where the engaged couple sat, hand
in hand, by the bed of the dead Councilor.

Again the door-bell rang and Doctor Roediger rose to answer it. While he was gone, Marianne, with her eyes on the floor, said, almost inaudibly: "I love you," and Fridolin answered by pronouncing her name tenderly. Then Roediger came back with an elderly couple, Marianne's uncle and aunt, and a few words, appropriate to the occasion, were exchanged, with the usual embarrassment in the presence of one who has just died. The little room suddenly seemed crowded with mourners. Fridolin felt superfluous, took his leave and was escorted to the door by Roediger who said a few words of gratitude and expressed the hope of seeing him soon again.

3

WHEN Fridolin stood on the street in front of the house, he looked up at the window which he himself had opened a little while before. The casements were swaying slightly in the wind of early spring, and the people who remained behind them up there, the living as well as the dead, all seemed unreal and phantomlike. He felt as if he had escaped from something, not so much from an adventure, but rather from a melancholy spell the power of which he was trying to break. He felt strangely disinclined to go home. The snow in the streets had melted, except where little heaps of dirty white had been piled up on either side of the curb. The gas-flame in the street lamps flickered and a nearby church bell struck eleven. Fridolin decided that before going to bed, he would spend a half hour in a quiet nook of a café near his residence. As he walked through Rathaus Park he noticed here and there on benches standing in the shadow, that couples were sitting, clasped together, just as if Spring had actually arrived and no danger were lurking in the deceptive, warm air. A tramp in tattered clothes was lying full length on a bench with his hat over his face. Suppose I wake him and give him some money for a night's lodging, Fridolin thought. But what good would that do? Then I would have to provide for the next night, too, or there'd be no sense in it, and in the end I might be suspected of having criminal relations with him. He quickened his steps to escape as rapidly as possible from all responsibility and temptation. And why only

this one? he asked himself. There are thousands of
such poor devils in Vienna alone. It's manifestly impossible to help all of them or to worry about all the
poor wretches! He was reminded of the dead man he
had just left, and shuddered; in fact, he felt slightly
nauseated at the thought that decay and decompo-
sition, according to eternal laws, had already begun
their work in the lean body under the brown flannel
blanket. He was glad that he was still alive, and in all
probability these ugly things were still far removed
from him. He was, in fact, still in the prime of youth,
he had a charming and lovable wife and could have
several women in addition, if he happened to want
them, although, to be sure, such affairs required more
leisure than was his. He then remembered that he
would have to be in his ward at the hospital at eight in
the morning, visit his private patients from eleven to
one, keep office hours from three to five, and that even
in the evening he had several appointments to visit
patients. Well, he hoped that it would be some time before he would again be called out so late at night. As he
crossed Rathaus Square, which had a dull gleam like a
brownish pond, and turned homeward, he heard the
muffled sound of marching steps in the distance. Then
he saw, still quite far away, a small group of fraternity
students, six or eight in number, turning a corner and
coming towards him. When the light of a street lamp
fell upon them he thought he recognized them, with
their blue caps, as members of the *Alemannia,* for although he had never belonged to a fraternity, he had
fought a few sabre duels in his time. In thinking of his
student days he was reminded again of the red dominoes who had lured him into a box at the ball the night
before and then had so shamefully deserted him. The

students were quite near now; they were laughing and talking loudly. Perhaps one or two of them were from the hospital? But it was impossible to see their faces plainly because of the dim light, and he had to stay quite close to the houses so as not to collide with them. Now they had passed. Only the one in the rear, a tall fellow with open overcoat and a bandage over his left eye, seemed to lag behind, and deliberately bumped into him with his raised elbow. It couldn't have been mere chance. What's got into that fellow? Fridolin thought, and involuntarily he stopped. The other took two more steps and turned. They looked at each other for a moment with only a short distance separating them. Suddenly Fridolin turned around again and went on. He heard a short laugh behind him and he longed to challenge the fellow, but he felt his heart beating strangely, just as it had on a previous occasion, twelve or fourteen years before. There had been an unusually loud knock on his door while he had had with him a certain charming young creature who was never tired of prattling about her jealous fiancé. As a matter of fact, it was only the postman who had knocked in such a threatening manner. And now he felt his heart beating just as it had at that time. What's the meaning of this? he asked himself, and he noticed that his knees were shaking a little. Am I a coward? Oh! nonsense, he reassured himself. Why should I go and face a drunken student, I, a man of thirty-five, a practising physician, a married man and father of a child? Formal challenge! Seconds! A duel! And perhaps because of such a silly encounter receive a cut in my arm and be unable to perform my professional duties?—Or lose an eye?—Or even get blood-poisoning?—And in a week perhaps be in the same

position as the man in Schreyvogel Strasse under the
brown flannel blanket? Coward—? He had fought
three sabre duels, and had even been ready to fight a
duel with pistols, and it wasn't at *his* request that the
matter had been called off. And what about his profession! There were dangers lurking everywhere and
at all times—except that one usually forgets about them.
Why, how long ago was it that that child with diphtheria had coughed in his face? Only three or four
days, that's all. After all, that was much more dangerous
than a little fencing match with sabres, and he hadn't
given it a second thought. Well, if he ever met that
fellow again, the affair could still be straightened out.
He was by no means bound by the code of honor to
take a silly encounter with a student seriously when on
an errand of mercy, to or from a patient. But if, for
instance, he should meet the young Dane with whom
Albertina—oh, nonsense, what was he thinking of?
Well, after all, it was just as bad as if she had been his
mistress. Even worse. Yes, just let that fellow cross his
path! What a joy it would be to face him somewhere
in a clearing in the woods and aim a pistol at his forehead with its smoothly combed blond hair.

He suddenly discovered that he had passed his destination. He was in a narrow street in which only a
few doubtful-looking women were strolling about in
a pitiful attempt to bag their game. It's phantomlike,
he thought. And in retrospect the students, too, with
their blue caps, suddenly seemed unreal. The same was
true of Marianne, her fiancé, her uncle and aunt, all of
whom he pictured standing hand in hand around the
deathbed of the old Councilor. Albertina, too, whom
he could see in his mind's eye soundly sleeping, her
arms folded under her head—even his child lying in

the narrow white brass bed, rolled up in a heap, and the red-cheeked governess with the mole on her left temple—all of them seemed to belong to another world. Although this idea made him shudder a bit, it also reassured him, for it seemed to free him from all responsibility, and to loosen all the bonds of human relationship.

One of the girls wandering about stopped him. She was still a young and pretty little thing, very pale with red-painted lips. She also might lead to a fatal end, only not as quickly, he thought. Is this cowardice too? I suppose really it is. He heard her steps and then her voice behind him. "Won't you come with me, doctor?"

He turned around involuntarily. "How do you know who I am?" he asked.

"Why, I don't know you," she said, "but here in this part of town they're all doctors, aren't they?"

He had had no relations with a woman of this sort since he had been a student at the Gymnasium. Was the attraction this girl had for him a sign that he was suddenly reverting to adolescence? He recalled a casual acquaintance, a smart young man, who was supposed to be extremely successful with women. Once while Fridolin was a student he had been sitting with him in an all-night café, after a ball. When the young man proposed to leave with one of the regular girls of the place, Fridolin looked at him in surprise. Thereupon he answered: "After all, it's the most convenient way—and they aren't by any means the worst."

"What's your name?" Fridolin asked the girl.

"Well, what do you think? Mizzi, of course." She unlocked the house-door, stepped into the hallway and waited for Fridolin to follow her.

"Come on," she said when he hesitated. He stepped

in beside her, the door closed behind him, she locked
it, lit a wax candle and went ahead, lighting the way.—
Am I mad? he asked himself. Of course I shall have
nothing to do with her.

An oil-lamp was burning in her room, and she turned
it up. It was a fairly pleasant place and neatly kept.
At any rate, it smelled fresher than Marianne's home,
for instance. But then, of course, no old man had been
lying ill there for months. The girl smiled, and without forwardness approached Fridolin who gently kept
her at a distance. She pointed to a rocking-chair into
which he was glad to drop.

"You must be very tired," she remarked. He nodded.
Undressing without haste, she continued: "Well, no
wonder, with all the things a man like you has to do
in the course of a day. We have an easier time of it."

He noticed that her lips were not painted, as he had
thought, but were a natural red, and he complimented
her on that.

"But why should I rouge?" she inquired. "How old
do you think I am?"

"Twenty?" Fridolin ventured.

"Seventeen," she said, and sat on his lap, putting
her arms around his neck like a child.

Who in the world would suspect that I'm here in
this room at this moment? Fridolin thought. I'd never
have thought it possible an hour or even ten minutes
ago. And—why? Why am I here? Her lips were seeking his, but he drew back his head. She looked at him
with sad surprise and slipped down from his lap. He
was sorry, for he had felt much comforting tenderness
in her embrace.

She took a red dressing-gown which was hanging
over the foot of the open bed, slipped into it and

folded her arms over her breast so that her entire body was concealed.

"Does this suit you better?" she asked without mockery, almost timidly, as though making an effort to understand him. He hardly knew what to answer.

"You're right," he said. "I am really tired, and I find it very pleasant sitting here in the rocking-chair and simply listening to you. You have such a nice gentle voice. Just talk to me."

She sat down on the couch and shook her head.

"You're simply afraid," she said softly—and then to herself in a barely audible voice: "It's too bad."

These last words made the blood race through his veins. He walked over to her, longing to touch her, and declared that he trusted her implicitly and saying so he spoke the truth. He put his arms around her and wooed her like a sweetheart, like a beloved woman, but she resisted, until he felt ashamed and finally gave it up.

She explained: "You never can tell, some time or other it's bound to get out. It's quite right of you to be afraid. If something should happen, you would curse me."

She was so positive in refusing the bank-notes which he offered her that he did not insist. She put a little blue woolen shawl about her shoulders, lit a candle to light him downstairs, went down with him and unlocked the door. "I'm not going out any more tonight," she said. He took her hand and involuntarily kissed it. She looked up to him astonished, almost frightened. Then she laughed, embarrassed and happy. "Just as if I were a young lady," she said.

The door closed behind Fridolin and he quickly made a mental note of the street number, so as to be able to send the poor little thing some wine and cakes the following day.

4

MEANWHILE it had become even milder outside. A fragrance from dewy meadows and distant mountains drifted with the gentle breezes into the narrow street. Where shall I go now? Fridolin asked himself, as though it weren't the obvious thing to go home to bed. But he couldn't persuade himself to do so. He felt homeless, an outcast, since his annoying meeting with the students . . . or was it since Marianne's confession? No, it was longer than that—ever since this evening's conversation with Albertina he was moving farther and farther away from his everyday existence into some strange and distant world.

He wandered about aimlessly through the dark streets, letting the breeze blow through his hair. Finally, he turned resolutely into a third-rate coffee-house. The place was dimly lighted and not especially large, but it had an old-fashioned, cozy air about it, and was almost empty at this late hour.

Three men were playing cards in a corner. The waiter who had been watching them helped Fridolin take off his fur coat, took his order and placed illustrated journals and evening papers on his table. Fridolin felt slightly more secure and began to look through the papers. His eyes were arrested here and there by some news-item. In some Bohemian city, street signs with German names had been torn down. There was a conference in Constantinople in which Lord Cranford took part about constructing a rail-

way in Asia Minor. The firm Benies & Weingruber
had gone into bankruptcy. The prostitute Anna Tiger,
in a fit of jealousy, had attempted to throw vitriol on
her friend, Hermine Drobizky. An Ash Wednesday
fish-dinner was being given that evening in Sophia
Hall. Marie B., a young girl residing at No. 28 Schönbrunn Strasse, had poisoned herself with mercuric
chloride.—Prosaically commonplace as they were, all
these facts, the insignificant as well as the sad, had a
sobering and reassuring effect on Fridolin. He felt
sorry for the young girl, Marie B. How stupid to take
mercuric chloride! At this very moment, while he was
sitting snugly in the café, while Albertina was calmly
sleeping, and the Councilor had passed beyond all human suffering, Marie B., No. 28 Schönbrunn Strasse,
was writhing in incredible pain.

He looked up from his paper and encountered the
gaze of a man seated opposite. Was it possible? Nachtigall—? The latter had already recognized him,
threw up his hands in pleased surprise and joined him
at his table. He was still a young man, tall, rather
broad, and none too thin. His long, blond, slightly
curly hair had a touch of gray in it, and his mustache
drooped in Polish fashion. He was wearing an open
gray top-coat, underneath which were visible a greasy
dress-suit, a crumpled shirt with three false diamond
studs, a crinkled collar and a dangling, white silk tie.
His eyelids were inflamed, as if from many sleepless
nights, but his blue eyes gleamed brightly.

"You here in Vienna, Nachtigall?" exclaimed
Fridolin.

"Didn't you know?" said Nachtigall with a soft,
Polish accent and a slightly Jewish twang. "How could
you miss it, and me so famous?" He laughed loudly

and good-naturedly, and sat down opposite Fridolin.

"What," asked Fridolin, "have you been appointed Professor of Surgery without my hearing of it?"

Nachtigall laughed still louder. "Didn't you hear me just now, just a minute ago?"

"What do you mean—hear you?—Why, of course." Suddenly it occurred to him that some one had been playing the piano when he entered; in fact, he had heard music coming from some basement as he approached the café. "So that was you playing?" he exclaimed.

"It was," Nachtigall said, laughing.

Fridolin nodded. Why, of course—the strangely vigorous touch, the peculiar, but euphonious bass chords had at once seemed familiar to him. "Are you devoting yourself entirely to it?" he asked. He remembered that Nachtigall had definitely given up the study of medicine after his second preliminary examination in zoölogy, which he had passed although he was seven years late in taking it. Since then he had been hanging around the hospital, the dissecting room, the laboratories and classrooms for some time afterwards. With his blond artist's head, his crinkled collar, his dangling tie that had once been white, he had been a striking and, in the humorous sense, popular figure. He had been much liked, not only by his fellow-students, but also by many professors. The son of a Jewish gin-shop owner in a small Polish town, he had left home early and had come to Vienna to study medicine. The trifling sums he received from his parents had from the very beginning been scarcely worth mention and were soon discontinued. However, this didn't prevent his appearing in the Riedhof Hotel at the table reserved for medical students where Fridolin

was a regular guest. At intervals, one after another of
his more well-to-do fellow-students would pay his bill.
He sometimes, also, was given clothes, which he accepted gladly and without false pride. He had already
learned to play in his home town from a pianist
stranded there, and while he was a medical student in
Vienna he had studied at the Conservatory where he
was considered a talented musician of great promise.
But here, too, he was neither serious nor diligent
enough to develop his art systematically. He soon became entirely content with the impression he made on
his acquaintances, rather with the pleasure he gave
them by his playing. For a while he had a position
as pianist in a suburban dancing-school. Fellow-
students and table-companions tried to introduce him
into fashionable houses in the same capacity, but on
such occasions he would play only what suited him
and as long as he chose. His conversations with the
young girls present were not always harmless, and he
drank more than he could carry. Once, playing for a
dance in the house of a wealthy banker, he embarrassed several couples with flattering but improper
remarks, and ended up by playing a wild cancan and
singing a risqué song with his powerful, bass voice.
The host gave him a severe calling down, but Nachtigall, blissfully hilarious, got up and embraced him.
The latter was furious and, although himself a
Jew, hurled a common insult at him. Nachtigall at
once retaliated with a powerful box on his ears, and
this definitely concluded his career in the fashionable
houses of the city. He behaved better, on the whole,
in more intimate circles, although sometimes when
the hour was late, he had to be put out of the place by
force. But the following morning all was forgiven and

forgotten. One day, long after his friends had graduated, he disappeared from the city without a word. For a few months he sent post cards from various Russian and Polish cities, and once Fridolin, who was one of Nachtigall's favorites, was reminded of his existence not only by a card, but by a request for a moderate sum of money, without explanation. Fridolin sent it at once, but never received a word of thanks or any other sign of life from Nachtigall.

At this moment, however, eight years later, at a quarter to one in the morning, Nachtigall insisted on paying his debt, and took the exact amount in banknotes from a rather shabby pocket-book. As the latter was fairly well filled, Fridolin accepted the repayment with a good conscience.

"Are you getting along well," he asked with a smile, in order to make sure.

"I can't complain," replied Nachtigall. Placing his hand on Fridolin's arm, he continued: "But tell me, why are you here so late at night?"

Fridolin explained that he had needed a cup of coffee after visiting a patient, although he didn't say, without quite knowing why, that he hadn't found his patient alive. Then he talked in very general terms of his duties at the hospital and his private practice, and mentioned that he was happily married, and the father of a six-year-old girl.

Nachtigall in his turn, explained that he had spent the time as a pianist in every possible sort of Polish, Roumanian, Serbian and Bulgarian city and town, just as Fridolin had surmised. He had a wife and four children living in Lemberg, and he laughed heartily, as though it were unusually jolly to have four children, all of them living in Lemberg, and all by one and the same woman. He had been back in Vienna since the preceding fall. The vaudeville company he had been with had suddenly gone to pieces. He was now playing anywhere and everywhere, anything that happened to come along, sometimes in two or three different houses the same night. For example, down there in that basement—not at all a fashionable place, as he remarked, really a sort of bowling alley, and with very doubtful patrons. . . . "But if you have to provide for four children and a wife in Lemberg"—he laughed again, though not quite as gaily as before, and added: "But sometimes I am privately engaged." Noticing a reminiscent smile on Fridolin's face, he continued: "Not just in the houses of bankers and such, but in all kinds of circles, even larger ones, both public and secret."

"Secret?" Fridolin asked.

Nachtigall looked straight before him with a gloomy and crafty air, and said: "They will be calling for me again in a minute."

"What, are you playing somewhere else tonight?"

"Yes, they only begin there at two."

"It must be an unusually smart place."

"Yes and no," said Nachtigall, laughing, but he became serious again at once.

"Yes and no?" queried Fridolin, curiously.

Nachtigall bent across the table.

"I'm playing tonight in a private house, but I don't know whose it is."

"Then you're playing there for the first time?" Fridolin asked with increasing interest.

"No, it's the third time, but it will probably be a different house again."

"I don't understand."

"Neither do I," said Nachtigall, laughing, "but you'd better not ask any more."

"Oh, I see," remarked Fridolin.

"No, you're wrong. It's not what you think. I've seen a great deal in my time. It's unbelievable what one sees in such small towns, especially in Roumania, but here . . ." He drew back the yellow curtain from the window, looked out on the street and said as if to himself: "Not here yet." Then he turned to Fridolin and explained: "I mean the carriage. There's always a carriage to call for me, a different one each time."

"You're making me very curious, Nachtigall," Fridolin assured him.

"Listen to me," said Nachtigall after a slight pause. "I'd like to be able to arrange it—but how can I do it—" Suddenly he burst out: "Have you got plenty of nerve?"

"That's a strange question," said Fridolin in the tone of an offended fraternity student.

"I don't mean that."

"Well, what do you mean?—Why does one need so much courage for this affair? What can possibly happen?" He gave a short and contemptuous laugh.

"Nothing can happen to *me*. At best this would be the last time—but perhaps that may be the case anyhow." He stopped and looked out again through the crevice in the curtain.

"Well, then where's the difficulty?"

"What did you say?" asked Nachtigall, as if coming out of a dream.

"Tell me the rest of the story, now that you've started. A secret party? Closed affair? Nothing but invited guests?"

"I don't know. The last time there were thirty people, and the first time only sixteen."

"A ball?"

"Of course, a ball." He seemed to be sorry he had spoken of the matter at all.

"And you're furnishing the music for the occasion?"

"What do you mean—for the occasion? I don't know for what occasion. I simply play—with bandaged eyes."

"Nachtigall, what do you mean?"

Nachtigall sighed a little and continued: "Unfortunately my eyes are not completely bandaged, so that I can occasionally see something. I can see through the black silk handkerchief over my eyes in the mirror opposite. . . ." And he stopped.

"In other words," said Fridolin impatiently and contemptuously, but feeling strangely excited, "naked females."

"Don't say females," replied Nachtigall in an offended tone, "you never saw such women."

Fridolin hemmed and hawed a little. "And what's the price of admission?" he asked casually.

"Do you mean tickets and such? There are none."

"Well, how does one gain admittance?" asked Fridolin with compressed lips and tapping on the table with his fingers.

"You have to know the password, and it's a new one each time."

"And what's the one for tonight?"

"I don't know yet. I'll only find out from the coachman."

"Take me along, Nachtigall."

"Impossible. It's too dangerous."

"But a minute ago you yourself spoke . . . of being

willing to . . . I think you can manage all right."

Nachtigal looked at him critically and said: "It would be absolutely impossible in your street clothes, for every one is masked, men and women. As you haven't a masquerade outfit with you, it's out of the question. Perhaps the next time. I'll try to figure out some way." He listened attentively, peered again through the opening in the curtain and said with a sigh of relief: "There's my carriage, good-bye."

Fridolin hung on to his arm and said: "You can't get away that way. You've got to take me along."

"But my dear man . . ."

"Leave it to me. I know that it's dangerous. Perhaps that's the very thing that tempts me."

"But I've already told you—without costume and mask—"

"There are places to rent costumes."

"At one o'clock in the morning?"

"Listen here, Nachtigall. There's just such a place at the corner of Wickenburg Strasse. I walk past it several times a day." And he added, with growing excitement: "You stay here for another quarter of an hour, Nachtigall. In the meantime I'll see what luck I have. The proprietor of the costume shop probably lives in the same building. If he doesn't—well, then I'll simply give it up for tonight. Let fate decide the question. There's a café in the same building. I think it's called Café Vindobona. You tell the coachman that you've forgotten something in the café, walk in, and I'll be waiting near the door. Then you can give me the password and get back into your carriage. If I manage to get a costume I'll take a cab and immediately follow you. The rest will take care of itself. I give you my word of honor, Nachtigall, that if you run any risk, I'll assume complete responsibility."

Nachtigall had tried several times to interrupt Fridolin, but it was useless——

The former threw some money on the table to pay his bill, including a generous tip which seemed appropriate for the style of the night, and left. A closed carriage was standing outside. A coachman dressed entirely in black with a tall silk hat, sat on the box, motionless. It looks like a mourning-coach, Fridolin thought. He ran down the street and reached the corner-house he was looking for a few minutes later. He rang the bell, inquired from the care-taker whether the costumer Gibiser lived in the house, and hoped in the bottom of his heart that he would receive a negative answer. But Gibiser actually lived there, on the floor below that of the costume shop. The care-taker did not seem especially surprised at having such a late caller. Made affable by Fridolin's liberal tip, he stated that it was not unusual during the carnival for people to come at such a late hour to hire costumes. He lighted the way from below with a candle until Fridolin had rung the bell on the second floor. Herr Gibiser himself opened the door for him, as if he had been waiting there. He was a bald-headed, haggard man and wore an old-fashioned, flowered dressing-gown and a tasselled, Turkish cap which made him look like a foolish old man on the stage. Fridolin asked for a costume and said that the price did not matter, whereupon Here Gibiser remarked, almost disdainfully: "I ask a fair price, no more."

He led the way up a winding staircase into the store. There was an odor of silk, velvet, perfume, dust and

withered flowers, and a glitter of silver and red out
of the indistinct darkness. A number of little electric
bulbs suddenly shone between the open cabinets of a
long, narrow passage, the end of which was enveloped
in darkness. There were all kinds of costumes hanging
to the right and to the left. On one side knights,
squires, peasants, hunters, scholars, Orientals and
clowns; on the other, ladies-at-court, baronesses, peasant women, lady's maids, queens of the night. The
corresponding head-dresses were on a shelf above the
costumes. Fridolin felt as though he were walking
through a gallery of hanged people who were on the
point of asking each other to dance. Herr Gibiser followed him. Finally he asked: "Is there anything special you want? Louis Quatorze, Directoire, or Old-
German?"

"I need a dark cassock and a black mask, that's all."

At this moment the clink of glasses rang out from
the end of the passage. Fridolin was startled and
looked at the costumer, as though he felt an explanation were due. Gibiser, however, merely groped for a
switch which was concealed somewhere. A blinding
light was diffused over the entire passage down to the
end where a little table, covered with plates, glasses
and bottles, could be seen. Two men, dressed in the
red robes of vehmic judges, sprang up from two chairs
beside the table and a graceful little girl disappeared at
the same moment. Gibiser rushed forward with long
strides, reached across the table and grabbed a white
wig in his hand. Simultaneously a young and charming girl, still almost a child, wearing a Pierrette costume, wriggled out from under the table and ran along
the passage to Fridolin who caught her in his arms.
Gibiser dropped the white wig and grabbed the two

vehmic judges by their robes. At the same time he
called out to Fridolin: "Hold on to that girl for me."
The child pressed against Fridolin as though sure of
protection. Her little oval face was covered with powder and several beauty spots, and a fragrance of roses
and powder arose from her delicate breasts. There was
a smile of impish desire in her eyes.

"Gentlemen," cried Gibiser, "you will stay here
while I call the police."

"What's got into you?" they exclaimed, and continued as if with one voice: "We were invited by the
young lady."

Gibiser released his hold and Fridolin heard him
saying: "You will have to explain this. Couldn't you
see that the girl was deranged?" Then turning to
Fridolin, he said: "Sorry to keep you waiting."

"Oh, it doesn't matter," said Fridolin. He would
have liked to stay, or, better, still, to take the girl
with him, no matter where—and whatever the consequences. She looked up at him with alluring and childlike eyes, as if spellbound. The men at the end of the
passage were arguing excitedly. Gibiser turned to
Fridolin and asked in a matter-of-fact way: "You
wanted a cassock, a pilgrim's hat and a mask?"

"No," said Pierrette with gleaming eyes, "you must
give this gentleman a cloak lined with ermine and a
doublet of red silk."

"Don't you budge from my side," answered Gibiser.
Then he pointed to a dark frock hanging between a
medieval soldier and a Venetian Senator, and said:
"That's about your size and here's the hat. Take it
quick."

The two strange men protested again: "You'll have
to let us out at once, Herr Chibisier." Fridolin noticed

with surprise the French pronunciation of the name Gibiser.

"That's out of the question," replied the costumer scornfully. "You'll kindly wait here until I return."

Meanwhile Fridolin slipped into the cassock and tied the white cords. Gibiser, who was standing on a narrow ladder, handed him the black, broad-rimmed pilgrim's hat, and he put it on. But he did all this unwillingly, being more and more convinced that danger was threatening Pierrette and that it was his duty to remain and help her. The mask which Gibiser gave him and which he at once tried on, smelt strange and rather disagreeable.

"You walk down ahead of me," Gibiser commanded the girl, pointing to the stairs. Pierrette turned and waved a gay, yet wistful farewell. Fridolin's eyes followed the direction of her gaze. The two men were no longer in costume but wore evening clothes and white ties, though their faces were still covered by their red masks. Pierrette went down the winding staircase with a light step, Gibiser behind her and Fridolin following in the rear. In the anteroom below Gibiser opened a door leading to the inner rooms and said to Pierrette: "Go to bed at once, you depraved creature. I'll talk to you as soon as I've settled with those two upstairs."

She stood in the doorway, white and delicate, and with a glance at Fridolin, sadly shook her head. He noticed with surprise, in a large wall-mirror to the right, a haggard pilgrim who seemed to be himself. At the same time he knew very well that it could be no other.

The girl disappeared and the old costumer locked

the door behind her. Then he opened the entrance door and hurried Fridolin out into the hallway.

"Well," said Fridolin, "how much do I owe you?"

"Never mind, sir, you can pay when you return the things. I'll trust you."

Fridolin, however, refused to move. "Swear that you won't hurt that poor child," he said.

"What business is it of yours?"

"I heard you, a minute ago, say that the girl was insane—and just now you called her a depraved creature. That sounds pretty contradictory."

"Well," replied Gibiser theatrically, "aren't insanity and depravity the same in the eyes of God?"

Fridolin shuddered with disgust.

"Whatever it is," he remarked, "there are ways and means of attending to it. I am a doctor. We'll have another talk about this tomorrow."

Gibiser laughed mockingly without uttering a sound. A light flared up in the hallway, and the door between them was closed and immediately bolted. Fridolin took off the hat, cassock and mask while going downstairs, carrying the bundle under his arm. The care-taker opened the outer door and Fridolin saw the mourning-coach standing opposite with the motionless driver on the box. Nachtigall was just on the point of leaving the café, and seemed somewhat taken aback at seeing Fridolin at hand so promptly.

"Then you did manage to get a costume?"

"You can see for yourself. What's the password?"

"You insist on knowing it?"

"Absolutely."

"Well then—it's Denmark."

"Are you mad, Nachtigall?"

"Why mad?"

"Oh, never mind—I was at the sea-shore in Denmark this summer. Get back into your carriage—but not too fast, so that I'll have time to take a cab over on the other side."

Nachtigall nodded and leisurely lighted a cigarette. Fridolin quickly crossed the street, hailed a cab in an offhand way, as though he were playing a joke, and told the driver to follow the mourning-coach which was just starting in front of them.

They crossed Alser Strasse, and drove on through dim, deserted side-streets under a railroad viaduct towards the suburbs. Fridolin was afraid that the driver might lose sight of the carriage, but whenever he put his head out of the open window, into the abnormally warm air, he always saw it. It was a moderate distance ahead of them, and the coachman with his high, black silk hat sat motionless on the box. This business may end badly, thought Fridolin. At the same time he remembered the fragrance of roses and powder that had arisen from Pierrette's breasts. What strange story is behind all that? he wondered. I shouldn't have left—perhaps it was even a great mistake—I wonder where I am now.

The road wound slowly up-hill between modest villas. Fridolin thought that he now had his bearings. He had sometimes come this way on walks, years ago. It must be the *Galitzinberg* that he was going up. Down to his left he could see the city indistinct in the mist, but glimmering with a thousand lights. He heard the rumbling of wheels behind him and looked out of the window back of him. There were two carriages following his. He was glad of that, for now the driver of the mourning-coach would certainly not be suspicious of him.

With a violent jolt, the cab turned into a side street and went down into something like a ravine, between iron fences, stone walls and terraces. Fridolin realized that it was high time to put on his costume. He took off his fur coat and slipped into the cassock, just as he slipped into the sleeves of his white linen coat every morning in his ward at the hospital. He was relieved to think that, if everything went well, it would be only a few hours before he would be back again by the beds of his patients, ready to give aid.

His cab stopped. What if I don't get out at all, Fridolin thought, and go back at once? But go where? To little Pierrette? To the girl in Buchfeld Strasse? Or to Marianne, the daughter of the deceased? Or perhaps home? He shuddered slightly and decided he'd rather go anywhere than home. Was it because it was farthest to go? No, I can't turn back, he thought. I must go through with this, even if it means death. And he laughed at himself, using such a big word but without feeling very cheerful about it.

A garden gate stood wide open. The mourning-coach drove on deeper into the ravine, or into the darkness that seemed like one. Nachtigall must, therefore, have got out. Fridolin quickly sprang out of the cab and told the driver to wait for him up at the turn, no matter how late he might be. To make sure of him, he paid him well in advance and promised him a large sum for the return trip. The other carriages drove up and Fridolin saw the veiled figure of a woman step out of the first. Then he turned into the garden and put on his mask. A narrow path, lighted up by a lamp

from the house, led to the entrance. Doors opened before him, and he found himself in a narrow, white
vestibule. He could hear an organ playing, and two
servants in dark livery, their faces covered by gray
masks, stood on each side of him.

Two voices whispered in unison: "Password?" He
replied: "Denmark." One of them took his fur coat
and disappeared with it into an adjoining room, while
the other opened a door. Fridolin entered a dimly
lighted room with high ceilings, hung on all sides with
black silk. Sixteen to twenty people masked and
dressed as monks and nuns were walking up and
down. The gently swelling strains of Italian church
music came from above. A small group, composed of
three nuns and two monks, stood in a corner of the
room. They watched him for a second, but turned
away again at once, almost deliberately. Fridolin, noticing that he was the only one who wore a hat, took
his off and walked up and down as nonchalantly as
possible. A monk brushed against him and nodded a
greeting, but from behind the mask Fridolin encountered a searching and penetrating glance. A
strange, heavy perfume, as of Southern gardens,
scented the room. Again an arm brushed against him,
but this time it was that of a nun. Like all the others
she had a black veil over her face, head and neck.
A blood-red mouth glowed under the black laces of
the mask. Where am I? thought Fridolin. Among
lunatics? Or conspirators? Is this a meeting of some
religious sect? Can it be that Nachtigall was ordered
or paid to bring along some stranger to be the target
of their jokes? But everything seemed too serious, too
intense, too uncanny for a masquerade prank. A
woman's voice joined the strains of the organ and an

Old Italian sacred aria resounded through the room.
They all stood still and listened and Fridolin surrendered himself for a moment to the wondrously
swelling melody. A soft voice suddenly whispered
from behind: "Don't turn around. There's still a
chance for you to get away. You don't belong here.
If it's discovered it will go hard with you."

Fridolin gave a frightened start. For a second he
thought of leaving, but his curiosity, the allurement
and, above all, his pride, were stronger than any of
his misgivings. Now that I've gone this far, he thought,
I don't care what happens. And he shook his head
negatively without turning around.

The voice behind him whispered: "I should feel
very sorry for you." He turned and looked at her. He
saw the blood-red mouth glimmering under the face.
Dark eyes were fixed on him. "I shall stay," he said in
an heroic voice which he hardly recognized as his own,
and he looked away again. The song was now ringing
through the room; the organ had a new sound which
was anything but sacred. It was worldly, voluptuous,
and pealing. Looking around Fridolin saw that all the
nuns had disappeared and that only the monks were
left. The voice had meanwhile also changed. It rose by
way of an artistically executed trill from its low and
serious pitch to a high and jubilant tone. In place of
the organ a piano had suddenly chimed in with its
worldly and brazen tunes. Fridolin at once recognized
Nachtigall's wild and inflammatory touch. The
woman's voice which had been so reverent a moment
before had vanished with a last wild, voluptuous out-
burst through the ceiling, as it were, into infinity.
Doors opened to the right and left. On one side Fridolin recognized the indistinct outlines of Nachtigall's

figure; the room opposite was radiant with a blaze
of light. All the women were standing there motionless. They wore dark veils over their heads, faces and
necks and black masks over their eyes, but otherwise
they were completely naked. Fridolin's eyes wandered
eagerly from voluptuous to slender bodies, from delicate figures to those luxuriously developed. He realized that each of these women would forever be a
mystery, and that the enigma of their large eyes peering at him from beneath the black masks would remain unsolved. The delight of beholding was changed
to an almost unbearable agony of desire. And the
others seemed to experience a similar sensation. The
first gasps of rapture had changed to sighs that held
a note very near anguish. A cry broke out somewhere.
Suddenly all of them, as though pursued, rushed from
the darkened room to the women, who received them
with wild and wicked laughter. The men were no
longer in cassocks, but dressed as cavaliers in white,
yellow, blue and red. Fridolin was the only one in
monk's dress. Somewhat nervously he slunk into the
farthest corner, where he was near Nachtigall whose
back was turned to him. Nachtigall had a bandage
over his eyes, but Fridolin thought he could see him
peering underneath the bandage into the tall mirror
opposite. In it the cavaliers with their gay-colored costumes were reflected, dancing with their naked partners.

A woman came up suddenly behind Fridolin and
whispered—for no one spoke aloud, as if the voices,
too, were to remain a secret—: "What is the matter?
Why don't you dance?"

Fridolin, seeing two noblemen watch fixedly from
another corner, suspected that this woman with the

boyish and slender figure, was sent to put him to the test. In spite of it he meant to dance with her, but at that moment another woman left her partner and walked quickly up to him. He knew at once that it was the same one who had already warned him. She pretended that she had just seen him and whispered, in a voice loud enough to be heard in the other corner: "Returned at last!" Laughingly, she continued: "All your efforts are useless. I know you." Then turning to the woman with the boyish figure, she said: "Let me have him for just two minutes, then he shall be yours again until morning, if you wish." In a softer voice she added: "It is really he." The other replied in astonishment: "Really?" and with a light step went to join the cavaliers in the corner.

Alone with Fridolin, the woman cautioned him, "Don't ask questions, and don't be surprised at anything. I tried to lead them astray, but you can't continue to deceive them for long. Go, before it is too late —and it may be too late at almost any moment—and be careful that no one follows you. No one must know who you are. There would be no more peace and quiet for you. Go!"

"Will I see you again?"

"It's impossible."

"Then I shall stay."

"My life, at most, is at stake," he said, "and I'm ready at this moment to give it for you." He took her hands and tried to draw her to him.

She whispered again, almost despairingly: "Go!"

He laughed, and he heard himself laughing as in a dream. "But I know what I'm doing. You are not all here just to make us mad by looking at you. You are doing this to unnerve me still more."

"It will soon be too late. You must go!"

But he wouldn't listen to her. "Do you mean to say that there are no rooms here for the convenience of congenial couples? Will all these people leave with just a courteous 'good-bye'? They don't look like it."

He pointed to the dancers, glowing white bodies closely pressed against the blue, red and yellow silks of their partners, circling, in the brilliant, mirrored room adjoining, to the wild tunes of the piano. It seemed to him that no longer was any attention paid to him and the woman beside him. They stood alone in the semi-dark middle room.

"You are hoping in vain," she whispered. "There are no such rooms here. This is your last opportunity to leave."

"Come with me!"

She shook her head violently, despairingly.

He laughed again, not recognizing his laughter. "You're making game of me. Did all these men and women come here merely to fan the flames of their desire and then depart? Who can forbid you to come away with me if you choose?"

She took a deep breath and drooped her head.

"Oh, now I understand," he said. "That's the punishment you impose on those who come here uninvited. You couldn't have invented a more cruel one. Please let me off and forgive me. Impose some other penalty, anything but that I must leave you."

"You are mad. I can't go with you, let alone any one else. Whomever I went with would forfeit his life and mine."

Fridolin felt intoxicated, not only with her, her fragrant body and her red-glowing mouth—not only with the atmosphere of this room and the voluptuous mysteries that surrounded him—he was intoxicated, his thirst unsatisfied, with all the experiences of the night, none of which had come to a satisfactory conclusion. He was intoxicated with himself, with his boldness, the change he felt in himself, and he touched the veil which was wound about her head, as though he intended to remove it.

She seized his hands. "One night during the dance here one of the men took it into his head to tear the veil from one of us. They ripped the mask from his face and drove him out with whips."

"And—she?"

"Did you read of a beautiful young girl, only a few weeks ago, who took poison the day before her wedding?"

He remembered the incident, even the name, and mentioned it. "Wasn't it a girl of the nobility who was engaged to marry an Italian Prince?"

She nodded.

One of the cavaliers, the most distinguished looking of them all and the only one dressed in white, suddenly stopped before them. With a slight bow, courteous but imperative, he asked the woman with whom Fridolin was talking to dance with him. She seemed to hesitate a moment, but he put his arm around her waist and they drifted away to join the other couples in the adjoining room.

A sudden feeling of solitude made Fridolin shiver as if with cold. He looked about him. Nobody seemed to be paying any attention to him. This was perhaps his last chance to leave with impunity. He didn't know, however, why it was that he remained spellbound in his corner where he now felt sure that he was not observed. It might be his aversion to an in-

glorious and perhaps ridiculous retreat, or the excruciating ungratified desire for the beautiful woman
whose fragrance was still in his nostrils. Or he may
have stayed because he vaguely hoped that all that
had happened so far was intended as a test of his courage and that this magnificent woman would be his
reward. It was clear at any rate that the strain was too
great to be endured, and that, no matter what the
danger, he would have to end it. It could hardly cost
him his life, no matter what he decided. He might
be among fools, or libertines, but certainly not among
rascals or criminals. The thought occurred to him to
acknowledge himself as an intruder and to place himself at their disposal in chivalrous fashion. This night
could only conclude in such a manner—with a har-
monious finale, as it were—if it were to mean more
than a wild, shadow-like succession of gloomy and
lascivious adventures, all without an end. So, taking a
deep breath, he prepared to carry out his plan.

At this moment, however, a voice whispered beside him: "Password!" A cavalier in black had stepped
up to him unseen. As Fridolin didn't reply, he repeated
his question. "Denmark," said Fridolin.

"That's right, sir, that's the password for admittance,
but what's the password of the house, may I ask?"

Fridolin was silent.

"Won't you be kind enough to tell me the password
of the house?" It sounded like a sharp threat.

Fridolin shrugged his shoulders. The other walked
to the middle of the room and raised his hand. The
piano ceased playing and the dance stopped. Two
other cavaliers, one in yellow, the other in red, stepped
up. "The password, sir," they both said simultaneously.

"I have forgotten it," replied Fridolin with a vacant smile but feeling quite calm.

"That's unfortunate," said the gentleman in yellow, "for here it doesn't matter whether you have forgotten it or if you never knew it."

The other men flocked in and the doors on both sides were closed. Fridolin stood alone in the garb of a monk in the midst of the gay-colored cavaliers.

"Take off your mask!" several of them demanded. Fridolin held out his arm to protect himself. It seemed a thousand times worse to be the only one unmasked amongst so many that were, than to stand suddenly naked amongst people who were dressed. He replied firmly: "If my appearance here has offended any of the gentlemen present, I am ready to give satisfaction in the usual manner, but I shall take off my mask only if all of you will do the same."

"It's not a question of satisfaction," said the cavalier in red, who until now had not spoken, "but one of expiation."

"Take off your mask!" commanded another in a high-pitched, insolent voice which reminded Fridolin of an officer giving orders, "and we'll tell you to your face what's in store for you."

"I shall not take it off," said Fridolin in an even sharper tone, "and woe to him who dares to touch me."

A hand suddenly reached out, as if to tear off the mask, when a door suddenly opened and one of the women—Fridolin did not doubt which one it was— stood there, dressed as a nun, as he had first seen her. The others could be seen behind her in the brilliantly lighted room, naked, with veiled faces, crowding together in a terrified group. The door at once closed again.

"Leave him alone," said the nun. "I am ready to redeem him."

There was a short, deep silence, as though something monstrous had happened. The cavalier in black who had first demanded the password from Fridolin turned to the nun, saying: "You know what you are taking upon yourself in doing this."

"I know."

There was a general sigh of relief from those present.

"You are free," said the cavalier to Fridolin. "Leave this house at once and be careful not to inquire further into what you have seen here. If you attempt to put any one on our trail, whether you succeed or not—you will be doomed."

Fridolin stood motionless. "How is this woman to redeem me?" he asked.

There was no answer. Hands pointed to the door indicated that he must go.

Fridolin shook his head. "Impose what punishment you wish, gentlemen, I won't let this woman pay for me."

"You would be unable, in any case, to change her lot," the cavalier in black said very gently. "When a promise has been made here there is no turning back."

The nun slowly nodded, as if to confirm the statement. "Go!" she said to Fridolin.

"No," replied the latter, elevating his voice. "Life means nothing to me if I must leave here without you. I shall not ask who you are or where you come from. What difference can it make to you, gentlemen, whether or not you keep up this carnival comedy, though it may aim at a serious conclusion? Whoever you may be, you surely lead other lives. I won't play a part, here or elsewhere, and if I have been forced to do so up to now, I shall give it up. I feel that a fate has overtaken me which has nothing to do with this foolery. I will tell you my name, take off my mask and be responsible for the consequences."

"Don't do it," exclaimed the nun, "you would only ruin yourself without saving me. Go!" Then she turned to the others, saying: "Here I am, take me—all of you!"

The dark costume dropped from her, as if by magic. She stood there in the radiance of her white body; reached for the veil which was wrapped about her head, face and neck and unwound it with a wonderful circular motion. It sank to the floor, dark hair fell in great profusion over her shoulders, breasts and hips— but before Fridolin could even glance at her face, he was seized by irresistible arms, and pushed to the door. A moment later he found himself in the anteroom, the door closed behind him. A masked servant brought him his fur coat and helped him put it on. The main door opened automatically, and as if driven by some invisible force, he hurried out. As he stood on the street the light behind disappeared. The house stood there in silence with closed windows from which not a glimmer issued. I must remember everything clearly, was his main thought; I must find the house again—the rest will follow as a matter of course.

Darkness surrounded him. The dull reddish glow of a street lamp was visible a slight distance above where the cab was to await for him. The mourning-coach drove up from the street below, as though he had called it. A servant opened the door.

"I have my own cab," said Fridolin. When the servant shook his head, Fridolin continued: "If it has already gone, I'll walk back to the city."

The man replied with a wave of his hand which was anything but servant-like, so that objection was out of the question. The ridiculously high silk hat of the coachman towered up into the night. The wind was blowing a gale; violet clouds raced across the sky. Fridolin felt that, after his previous experience, there was nothing for him to do but to get into the carriage. It started the moment he was inside.

He resolved, as soon as possible, to clear up the mystery of his adventure, no matter how dangerous it might be. His life, it seemed, would not have the slightest meaning any more, if he did not succeed in finding the incomprehensible woman who at this very moment was paying for his safety. It was only too easy to guess the price. But why should she sacrifice herself for him? To sacrifice—? Was she the kind of woman to whom the things that were facing her, that she was now submitting to, could mean a sacrifice? If she attended these affairs—and since she seemed to understand the rules so well it could not be her first time—what difference could it make to her if she belonged to one of the cavaliers, or to all? Indeed, could she possibly be anything but a woman of easy virtue? Were any of them anything else? That's what they were, without a doubt, even if all of them led another, more normal life, so to speak, besides this one of promiscuity. Perhaps everything he had just gone through had been only an outrageous joke. A joke planned, prepared and even rehearsed for such an occasion when some bold outsider should be caught intruding? And yet, as he thought of the woman who had warned him from the very beginning, who was now ready to pay for him—he remembered something in her voice, her bearing, in the royal nobility of her nude body which could not possibly have been false. Or was it possible that only his sudden appearance had caused her to change? After everything that had happened, such a supposition did not seem impossible. There was no conceit in this idea. There may be hours or nights, he thought, in which some strange, irresistible charm emanates from men who under normal circumstances have no special power over the other sex.

The carriage continued up-hill. If all were well, he should have turned into the main street long ago. What were they going to do with him? Where was the carriage taking him? Was the comedy to be continued elsewhere? And what would the continuation be? A solution of the mystery and a happy reunion at some other place. Would he be rewarded for passing the test so creditably and made a member of the secret society? Was he to have unchallenged possession of the lovely nun? The windows of the carriage were closed and Fridolin tried to look out—but they were opaque. He attempted to open them, first on one side, then on the other, but it was impossible. The glass partition between him and the coachman's box was just as thick and just as firmly closed. He knocked on the glass, he called, he shouted, but the carriage went on. He tried to open both the doors, but they wouldn't budge. His renewed calling was drowned by the rattling of the wheels and the roaring of the wind. The carriage began to jolt, going down-hill, faster and faster. Fridolin, uneasy and alarmed, was on the point of smashing one of the blind windows, when the carriage suddenly stopped. Both doors opened together, as if by some mechanism, and as though Fridolin had been ironically given the choice between one side or the other. He jumped out, the doors closed with a bang—and without the coachman paying the slightest attention to him, the carriage drove away across the open field into the darkness of the night.

The sky was overcast, clouds raced across it, and the wind whistled, Fridolin stood in the snow which shed a faint light round about. He was alone, his open fur coat over his monk's costume, the pilgrim's hat on his head; and an uncanny feeling overcame him. The main street was a slight distance away, where a row of dimly flickering street lamps indicated the direction of the city. However, he ran straight down across the sloping, snow-covered field, which shortened the way, so as to get among people as quickly as possible. His feet soaked, he came into a narrow, almost unlighted street, and at first walked along between high board fences which groaned in the wind. Turning the next corner, he reached a somewhat wider street, where scattered little houses alternated with empty building lots. Somewhere a tower clock struck three. Some one was coming towards him. The person wore a short jacket, he had his hands in his trouser pockets, his head was down between his shoulders, and his hat was pulled over his forehead. Fridolin got ready for an attack, but the tramp unexpectedly turned and ran. What does that mean? he asked himself. Then he decided that he must present a very uncanny appearance, took off the pilgrim's hat and buttoned his coat, underneath which the monk's gown was flapping around his ankles. Again he turned a corner into a suburban main street. A man in peasant's dress walked past and spoke to him, thinking him a priest. The light of a street lamp fell upon a sign on a corner house, *Lieb-*

hartstal—then he wasn't very far from the house which he had left less than an hour before. For a second he felt tempted to retrace his steps and to wait in the vicinity for further developments. But he gave up the idea when he realized that he would only expose himself to grave danger without solving the mystery. As he imagined what was probably taking place in the villa at this very moment he was filled with wrath, despair, shame and fear. This state of mind was so unbearable that it almost made him sorry the tramp had not attacked him; in fact, he almost regretted that he wasn't lying against the fence in the deserted street with a knife-gash in his side. That, at least, might have given some significance to this senseless night with its childish adventures, all of which had been so ruthlessly cut short. It seemed positively ridiculous to return home, as he now intended doing. But nothing was lost as yet. There was another day ahead, and he swore that he would not rest until he had found again the beautiful woman whose dazzling nakedness had so intoxicated him. It was only now that he thought of Albertina, but with a feeling that she, too, would first have to be won. He could not, must not, be reunited with her until he had deceived her with all the other women of the night. With the naked woman, with Pierrette, with Marianne, with Mizzi in the narrow street. And shouldn't he also try to find the insolent student who had bumped into him, so that he might challenge him to a duel with sabres or, better still, with pistols? What did some one else's life, what did his own, matter to him? Is one always to stake one's life just from a sense of duty or self-sacrifice, and never because of a whim or a passion, or simply to match oneself against Fate?

Again the thought came to him that even now the germ of a fatal disease might be in his body. Wouldn't it be silly to die just because a child with diphtheria had coughed in his face? Perhaps he was already ill. Wasn't he feverish? Perhaps at this moment he was lying at home in bed—and everything he thought he had experienced was merely delirium?

Fridolin opened his eyes as wide as possible, passed his hand over his forehead and cheeks and felt his pulse. It scarcely beat faster. Everything was all right. He was completely awake.

He continued along the street, towards the city. A few market-wagons rumbled by, and now and then he met poorly dressed people whose day was just beginning. Behind the window of a coffee-house, at a table over which a gas-flame flickered, sat a fat man with a scarf around his neck, his head on his hands, fast asleep. The houses were still enveloped in darkness, though here and there a few windows were lighted and Fridolin thought he could feel the people gradually awaking. It seemed that he could see them stretching themselves in their beds and preparing for their pitiful and strenuous day. A new day faced him, too, but for him it wasn't pitiful and dull. And with a strange, happy beating of his heart, he realized that in a few hours he would be walking around between the beds of his patients in his white hospital coat. A one-horse cab stood at the next corner, the coachman asleep on the box. Fridolin awakened him, gave his address and got in.

5

It was four o'clock in the morning when Fridolin
walked up the steps of his home. Before doing anything
else he went into his office and carefully locked the
masquerade costume in a closet. As he wished not to
wake Albertina, he took off his shoes and clothes before going into the bedroom, and very cautiously
turned on the light on the little table beside his bed.
Albertina was lying there quietly, with her arms
folded under her head. Her lips were half open, and
painful shadows surrounded them. It was a face that
Fridolin did not know. He bent down over her, and
at once her forehead became lined with furrows, as
though some one had touched it, and her features
seemed strangely distorted. Suddenly, still in her sleep,
she laughed so shrilly that he became frightened. Involuntarily he called her name. She laughed again, as
if in answer, in a strange, almost uncanny manner.
Fridolin called her in a louder voice, and she opened
her eyes, slowly and with difficulty. She stared at him,
as though she did not recognize him.

"Albertina!" he cried for the third time. As she
gained consciousness, an expression of fear, even of
terror came into her eyes. Half awake, and seemingly
in despair, she raised her arms.

"What's the matter?" asked Fridolin with bated
breath. As she still stared at him, terrified, he added, to
reassure her: "It is I, Albertina." She breathed deeply,

tried to smile, dropped her arms on the bed cover and said, in a far away voice: "Is it morning yet?"

"It will be very soon," replied Fridolin, "it's past four o'clock. I've just come home." She was silent and he continued: "The Councilor is dead. He was dying when I arrived, and naturally I couldn't—leave immediately."

She nodded, but hardly seemed to have heard or understood him. She stared into space, as though she could see through him. He felt that she must know of his recent experiences—and at the same time the idea seemed ridiculous. He bent down and touched her forehead. She shuddered slightly.

"What's the matter?" he asked again.

She shook her head slowly and he passed his hand gently over her hair. "Albertina, what's the matter?"

"I've been dreaming," she said distantly.

"What have you been dreaming?" he asked mildly.

"Oh, so much, I can't quite remember."

"Perhaps if you try?"

"It was all so confused—and I'm tired. You must be tired, too."

"Not in the least. I don't think I shall go to bed at all. You know, when I come home so late—it would really be best to sit right down to my desk—it's just in such morning hours—" He interrupted himself. "Wouldn't it be better if you told me your dream?" He smiled a little unnaturally.

She replied: "You really ought to lie down and take a little rest."

He hesitated a moment, then he did as she suggested and stretched himself beside her, though he was careful not to touch her. There shall be a sword between us, he thought, remembering a remark he had once made, half joking, on a similar occasion. They lay there silently with open eyes, and they felt both their proximity and the distance that separated them. After a while he raised his head on his arm and looked at her for a long time, as though he could see much more than just the outlines of her face.

"Your dream!" he hinted, once more. She must just have been waiting for him to speak. She held out her hand to him, he took it and, more absent-mindedly than tenderly, clasped his hand about her slender fingers, as he had often done before. She began: "Do you still remember the room in the little villa on Lake Wörther, where I lived with Mother and Father the summer we became engaged?"

He nodded.

"Well, it was there the dream began. I was entering this house, like an actress stepping onto the stage—I don't know where I came from. My parents seemed to have gone on a journey and left me alone. That surprised me, for our wedding was the next day. But my wedding-dress hadn't yet arrived. I thought I might be mistaken, and I opened the wardrobe to look. Instead of the wedding dress a great many other clothes, like fancy dress costumes, were hanging there, opera-like, gorgeous, Oriental. Which shall I wear for the wedding? I thought. Then the wardrobe was suddenly closed again, or it disappeared, I don't remember. The room was brightly lighted, but outside the window it was pitch black. . . . Suddenly you were standing out there. Galley slaves had rowed you to the house. I had just seen them disappearing in the darkness. You were dressed in marvelous gold and silver clothes, and had a dagger in a silver sheath hanging by your side. You lifted me down from the window. I, too, was gorgeously dressed, like a princess. We stood outside in the twilight, and a fine gray mist reached up to our ankles. The country-side was perfectly familiar to us: there was the lake, the mountain rose above us, and I could even see the villas which stood there like little toy houses. We were floating, no, flying, along above the mist, and I thought: so this is our honeymoon trip. Soon, however, we stopped flying and were walking along a forest path, the one leading to Elizabeth Heights. Suddenly, we came into a sort of clearing in the mountains enclosed on three sides by the forest, while a steep wall of rock towered up in the back. The sky was blue and starry, with an expanse far greater than it ever has in reality; it was the ceiling of our bridal-chamber. You took me into your arms and loved me very much."

"I hope you loved me, too," remarked Fridolin with an invisible, malicious smile.

"Even more than you did me," replied Albertina seriously, "but, how can I explain it—in spite of the intensity of our happiness our love was also sad, as if filled with some presentiment of sorrow. Suddenly, it was morning. The meadow was light and covered with flowers, the forest glistened with dew, and over the rocky wall the sun sent down quivering rays of light. It was now time to return to the world and go among people. But something terrible happened: our clothes were gone. I was seized with unheard of terror and a shame so burning that it almost consumed me. At the same time I was angry with you, as though you were to blame for the misfortune. This sensation of terror, shame and anger was much more intense than anything I had ever felt when awake. Conscious of your guilt, you rushed away naked, to go and get clothes for

us. When you had gone I was very gay. I neither felt
sorry for you, nor worried about you. Delighted to
be alone, I ran happily about in the meadow singing
a tune we had heard at some dance. My voice had a
wonderful ring and I wished that they could hear me
down in the city, which I couldn't see but which nevertheless existed. It was far below me and was surrounded by a high wall, a very fantastic city which I
can't describe. It was. not Oriental and not exactly
Old-German, and yet it seemed to be first one, and
then the other. At any rate, it was a city buried a long
time ago and forever. Suddenly I was lying in the
meadow, stretched out in the sunlight—far more beautiful than I ever was in reality, and while I lay there, a
young man wearing a light-colored fashionable suit of
clothes walked out of the woods. I now realize that he
looked like the Dane whom I mentioned yesterday. He
walked up and spoke to me courteously as he passed,
but otherwise paid no particular attention to me. He
went straight to the wall of rock and looked it over
carefully, as though considering how to master it. At
the same time I could see you hurrying from house to
house, from shop to shop in the buried city, now walking underneath arbors, then passing through a sort of
Turkish bazaar. You were buying the most beautiful
things you could find for me: clothes, linen, shoes, and
jewelry. And then you put these things into a little
hand-bag of yellow leather that held them all. You were
being followed by a crowd of people whom I could
not see, but I heard the sound of their threatening
shouts. The Dane, who had stopped before the wall of
rock a little while before, now reappeared from the
woods and apparently in the meantime he had en-
circled the whole globe. He looked different, but he

was the same, nevertheless. He stopped before the wall of rock, vanished and came out of the woods again, appearing and disappearing two, or three, or a hundred times. It was always the same man and yet always different. He spoke to me every time he passed, and finally stopped in front of me and looked at me searchingly. I laughed seductively as I have never laughed in my life, and he held out his arms to me. I wished to escape but it was useless—and he sank down beside me on the meadow."

She was silent. Fridolin's throat was parched. In the darkness of the room he could see she had concealed her face in her hands.

"A strange dream," he said, "but surely that isn't the end?" When she said "no," he asked: "Then why don't you continue?"

"It's not easy," she began again. "Such things are difficult to express in words. Well, to go on—I seemed to live through countless days and nights; there was neither time nor space. I was no longer in the clearing, enclosed by the woods and rock. I was on a flower-covered plain, that stretched into infinite distance and, finally, into the horizon in all directions. And for a long time I had not been alone with this one man on the meadow. Whether there were three, or ten, or a thousand other couples I don't know. Whether I noticed them or not, whether I was united only with that particular man or also with others, I can't say. Just as that earlier feeling of terror and shame went beyond anything I have ever felt in the waking state, so nothing in our conscious existence can be compared with the feeling of release, of freedom, of happiness, which I now experienced. Yet I didn't for one moment forget you. In fact, I saw that you had been seized—by soldiers, I think—and there were also priests among them. Somebody, a gigantic person, tied your hands, and I knew that you were to be executed. I knew it, without feeling any sympathy for you, and without shuddering. I felt it, but as though I were far removed from you. They led you into a yard, a sort of castle-yard, and you stood there, naked, with your hands tied behind your back. Just as I saw you, though I was far away, you could also see me and the man who was holding me in his arms. All the other couples, too, were visible in this infinite sea of nakedness which foamed about me, and of which my companion and I were only a wave, so to speak. Then, while you were standing in the castle-yard, a young woman, with a diadem on her head and wearing a purple cloak, appeared at a high arched window between red curtains. It was the queen of the country, and she looked down at you with a stern, questioning look. You were standing alone. All the others stood aside, pressed against the wall, and I heard them whispering and muttering in a malicious and threatening manner. Then the queen bent down over the railing. Silence reigned, and she signaled to you, commanding you to come up to her, and I knew that she had decided to pardon you. But you either didn't notice her, or else you didn't want to. Suddenly you were standing opposite her, with your hands still tied. You were wrapped in a black cloak, and you were not in a room, but in the open, somehow, floating, as it were. She held a piece of parchment in her hand, your death-sentence, which stated your crime and the reasons for your conviction. She asked you—I couldn't hear the words, but I knew it was so—whether you were willing to be her lover, for in that case the death-penalty would be remitted. You shook your head, re-

fusing. I wasn't surprised, for it seemed natural and in-
evitable that you should be faithful to me, under all
circumstances. The queen shrugged her shoulders,
waved her hand, and suddenly you were in a subter-
ranean cellar, and whips were whizzing down upon
you, although I couldn't see the people who were
swinging them. Blood flowed down you in streams. I
saw it without feeling cruel, or even surprised. The
queen now moved towards you, her loose hair flowing
about her naked body, and held out her diadem to you
with both hands. I realized that she was the girl at
the sea-shore in Denmark, the one you had once seen
nude, in the morning, on the ledge of a bathing-hut.
She didn't say a word, but she was clearly there to
learn if you would be her husband and the ruler of the
land. When you refused again, she suddenly disappeared. At the same time I saw them erecting a cross
for you—not down in the castle-yard, but on the
meadow, where I was resting with my lover among
all the other couples. I saw you walking alone through
ancient streets without a guard, but I knew that your
course was marked out for you and that it was impossible for you to turn aside. Next, you were coming
up the forest path, where I anxiously awaited you, but
I did not feel any sympathy for you, though your body
was covered with the weals which had stopped bleed-
ing. You went higher and higher, the path widened,
the forest receded on both sides, and you stood at the
edge of a meadow at an enormous incomprehensible
distance. Your eyes smiled at me as if to show that you
had fulfilled my wish and had brought me everything
I needed: clothing and shoes and jewels. But I thought
your actions senseless beyond description and I wanted
to make fun of you, to laugh in your face—because

you had refused the queen's hand out of faithfulness
to me. And because you had been tortured and now
came tottering up here to a horrible death. As I ran to
meet you, you came near moré and more quickly. We
were floating in the air, and then I lost sight of you;
and I realized we had flown past each other. I hoped
that you would, at least, hear my laughter when they
were nailing you to the cross.—And so I laughed, as
shrill and loud as I could—that was the laugh, Fridolin, that you heard—when I awoke."

Neither of them spoke or moved. Any remark at
this moment would have seemed futile. The further
her story progressed, the more ridiculous and insignificant did his own experiences become, at least up to
date. He swore to himself that he would resume and
conclude all of them. He would then faithfully report
them and so take vengeance on this woman who had
revealed herself as faithless, cruel and treacherous,
and whom he now believed he hated more than he
had ever loved her.

He realized that he was still clasping her fingers.
Ready as he was to hate her, his feeling of tenderness
for these slender, cool fingers was unchanged except
that it was more acute. Involuntarily, in fact against
his will, he gently pressed his lips on this familiar hand
before he let it go.

Albertina still kept her eyes closed and Fridolin
thought he could see a happy, innocent smile playing
about her mouth. He felt an incomprehensible desire
to bend over her and kiss her pale forehead. But he
checked himself. He realized that it was only the natural fatigue of the last few hours which disguised itself as tenderness in the familiarity of their mutual
room.

But whatever his present state of mind—whatever
decisions he might reach in the next few hours, the
urgent demand of the moment was for sleep and for-
getfulness. He had been able to sleep long and dreamlessly the night following the death of his mother, so
why not now? He stretched himself out beside his wife
who seemed already asleep. A sword between us, he
thought, we are lying here like mortal enemies. But it
was only an illusion.

6

At seven o'clock Fridolin was awakened by the maid gently knocking on the door, and he cast a quick glance at Albertina. Sometimes this knocking awakened her too. But today she was sleeping soundly; too soundly Fridolin thought. He dressed himself quickly, intending to see his little daughter before leaving. The child lay quietly in her white bed, her hands clenched into little fists, as children do in sleep, and he kissed her on her forehead. Tip-toeing to the door of the bedroom he found Albertina still sleeping soundly; then he went out. The cassock and pilgrim's hat were safely concealed in his black doctor's bag. He had drawn up a program for the day with great care, indeed, even a bit pedantically. First of all he had to see a young attorney in the neighborhood who was seriously ill. Fridolin made a careful examination and found his condition somewhat improved. He expressed his satisfaction with sincere joy and ordered an old prescription to be refilled. Then he went to the house in the basement of which Nachtigall had played the piano the night before. The place was still closed, but the girl at the counter in the café above said that Nachtigall lived in a small hotel in *Leopoldstadt*. He took a cab and arrived there a quarter of an hour later. It was a very shabby place, smelling of unaired beds, rancid lard and chicory. A tough looking concierge, with sly, inflamed eyes, wishing to keep on good terms with the police, willingly gave information. Herr Nachtigall had arrived in a cab at five o'clock in the morning, accompanied by two men who had disguised their faces, perhaps intentionally so, with scarfs which they wore wrapped about their heads and necks. While Nachtigall was in his room, the two men had paid his bill for the last four weeks. When he didn't appear after half an hour, one of them had gone up to fetch him, whereupon they all three took a cab to North Station. Nachtigall had seemed highly excited, in fact—well, why not tell the whole truth to a man who gave one so much confidence—he had tried to slip a letter to the concierge, but the two men stopped that. Any letters for Herr Nachtigall—so the men had explained—would be called for by a person properly authorized to do so. Fridolin took his leave. He was glad that he had his doctor's bag with him when he stepped out of the door, for any one seeing him would not think that he was staying at the hotel, but would take him for some official person. There was nothing to be done about Nachtigall for the time being. They had been extremely cautious, probably with good reason.

At the costume shop, Herr Gibiser himself opened the door. "I'm bringing back the costume I hired," said Fridolin, "and would like to pay my bill." The proprietor mentioned a moderate sum, took the money and made an entry in a large ledger. He looked up, evidently surprised, when Fridolin made no move to leave.

"I would also like," said Fridolin in the tone of a police magistrate, "to have a word with you about your daughter."

There was a peculiar expression about the nostrils of Herr Gibiser—it was difficult to say whether it was displeasure, scorn or annoyance.

"What did you say?" he asked in a perfectly indefinite voice.

"Yesterday you said," remarked Fridolin, one hand with outstretched fingers resting on the desk, "that your daughter was not quite normal mentally. The situation in which we discovered her actually indicates some such thing. And since I took part in it, or was at least a spectator, I would very much like to advise you to consult a doctor."

Gibiser surveyed Fridolin insolently, twirling an unnaturally long pen-holder in his hand.

"And I suppose the doctor himself would like to take charge of the treatment?"

"Please don't misunderstand me," replied Fridolin in a sharp voice.

At this moment the door which led to the inner rooms was opened, and a young man with an open top-coat over his evening clothes stepped out. Fridolin decided it could be none other than one of the vehmic judges of the night before. He undoubtedly came from Pierrette's room. He seemed taken back when he caught sight of Fridolin, but he regained his composure at once. He waved his hand to Gibiser, lighted a cigarette with a match from the desk, and left the apartment.

"Oh, that's how it is," remarked Fridolin with a contemptuous twitch of his mouth and a bitter taste on his tongue.

"What did you say?" asked Gibiser with perfect equanimity.

"So you have changed your mind about notifying the police," said Fridolin as his eyes wandered significantly from the entrance door to that of Pierrette.

"We have come to another agreement," remarked

Gibiser coldly, and got up as though this were the end of an interview. He obligingly opened the door as Fridolin turned to go and said, without changing his expression: "If the doctor should want anything again . . , it needn't necessarily be a monk's costume."

Fridolin slammed the door behind him. So that is settled, he thought, as he hurried down the stairs with a feeling of annoyance which, even to him, seemed exaggerated. The first thing he did on arriving at the Polyclinic was to telephone home to inquire whether any patients had sent for him, if there was any mail, or any other news. The maid had scarcely answered him when Albertina herself came to the phone to answer Fridolin's call. She repeated everything the maid had already told him, and then said casually that she had just got up and was going to have breakfast with the child. "Give her a kiss for me," said Fridolin, "and I hope you enjoy your breakfast."

It had been pleasant to hear her voice but he quickly hung up the receiver. Although he had really wanted to know what she planned to do during the forenoon, what business was it of his? Down in the bottom of his heart he was through with her, no matter how their surface life continued. The blonde nurse helped him to take off his coat and handed him his white linen one, smiling at him just as they all did, whether one paid attention to them or not.

A few minutes later he was in the ward. The physician in charge had suddenly sent word that he had to leave the city for a conference, and that the assistants should make the rounds without him. Fridolin felt almost happy as he walked from bed to bed, followed by the students, making examinations, writing prescriptions, and having professional conversations with the assistants and nurses. Various changes had taken place. The journeyman-locksmith, Karl Rödel, had died during the night and the autopsy was to take place at half past four in the afternoon. A bed had become vacant in the woman's ward, but was again occupied. The woman in bed seventeen had had to be transferred to the surgical division. Besides this, there was a lot of personal gossip. The appointment of a man for the ophthalmology division would be decided day after tomorrow. Hügelmann, at present professor at the University of Marburg, had the best chances, although four years ago he had been merely a second assistant to Stellwag. That's quick promotion, thought Fridolin. I'll never be considered for the headship of a department, if for no other reason than that I've never been a *Dozent*. It's too late. But why should it be? I really ought to begin again to do scientific work or take up more seriously some of the things that I have already started. My private practice would leave me ample time for it. He asked Doctor Fuchstaler if he would please take charge of the dispensary. He confessed to himself that he would rather have stayed there than drive out to *Galitzinberg*. And yet, he must. He felt obliged, not only for his own sake, to investigate this matter further, but there were all sorts of other things to be settled that day. He decided to ask Doctor Fuchstaler to take charge of the afternoon rounds, too, so as to be prepared for all emergencies. The young girl, over there, with suspected tuberculosis was smiling at him. It was the same one who had recently pressed her breasts so confidingly against his cheek when he examined her. Fridolin gave her a cold look and turned away with a frown. They are all alike, he thought bitterly, and Albertina is like the rest of them—if not the worst. I won't live with her any longer. Things can never be the same again.

On the stairs he spoke to a colleague from the surgical division. Well, how was the woman who had been transferred during the night getting along? As far as he was concerned, he didn't really think it was necessary to operate. They would, of course, tell him the result of the histological examination?

"Why certainly, doctor."

He took a cab at the corner, consulting his notebook and pretending to the cabman that he was making up his mind where to go. "To *Ottakring,*" he then said, "take the street going out to *Galitzinberg.* I'll tell you where to stop."

When he was in the cab he suddenly became terribly restless. In fact, he almost had a guilty conscience, because, during the last few hours, he had nearly forgotten the beautiful woman who had saved him. Would he now find the house? Well, that shouldn't be particularly difficult. The only question was what to do when he had found it. Notify the police? That might have disastrous consequences for the woman who had sacrificed herself for him, or had, at least, been ready to do so. Should he go to a private detective agency? He thought that would be in rather bad taste and not particularly dignified. But what else could he possibly do? He hadn't the time or the skill to make the necessary investigations. A secret club? Well, yes, it certainly was secret, though they seemed to know each other. Were they aristocrats, or perhaps even members of the court? He thought of certain archdukes who might easily be capable of such behavior. And what about the women? Probably they were recruited from brothels. Well, that was not by any means certain, but at any rate, they seemed very attractive. But how about the woman who had sacrificed herself for him? Sacrificed? Why did he try, again and again, to make himself believe that it really was a sacrifice? It had been a joke, of course; the whole thing had been a joke and he ought to be grateful to have gotten out of the scrape so easily. Well, why not? He had preserved his dignity, and the cavaliers probably realized that he was nobody's fool. And she must have realized it also. Very likely she had cared more for him than for all those archdukes or whatever they were.

He got out at the end of *Liebhartstal,* where the road led sharply up-hill, and took the precaution of sending the cab away. There were white clouds in the pale-blue sky and the sun shone with the warmth of spring. He looked back—there was nothing suspicious in sight, no cab, no pedestrian. He walked slowly up the road. His coat became heavy. He took it off and threw it over his shoulder just as he came to the spot where he thought the side-street, in which the mysterious house stood, branched off to the right. He could not go wrong. The street went down-hill but not nearly so steeply as it had seemed during the night. It was a quiet little street. There were rose-bushes carefully covered with straw in a front garden, and in the next yard stood a baby carriage. A boy in a blue jersey suit was romping about and a laughing young woman watched him from a ground-floor window. Next came an empty lot, then an uncultivated fenced-in garden, then a little villa, next a lawn, and finally—there was no doubt about it—the house he was looking for. It certainly did not seem large or magnificent. It was a one-story villa in modest Empire style and obviously renovated a comparatively short time before. The green

blinds were down and there was nothing to show that
any one lived there. Fridolin looked around. There
was no one in the street, except farther down where two
boys with books under their arms were going in the opposite direction. He stopped in front of the garden
gate. And what was he to do now? Simply walk back
again? That would be too ridiculous, he thought,
looking for the bell-button. Supposing some one answered it, what was he to say? Well, he would simply
ask if the pretty country house was to let for the summer. But the house-door had already opened and an
old servant in plain morning livery came out and
slowly walked down the narrow path to the gate. He
held a letter in his hand and silently pushed it through
the iron bars to Fridolin whose heart was beating
wildly.

"For me?" he asked, hesitantly. The servant nodded,
went back to the house, and the door closed behind
him. What does that mean? Fridolin asked himself.
Can it possibly be from her? Does she, herself, own
the house? He walked back up the street quickly and
it was only then that he noticed his name on the envelope in large, dignified letters. He opened it, un-
folded a sheet and read the following:

> *Give up your inquiries which are perfectly useless,*
> *and consider these words a second warning. We hope,*
> *for your own good, that this will be sufficient.*

This message disappointed him in every respect,
but at any rate it was different from what he had
foolishly expected. Nevertheless, the tone of it was
strangely reserved, even kindly, and it seemed to
show that the people who had sent it by no means felt
secure.

Second warning—? How was that? Oh yes, he had received the first one during the night. But why *second* warning—and not the last? Did they want to try his courage once more? Was he to pass a test? And how did they know his name? Well, that wasn't difficult. They had probably forced Nachtigall to tell. And besides—he smiled at his absent-mindedness—his monogram and his full address were sewn into the lining of his fur coat.

But, though he had made no progress, the letter on the whole reassured him, just why he couldn't say. At any rate he was convinced that the woman he was so uneasy about was still alive, and that it would be possible to find her if he went about it cautiously and cleverly.

He went home, feeling rather tired but with a strange sense of security which somehow seemed deceptive. Albertina and the child had finished their dinner, but they kept him company while he ate his meal. There she sat opposite him, the woman who had calmly allowed him to be crucified the preceding night. She was sitting there with an angelic look, like a good housewife and mother, and to his surprise he did not hate her. He enjoyed his meal, being in an excited, cheerful mood, and, as he usually did, gave a very lively account of the little professional incidents of the day. He mentioned especially the gossip about the doctors, about whom he always kept Albertina well informed. He told her that the appointment of Hügelmann was as good as settled, and then spoke of his own determination to take up scientific work again with greater energy. Albertina knew this mood. She also knew that it usually didn't last very long and betrayed her doubts by a slight smile. When Fridolin

became quite warm on the subject, she gently smoothed
his hair to calm him. He started slightly and turned to
the child, so as to remove his forehead from the em-
barrassing touch. He took the little girl on his lap and
was just beginning to dance her up and down, when
the maid announced that several patients were waiting. Fridolin rose with a sigh of relief, suggesting to
Albertina that she and the child ought to go for a
walk on such a beautiful, sunny afternoon, and went
to his consulting room.

During the next two hours he had to see six old
patients and two new ones. In every single case he had
his whole mind on the subject. He made examinations,
jotted down notes and wrote prescriptions—and he
was glad that he felt so unusually fresh and clear in
mind after spending the last two nights almost without sleep.

At the end of his consultation period, he stopped to
see his wife and little daughter once more. He noted
with satisfaction that Albertina's mother was with her,
and that the child was having a French lesson with her
governess. It was only when he reached the front steps
that he realized that all this order, this regularity, all
the security of his existence, was nothing but deception
and delusion.

Although he had excused himself from his afternoon duties at the hospital, he felt irresistibly drawn
to his ward. There were two cases there of special importance to the piece of research he was planning. He
was busy for some time making a more detailed study
of them than he had yet done, and following that he
still had to visit a patient in the heart of the city. It
was already seven o'clock in the evening when he

stood before the old house in Schreyvogel Strasse. As
he looked up at Marianne's window, her image, which
had completely faded from his mind, was revived—
more clearly than that of all the others. Well—there
was no chance of failure here. He could begin his
work of vengeance without any special exertion and
with little difficulty or danger. What might have deterred others, the betrayal of her fiancé, only made
him keener. Yes, to betray, to deceive, to lie, to play a
part, before Marianne, before Albertina, before the
good Doctor Roediger, before the whole world. To
lead a sort of double life, to be the capable, reliable
physician with a future before him, the upright husband and head of a family. And at the same time a
libertine, a seducer, a cynic who played with people,
with men and women, just as the spirit moved him—
that seemed to him, at the time, very delightful. And
the most delightful part was that at some future time,
long after Albertina fancied herself secure in the peace-
fulness of marriage and of—family life—he would
confess to her, with a superior smile, all of his sins,
in retribution for the bitter and shameful things she
had committed against him in a dream.

On the steps he met Doctor Roediger who held out
his hand cordially.

"How is Fräulein Marianne?" asked Fridolin, "is
she a little more composed?"

Doctor Roediger shrugged his shoulders, "She was
prepared for the end long enough, doctor.—Only when
they came this noon to call for the corpse—"

"So that's already been done?"

Doctor Roediger nodded. "The funeral will be at
three o'clock tomorrow afternoon."

Fridolin looked down. "I suppose—Fräulein Marianne's relatives are with her?"

"No," replied Doctor Roediger, "she is alone now. She will be pleased to see you once more, for tomorrow my mother and I are taking her to Mödling." When Fridolin raised his eyes with a politely questioning look, Doctor Roediger continued: "My parents have a little house out there. Good-bye, doctor. I still have many things to attend to. It's unbelievable how much trouble is connected with such a—case. I hope I shall still find you upstairs when I return." And as he said this he reached the street.

Fridolin hesitated a moment, then slowly went up the stairs. He rang the bell and Marianne herself opened the door. She was dressed in black and had on a jet necklace which he had never seen before. Her face became slightly flushed.

"You made me wait a long time," she said, smiling feebly.

"Forgive me, Fräulein Marianne, this was a particularly busy day for me."

They passed through the death-chamber, in which the bed was now empty, into the adjoining room where under the picture of the officer in a white uniform, he had, the day before written the death-certificate of the Councilor. A little lamp was burning on the writing desk, and it was nearly dark. Marianne offered him a seat on the black leather divan and sat down opposite him.

"I have just met Doctor Roediger. So you are going to the country tomorrow?"

Marianne seemed little surprised at the cool tone of his question and her shoulders drooped when he continued almost harshly: "I think that's very sensible."

And he explained in a matter-of-fact way what a favorable effect the good air and the new environment would have on her.

She sat motionless, and tears streamed down her cheeks. He saw them, feeling impatient rather than sympathetic. The thought that the next minute, perhaps, she might be lying at his feet, repeating her confession of the night before, filled him with fear. When she said nothing he got up suddenly. "Much as I regret it, Fräulein Marianne—" He looked at his watch.

Still crying, she raised her head and looked at Fridolin. He would gladly have said something kind to her, but found it difficult to do so.

"I suppose you will stay in the country for several days," he began rather awkwardly. "I hope you will write to me. . . . By the way, Doctor Roediger says the wedding is to be soon. Let me offer you my best wishes."

She did not move, as though she had understood neither his congratulations nor his farewell. He held out his hand but she refused it, and he repeated almost reproachfully: "Well then, I sincerely hope that you will keep me posted about your health. Good-bye, Fräulein Marianne."

She sat there as if turned to stone and he left the room, stopping for a second in the doorway, as though to give her a last opportunity to call him back. But she turned her head away, and he closed the door behind him. When he was out in the hallway he felt rather remorseful and for a moment he thought of going back, but he felt that it would have been ridiculous to do so.

But what was he to do now? Go home? Where else could he go? Anyhow, there was nothing more

he could do today. And what about tomorrow? What
could he do and how should he go about it? He felt
awkward and helpless. Everything he put his hands
to turned out a failure. Everything seemed unreal:
his home, his wife, his child, his profession, and even
he himself, mechanically walking along through the
nocturnal streets with his thoughts roaming through
space.

The clock on the Rathaus tower struck half past
seven. It didn't matter how late it was; he had more
time on his hands than he needed. There was nothing
and no one that interested him, and he pitied himself
not a little. Then the idea occurred to him—not deliberately but as a flash across his mind—to drive to
some station, take a train, no matter where, and to disappear, leaving every one behind. He could then turn
up again, somewhere abroad, and start a new life, as
a different personality. He recalled certain strange
pathological cases which he had read in books on
psychiatry, so-called double-lives. A man living in
normal circumstances suddenly disappeared, was not
heard from, returned months or years later and didn't
remember where he had been during this time. Later,
however, some one who had run across him, somewhere, in a foreign country, recognized him, but the
man himself remembered nothing. Such things certainly didn't happen very often, but just the same
they were authentic. Many others probably experienced
the same things in a lesser degree. For instance, when
one comes back out of dreams. Of course, one remem-
bers some dreams, but there must be others one completely forgets, of which nothing remains but a mysterious mood, a curious numbness. Or one doesn't

remember until very much later, and doesn't even then know whether it was real or only a dream. *Only* a dream!

While Fridolin wandered along, drifting aimlessly towards his home, he entered the neighborhood of the dark, rather questionable street, where he had accompanied the forlorn little girl to her humble room less than twenty-four hours before. Why was she "forlorn"? And why was just *this* street "questionable"? Isn't it strange how we are misled by words, how we give names to streets, events and people, and form judgments about them, just because we are too lazy to change our habits? Wasn't this young girl in reality the most charming, if not actually the purest of all those with whom he had come in contact during the past night? He felt rather touched when he thought of her, and remembering his plan of the night before, he turned into the nearest store and bought all kinds of delicacies. Walking along with his package, the consciousness of performing an act which was at least sensible, and perhaps actually laudable, made him feel glad. Nevertheless, he turned up his coat collar when he stepped into the hallway and went upstairs several steps at a time. The bell of the apartment rang with unwelcome shrillness and he felt relieved when a disreputable looking woman informed him that Fräulein Mizzi was not at home. But before the woman had an opportunity of taking charge of the package for Mizzi, another woman joined them. She was still young and not bad-looking, and had on a sort of bathrobe. "Whom are you looking for?" she said, "Fräulein Mizzi? Well, she won't be home again for some time."

The older woman made a sign to her to keep quiet,

but Fridolin, anxious to confirm what he had already half guessed asked very simply: "She's in the hospital, isn't she?"

"Well, as long as you know it anyhow. But there's nothing wrong with *me,* thank heaven," she exclaimed vivaciously and stepped quite close to Fridolin. Her lips were half open, and as she boldly drew up her voluptuous body the bath-robe parted. Fridolin declined and said: "I was passing by and I stopped to bring something for Mizzi." He suddenly felt very young, but asked in a matter-of-fact voice: "In which ward is she?"

The younger woman mentioned the name of a professor in whose clinic Fridolin had been an assistant several years before, and added good-naturedly: "Just let me have those packages, I'll take them to her tomorrow. And I promise that I won't snitch any of it. I'll give her your regards too and tell her that you're still true to her."

She stepped closer to him and laughed invitingly but when he drew back a little she gave it up at once and said, as if to console him: "The doctor said she'd be home in six or, at most, eight weeks."

When Fridolin returned to the street he felt choked with tears. He knew that this was not because he was deeply affected, but because his nerves were gradually giving way, and he intentionally struck up a quicker and more lively pace than he was in the mood for. Was this another and final sign that everything was bound to turn out a failure for him? But why should it? The fact that he had escaped such a great danger might just as well be a good sign. Was it the all-important thing to escape danger? He could expect to face many others, as he was by no means ready to give up the search for the marvelous woman of the night before.

Of course, it was too late to do anything about it now. Besides, he had to consider carefully just how to continue the search. If only there were some one he could consult in the matter! But he knew of no one to whom he was willing to confide his adventures of the preceding night. For years he had not exchanged confidences with any one except his wife, and of course, he could hardly discuss this case with her. Neither this nor any other. For, no matter how one looked at it, she had permitted him to be crucified the night before.

And he suddenly realized why he was walking, not towards his house, but, unconsciously, farther and farther in the opposite direction. He would not, and could not, face Albertina now. The most sensible thing to do was to have supper away from home, then he could go to his ward and look after his two cases. But under no circumstances would he go home—"home"? —until he could be certain of finding Albertina asleep.

He entered a café, one of the more quiet and select ones near the Rathaus. He telephoned home not to expect him for supper, and hung up the receiver quickly so that Albertina wouldn't have a chance to come to the phone.

Then he sat down by a window and drew the curtain. A man had just taken a seat in a distant corner. He wore a dark overcoat and inconspicuous clothes and Fridolin thought he had seen his face before, during the day. It might, of course, be just a fancy. He picked up an evening paper, read a few lines here and there, just as he had done the night before in a different place. Reports on political events, articles on the theatre, art and literature, accounts of accidents and disasters. In some city that he had never heard of in the

United States a theatre had burned down. Peter Ko-
rand, a chimney-sweep, had thrown himself out of a
window. Somehow, it seemed strange to Fridolin that
even chimney-sweeps occasionally commit suicide. Involuntarily he wondered whether the man had first
washed himself properly or whether he had plunged
into nothingness just as he was, black and dirty. A
woman had taken poison that morning in a fashionable hotel in the heart of the city. She was an unusually
good-looking woman and had registered there a few
days before under the name of Baroness D. At once
Fridolin felt a strange presentiment. The woman had
returned to the hotel at four o'clock in the morning,
accompanied by two men who had left her at the door.
Four o'clock! That was exactly the time that he, too,
had reached home. About noontime—the account continued—she had been found unconscious in her bed
with every indication of serious poisoning. . . . An
unusually good-looking woman. . . . Well, there were
many unusually good-looking women. . . . There was
no reason to believe that Baroness D., or rather the
woman who had registered as such, and a certain
other person, were one and the same. And yet—his
heart throbbed and his hand trembled as it held the
paper. In a fashionable hotel . . . which one—? Why
so mysterious?—so discreet? . . .

He put the paper down and at the same time the
man in the far corner raised his, a large, illustrated
journal, and held it to shield his face. Fridolin at
once picked up his paper again and decided that the
Baroness D. must certainly be the woman he had seen
the night before. In a fashionable hotel. . . . There
were not many which would be considered—by a
Baroness D. . . . Whatever happened now, this clue

had to be followed up. He called for the waiter, paid his bill and left. At the door he turned to look for the suspicious character in the corner, but strange to say, he was already gone. . . .

Serious poisoning. . . . But she was still living. . . . She was living when they found her. There was really no reason to suppose that she had not been saved. In any case, he would find her—whether she lived or not. And he would see her—dead or alive. He would see her; no one in the world could stop his seeing the woman who had died on his account; who had, in fact, died *for him*. He was the cause of her death—he alone —if it were she. Yes, it was she. Returned to the hotel at four o'clock in the morning, accompanied by two men! Very likely the same men who had taken Nachtigall to the station a few hours later. This did not seem to point to a very clear conscience.

He stood in the large Square before the Rathaus and looked around. There were only a few people in sight and the suspicious looking man from the café was not among them. But even if he were—the men had been afraid—Fridolin had the upper hand. He hurried on, took a cab when he reached the Ring, and driving first to the Hotel Bristol, asked the concierge, as though he were fully authorized to do so, whether the Baroness D. who had taken poison that morning, had stopped at this hotel. The concierge didn't seem at all surprised; perhaps he thought Fridolin was a police officer or some other official. At any rate, he replied courteously that the sad case had not occurred there, but in the Hotel Erzherzog Karl. . . .

Fridolin at once went there and found that Baroness D. had been taken to the General Hospital immediately after they found her. He also inquired how they had

discovered her attempt at suicide. Why had they disturbed at noon a lady who had not returned until four
in the morning? Well, it was quite simple; two men
(the two men again!) had asked for her at eleven
o'clock in the morning. The lady had not answered
her telephone, although they had rung several times,
and when the maid knocked on her door, there was no
answer. It was locked on the inside. Finally, they had
had to break it open, and they found the Baroness in
her bed, unconscious. They had at once called an am-
bulance and notified the police.

"And the two men?" asked Fridolin, rather sharply.
He felt like a detective.

Yes, of course the two men looked rather suspicious.
In the meantime they had completely disappeared.
Anyhow, it was unlikely that she was really the Baroness Dubieski, the name under which she had registered. This was the first time she had stopped at the
hotel. Besides, there wasn't a family by that name;
at least none belonging to the nobility.

Fridolin thanked the concierge for the information
and left quickly, for one of the hotel managers had just
come up and looked him over with unpleasant curiosity. He got back into the cab and told the cabman to
take him to the hospital. A few minutes later, in the
outside office, he learned that the alleged Baroness
Dubieski had been taken to the second clinic for internal medicine. In spite of all the efforts of the doctors, she had died at five in the afternoon—without
having regained consciousness.

Fridolin breathed a sigh of relief that sounded now
like a deep groan. The official on duty looked up,
startled, and Fridolin pulled himself together and
courteously took his leave. A minute later he stood

again out-doors. The hospital park was empty except where a nurse, in her blue and white uniform and cap, was walking along a near-by path. "She is dead," Fridolin said to himself.—"If it *is* she. And if it is not? If she still lives, how can I find her?"

Only too easily could Fridolin answer the question as to where at that moment he could find the body of the unknown woman. As she had died so recently, she was undoubtedly lying in the hospital morgue, a few hundred paces away. As a doctor, there would, of course, be no difficulty in gaining admittance there, even at such a late hour. But—what did he want there? He had never seen her face, only her body. He had only snatched a hasty glance at the former when he had been driven out. Up to this moment he hadn't thought of that fact. During the time since he had read the account in the paper he had pictured the suicide, whose face he didn't know, as having the features of Albertina. In fact, he now shuddered to realize that his wife had constantly been in his mind's eye as the woman he was seeking. He asked himself again why he really wanted to go to the morgue. He was sure that if he had met her again alive—whether days or years later, whatever the circumstances—he would un-questionably have recognized her by her gait, her bearing, and above all by her voice. But now he was to see only the body again, the dead body of a woman, and a face of which he remembered only the eyes, now lifeless. Yes—he knew those eyes, and the hair which had suddenly become untied and had enveloped her naked body as they had driven him from the room. Would that be enough to tell him if it were unmis-takably she?

With slow and hesitating steps he crossed the familiar courtyards to the Institute of Pathological Anatomy. Finding the door unlocked, it was unnecessary to ring the bell. The stone floor resounded under his footsteps as he walked through the dimly lighted hall. A familiar, and to a certain extent homelike, smell of all kinds of chemicals pervaded the place. He knocked on the door of the Histological Room where he expected to find some assistant still at work. A rather gruff voice called, "Come in." Fridolin entered the high-ceilinged room which seemed almost festively illuminated. As he half expected, Doctor Adler, an assistant in the Institute and an old fellow-student of his, was in the center of the room. He raised his eyes from the microscope and arose from his chair.

"Oh, it's you," he said to Fridolin, a little annoyed, but also surprised, "to what do I owe the honor of your visit at such an unaccustomed hour?"

"Forgive me for disturbing you," said Fridolin. "I see you are just in the midst of some work."

"Yes, I am," replied Alder in the sharp voice which he retained from his student days. He added in a lighter tone: "What else could one be doing in these sacred halls at midnight? But, of course, you're not disturbing me in the least. What can I do for you?"

When Fridolin did not answer, he continued: "That Addison case you sent down to us today is still lying over there, lovely and inviolate. Dissection tomorrow morning at eight-thirty."

With a gesture Fridolin indicated that that was not the reason of his visit. Doctor Adler went on: "Oh, then it's the pleural tumor. Well, the histological examination has unmistakably shown sarcoma. So you needn't worry about that either."

Fridolin again shook his head. "My visit has nothing to do with—official matters."

"Well, so much the better," said Alder. "I was beginning to think that your bad conscience brought you down here when all good people should be sleeping."

"It *has* something to do with a bad conscience, or at least with conscience in general," Fridolin replied.

"Oh!"

"Briefly, and to the point,"—he spoke in a dry, offhand tone—"I should like to have some information about a woman who died of morphine poisoning in the second clinic this evening. She is likely to be down here now, a certain Baroness Dubieski." He continued more hurriedly: "I have a feeling that this so called Baroness is a person I knew casually years ago, and I am interested to know if I am right—."

"Suicidium?" asked Adler.

Fridolin nodded. "Yes, suicide," he translated, as though he wished to restore the matter to a personal plane.

Adler jokingly pointed his finger at him. "Was she unhappily in love with your Excellency?"

Fridolin was a little annoyed and answered, "The suicide of the Baroness Dubieski has nothing whatever to do with me personally."

"I beg your pardon, I didn't mean to be indiscreet. We can see for ourselves at once. As far as I know, no request from the coroner has come tonight. Very likely—"

Post-mortem examination—flashed across Fridolin's mind. That might easily be the case. Who knows whether her suicide was in any sense voluntary? He thought again of the two men who had so suddenly disappeared from the hotel after learning of her attempt at suicide. The affair might still develop into a criminal case of great importance. And mightn't he —Fridolin—perhaps be summoned as a witness?—In fact, wasn't it really his duty to report to the police?

He followed Doctor Alder across the hallway to the door opposite, which was ajar. The bare high room was dimly lighted by the low, unshaded flames of a two-armed gas-fixture. Less than half of the twelve or fourteen morgue tables were occupied by corpses. A few bodies were lying there naked. Others were covered with linen sheets. Fridolin stepped up to the first table by the door and carefully drew back the covering from the head of the corpse. A glare from Doctor Adler's flashlight suddenly fell upon it and Fridolin saw the yellow face of a gray-bearded man. He immediately covered it again with the shroud. On the next table was the naked, emaciated body of a young man, and Doctor Adler called out from farther down: "Here's a woman between sixty and seventy, so I suppose she isn't the one either."

Fridolin suddenly felt irresistibly drawn to the end of the room where the sallow body of a woman faintly glowed in the darkness. The head was hanging to one side and the long dark hair almost touched the floor. He instinctively stretched out his hand to put the head in its proper position, but feeling a certain dread which, as a doctor, was otherwise unknown to him he drew back his hand. Doctor Adler came up and, pointing to the corpses behind him, remarked: "All those are out of the question, so it's probably this one?" He pointed his flashlight at the woman's head. Overcoming his dread, Fridolin raised it a little with his hands. A white face with half-closed eyelids stared at him. The lower jaw hung down limply, the narrow upper lip was drawn up, revealing the bluish gums and a number of white teeth. Fridolin could not tell whether this face had ever been beautiful, even as lately as the day before. It was a face without any expression or character. It was dead. It could just as easily have been the face of a woman of eighteen, as of thirty-eight.

"Is it she?" asked Doctor Adler.

Fridolin bent lower, as though he could, with his piercing look, wrest an answer from the rigid features. Yet at the same time he knew that if it were *her* face, and *her* eyes, the eyes that had shone at him the day before with so much passion, he would not, could not —and in reality did not, want to know. He gently laid the head back on the table. His eyes followed the moving flashlight, passing along the dead body. Was it her body?—the wonderful alluring body for which, only yesterday, he had felt such agonizing desire? Fridolin touched the forehead, the cheeks, the shoulders and arms of the dead woman, doing so as if compelled and directed by an invisible power. He twined his fingers about those of the corpse, and rigid as they were, they seemed to him to make an effort to move, to seize his hand. Indeed, he almost felt that a vague and distant look from underneath her eyelids was searching his face. He bent over her, as if magically attracted.

Suddenly he heard a voice behind him whispering: "What on earth are you doing?"

Fridolin regained his senses instantly. He freed his fingers from those of the corpse, and taking her thin wrists, placed the ice-cold arms alongside of the body very carefully, even a little scrupulously. It seemed to him that she had just at that moment died. He turned away, directed his steps to the door and across the resounding hallway back into the room which they had

left a little while before. Doctor Adler followed in
silence and locked the door behind them.

Fridolin stepped up to the wash-basin. "With your
permission," he said and carefully washed his hands
with disinfectant. Doctor Adler seemed anxious to
continue his interrupted work without further cere-
mony. He switched on his microscope lamp, turned
the micrometer screw and looked into the microscope.
When Fridolin went up to him to say good-bye he was
already completely absorbed.

"Would you like to have a look at this preparation?"
he asked.

"Why?" asked Fridolin absent-mindedly.

"Well, to quiet your conscience," replied Doctor
Adler—as if he assumed that, after all, the purpose of
Fridolin's visit had been a medical-scientific one.

"Can you make it out?" he asked, as Fridolin looked
into the microscope. "It's a fairly new staining
method."

Fridolin nodded, without raising his eyes from the
glass. "Perfectly ideal," he said, "a colorful picture,"
one might say."

And he inquired about various details of the new
technique.

Doctor Adler gave him the desired explanations.
Fridolin told him that the new method would most
probably be very useful to him in some work he was
planning for the next few months, and asked permission to come again to get more information.

"I'm always at your service," said Doctor Adler. He
accompanied Fridolin over the resounding flag-stones
to the locked outer door, and opened it with his own
key.

"You're not going yet?" asked Fridolin.

"Of course not," replied Doctor Adler. "These are the very best hours for work—from about midnight until morning. Then one is at least fairly certain not to be disturbed."

"Well"—said Fridolin, smiling slightly, as if he had a guilty conscience.

Doctor Adler placed his hand on Fridolin's arm reassuringly, and then asked, with some reserve: "Well —was it she?"

Fridolin hesitated for a moment, and then nodded, without saying a word. He was hardly aware that by this action he might be guilty of untruthfulness. It did not matter to him whether the woman—now lying in the hospital morgue—was the same one he had held naked in his arms twenty-four hours before, to the wild tunes of Nachtigall's playing. It was immaterial whether this corpse was some other unknown woman, a perfect stranger whom he had never seen before. Even if the woman he had sought, desired and perhaps loved for an hour were still alive, he knew that the body lying in the arched room—in the light of flickering gas-flames, a shadow among shadows, dark, without meaning or mystery as the shadows themselves—could only be to him the pale corpse of the preceding night, doomed to irrevocable decay.

7

FRIDOLIN hurried home through the dark and empty streets. After undressing in the consultation room, as he had done twenty-four hours before, he entered the bedroom as silently as possible.

He heard Albertina breathing quietly and regularly and saw the outlines of her head on the soft pillow. Unexpectedly, his heart was filled with a feeling of tenderness and even of security. He decided to tell her the story of the preceding night very soon—perhaps even the next day—but to tell it as though everything he had experienced had been a dream. Then, when she had fully realized the utter futility of his adventures, he would confess to her that they had been real. Real? he asked himself—and at this moment he noticed something dark quite near Albertina's face. It had definite outlines like the shadowy features of a human face, and it was lying on *his* pillow. For a moment his heart stopped beating, but an instant later he saw what it was, and stretching out his hand, picked up the mask he had worn the night before. He must have lost it in the morning when making up his bundle, and the maid or Albertina herself had found it. Undoubtedly Albertina, after making this find, suspected something—presumably, more and worse things than had actually happened. And she intimated this, by placing the mask on the pillow beside her, as though it signified *his* face, the face of her husband who had become an enigma to her. This playful, almost joking action seemed to express both a gentle warning and her readiness to forgive. Fridolin confidently hoped that, remembering her own dream, she would not be inclined to take his too seriously, no matter what might have happened. All at once, however, he reached the end of his strength. He dropped the mask, uttered a loud and painful sob—quite unexpectedly—sank down beside the bed, buried his head in the pillows, and wept.

A few minutes later he felt a soft hand caressing his hair. He looked up and from the depths of his heart he cried: "I will tell you everything."

She raised her hand, as if to stop him, but he took it and held it, and looked at her both questioningly and beseechingly. She encouraged him with a nod and he began his story.

The gray dawn was creeping in through the curtains when Fridolin finished. Albertina hadn't once interrupted him with a curious or impatient question. She probably felt that he could not, and would not, keep anything from her. She lay there quietly, with her arms folded under her head, and remained silent long after Fridolin had finished. He was lying by her side and finally bent over her, and looking into her immobile face with the large, bright eyes in which morning seemed to have dawned, he asked, in a voice of both doubt and hope: "What shall we do now, Albertina?"

She smiled, and after a minute, replied: "I think we ought to be grateful that we have come unharmed out of all our adventures, whether they were real or only a dream."

"Are you quite sure of that?" he asked.

"Just as sure as I am that the reality of one night,

let alone that of a whole lifetime, is not the whole truth."

"And no dream," he said with a slight sigh, "is entirely a dream."

She took his head and pillowed it on her breast. "Now I suppose we are awake," she said—"for a long time to come."

He was on the point of saying, "Forever," but before he could speak, she laid her finger on his lips and whispered, as if to herself: "Never inquire into the future."

So they lay silently, dozing a little, dreamlessly, close to one another—until, as on every morning at seven, there was a knock on the door; and, with the usual noises from the street, a victorious ray of light through the opening of the curtain, and the clear laughter of a child through the door, the new day began.

BEATRICE

Translated from the German of
FRAU BEATE

by

AGNES JACQUES

I

SHE thought she heard a sound in the next room. She left her half-finished letter, went softly towards the partly open door and peered into the darkened room, where her son lay fast asleep on the divan. As she stepped inside, she could see how Hugo's breast rose and fell regularly in the healthy sleep of youth. His soft, rather crumpled collar lay open at his throat; he was fully clothed, even to the heavy spiked boots which he always wore in the country. Obviously he had intended to lie down for just a short time during the heat of midday, and then to resume his studies, for his books and papers lay open around him. Now he threw his head from side to side as if trying to awaken, but he only stirred a little and slept on. The mother's eyes, by this time accustomed to the darkness, could no longer ignore the fact that the strange, painfully intent expression around the boy's lips that she had noticed again and again during the past days, did not leave him even in sleep. Beatrice sighed and shook her head. Then she went back to her room, shutting the door quietly behind her. She looked at the letter, but had no desire to go on with it. Dr. Teichmann, for whom it was intended, was certainly not the man with whom she could speak unreservedly —in fact, she already regretted the all too friendly smile with which she had bidden him farewell from the train. For just now, during these summer weeks in the country, the memory of her husband, who had

died five years before, was more than ever alive within
her, and she laid aside all thoughts of the lawyer's
wooing and the proposal of marriage—which he had
not yet made, but which was bound to come—together
with all similar thoughts concerning her own future.
She felt she could speak of her concern for Hugo least
of all with the man who would see in it not so much
a proof of confidence as a definite sign of encouragement. Therefore she destroyed the letter and went
irresolutely to the window.

The line of mountains across the lake dissolved in
tremulous rings of air. Below, in the water, sparkled
the reflection of the sun, broken into a thousand rays.
Beatrice turned away her eyes, blinded by the light,
after casting a fleeting glance over the narrow meadow
land, the dust-exhaling country road, the blinking
roofs of the villas, and the motionless field of young
corn in her garden. Her glance rested on the white
bench under her window—and she recalled the many
times when her husband had sat there dreaming over
some rôle, or dozing, especially when the air was so
redolent of summer as it was today. She remembered
how she would lean over the sill to stroke the gray-
black curly hair and run her fingers tenderly through
it, till Ferdinand, who though immediately awake,
but feigning sleep so that he might not interrupt her
caresses, would slowly turn around and look up at her
with his bright child's eyes, which could look so heroic
or heavy with death on those long ago, but never to
be forgotten magic evenings. She loved to think of those
times, though she knew she should not, certainly not
with those sighs which in spite of herself came from
her lips. For Ferdinand himself—in the days that were
past, he had made her swear to it—wanted his memory

to be celebrated only by pleasant recollections, and by an untroubled acceptance of new happiness. And Beatrice thought: "How dreadful it is to think that we could speak of such horror in such bright times, jokingly and lightly, as if it concerned only others and could never fall upon us. And then when it really comes, we do not grasp it—and yet we endure it—and time passes, and we live on, and we sleep in the same bed that we shared once with our beloved, drink out of the same glass that he touched with his lips, pick strawberries in the shade of the same pine where we picked them with one who will never pick them again —and still we never quite understand either the meaning of death or life."

She had often sat on this bench at Ferdinand's side, while the child, followed by the loving glances of his parents, had romped in the garden with ball or hoop. But as well as she knew in her mind that that Hugo who lay asleep there on the divan with the new painful expression around his mouth was the same child that played in the garden but a few years ago, in her heart she could not comprehend it any more than that Ferdinand was dead—more truly dead than Hamlet or Cyrano or King Richard in whose masks she had so often seen him die. But that she would probably never quite grasp, for between the bright full present and the dark mystery of death, there had not even elapsed weeks or days of suffering. Healthy and happy, Ferdinand had left the house one day to attend a theatrical performance, and within an hour they had brought him back from the railroad station, where the stroke had felled him.

While Beatrice clung to these memories, in her heart she felt all the time some other ghostly tormenting thing which awaited her solution. It was only after much meditation, that she knew that the last sentence in her unfinished letter, in which she had wanted to mention Hugo, would not leave her in peace, and that she must think it through to the end. It was clear to her that something either had happened or was about to happen to Hugo, something she had long awaited, but still had not considered possible. In earlier years, when he was still a child, she had dearly cherished the thought that later she would be not only mother, but friend and confidante to her boy—and till just recently, when he would come to her with his tales of school mishaps or to confess his first boyish love affairs, she dared imagine that her wish might be gratified. Had he not let her read those touching childish verses which he had written to little Elise Weber, the sister of a schoolmate of his, and which Elise herself had never seen? And even last winter, had he not told his mother that a little girl, whose name he gallantly kept secret, had kissed him on the cheek during a dance? And last spring, had he not come to her much disturbed to tell her of two boys in his class who had spent an evening at the Prater in questionable company, and who had boasted of coming home at three in the morning? And so Beatrice had dared hope that Hugo would choose her as confidante in his more serious emotional experiences, and that she would be able by encouragement and advice to keep him from the many sorrows and dangers of youth. But now she saw that these had been the dreams of an over-indulgent mother's heart, for at the first real conflict of the soul, Hugo showed himself strange and taciturn and his mother remained shy and helpless before these new events.

She shuddered, for at the first breath of wind, like

a sneering confirmation of the fear in her heart, she saw down in the valley the hated white banner fluttering from the roof of the bright villa on the lake shore. Rippling jauntily, it waved the importunate restless greeting of a depraved woman to the boy whom she wanted to ruin. In spite of herself, Beatrice raised a menacing hand, then hurried back into the room in eager haste to see her son and have it out with him at once. She listened at the connecting door for a moment, for she did not want to awaken him from his good sleep, and she thought she heard his regular boyish breathing as before. Carefully she opened the door, intending to await Hugo's awakening, and then sitting beside him on the divan, with motherly tact, to win his secret from him. But to her astonishment, she discovered that Hugo was no longer there. He had gone out without saying even adieu to his mother, as he had always done before, and without the accustomed farewell kiss—evidently he, too, feared the question which for days had been visible on her lips and which, as she knew now for the first time, she had expected to put to him at that moment. Was he already so far from her, already torn away by restless desire? That was what the first hand-clasp of that woman had made of him, when he met her recently on the wharf. That was what her look had done to him yesterday, when she smilingly greeted him from the gallery of the swimming pool, as his glowing boyish body had come swimming up out of the waves. Of course—he was more than seventeen, and she had never imagined that he would be spared for one certain girl who was destined for him from the beginning of time, and who would meet him as young and pure as he himself was. But only this had she wished for him: that his youth should not fall a victim to the lust of such a woman, who owed her half-forgotten stage reputation only to a glittering wantonness, and whose life and calling had not been changed even by her late marriage.

Beatrice sat on Hugo's divan in the half-darkened room, her eyes closed, her head in her hands, deliberating. Where might Hugo be? With the Baroness perhaps? That was unbelievable. These things could not develop so rapidly. But was there still any possibility of saving her beloved boy from this miserable affair? She was afraid not. For indeed she had forebodings: just as Hugo had the features of his father, so did his father's blood run through his veins, that dark blood of those men from a different world, a lawless world, where boys were inflamed with the dark passions of men, while their eyes even in maturity gleamed with childish dreams. Was it only the father's blood? Did hers run more coolly? Dared she say that, simply because since the death of her husband no temptation had come to her? And because she had never belonged to another, was what she had once told her husband therefore any less true: that he alone had filled her whole life for her, because when his features were veiled by night, he represented many different characters to her—because in his arms she was the beloved of King Richard and Cyrano and Hamlet and all the others whose rôles he played—the beloved of heroes and scoundrels, the blessed and the damned, the naïve and the sophisticated. In fact, in her early girlhood had she not wished to be the wife of the actor because union with him offered the only possibility for her to live the decorous life which her bourgeois upbringing had intended her for, and at the same time to lead the wild adventurous existence for which she longed in her

secret dreams? And she remembered how she had
taken Ferdinand not only against the wishes of her
parents, whose pious bourgeois minds could not quite
overcome a slight repugnance at the thought of the
actor, even after her marriage had been consummated,
but how she had won him besides from a much more
dangerous enemy. For at the time when she met Ferdinand, he was in the midst of a liaison (which was
no secret in the town) with a not very young but
wealthy widow, who had assisted him greatly in his
early days and who had often paid his debts. It was
only lack of will power that kept him bound to her. It
was then that Beatrice had made the romantic decision
to free her hero from such unworthy bondage and to
dissolve the ties of a relationship which, owing to its
unstable foundation, was bound to break sooner or
later, but which she feared might come too late for the
good of the artist and his art. It was a never-to-be-
forgotten occasion for her, and although she received a
half insulting and joking refusal which she never forgot, and though it was a whole year till Ferdinand was
really finally freed, still she could not doubt that that
conversation was the first step towards the break. In
fact her husband did the story full justice and boasted
of it proudly even to people who were not in the least
concerned.

Beatrice removed her hands from her eyes, and stood
up in sudden passion. Almost twenty years lay between
that madly bold adventure and the present—but had
she become a different creature since then? Did she not
dare to trust herself to steer the course of one who was
so dear to her, as she saw fit? Was she the woman to
stand humbly by, while her son's young life was being
besmirched and broken, instead of acting as she had

formerly acted with the other? She would go today to the Baroness, who after all was only a woman and must have somewhere, though it be in the nethermost corner of her soul, some understanding of the meaning of motherhood. And happy in her sudden decision, which came to her like a beam of light, she went to the window, opened the blinds, and full of new hope, she greeted as a good omen the charming landscape before her eyes. And she felt that she must carry out her sudden decision immediately, while her determination was fresh and strong. Without further hesitation, she went into her bedroom and rang for her maid, whom she bade be especially careful in helping her dress that day. As soon as this was done to her satisfaction, she put on her broad-brimmed panama hat with its narrow black band, over her dark-blonde, thickly waved hair, chose the freshest of three red roses from a vase on her night table, slipped it into her white leather belt, took her slender mountain cane in her hand, and left the house. She felt young, happy, and sure of the outcome of her mission.

As she stepped out of the door, she saw Herr and Frau Arbesbacher at the garden gate. He was in a waterproof shooting jacket and leather breeches; she wore a dark flowered cotton gown which, in style and cut, was too matronly for her rather careworn but still youngish face.

"Greetings, Frau Heinold," called out the architect, raising his green Tyrolean hat with its cockade of goat's hair, and holding it in his hand so that his white head remained uncovered for a moment. "We have just come to call for you." And to her inquiring look: "Have you forgotten that today is Thursday, the day of the tarock party at the Director's?"

"Yes, that is so," said Beatrice, remembering.

"We just met your son," remarked Frau Arbesbacher, and over her faded features passed a tired smile.

"He went up that way, with two thick books under
his arm," finished the architect, pointing to the path
which led over the sunny meadow, upwards toward the
wood. "An industrious boy!"

Beatrice smiled in unrestrained happiness. "Next
year he will finish the 'gymnasium,'" she said.

"How pretty Frau Heinold looks today," remarked
Frau Arbesbacher naïvely, in a voice that was almost
humble with surprise.

"Yes, how are we going to feel, Frau Beatelinde,
when we suddenly find we have a grown son who
fights duels and turns the heads of the women?"

"But did you fight duels?" interrupted his wife.

"Oh, well, I've had my little battles. Those things
come of themselves. You get into trouble either way."

They walked along the road, which with its splendid
view of the lake, led up past the town to the villa of
Herr Welponer, Bank Director.

"Well—here I seem to be going along with you, when
instead I should go down to the village first—to the
post-office—in regard to a package which was sent
from Vienna a week ago, and has not yet arrived. And
it was sent special delivery too," she added naturally,
as if she believed the story which she had so suddenly
invented, she knew not why.

"Perhaps it will come on this train— your package,"
said Frau Arbesbacher, pointing down below where
the little train came puffing pompously from behind
the cliffs, up to the station which was slightly elevated
from the meadow land. Travelers put their heads out
of the windows, and Herr Arbesbacher waved his hat.

"What are you doing?" asked his wife.

"There are surely friends of ours among them and one must be polite."

"Well, then, auf Wiedersehen," said Beatrice suddenly. "I'll come up directly, of course. Take them my greetings in the meantime."

She departed quickly and went down the road she had just ascended. She felt that the architect and his wife, who had remained standing on the road, followed her with their eyes almost to the villa which Arbesbacher had built for his friend and hunting companion, Ferdinand Heinold.

Here Beatrice took the narrow wagon road which led steeply past unassuming country houses to the town, but she had to wait before crossing the tracks, for the train was just leaving the station. Now she realized that she really had nothing to do at the post-office, but had much more important work—to speak with the Baroness. But now that she knew her son was in the woods with his books, that did not seem so pressing as it had seemed an hour earlier. She crossed the tracks to the station and found the usual excitement which follows the arrival of a train. The two busses from the Lake Hotel and the Posthof were just rumbling away with their passengers. Other arrivals, high-voiced and excited, followed by porters, and happy-go-lucky picnickers, crossed Beatrice's path. She watched in amusement a whole family, father, mother, three children, nurse, and maid, trying to get into one cab, together with trunks, satchels, bags, umbrellas, and canes, and a snapping little fox-terrier. From another cab, a young married couple—friends of the year before—waved to her with the irresistible good spirits of summer resorters. A young man in a light gray summer suit, a very new yellow leather bag in his hand, raised his straw hat to Beatrice. She did not recognize him and greeted him coolly.

"How do you do, Frau Heinold," said the stranger, shifting his bag from one hand to the other and awkwardly offering Beatrice his free right one.

"Why, Fritzl!" cried Beatrice, suddenly recognizing him.

"Certainly, Frau Heinold, it's I—Fritzl himself!"

"Do you know—I really did not know you. You've become quite a dandy."

"Well, that's not so bad, is it?" answered Fritz, changing his bag back again to the other hand. "But didn't Hugo receive my card?"

"I don't know, but he told me recently that he was expecting you."

"Naturally, it was arranged in Vienna that I should come here for a few days from Ischl. But yesterday I wrote expressly that I expected to arrive this afternoon."

"In any case, he will be very happy. Where are you staying, Herr Weber?"

"No, no, please, Frau Heinold—don't say Herr Weber."

"Well then, where—Herr—Fritz?"

"I sent my trunk on in advance to the Posthof, but as soon as I have seen to my affairs, I shall be free to make my headquarters at the Villa Beatrice."

"Villa Beatrice? There is no villa by that name here."

"But what else can it be called when a person with such a charming name lives in it?"

"It has no name—I don't like such things—No. 7 Oak Road is its name—see—there it is—up there—with the green balcony——"

Fritz Weber looked thoughtfully in the direction designated. "The view must be delightful— But I shall not stop longer now. In an hour I shall find Hugo at home I hope?"

"I believe so. Just now he is in the woods studying."

"Studying, is he? Well, we shall have to cure him of that habit as soon as possible."

"Oho!"

"You see, I want to take trips with him. Do you know that I climbed the Dachstein recently?"

"Unfortunately not, Herr Weber. It was really not in the newspapers."

"But please—not Herr Weber."

"I'm afraid it shall have to be that since I'm neither your aunt nor governess."

"An aunt like you might not be a bad thing to have."

"Dear me, what a gallant gentleman he is—and at his age too." She laughed aloud; and instead of the well-dressed young man, the boy suddenly stood before her, the child whom she had known since he was twelve; and his little blond mustache looked as if it were pasted to his lip. "Well, then, auf Wiedersehen, Fritzl," she said, holding out her hand. "This evening at supper you'll tell us about your Dachstein party, won't you?"

Fritz bowed a trifle stiffly, then kissed Beatrice's hand, which she allowed as if in submission to the quick passing of time. Then he went away with heightened self-respect, which was evident from his carriage and walk. "And he," thought Beatrice, "he is the friend of my Hugo. Of course he is a bit older—about a year

and a half or two, at least. He was always in a higher
class than Hugo at school," Beatrice remembered, "and
he had to repeat one year." In any case, she was glad
that he was there and expected to go on excursions
with Hugo—if she could only send the two boys immediately on a two weeks' walking tour! Ten hours'
walking a day, with the mountain wind blowing
through one's hair—evenings to fall exhausted on a
straw pallet, and in the morning to start again with the
sun! How excellent and wholesome that was! She was
tempted to go with them. But that would not do. The
boys would not wish to have an aunt or governess with
them. She sighed gently and passed her hand over her
forehead.

She walked down the street which ran along the
lake. The little steamboat had just left the landing and
was floating sprucely and brightly across the water
toward the place known as Grassy Meadow, where a
few quiet houses lay almost hidden under the chestnut
and fruit trees, and where it was already almost dark.
On the diving-board over the swimming pool, a lonely
figure in a white bath-robe bobbed up and down.
There were still some swimmers in the lake. "They are
enjoying themselves more than I," thought Beatrice,
looking enviously at the water from which came a cool
peace-bringing breath. But she quickly turned the
temptation from her, and in firm determination continued on her way, until she unexpectedly found herself before the villa where Baroness Fortunata was
living this summer. Through the commonplace garden
of bright mallow and gillyflowers, she could see the
veranda extending all along the front of the house and
she caught the shimmer of white dresses shining
through. Her eyes fixed straight ahead, Beatrice walked

on past the white fence. To her shame, she felt her heart beating wildly. The sound of women's voices came to her ear. Beatrice hastened her steps and suddenly found herself beyond the house. She decided to go first to the village grocery, where she usually had some purchases to make, and especially today, as she expected a guest for supper. In a few minutes she was in Anton Meissenbichler's shop, had bought cold meat, fruit, and cheese, and had given little Lisle the package and a tip with instructions to deliver it at once to Oak Road. "And now what?" she asked herself as she stood outside in the church square, facing the open cemetery gate, where the gilded crosses glimmered reddish in the afternoon sunlight. Should she let her plans fall through merely because her heart had begun to beat faster? Never should she be able to forgive such weakness. And the punishment of fate—she felt it—would be upon her. Then there was nothing left to do, but to go back—and without further delay—back to the Baroness.

In a few moments Beatrice was down at the lake shore. Now she passed by the Lake Hotel on whose high terrace guests sat drinking coffee or ices, then past two huge modern villas that she detested—and two seconds later her eyes met those of the Baroness who lay on the veranda on a chaise-longue under a white sun-shade trimmed in red. Leaning against the wall, stood another woman, like a statue, with an ivory yellow face, in a billowy white dress. Fortunata had been speaking gayly, but now she was suddenly silent, and her features hardened. But her look immediately softened again, and she broke into a smile of greeting that glowed with genuine friendliness and welcome. "You jade," thought Beatrice, a bit indignant at her own expression. And she girded herself for the struggle. Fortunata's voice rang too happy in her ears. "How do you do, Frau Heinold."

"How do you do," answered Beatrice in a voice that could scarcely be heard, and as if she cared little whether her greeting reached the veranda or not. Then she pretended to go on.

"Apparently you are out for a sun and dust bath today, Frau Heinold." Beatrice did not doubt that Fortunata had only said this in order to start a conversation with her. For the friendship between these two was so superficial, that the joking tone did not seem particularly in place. Many years ago Beatrice had met the young actress, Fortunata Schon, a colleague of Ferdinand's, at a theatre party, and in the good fellowship of that festive evening the young couple had sat at the same table with her and her lover of that time, and had had supper and drunk champagne together. Later, there had been fleeting meetings in the theatre or on the street, but these had never led to real conversation even of a moment's duration. Eight years ago, after her marriage to the Baron, Fortunata had left the stage and disappeared from Beatrice's vision until she had met her accidentally, here at the watering place a few weeks ago; and after that meeting, since she could hardly avoid it, she had exchanged a few words with her on the street, in the woods, or while bathing. But today it pleased Beatrice that the Baroness herself seemed disposed to start a conversation and so she answered as indifferently as possible:

"A sun bath?—The sun has already set, and in the evening it's not as sultry near the lake as up above in the wood."

Fortunata had stood up; she leaned her slender well-

formed little figure over the railing and answered
quickly that for her part she preferred walks in the
wood and that she found especially the one to the
Hermitage quite impressive.

"What a stupid word," thought Beatrice, and asked
politely why the Baroness had not taken a villa at the
edge of the forest since she preferred it.

The Baroness explained that she, or rather her husband, had rented the house from an advertisement,
and that besides, she was quite well satisfied in every
respect. "But why not end your walk, and drink a cup
of tea with me and my friend?" And without awaiting an answer, she went towards Beatrice, gave her a
smooth, white, somewhat restless hand, and led her
with exaggerated friendliness to the veranda, where
in the meantime, the other woman still leaned motionless against the wall in her billowy white muslin dress,
in a sort of gloomy seriousness, that struck Beatrice as
half sinister, half ridiculous. Fortunata presented her:
"Fräulein Wilhelmine Fallehn—Frau Beatrice Heinold. You must know the name, dear Willy."

"I had the greatest regard for your husband," said
Fräulein Fallehn, coolly and in a dark voice.

Fortunata offered Beatrice an upholstered wicker
chair, and apologized as she stretched herself out again
as comfortably as before. Never had she felt so tired
and languid as here, especially in the afternoons. Most
probably it was because she could not stand the experi-
ment she was making of bathing twice a day and remaining in the water an hour each time. But when
one knew so many waters as she—inland lakes, and
rivers, and seas—one must finally discover that each
water had its own definite character. So she continued,
carefully and too elegantly as it seemed to Beatrice,

while she stroked her red-dyed hair with one hand.
Her long white dress, trimmed with crocheted lace,
hung down over both sides of the low chair to the
floor. Around her bare neck she wore a modest string
of small pearls. Her pale narrow face was heavily
powdered; only the tip of her nose showed pink, and
her frankly painted lips were a dark red. Beatrice
could not help thinking of a picture in an illustrated
magazine, representing a Pierrot hanging on a lamp-
post, an impression that was strengthened by the fact
that Fortunata kept her eyes half closed while she
spoke.

Tea and pastry were served and the conversation
continued, with Wilhelmine Fallehn, who now leaned
over the railing, her cup in her hand, joining in the
talk even more informally than before. The subject
changed from summer to winter; they spoke of the
city, of the theatre, of the stupid disciples of Ferdinand Heinold, and about his unfortunate and prema-
ture death. Wilhelmine expressed in measured tones
her surprise that a woman could survive the loss of
such a husband, whereupon the Baroness, noticing
Beatrice's surprise, smoothly remarked: "You must
know, Willy, Frau Heinold has a son."

At that moment Beatrice looked at her with un-
bridled hostility in her eyes and she returned the look
with the wicked slyness of a malicious water-sprite;
in fact Beatrice imagined that Fortunata exhaled a
damp breath like that from reeds or water-lilies. At
the same time, she noticed that Fortunata's feet were
bare in their sandals and that under her white linen
dress she had nothing else on. In the meantime the
Baroness continued speaking, incessantly, in her
smooth and well-bred manner. She believed that life

was stronger than death, and that therefore it must always win out in the end. But Beatrice felt that this was a creature who had never loved a soul, man or woman.

Wilhelmine Fallehn suddenly put down her cup. "I must finish packing," she explained, said a curt farewell, and disappeared through the sun-porch.

"You see, my friend is going back to Vienna today," said Fortunata. "She is engaged—so to speak."

"Ah," said Beatrice politely.

"What would you take her for?" asked Fortunata with half-closed eyes.

"She is evidently an actress."

Fortunata shook her head. "She was in the theatre for a while. She is the daughter of a high official. Or rather—an orphan. Her father put a bullet through his head in grief over the life she was leading. That was ten years ago. Now she is twenty-seven. She can still go far— Will you have another cup of tea?"

"No thank you, Baroness." She took a deep breath. Now the moment had come. Her face suddenly became so determined that Fortunata unconsciously half sat up. And Beatrice began with decision: "It is really not an accident that I was passing by your house today. I have something to say to you, Baroness."

"Oh," said Fortunata; and a faint red showed under the powdered Pierrot face. She threw one arm over the back of the chaise-longue and twisted her restless fingers.

"Please allow me to be very brief," began Beatrice.

"Just as you wish. As brief or as lengthy as you like, dear Frau Heinold."

Beatrice was provoked at these rather condescending words and said sharply: "To put it simply and briefly, it is this: Baroness, I do not wish my son to become your lover."

She was very calm; yes, exactly so had she felt when, nineteen years before, she had taken her future husband from the elderly widow.

The Baroness returned Beatrice's look no less calmly. "Oh," she said, half to herself, "you do not wish it? What a pity— Really, to tell the truth, I had not yet thought of it myself."

"Then it will be all the easier for you to grant my wish," answered Beatrice, a bit more heatedly.

"Certainly, if it depends on me alone."

"Baroness, it depends only on you. You know that very well. My son is still only a child."

A look of pain appeared around Fortunata's painted lips. "What a terrible woman I must be," she said thoughtfully. "Shall I tell you why my friend is leaving? She had intended to spend the whole summer with me—and her fiancé was to have visited her here. And imagine—suddenly she became frightened. Afraid of me. Yes, perhaps she is right. That is how I am. I cannot answer for myself."

Beatrice sat motionless. She had not expected such frankness that was almost shamelessness. And she answered bitingly, "Then, Baroness, since you feel that way, it will mean very little to you to—"

Fortunata rested her childish glance on Beatrice. "What you are doing, Frau Heinold," she said in a quiet new-found voice, "is touching indeed. But clever, on my soul, it is not. Besides, I repeat that I had not even entertained the thought. In truth, Frau Heinold, I believe that women like you have no conception of women—of my kind. Look here—two years ago, for example, I spent three whole months in a Dutch fish-

ing village—quite alone. And I believe I was never so
happy in my whole life. And so it could have happened that this summer too— Oh, I want to think it
possible—I never have schemed—never in my life.
Even my marriage, I assure you, was a matter of pure
chance." And she looked up as if a sudden thought
had come to her. "Or perhaps you are afraid of the
Baron—are you afraid that there may be some unpleasantness for—ah—for your son on that score? As
far as that is concerned—" And she smilingly closed
her eyes.

Beatrice shook her head. "I had really not thought
of anything of the sort."

"Still, one might think of such things. There's no
telling what husbands will do. But look you, Frau
Heinold," and she opened her eyes again, "if that question has really played no part, then it is all the more
incomprehensible to me— Seriously—if I had a son
of the same age as your Hugo—"

"You know his name?" asked Beatrice severely.

Fortunata smiled. "You told it to me yourself—
recently at the pier."

"Quite right. I beg your pardon, Baroness."

"Well then, dear Frau Heinold, I wanted to say—
that if I had a son and he were to fall in love with a
woman like you, for example—I don't know—but I
think I could hardly picture a better début for a young
man."

Beatrice moved in her chair, as if to stand up.

"We are just two women between ourselves," said
Fortunata soothingly.

"You have no son, Baroness—and then—" She
stopped.

"Ah, yes, you mean that there would be another

very great difference. But that difference would make the affair—for my son—even more dangerous. For you, Frau Heinold, would probably take such an affair seriously. But I, on the contrary—I— Really, Frau Heinold, the more I think about it, the more it seems to me, it would have been wiser of you to come to me with the opposite request—if you had brought your son, so to speak, to my very arms."

"Baroness!" Beatrice was dumbfounded. She could have screamed.

Fortunata leaned back, crossed her arms under her head, and completely shut her eyes. "Such things do happen"— And she began to tell a story. "Many years ago, somewhere in the provinces, I had a friend, an actress, who was at that time about as old as I am now. She played the heroic-sentimental rôles. One day a countess came to her—the name does not concern us. You see, her son, the young count, had fallen in love with a girl of the middle classes, of good but rather poor family—civil service, or something of the sort. And the young count wanted to marry the girl at once. Besides, he was under twenty. And the countess—do you know what that clever woman did? One fine day she appeared before my friend and spoke with her, and asked her— Well, to make it short—she arranged it so that her son forgot the girl in the arms of my friend and—"

"I beg you, Baroness, to desist from such anecdotes."

"It is not an anecdote. It is a true story and a very moral one besides. A mésalliance was prevented, and an unhappy marriage, perhaps a suicide, or a double suicide."

"That may be," said Beatrice, "but all that does not concern us. In any case, I am different from the count-

ess. And for me, the thought is simply unbearable—
unbearable—"

Fortunata smiled and was silent for a while, as if
she wished to force an end to the sentence. Then she
said, "Your son is sixteen—or seventeen?"

"Seventeen," answered Beatrice and was immediately angry with herself for having given the information so meekly.

Fortunata half closed her eyes, as if she were seeing
a vision. And she said as if out of a dream, "Then you
must get used to the thought. If it is not I, it will be
another—and who can tell you"—(out of the suddenly opened eyes came a green flash)—"that it will
be a better one?"

"Will you have the kindness, Baroness," answered
Beatrice with labored superiority, "to leave that problem to me?"

Fortunata sighed softly. Suddenly she seemed tired
and said, "Well, then, why talk of it any more? I am
willing to be agreeable. Your son has nothing to fear
from me—or as we might also put it—to hope—if you
are not"—and now her eyes were large, gray, and
clear—"entirely on the wrong track, Frau Heinold.
For I—honestly, till now I had never thought that I
had made any particular impression on Hugo." She
let the name slip slowly out of her mouth. And she
looked innocently into Beatrice's face. Beatrice had
blushed darkly, and speechlessly pressed her lips together. "Then what shall I do?" asked Fortunata piti-
fully. "Go away? I could write my husband that the
air here does not agree with me. What do you think,
Frau Heinold?"

Beatrice shrugged her shoulders. "If you really are
willing, I mean if you will really have the kindness

not to concern yourself with my son, it will not be so
very hard, Baroness—your word will suffice."

"My word? Don't you think, Frau Heinold, that in
such affairs words and oaths—oh, even of women
different from myself—mean very little?"

"You do not love him at all," Beatrice suddenly
cried, losing all her self-control. "It would have been a
whim, no more. And I am his mother. Baroness, you
will not permit me to have made this step in vain."

Fortunata stood up, looked long at Beatrice, and
offered her hand. She seemed suddenly to admit de-
feat. "Your son, from this hour, does not exist for me,"
she said earnestly. "Forgive me for having caused you
to wait so long for this self-evident answer."

Beatrice took her hand and at that moment felt a
sort of sympathy, even of pity for the Baroness. She
almost felt as if she owed her an apology. But she
restrained this impulse, even avoided saying anything
that might be taken as thanks, and said instead, rather
lamely, "Then the affair is in order, Baroness." And
she stood up.

"Must you go?" asked Fortunata in her most proper
voice.

"I have detained you long enough," answered Beatrice equally politely.

Fortunata smiled and Beatrice felt rather stupid. She
allowed the Baroness to accompany her to the garden-
gate, and gave her her hand once more. "Thank you
for your visit," said Fortunata cordially and added, "If
I shall not be able to return it in the near future, I hope
you will not take it amiss."

"Oh," said Beatrice and returned again from the
street the friendly nod of the Baroness who remained
standing at the gate. Involuntarily Beatrice walked

more rapidly than usual and kept to the level road. She could turn off later to the narrow forest path that led steep and straight to the Director's villa. "How do matters really stand?" she asked herself excitedly. "Am I the victor? She gave me her word. Yes. But did she not herself say that the promises of women did not mean much? No, she will not dare. She has seen to what lengths I can go." Fortunata's words kept ringing in her ears. How queerly she spoke of that summer in Holland! As if of a peaceful respite from a wildly sweet, but very difficult time. And she imagined Fortunata in a white linen dress over her naked body, running along the seashore, as if pursued by evil spirits. Perhaps it was not always pleasant, the life that was Fortunata's lot. In a way, as was the case with women of her sort, she was probably half-insane and hardly answerable for the harm that she did. Well, she could do what she wished, only she must leave Hugo in peace. Why did it have to be just he? And Beatrice smiled as she thought that she could have offered the Baroness as compensation a handsome young man, newly arrived, named Fritz Weber, with whom she would surely be just as well satisfied. Yes, she should have made the proposal. Truly, that would have put the proper spice into the conversation. What women there were! What a life they led! So that they had to go to Dutch fishing villages from time to time to recuperate. For others all life was just such a fishing village. And Beatrice smiled, but without real joy.

She stood before the gate of Welponer's villa and entered. From the tennis court which was quite near the entrance, Beatrice could see white figures shimmering through the thin shrubbery and could hear familiar voices. As she came closer, she saw two couples standing facing each other. On one side stood the son and daughter of the house, nineteen and eighteen years of age, both resembling their father in their dark eyes and heavy brows, and betraying by features and bearing, the Italian-Jewish stock from which they came. On the other side played Dr. Bertram and his slender little sister, Leonie, the children of a well-known physician, who also had a home in the vicinity. At first Beatrice stood off a little to enjoy the strong free movement of their young bodies and the sharp flight of the balls. The fresh grace of the battle refreshed and pleased her. In a few moments the set was ended. Both couples met at the net, racquets in hand, and stood there, chatting. Their features, earlier made tense by the excitement of the game, now melted into vacuous smiles; their eyes, which before had followed the spring of the balls so keenly, now met dreamily. Beatrice realized this with strange uneasiness: it was as if the atmosphere, formerly so clean and pure, had suddenly become stormy and misty, and she could not help thinking: "How well this evening would end if suddenly, by some magic, all the inhibitions of society should be done away with, and these young people might follow without hindrance the secret, perhaps even unsuspected urge which impels them." And suddenly she realized that there was a lawless world—that she had just stepped out of just such a one, and that its breath still hung around her. It was only because of that, that she saw today what otherwise would have escaped her innocent eyes. Only because of that?— Had she not herself secretly desired these worlds? Was she not herself once the beloved of the blessed and the damned, the naïve and the sophisticated, of scoundrels and heroes?

She was seen. They waved their hands to her in greeting. She went closer to the wire netting and the others walked towards her. She heard their light chatter around her. But she felt as if both young men looked at her in a new way. Especially young Dr. Bertram had a sort of superior scorn about his mouth and looked her up and down as he had never done before, or at least in a way that she had never before noticed. And when she left them to go at last up to the house, he jokingly caught her finger through the net and kissed it long, as if he could never stop. And he laughed insolently as a dark look of displeasure appeared on her face.

Up above, on the roofed, almost too handsome balcony, Beatrice found both couples, the Welponers and the Arbesbachers, playing tarock. She would not let them be disturbed, pushed the Director back into his chair when he tried to lay aside his cards, and then sat down between him and his wife. She said she wanted to look on at their game, but she hardly did—her glance soon wandered over the stone balustrade far over the hills which the sun was gilding. Here a feeling of security and fitness came over her that she had not felt out there among the young people—a feeling that rendered her calm, but at the same time sad. The Director's wife offered her tea in her rather condescending manner to which one had to become accustomed. But Beatrice thanked her: she had just had some. Just! How many miles away lay that house with its insolently fluttering flag? How many hours, or days ago, had she left that place for this? Shadows sank upon the park, the sun suddenly disappeared behind the mountains; from the street below, invisible from here, came indefinite sounds. Beatrice suddenly felt so alone as she had only felt in twilight hours in the country immediately after Ferdinand's death and never since. Even Hugo seemed suddenly to disappear into unreality and to be unattainably far away. She wanted him urgently and hastily took her leave of the party. The Director insisted on accompanying her. He went down the broad staircase with her, then along the pond, in the center of which the fountain was now silent, then past the tennis court where the two couples, in spite of the falling evening, still played so eagerly that they did not notice them as they went by. Herr Welponer threw a troubled look towards them, which Beatrice had noticed on his face before. But she felt that today she understood him for the first time. She knew that in the midst of the strenuous powerful life of a keen financier, the Director was disturbed by the melancholy fear of advancing age. And while he walked at her side, his tall figure bent forward slightly as if only in affectation, and while he conversed lightly with her about the wonderful summer weather, and about the excursions which they really must under-take, but for which the energy always failed them, Beatrice felt that they were both being enmeshed in an invisible net. And when he kissed her hand at the gate of the park, he left a feeling of gentle sadness upon her, that accompanied her all the way home.

At the door, the maid told her that Hugo and an-other young man were in the garden, and besides, that a package had been left by the postman. Beatrice found it in her room, and smiled with pleasure. Was it not a good omen that fate had made the truth out of her un-necessary small lie? Or should it be taken as a warn-ing: this time you were lucky. The package was from Dr. Teichmann. It contained books that he had prom-

ised to send her, the memoirs and letters of great
statesmen, of people, therefore, whom the little lawyer
tremendously admired. Beatrice merely looked at a
title page, took off her hat in her bedroom, threw a
shawl around her shoulders and went into the garden.
She saw the boys below near the hedge. Without noticing her, they continued to jump high up in the air
like madmen. When Beatrice came nearer, she saw
that both had taken off their coats. Now Hugo ran
towards her and kissed her for the first time in weeks,
childishly and stormily on both cheeks. Fritz quickly
slipped his coat on, bowed, and kissed Beatrice's hand.
She smiled. It seemed to her that he wanted to wipe
away that other melancholy kiss by the touch of his
young lips.

"What are you children doing there?" asked Beatrice.

"Contest for the world's championship in high-
jumping," explained Fritz.

The high cornstalks on the other side of the hedge
moved in the evening breeze. Below lay the lake, dull
gray and misty. "You might put on your coat too,
Hugo," said Beatrice, gently pushing his damp blond
hair off his forehead. Hugo obeyed. Beatrice thought
that her boy looked rather unkempt and childish next
to his friend, but it pleased her at the moment.

"Just think, Mother," said Hugo, "Fritz wants to
take the half-past nine train back to Ischl."

"But why?"

"There are no rooms to be found, Frau Heinold.
There may be one in two or three days at the earliest."

"But you are not going away just because of that,
Herr Fritz? We have room for you."

"I have already told him, Mother, that you certainly would not object to his staying."

"Why should I? Certainly you shall spend the night here, in the guest room. What is it for, if not for just such occasions?"

"Frau Heinold, I shouldn't like to inconvenience you in any way. I know that my mother is always much upset when we have unexpected house guests in Ischl."

"Well, that is not the case here, Herr Fritz."

They finally agreed that Herr Weber's baggage should be sent for from the Posthof where it had been checked, and that he should live from that time on in the attic bedroom, in exchange for which Beatrice solemnly promised to call him plain "Fritz" without the "Herr."

Beatrice gave the necessary orders in the house, and feeling it more fitting that the young friends be left to themselves for a while, did not appear until supper was served on the sun-porch. For the first time in many days, Hugo was in the best of spirits, and Fritz, too, had given up playing the grown-up man. Two school boys sat at the table, and as usual began first to criticize all their teachers, and then to discuss the outlook for their last year in school and plans for the more distant future. Fritz Weber, who wanted to be a physician, had already visited the dissecting room one day last winter, and he implied that no one else could have had such impressive experiences as he. Hugo, for his part, had long ago decided to dedicate his life to archæology. He already had a small collection of relics—a Pompeian lamp, a piece of mosaic from the Baths of Caracalla, a pistol lock from the French invasion, and a few other things. He was planning to excavate here at the lake shore, and of course, over in Grassy Meadow where the remains of lake dwellings had been found. Fritz did not conceal his suspicions as to the authenticity of Hugo's museum pieces—above all he had always been doubtful of the pistol lock which Hugo had found in the Turkish entrenchments. Beatrice said that Fritz was too young for such scepticism, whereupon he answered that it had nothing to do with age— it was just his natural tendency. "I prefer my Hugo to this precocious cub," thought Beatrice, "but in truth, life will be much more difficult for him." She looked at him. His eyes were staring far off into the distance, whither Fritz surely could not follow him. Beatrice thought further: "Naturally he has no suspicion as to the kind of person this Fortunata really is. Who knows what he imagines about her? Perhaps to him she is a sort of fairy princess whom a cruel wizard holds in captivity. How he sits there, with his mussed blond hair and his untidy neck-tie! He still has the child's mouth—the sweet red child's mouth— It is his father's —the same mouth and eyes." And she looked out into the darkness that hung so heavy and black over the meadow that it seemed as if a deep forest stood around the windows.

"May I smoke?" asked Fritz. Beatrice nodded, whereupon Fritz took out a silver cigarette case with a golden monogram and offered it politely to his hostess. Beatrice took a cigarette and let him light it for her, and was informed that Fritz got his tobacco directly from Alexandria. Hugo smoked today too. It was, he said, the seventh cigarette of his life. Fritz had given up counting his long ago. Besides, he announced that these cigarettes were given him by his father, who, he said, had excellent business prospects for the next

year. Then he told the latest news—that his sister
was going to finish her "gymnasium" in three years,
and then would probably study medicine just as he
himself was going to do. Beatrice glanced quickly at
Hugo, who blushed slightly. Was it perhaps still the
love for little Elise that he had in his heart, and which
caused the painful look about his mouth?

"Couldn't we go for a little row?" asked Fritz. "It's
such a beautiful night, and so warm."

"Why not wait for moonlight," said Beatrice. "It's
gloomy, floating around out there on such a dark
night."

"I think so too," said Hugo. Fritz's nostrils twitched
contemptuously. But then the boys decided to celebrate
the day by having an ice on the terrace of the Lake
Hotel.

"You young scamps," said Beatrice smilingly as they
left.

Then she looked over the attic room to see that
everything was in order, and attended to all her final
housewifely duties before going to bed. She went to
her room, undressed, and lay down in bed. Soon she
heard voices outside—evidently those of the porters
who were bringing Fritz's trunk, which was now being carried up the wooden steps. Then followed a conversation between the porter and maid that lasted
longer than was absolutely necessary—and then—all
was silent. Beatrice took up one of the books of heroes
that Dr. Teichmann had sent her and began to read
the memoirs of a French general. But her mind was
not on it—she was restless and tired, and she felt as if
the very stillness around would not let her sleep. After
some time she heard the front door open, then footsteps, whispering, and laughter. The boys! They tip-

toed upstairs as quietly as possible. Then from above came sounds of movement, a clatter, a murmur—then footsteps descending the stairs. That was Hugo going down to bed. Now all was quiet in the house. Beatrice put aside her book, turned out the light, and fell asleep, calm, and almost happy.

2

THEY had finally reached their goal. As all had prophesied, the journey lasted longer than the architect had said. But he countered with: "Well, what'd I say? Three hours from Oak Road. It's not my fault if we started at nine instead of eight."

"But now it's half past one," remarked Fritz.

"Yes," said Frau Arbesbacher sadly, "that's always how he measures time."

"When there are women about," answered her husband, "you always have to add fifty per cent. It's an old, old story, especially when you go shopping with them." And he laughed dully.

Young Dr. Bertram, who since the beginning of the excursion had steadily kept near Beatrice, spread his green coat out on the grass. "Please, Frau Heinold," he said, pointing to it with a gentle smile. His words and looks had been full of meaning ever since the day two weeks ago, when he had kissed her finger through the tennis net.

"No, thanks," answered Beatrice, "I have my own, you see." And at a glance from her, Fritz flung open her Scotch plaid, which he had been carrying on his arm. But the wind was so strong up there on the mountain side, that the blanket flapped like a giant veil until Beatrice caught it at the other end, and with Fritz's help, spread it out on the ground.

"There's always a nice little breeze blowing up here," said the architect. "But what a pretty sight, eh what?" And he made a sweeping gesture over the whole landscape. They were on a broad, closely cropped meadow that sloped gently and left the view free on all sides. All of them contemplated the scene for some time in silent pleasure. The men had taken off their waterproof hats. Hugo's hair was more untidy than ever, the bristling white hair of the architect was stirred too by the wind, even Fritz's well-combed crop underwent some damage, and it was only Bertram's straight blond hair that the wind could not disturb, though it blew so steadily over the height. Arbesbacher named several of the mountain peaks across the lake together with their respective heights, and pointed out one peak which, he said, had never been reached from the north. Dr. Bertram said this was a mistake, for he himself had climbed it last year.

"Then you were the first," said the architect.

"That's possible," answered Bertram, nonchalantly, and called attention immediately to another mountain that looked much less formidable, but that he had never dared climb. He knew just how much he dared attempt. Above all, he was not foolhardy, and had no especial fondness for death. He pronounced the word "death" very lightly, in the voice of the expert who disdains to speak seriously of his specialty before the layman.

Beatrice had stretched out on the plaid and looked up at the dull, blue sky over which thin white summer clouds were passing. She knew that Dr. Bertram was speaking only to her—that he was placing at her disposal all his most interesting qualities—pride and knowledge, contempt of death, and love of life—to choose from as she would. But it had not the slightest effect on her.

The youngest members of the party—Fritz and Hugo
—had brought the lunch in their packs. Leonie helped
them unpack and then buttered the bread in her graceful motherly way, not forgetting to take off her tan
gloves and slip them into her brown leather belt. The
architect uncorked the bottles, Dr. Bertram poured
the wine and offered the full glasses to the ladies, looking past Beatrice with deliberate indifference, towards
the mountain tops across the lake. They all found it
delightful to be partaking of bread and butter sand-
wiches and tangy Terlan wine up there, with the
mountain wind blowing around them. To finish off
the lunch, there was a large cake that Frau Director
Welponer had sent to Beatrice that morning, together
with an apology for herself and her family, because
they were unable to join them, although they should
have enjoyed it so much. Their refusal was not unexpected. To pry the Welponer family loose from
their garden was no easy task, as Leonie said. The
architect took the liberty of reminding the honorable
ones present that they too could not boast much of
their enterprise. How had they been spending these
beautiful summer days?—"lackadaisied," as he put it,
around on the forest paths, or bathed in the lake, or
played tennis and tarock—but how many plans and
preparations had been necessary before they finally
decided to undertake even this little excursion—which,
all told, was but a short walk?

Beatrice thought to herself that she had only been
here once before—with Ferdinand—ten years ago—
the same summer, therefore, when they had moved
into their new home. But it was hard to realize that
it was the same meadow where she was today—in her
memory it had been so different—so much broader

and lighter. A soft melancholy crept into her heart.
How alone she was amongst all these people! What
did the happy chatter all around mean to her? There
they all sat on the meadow, letting their glasses clink!
Fritz touched his glass to Beatrice's; but after she had
long emptied hers, he still stood motionlessly holding
his in his hand and staring at her. "What a look,"
thought Beatrice. "Even more enraptured and thirsty
than those that he has been directing towards me for
the past few days—or do I just imagine it, because I
have drunk three glasses of wine in such quick succession?" She stretched out again on her plaid beside
Frau Arbesbacher, who had fallen fast asleep, and
looked blinkingly into the air, where she saw a tiny
smoke cloud rising gracefully—probably from Bertram's cigarette, though she could not see him. But
she felt his glance running along the whole length of
her body to the nape of her neck, until she almost
thought she felt his touch, but realized that it was only
the long grass that was tickling her.

The voice of the architect came to her as if from a
great distance, as he told the boys of the time when the
little train did not yet come to the village below. And
although hardly fifteen years had gone by, he tried
to spread an atmosphere of gray antiquity over that
period. Among other stories, he told one of a drunken
coachman who had once driven him right into the
lake and whom he had thrashed almost to death for
it. Then Fritz related the following heroic anecdote in
his best manner: once in the Wiener Wald, he had
made a very timid boy take to his heels by merely putting his hand into his pocket as if he had a revolver
there. For it was a question, as he enlighteningly ex-

plained, not of the revolver, but of presence of mind.
"It's a pity," said the architect, "that one does not always have a six-barreled, loaded presence of mind
about one." The boys laughed. How well Beatrice
knew that laugh, that double laugh, that she could
now enjoy so often at home during meal times and in
her garden; and how happy she was that the boys got
along so well together! Recently they had gone away
together for two days, fully equipped, on an excursion
to Gosauseen, as a preparation for the September tour
that they were planning. Besides, they had been better
friends in Vienna than Beatrice had known. She had
learned from others something that Hugo had stub-
bornly kept silent—that some evenings, after an hour
in the gymnasium, both would go to a coffee house on
the other side of the village to play billiards. But in any
case, she was deeply grateful to Fritz for coming to
them at that time. Hugo's mood had become again as
fresh and untroubled as ever, the painful look had left
his face, and surely he did not think of the terrible
woman with the Pierrot face and the red-dyed hair.
And Beatrice could not deny that she had comported
herself blamelessly. Just a few days ago she had by
chance been standing near her on the gallery of the
bath house, just when Hugo and Fritz had come rac-
ing in as usual from the open lake. They reached the
slippery steps simultaneously and supporting themselves with one arm, they had splashed each other's
faces, dived and appeared again far out in the open
lake. Fortunata, in her white bathrobe, had looked on
carelessly with an absent smile, as at the play of children, and then had looked again out over the lake
with lost sad eyes, so that Beatrice in mild discontent,

and with an almost guilty feeling, recalled the talk in
the white-flagged villa, that was ever becoming dim-
mer and less important to her, and that the Baroness
herself seemed to have long forgiven and forgotten.
One evening Beatrice had seen the Baron seated on a
bench in the wood. He evidently had come for a short
visit. He had light blond hair, a beardless, wrinkled,
and yet young looking face with steel-gray eyes, wore a
light blue flannel suit, smoked a short pipe, and had
beside him on the bench, a sailor's cap. He looked to
Beatrice like a captain who had come from a distant
land, and who must immediately go back to sea. Fortunata sat beside him, small and well-bred, her nose
pinkish as usual, with tired arms, like a doll that the
distant captain could take out or put back into its case
according to his pleasure.

All of this went through Beatrice's mind as she lay
on the meadow while the wind blew and grass-blades
tickled her neck. Around her now everything was
silent; all of them seemed to be asleep; only at a short
distance away somebody was whistling. Unconsciously
Beatrice looked with blinking eyes for the small smoke
cloud, and immediately saw it rising thin and silver-
gray into the air. Beatrice raised her head slightly—
she saw Dr. Bertram leaning his head on both arms,
his eyes fastened on the low cut neck of her dress.
He was speaking and it was quite possible that he had
been speaking for a long time, in fact that his speech
had awakened her out of her half-sleep. Now he asked
her whether she would be interested in a mountain
climbing party, in a real climb, or whether she were
afraid of dizziness—it didn't have to be a peak, it could
be a plateau as well; only he wanted to go higher than
the others, so much higher, that they could not follow.

To look with her from a high peak into the valley—
that would be divine. When he got no answer, he
said: "Well, Frau Beatrice?"

"I'm asleep," answered Beatrice.

"Then allow me to be your dream," he began and
continued—he could picture no more beautiful death
than to jump into the deep—one's whole life would
rush by in such frightful clearness, and it would naturally be more pleasant in proportion as to how one
lived, and if one had not the slightest fear, only a
never before experienced thrill, and a sort—yes, a sort
of metaphysical curiosity. And he buried his burned
out cigarette stub in the ground with quick fingers.
Besides, he continued, he was not particularly interested in such an end. On the contrary, even if he were
obliged to see so much misery and horror in his work,
for that reason, he treasured everything light and pure
in life all the more. Wouldn't Frau Beatrice like to
see the hospital garden? There was a very curious
and charming atmosphere about it, especially on
autumn evenings. You see, he was now living in the
hospital. And if Beatrice would like to take tea with
him at the same time—

"You're quite mad," said Beatrice, sitting up and
looking with clear eyes into the blue-gold atmosphere
which the dull mountain-peaks seemed to absorb.
Drunk with the sun, a little weak, she stood up, shook
out her dress, and noticed, how, quite against her
will, she looked wearily down at Dr. Bertram. She
quickly looked away toward Leonie, who stood quite
alone at some distance from them, like a picture, a
fluttering veil thrown about her head. The architect
sat with crossed legs on the grass, playing cards with
the boys.

"I say, Frau Beatrice, soon you won't have to give Hugo any more pocket money," he called out, "he can support himself comfortably out of today's winnings in tarock."

"Then it would be wise for us to start homeward before you are completely ruined." Fritz looked at Beatrice with glowing cheeks. She smiled at him. Bertram stood up, looked at the sky, and then down over her bit by bit. "What is the matter with you all?" she thought. "And what is the matter with me?" For suddenly she noticed that she allowed the lines of her body to play as alluringly as possible. Seeking assistance, she turned her look towards her son, who was playing out his last card, his childish face aglow, his clothes unspeakably untidy. He won the game and proudly collected one crown and twenty heller from the architect. They got ready for the descent, all except Frau Arbesbacher who was still asleep. "Let her lie," joked the architect. But at that moment, she stirred, rubbed her eyes, and was ready for the homeward journey long before the others.

For a while the path led sharply downhill, then it ran almost level through young forests; at the next bend, they could see the lake which disappeared at once. Beatrice, who at first had joined Hugo and Fritz and had run ahead with them, soon remained behind; Leonie came up to her and spoke of a sailing regatta that was to take place soon. Beatrice still remembered clearly the race seven years ago in which Ferdinand had won second prize in his boat, "The Roxana." Where was she now? After so many triumphs she led a lonely inglorious life down there in the boat-house. The architect took advantage of this opportunity to say that this year boating was as much neglected as

all other sports. Leonie expressed the opinion that
there was some enervating influence coming from the
Welponer house, whose effect no one could escape.
The architect, too, believed that the Welponers were in
no way suited to agreeable society, and his wife said
it was due most of all to Frau Welponer's arrogance
and because she had not the slightest need for amusement. They suddenly were silent, as they saw the Director sitting on a worm-eaten, broken down bench at
the turn in the road. He stood up; and his monocle on
its narrow silk ribbon hung down over his white
piqué vest. He said that he had taken the liberty of
coming to meet them and invite them in the name
of his wife to partake of a small "Jause," which was
awaiting the tired wanderers on the shady veranda.
At the same time, he looked wearily at them all, and
Beatrice noted that when he looked at Bertram, his
face darkened; and she suddenly knew that the Director was envious of the young man. But she was immediately ashamed of such a foolish assumption. She
lived on in the present, quietly and unquestioningly,
in undisturbed faithfulness to him alone whose voice
even now rang clearer in her memory than all the
voices of the living, and whose eyes still shone brighter
than all those living ones.

The Director remained behind with Beatrice. First
he talked of various unimportant events of the day,
of some friends who had recently arrived, of the death
of the miller, aged ninety-five, about the ugly house
that a Salzburg architect was building in Grassy Meadow, and then, as if by accident, reminded her of the
time when neither his house, nor the Heinold house
had yet been built, and when both families had lived
all summer in the Lake Hotel. He recalled several trips

they had taken together on the then little known roads, and one sailing party in "The Roxana," which ended in a terrible storm; spoke of the housewarming party at the Heinold house when Ferdinand had made two of his fellow actors dead drunk, and finally, of Ferdinand's last rôle in a modern, rather tragic play, in which he had so perfectly played the part of a youth of twenty. What an inimitable artist he had been! And what an excellent man! A man of eternal youth, one might say. A wonderful contrast to that class of people in whose numbers he must unfortunately include himself, of people who were not made to bring either themselves or others happiness. And as Beatrice looked at him questioningly, he said: "I, dear Frau Beatrice. I was born old, so to speak. Do you know what that means? I shall try to explain. You see, we who were born old—during our lives we let one mask after another fall from us, until, at the age of eighty or thereabouts, sometimes sooner, we show our real faces to the world. The others, the youthful ones—and such a one was Ferdinand" (quite contrary to his habit he called him by his Christian name) "they always remain young, remain children, and therefore are obliged to put on one mask after another if they do not wish to astonish other people too much. Perhaps these masks come of themselves over their faces, and they do not know that they wear them, and only have a strange dark feeling that something does not fit in their lives—because they always feel young. Such a man was Ferdinand."

Beatrice listened to the Director in surprise and with rising defiance. She could not help feeling that he had conjured up Ferdinand's shadow intentionally, as if he had been assigned to guard her honor, to warn her of some near danger, and to protect her. Really, he might have spared himself the trouble. What gave him the right, what grounds had he for appointing himself the representative and guardian of Ferdinand's memory? What was there in her actions that aroused such insulting suspicions in his mind? If she could play and laugh today and wear bright colors again, could any unprejudiced onlooker interpret it as anything but the necessity of living on in conformity with the others? But the thought that she might ever be really happy again, or might belong again to any man, filled her with disgust and horror; and that horror, as she learned in many sleepless nights, became only deeper, when some inexplicable flashes of longing rushed through her blood and passed by unfulfilled. And again she glanced quickly at the Director, who now walked silently beside her. But she was terrified to discover the smile on her lips, that in spite· of herself, came from the depths of her soul, and that unerringly, almost shamelessly, said more plainly than words: "I know that you desire me, and I am glad." She saw his eyes suddenly flare up into a burning question, which he immediately controlled and quieted. And he addressed an indifferent polite word to Frau Arbesbacher, who was just a few steps ahead of them, for the small party, now that they were nearing their goal, had all come together again. Suddenly young Dr. Bertram was at Beatrice's side and by his bearing, look, and speech, implied that the relations between him and Beatrice had become more closely bound on this picnic, and that she must admit the fact that she was beginning to yield to his graces. But she remained cool and distant and grew more distant at each step. And when they reached the gate of Welponer's Villa, she

announced, to the surprise of everyone, including herself, that she was tired and would prefer to go home.
They tried to dissuade her. But since the Director
himself expressed only mild disappointment, they did
not insist. She was undecided as to whether she would
return for supper, which they had agreed to take together at the Lake Hotel, but had no objections to
Hugo's joining them in any case. "I'll take good care,"
said the architect, "that he does not drink himself
silly." Beatrice took her leave. A feeling of great relief came over her as she took the road homewards and
she was happy in the prospect of the few undisturbed
hours that were to be hers.   ·

At home she found a letter from Dr. Teichmann,
and was mildly surprised, not so much that he again
gave a sign of life, as that she had almost forgotten
his existence in the excitement of the past days. It
was only after she had removed the dust of the day's
journey and was sitting before her toilet table in a comfortable house gown, that she opened the letter about
whose contents she was not in the least bit curious.
The letter opened, as usual, with reports on business
matters, for Dr. Teichmann believed it his duty to
serve Beatrice first of all as her solicitor, and he informed her with misplaced humor of the success of a
little venture of hers in which he was able to gain
quite a sum of money for her. Finally, he told her,
in an elaborately casual tone, that his vacation journey
that year would take him past Oak Road, and that he
dared hope—as he wrote—that through the bushes he
might catch sight of a gay garment, or that a friendly
eye might smile at him and might invite him to linger,
even though it be for just a moment's chat. He did
not forget to send regards to the Arbesbachers and

the "noble Lord and Lady of the castle, together with their worthy offspring," as he expressed it, and the other friends, whose acquaintance he had made last year when he spent three days at the Lake Hotel. Beatrice found it strange that last year seemed so far away and like a different period of her life, although it had been hardly any different from this summer. Even the flirtations on the part of the Director and young Dr. Bertram had not been wanting. It was only that she herself had gone on unperturbed amongst all their looks and words; yes, that she had hardly noticed them, and was only now conscious of them in reminiscence. This might be due to the fact that she had very little to do with all these summer acquaintances in the city. Since the death of her husband, after she had broken connections with the circle of artists and theatrical people, she had led a retiring and monotonous life. Only her mother, who lived in a suburb in an old mansion near the factory that her father had once managed, and a few distant relatives, found their way to her quiet home which had become quite bourgeois and commonplace again. And when Dr. Teichmann would appear for tea and a little chat, it meant a diversion to her that gave her real pleasure, she realized now with surprise.

Thoughtfully shaking her head, she laid the letter down and looked into the garden over which the early August twilight was spreading. The comfortable feeling of solitude had gradually left her and she wondered whether it would not be wiser to go back to the Welponer's, or later to go to the Lake Hotel. But then she restrained the impulse, a little ashamed that she should have succumbed so completely to the allurement of society and that the pensive magic of such soli-

tary summer evenings that formerly had so charmed
her, should have disappeared forever. She threw a thin
shawl over her shoulders and went into the garden.
Here the melancholy she had been seeking came over
her, and she knew in the depths of her soul that she
could never walk up and down these paths that she
had so often walked with Ferdinand, on the arm of
another man. At this moment, one thing above all was
clear to her: if Ferdinand in those distant days had
made her swear not to cast aside any opportunity for
happiness, certainly he had not pictured a marriage
with such a man as Dr. Teichmann; any passionate,
though perhaps merely passing adventure would be
much more likely to win his approval in his celes-
tial realm. And with horror she realized that a picture
had sprung up in her mind: she saw herself upon the
meadow in the twilight in the arms of Dr. Bertram.
But she merely saw the picture, no wish accompanied
it; cool and distant, it hung in the air like a vision
and disappeared.

She stood at the lower end of the garden, leaned
her arms on the fence, and looked downwards to
the lights of the town blinking below. The voices of
an evening boating party, singing out on the lake,
came to her with startling clearness through the quiet
air. The clock in the church tower struck nine. Beatrice
sighed softly, then turned around and slowly went
back across the lawn to the house. On the veranda,
she found the table set with the usual three places. She
let the maid bring her her supper and ate it without
any particular relish, feeling a useless, aimless sadness. While eating, she picked up a book—it was the
memoirs of a French general, which interested her
today even less than usual. The clock struck half past

nine, and loneliness depressing her more every moment, she decided to leave the house after all, and to
find the party at the Lake Hotel. She stood up, put
her long silk coat over her house gown, and started
out. As she went past the Baroness' house at the lake,
she noticed that it was completely dark; and she remembered that she had not seen Fortunata for several days. Had she gone away with the distant Captain? But as Beatrice looked back again, she thought
she saw a light behind one of the closed blinds. Why
did it trouble her? She didn't care any more.

On the high terrace of the Lake Hotel, whose electric arc lights were already out, she found her party,
seated around a table, in the faint light of two wall
brackets. Conscious suddenly of the too serious expression on her face, she forced an empty smile to her
lips. She was greeted warmly, shook hands with all of
them in a row, the Director, the architect, their wives,
and young Fritz Weber. There was no one else present. "Where is Hugo?" she asked, somewhat per-
turbed.

"He left this very moment," answered the architect.
"Queer that you didn't meet him."

Unconsciously Beatrice glanced at Fritz, who with
an embarrassed, stupid, childish smile, twirled his
beer glass and averted his eyes with obvious intent.
Then she sat down between him and Frau Welponer, and in order to overcome the menacing
thoughts that were arising in her, she began to talk
with exaggerated cheerfulness. She was very sorry
that Frau Welponer had not been with them on the
charming picnic; she asked about the brother and
sister, Bertram and Leonie; and finally related that
at supper she had read some French memoirs and

letters of great men. She found no pleasure in novels and such things any more. It seemed that the others agreed with her. "Love stories are only for young folks," said the architect— "I mean for children, for in a way, we are all still young folks." Fritz too said that he preferred scientific works, or especially books on travel. While he spoke, he moved quite close to Beatrice, and pressed his knee against hers as if by accident; his napkin fell down, he bent down to pick it up, and tremblingly stroked her ankle. Was the boy mad? And he continued speaking, excitedly, with glowing eyes: as soon as he was a doctor, he would join some large expedition, perhaps to Tibet or darkest Africa. The others smiled indulgently at his words; only the Director—Beatrice noted it well—looked at him with sullen envy. As the party arose to go home, Fritz said that he would first take a solitary walk on the lake shore. "Alone?" asked the architect, "that isn't so easy to believe." But Fritz answered that walking alone on summer evenings was one of his particular passions; just recently he had come home about one in the morning, and in fact with Hugo, who at times accompanied him on these nightly jaunts. And as he saw the restless, questioning glance that Beatrice turned to him, he added: "It is quite possible that I shall meet Hugo somewhere down at the lake tonight, if he hasn't gone rowing as he sometimes does."

"This is interesting news," said Beatrice, shaking her head doubtfully.

"Yes, these summer evenings," sighed the architect.

"What have you to say about it?" asked his wife enigmatically.

Frau Welponer, who had gone down the steps of

the terrace ahead of the others, remained standing for a moment and looked at the heavens, as if seeking something. Then she let her head sink again in a strange hopeless way. The Director was silent. But in his silence, burned hatred of summer nights, youth, and happiness.

They had hardly reached the lake shore, when Fritz slipped away, as if in fun, and disappeared into the dark. The two couples accompanied Beatrice home. Slowly and with difficulty, they climbed the steep road up the hill. "Why did Fritz run away so suddenly?" Beatrice wondered. "Will he find Hugo at the shore? Did he ever go rowing with him in the evening? Is there a compact between them? Does Fritz know where Hugo is at this moment? Does he know?" And she had to pause a moment, for it seemed to her that her heart had suddenly stopped beating. "As if I did not know where Hugo is! As if I had not known it for days!" . . .

"'Twould be mighty nice if they'd build a railway up this hill," said the architect. He had taken his wife's arm, which, as far as Beatrice could remember, he had never done before. The Director and his wife walked together, in step, both bent and silent. As Beatrice stood before her door, she suddenly knew why Fritz had stolen away down there. He had wanted to avoid going alone into the house with her at night, in the presence of all the others. And she was grateful for the wise gallantry of the young man.

The Director kissed Beatrice's hand. "Whatever may happen to you," trembled in his silence, "I shall understand, and you will have a friend in me."

"Let me alone," answered Beatrice as silently as he. The two couples parted. The Director and his wife

disappeared with strange suddenness into the darkness, where wood, mountains, and heaven all ran together. The Arbesbachers took the road towards the
other side, where the path was more open, and over
which the soft, blue starry night spread on high.

When the door had closed behind her, Beatrice
thought: "Shall I look in Hugo's room? What for?
I know that he is not at home. I know that he is there
where the light shone from behind closed blinds." And
she remembered that just now, on her return walk,
she had again passed the house, and that it had seemed
a house in the dark to her, like the others. But she did
not doubt any more that at this hour her son was in
the villa that she had passed thoughtlessly, and yet
full of foreboding. And she knew too that she was
to blame—yes she alone—for she had let it happen.
With that one visit to Fortunata, she had imagined
that she had fulfilled all her motherly duties; after
that she had let it go on as it would—out of laziness,
out of weariness, out of cowardice—she had seen nothing, known nothing, thought nothing. Hugo was at
Fortunata's at this moment, and not for the first time.
A picture came to her, that made her shudder and she
hid her face in her hands as if to banish it in that way.
Slowly she opened the door to her bedroom. A sadness came over her, a feeling that she had taken leave
of something that would never return. The time was
past when Hugo was a child, her child. Now he was
a young man, one who lived his own life, of which he
could no longer tell his mother. Never more would
she stroke his cheeks and hair—never more could she
kiss his sweet child's mouth as before. Now for the
first time, since she had lost him, she was alone.

She sat on her bed and slowly began to undress.

How long would he stay away? Probably the whole
night. And in the gray of early morning, very quietly,
in order not to awaken his mother, he would slip
through the hall into his room. How often had it happened already? How many nights had he been with
her? Many? No, not many. For a few days he had
been on a walking tour through the country. Yes, if
he had spoken the truth! But he had not been telling
the truth lately. Not for a long time. In the winter he
played billiards in a coffee house in the suburbs, and
where else he might have been, who knew? And suddenly a thought made the blood run faster through
her veins: Was he perhaps even then Fortunata's
lover: On the day when she had paid her ridiculous
visit to the villa down near the lake? And had the
Baroness played a shabby trick on her, and then, heart
to heart with Hugo, had she scoffed and laughed at
her? Yes—even that was possible. For what did she
know today of her boy who had grown to manhood in
the arms of a wanton? Nothing—nothing.

She leaned on the sill of her open window, and
looked into the garden and far away to the dark mountain peaks on the other side of the lake. Sharply outlined, towered the one that Dr. Bertram had never
dared attempt to climb. How did it happen that he
was not there at the hotel? If he had guessed that she
might return, he would surely have been there. Was
it not strange that they should still desire her, who
was the mother of a boy who already spent his nights
with a mistress? Why strange? She was as young,
perhaps younger than, Fortunata. And all at once, she
felt the outlines of her body under her light garment,
with agonizing distinctness, and even a sort of painful pleasure. A noise outside on the path made her

jump. She knew it was Fritz coming home. Where
could he have been all this time? Did he too perhaps
have his little adventure here in the country? She
smiled wearily. No, surely not he. For he was a little
in love with her. And really—no wonder. She was
just at the age that would appeal to so green a youth.
Evidently he had wanted to cool his longing out in
the night air; and she was a little sorry for him because just tonight the heavens hung so heavy and
misty over the lake. And suddenly she remembered
such a sultry summer night a long time ago, when her
husband had forced her against her will to go with
him from the soft privacy of their chamber into the
garden, and there, in the dark black shadows of the
trees, to exchange wild and tender caresses. Then she
thought of the cool morning when a thousand birds
had awakened her to a sweet heavy sadness, and she
trembled. Where was all that now? Did it not seem
that the garden into which she was looking had preserved the memory of that night better than she herself, and that it might be able in some wonderful way
to betray her to those who understood the language
of the dumb? And she felt as if night in person stood
out in the garden, ghostly and mysterious—yes, as if
each house, each garden, had its own night, that was
quite different from, deeper and more trustworthy
than, that meaningless blue darkness that spread above
the sleeping world, unattainably far away. And that
night that belonged to her, stood full of secrets and
dreams before her window, and stared into her face
with blind eyes. She unconsciously put out her hands
as if to ward off the vision; then she returned to her
room, went slowly to her mirror, and with a tired
droop of the shoulders, began to take down her hair.

It must be past midnight. She was very tired, and at the same time far too wide awake. Of what use were all her meditations, all her memories, all her dreams? Of what use were all her fears and hopes? Hopes? Where was there any hope for her? She went again to the window and carefully pulled the blinds. "Even from here, it shines out into the night, into my night," she thought. She locked the door leading to the hall; then according to her old careful habit, she opened the door into her little parlor for a last look. She drew back, frightened. In the semi-darkness, she saw the figure of a man, standing upright in the middle of the room. "Who is there?" she asked. The figure moved. She recognized Fritz. "What are you doing here?" she asked.

He rushed to her and snatched both of her hands. Beatrice pulled them away. "You are not in your right mind," she said.

"Pardon me, dear Frau Heinold," he whispered, "but I—I don't know what to do any more."

"That is very simple," answered Beatrice. "Go to bed." He shook his head. "Go, go," she said, and turned back to her room, and was about to lock the door behind her. Then she felt his arms thrust gently but awkwardly around her neck. She shrank away, but turned around involuntarily and put out her arm, as if to push Fritz back. He took her hand and put it to his lips. "But Fritz," she said, more mildly than had been her intention.

"I shall go quite mad," he whispered.

She smiled. "I believe you are already mad."

"I should have waited here all night," he whispered again. "I had not dreamt that you would open this door. I just wanted to be here near you."

"Now go to your room at once. Do you hear me? Or you will make me really angry." He had taken both her hands.

"I beg you, Frau Heinold."

"Don't be ridiculous, Fritz! That's enough. Let go my hands. That's right. And now, go."

He had let her hands drop; and then she felt the warmth of his lips on her cheek. "I'm going mad. I've been in this room before."

"What?"

"Yes, I spent half of the night here recently, until it was almost light. I couldn't help it. I should like always to be near you."

"Don't say such foolish things."

He stammered on: "I beg of you, Frau Heinold, Frau Beatrice—Beatrice!"

"That's enough—really you are—what is the matter with you? Shall I call? But for God's sake! Think then—think of Hugo."

"Hugo is not at home. No one hears us."

Quickly that burning pain again rose within her. Then suddenly, with shame and fright she realized that she was glad of Hugo's absence. She felt Fritz's warm lips on hers, and a longing sprang up in her which she had never felt to such an extent before, not even in those far-off days. "Who can blame me for it?" she thought. "To whom am I accountable?" And with desirous arms, she drew the glowing boy to her.

3

As BEATRICE came out of the dark shadow of the forest
into the open, the gravel road stretched out before
her, white and burning hot, and she was almost sorry
that she had left the Welponers so early in the afternoon. But since Frau Welponer had departed for her
usual after-dinner nap as soon as they left the table,
and since her son and daughter had also disappeared
without any apology, Beatrice would have been obliged to remain alone with the Director, a thing that
she must avoid at all events, after the occurrences
of the past few days. His attempts to win her favor
had become altogether too open; in fact, he had
dropped certain hints that gave her to believe that
he would be ready to leave his wife and children at
her will—and not only that, but that union with her
would mean above all that wished for flight from unbearable houschold ties. For, with her lately acquired
painful insight into the relationships of man, Beatrice
had realized that that marriage had been deeply un-
dermined, and that a collapse could follow at any time,
unexpectedly and without any special reason. She had
often noticed the exaggerated care with which the
husband and wife spoke to each other, as if the hatred
which lowered quiveringly in the hard lines around
their mouths might break out at any moment into
words that could never be made good again. But not
until Fritz had told her last night of the almost incredible rumor, which she still did not believe—of a

love affair between her dead husband and Frau Welponer, did she allow herself to take part with any real interest in the cause for the disturbance. And although the rumor had been troubling her even during dinner, while indifferent conversation went on around the table, now as she walked homewards down the path through the glittering summer air, from whose burning breath every living being seemed to have fled to the shelter of closed rooms, Fritz's rude intimations began to work with painful activity on her mind. Why, she asked herself, had he spoken of it, and especially that night? Was it in revenge because she had told him jokingly that he had better remain at Ischl with his parents, whom he was going to visit in the morning, instead of coming back the same evening as he had intended? Had a jealous suspicion awakened in him, that with all the charm of his youth, still he meant nothing to her but a handsome young boy, whom she could send home without further ado, when the game was at an end? Or had he only succumbed to his inclination to indiscreet talk, which she had been obliged to curb several times before, and even quite recently, when he evinced a desire to tell her about Hugo's relations with Fortunata? Or was the conversation between Fritz's parents, that he said he had recently overheard, just a child of his fanciful brain—just as his visit to the dissection room, of which he had told her on the day of his arrival, had recently turned out to be empty boasting? But although he had undertaken to tell of the talk of his parents in good faith, might he not have heard wrongly, or misunderstood? This last idea was all the more probable, since not the slightest whisper of that rumor had come to Beatrice before.

Busied with such thoughts, Beatrice reached her villa. Since Hugo had ostensibly gone on a tour, and the maid was having the day off, Beatrice found herself alone in the house. She undressed in her room, and submitting to the heavy weariness that often came over her these summer afternoons, she stretched out on her bed. Consciously enjoying the solitude, the peace, the very faint light, she lay there a while with open eyes. In the large mirror that hung opposite her, she could see the life-size bust-portrait of her husband reflected in faint outline from the wall over her bed. She could see clearly only a red spot that she knew represented the carnation in his button-hole. In the early days after Ferdinand's death, this picture had continued to lead a strangely personal life for Beatrice. She saw it smiling or sad, happy or distressed—in fact, at times, she imagined that in some way the painted features expressed unconcern or despair over their own death. In the course of years, however, it had become dumb and silent, and remained a piece of painted canvas and nothing more. But at this hour, it seemed to want to live again. And although Beatrice could not see very clearly in the mirror, it seemed to her that it sent an ironic look down over her; and memories awoke within her that, though they had seemed harmless, or even gay before, now came to her mind with a new bitter meaning. And in place of the one on whom her suspicions had been fastened, a whole row of women went by, whose features she had forgotten, but who, as she suddenly realized, had all been Ferdinand's loves—admirers who wanted his autograph or photograph, young actresses who took lessons from him, society women whose salons he and Beatrice had often frequented, fellow actresses who had fallen into his arms as wives, brides, or betrayed ones. And she asked herself whether it were not his consciousness of guilt that had made him so mild and so wisely indifferent, as it seemed, to any unfaithfulness that Beatrice might commit against his memory. And all of a sudden, as if he had thrown aside the useless uncomfortable mask that he had worn long enough, both alive and dead, he stood before her mind with his red carnation and all—a silly comedian for whom she was nothing but an industrious housewife, the mother of his son, and a woman whom one embraced once in a while when, on a mild summer evening, the magic of propinquity so disposed one. And like his picture, his voice suddenly changed mysteriously. It no longer had the noble ring that sounded more beautiful in her memory than the voices of all the living. It rang empty, affected, and false. But at once she knew that it was not really his voice that she now heard, but that of another who recently had ventured—here in her own house—had ventured to ape the voice, intonation, and actions of her dead husband.

She sat up in bed, threw one arm over the pillow, and stared in horror into the darkness of her chamber. Now for the first time, in this peaceful hour, she recalled that event in all its atrocity. It had happened a week ago, on a Sunday as today—she was sitting in the garden with her son and—she thought the word with a grimace—her lover. Suddenly a young man had appeared, tall and dark, with shining eyes, in a sport outfit, with a yellowish-red tie. She did not recognize him until the cheerful greeting of the others informed her that Rudi Beratoner stood before her, the same young man who had visited Hugo several times the past winter to borrow books from him, and who, as

she knew, was one of the two who Hugo had told her
had spent that spring night in the Prater with the girls
of questionable repute. He was just coming from Ischl,
where he had looked for Fritz in vain at his parents'
home. Naturally he was invited to dinner. He accepted
gladly, a little too boisterously, and proved to be in-
defatigable in relating hunting stories and all sorts
of anecdotes; and his younger friends who seemed like
children in comparison with his precociousness, looked
at him in astonishment. He also showed a capacity for
drink that was far beyond his years. Since the boys
did not want to remain behind him, and since even
Beatrice allowed herself to drink more than usual, the
spirit in the house was much easier than was usual.
Beatrice, who noticed with gratitude and emotion that
in spite of all her gayety her guest acted with great
respect for her, imagined, as she often did in these
days, that all that had happened recently, the truth of
which she could not doubt, was only some sort of
dream that could be repaired. For a moment, as formerly, she had put her arm around Hugo's shoulders
and played with his hair, but she looked coquettishly
at Fritz at the same time, and forthwith felt strange
emotions over her own fate and the world. Later she
noticed that Fritz was whispering very eagerly to
Rudi and seemed to be persuading him to do something very important. She asked gayly what terrible
thing the two young men were plotting; Beratoner
did not want to answer, but Fritz explained—there
was no reason for keeping it a secret—the fact was
commonly known that Rudi could impersonate actors
remarkably well, not only the living, but even the—
but now he stopped. But Beatrice, very much excited
and already slightly intoxicated, turned quickly to

Rudi Beratoner, and asked somewhat hoarsely, "Then you can impersonate Ferdinand Heinold too?" She pronounced the famous name as if it belonged to a stranger. Beratoner did not want to hear of it. He did not understand Fritz at all—formerly he had practiced such tricks, but not for a long time now; besides, he naturally could not recall the voices of those he had not heard for a long time, and if he had to do something, he preferred to sing a couplet in the style of any comedian they might choose. But Beatrice would not allow any evasion. She wanted nothing more than to take advantage of this opportunity. She trembled with longing to hear the beloved voice, at least in reflected splendor. That that desire might mean something blasphemous did not strike her in her befogged state of mind. At last Beratoner let himself be persuaded. And with beating heart, Beatrice heard at first Hamlet's monologue, "To be or not to be" ringing through the free summer air in Ferdinand's heroic sounding voice, then verses from Tasso, then some long forgotten words out of a long forgotten play—she heard the beloved voice, deeply booming and melting softly away. With closed eyes, she drank it in, full of wonder, until suddenly she heard, still in Ferdinand's voice, but now in his familiar everyday tone: "Grüss Gott, Beatrice!" Then she opened her eyes in great fright and saw before her an insolent, spoiled face, around whose lips there still remained fading traces, like ghostly reminders, of Ferdinand's smile; she met Hugo's wandering glance and the half tragic, half stupid simper on Fritz's face; and heard herself saying as if from afar, a polite word of thanks to the wonderful mimic. The silence that followed was dark and oppressive; they could not bear it very long and soon gay words about summer weather and picnics were flying back and forth. But Beatrice soon arose and went back to her room, where she sank wearily into her armchair and then fell into a sleep from which she awoke hardly an hour later as if from an abysmally deep night. When she walked later in the garden, in the cool of evening, the young people had gone away. They came back soon without Rudi Beratoner, whom they took elaborate pains not to mention further, and it was deeply consoling to Beatrice to see how her son and lover tried with un-usual consideration and delicacy to wipe away the dis-tressing impression of the afternoon.

And now, in the quiet solitude of twilight, when Beatrice tried to recall the real voice of her husband, she could not do it. It was always the voice of that unwelcome guest that she heard, and she realized more deeply than ever what a crime she had committed against the dead man, worse than any that he could have committed during his life-time against her, more cowardly and inexpiable than unfaithfulness and be-trayal. He was rotting deep in the ground and his widow allowed stupid boys to make fun of him, of that wonderful man who had loved her—her alone, in spite of everything that had happened, just as she had loved no other but him, and would never love any other. Now she knew it for the first time—since she had a lover. A lover! Oh, if he would never come back, that lover of hers—if he would only go away forever out of her sight and out of her blood, and if she could live again in her villa with Hugo in the quiet peace of summer, as before! As before? And if Fritz were no longer there, would she have her son back? Did she still have the right to expect it? Had she troubled

much about him recently? Had she not been much
happier that he went his own way? And she remembered now, recently, when she had been walking in
the wood with the Arbesbachers, she had seen her son
hardly a hundred steps away together with Fortunata,
Wilhelmine Fallehn, and a strange man; and she had
hardly been ashamed, only had talked more eagerly
with her friends so that they might not notice Hugo.
And in the evening of the same day, yesterday—yes,
certainly it was only yesterday—how slowly time went
by—she had met Fräulein Fallehn and that strange
man, who, with his black shiny hair, his sparkling
white teeth, his mustache cut English fashion, his pon-
gee silk suit, and his red silk tie, looked like a circus-
rider, a swindler, or a Mexican millionaire. When
Wilhelmine nodded in greeting with her never-
changing deep solemnity, he had taken off his hat,
bared his white teeth, and looked at Beatrice with an
insolent smile that made her blush even in recollection. What a pair they were! She believed them capable of any vice, any crime. And these were the friends
of Fortunata, these were people with whom her son
now went walking and whose company he now frequented! Beatrice covered her face with her hands,
sighed and whispered to herself: "Away, away, away!"
She said the word without really knowing what it
meant. Gradually she began to realize its full meaning
and thought that perhaps in it lay her and Hugo's salvation. Yes, they must go away, both of them, mother
and son, and as quickly as possible. She must take him
with her—or he must take her. Both of them must
leave this place before something would happen to
them that could never be repaired, before she would
lose all rights of motherhood, before her son's youth

would be completely ruined, before fate would fall crashing down upon them both. There was still time. No one knew of her own adventure, otherwise she would have noticed it in some way, at least in the actions of the architect. And the adventure of her son was doubtless also not yet known. And if they did know it, they would excuse it in so inexperienced a youth; and they could not even reproach a mother who had been so careless up to this time, if she should flee with him now, as if she had just discovered it. Therefore it was not too late. The difficulty lay elsewhere: to persuade Hugo to undertake such a sudden journey. Beatrice could not guess how far the power of the Baroness extended over Hugo's heart and mind. She knew nothing, nothing about him, since she had her own love affairs to worry over. But Hugo was clever, and he would not deceive himself into thinking that his adventure with Fortunata was to last forever, and so he could easily see that a few days more or less did not matter. And in her thoughts, she spoke to him: "We cannot go directly to Vienna. Oh, we can't think of it, my child. We shall go South. We have been planning that for a long time. To Venice, to Florence, to Rome. Just think, you will see the old palaces, and St. Peter's! Hugo, let's go tomorrow! You and I alone. Another journey like that one two years ago in the spring. Do you remember? Over Murrensteig by carriage to Mariazell. Wasn't it beautiful? And this time it will be still more beautiful. And if it'll be hard at first, oh, God, I'll understand, and I'll not ask you anything and you'll not have to tell me anything. But seeing so much beauty and novelty, you'll forget. You'll forget very soon. Much sooner than you think—"

"And you, Mother—you?" She heard Hugo's voice saying it. She shuddered. And she dropped her hands from her eyes as if to assure herself that she was alone. Yes, she was alone, quite alone in the house in the half darkened room; outside, the summer day breathed heavily and sultrily; no one could disturb her. She had plenty of quiet and time to plan what to say to her son. Of one thing she was certain: she need not fear a response such as she had imagined in her excitement: "And you, Mother?" That he could not ask. For he knew nothing—he could know nothing. And he would never know. Even if some suggestive whisper should come to his ear, he would not believe it. He would never believe anything like it of his mother. On that score she could be quite at ease. And she saw herself wandering with him through some fantastic landscape that she remembered from a painting—a grayish-yellow road with a town all in blue and with many towers swimming in the distance. Then she saw themselves walking in a large square under arched passages—strange people met them and looked at her and her son. They looked at her meaningly with bold teethy smiles, and as if they thought: "Ah, she has brought a nice youth with her on her journey! She might be his mother." What? Did the people take them for lovers? Well, why not? They could not know that the boy was her son, and they would know her for one of those over-ripe women who desire such young blood. And there they would be, walking around a strange city among strange people and he would think of his beloved with the Pierrot face, and she, of her sweet blond boy. She groaned aloud. She wrung her hands. Whither? Whither? All of a sudden, one of the love-words with which she had

held him to her bosom last night slipped treacherously
from her lips—the boy whom she would bid farewell
forever and whom she would never—never see again.
Yet, just once more, if he came back today. Or tomorrow morning. But tonight her door would be
locked. It was over forever. And she would say at
parting that she had loved him very much—with a
love that he would never meet again. And with that
proud feeling, he would realize all the more his gallant duty to eternal silence. And he would understand
that it must be thus, and he would kiss her hand once
more and would go. Would go. And then what? Then
what? And she lay there with parted lips, her arms
outstretched, her body trembling, and she knew that
if he would come at that moment into the door, young
and full of longing, she would not be able to resist
him and would again belong to him with all the ardor
that was now awakened in her like something long
forgotten, in fact, like something that she had never
before known. And now she knew too, in simulta-
neous agony and ecstasy, that the youth to whom she
had given herself would not be her last lover. Already
hot curiosity raged within her: who would the next
one be? Dr. Bertram? She remembered an evening—
was it three or eight days ago?—she did not know—
time dragged so—went by so quickly—the hours
melted into each other and meant nothing—it happened in Welponer's garden—Bertram had suddenly
run up to her on a dark path, had drawn her to him,
and embraced and kissed her. And even though she
had angrily pushed him away, what did that matter
to him, who in spite of that must have felt the sub-
missive pressure of her lips, so accustomed to kisses?
That was why he had immediately become so quiet,

and patient, as if he well knew just where he stood, and she could read in his look: "Winter belongs to me, dear lady. We have been in agreement for a long time. We both know that death is bitter and virtue only an empty word, and that one should let nothing go by." But it was not Bertram who spoke to her. Suddenly, while she lay there with closed eyes, another face had pushed Bertram's out of the way, that of the circus-rider or gambler or Mexican who had recently looked at her so boldly, just as Bertram had done and every one else. They all had the same look—all—and that look always said and wished and knew the same thing; and if one gave in to one of them one was lost. They took the one who happened to please them, and threw her away again. Yes, if one let herself be taken and thrown away. But she was not of that class. No, it had not gone that far with her. Passing adventures were not her style. If she had been created for that, how could she take the affair with Fritz so much to heart? And if she suffered such pangs of remorse and fear, it was only because that which she had done was so much against her nature. She hardly understood that it all had happened. There was no other way to explain it, than that it had come over her like a disease in these unbearably hot summer days, and had left her defenseless and weak. And just as the disease had come, so it would leave her again. Soon, soon. She felt in all her pulses, all her senses, in her whole body, that she was not the same as she had been formerly. She could hardly collect her thoughts. How feverishly they ran through her mind! She did not know what she wanted, what she hoped for, what she regretted, hardly knew if she were happy or unhappy. It could only be a disease. There were women in whom such

a condition lasted a long time, and would hardly ever
improve; such a one was Fortunata and that marble-
white Fräulein Fallehn. There were others again
whom it invaded or attacked and left soon after. That
was her case. Most certainly. How otherwise could
she have lived all these years since Ferdinand had
gone, as chaste as a young girl and without desire?
It only came over her this summer. All the women
looked differently this year; the girls too—their eyes
were brighter and bolder, and their behavior was
lighter, more enticing and seductive. And one heard
such stories! What was that one about the doctor's
young wife, who went out on the lake evenings with
an oarsman and did not come home till the next morning? And about the two young girls who lay naked
on the meadow just as the little steam-boat went by,
and suddenly, before any one could recognize them,
had disappeared into the forest? Really, it was in the
air this year. The sun had unusual strength, and the
waves of the lake caressed her body more tenderly
than ever before. And when that secret curse was
lifted, would she again be as she had been, and could
she slip through the hot adventures of these days and
nights as if through an easily forgotten dream? And
if she felt it coming again as she had felt it coming on
this time, far in advance, when longing began to rage
in her blood with dangerous intensity, she would be
able to choose a much better and cleaner salvation
than this time—she would marry again as other
women did when they felt as she did. Then an ironic
smile came to her lips, as if taken unawares. She
thought of some one who had recently been there,
one whom she credited with the most honorable intentions, the lawyer, Dr. Teichmann. She saw him

before her in a brand new green and brown sport suit, with a plaid tie, his green hat with the fur cockade placed dashingly on his head—in short in an outfit by which he openly wanted to show that he knew how to look very fetching, even though he, a very serious man under ordinary circumstances, placed no worth upon such superficialities. Then she saw him sitting at dinner on the veranda between her son and her lover, addressing now one, now the other, with the seriousness of a senior assistant master, and saw him in his ridiculous innocence which had tempted her to exchange handclasps playfully with her Fritz under the table. He had left the same evening, since he was to meet friends in Bozen, and although Beatrice had not invited him to remain, he seemed very much puffed up and full of hope on leaving, for in the gay mood of that summer day she had not deprived even him of encouraging and exciting looks. Now she regretted it as she regretted so much else; and her next conversation with him appeared all the more uncertain because in the complete relaxation of that hour, she was more painfully conscious of the gradual weakening of her will-power. With a similar feeling of shame, she recalled the feeling of helplessness that had at times come over her during her last talks with Director Welponer, and then it seemed to her that if she were to choose, she could sooner think of herself as the wife of the Director—yes she must admit that the notion did not lack charm for her. Today she felt as if this man had interested her from earliest times. The things that the architect had told her about the grandiose speculations and battles of the Director, in which he had been victor over ministers and members of the court, were especially well calculated to arouse

Beatrice's curiosity and admiration. Besides, Dr. Teichmann, too, had called him a genius when speaking of
him, and had compared him in the daring of his un-
dertakings, which always meant everything to Teichmann, to a valiant cavalry-general. And so it flattered
Beatrice a little that just this man seemed to want
her, apart from the satisfaction that it would offer her
of taking the husband away from the woman who had
once robbed her of hers. "Has robbed me of mine?"
she asked herself in confused surprise. "What is wrong
with me? What am I thinking of? Do I believe it,
then? It may not be true. Everything else, but not
that. I should have noticed something of it. Noticed
something? Why? Wasn't Ferdinand an actor, and a
great one too? Why couldn't it have happened without
my noticing it? I was so trusting, that it was not difficult to betray me. Not difficult—but that does not
mean that it actually happened. Fritz is a gossip, a liar,
and these rumors are false and stupid. And even
though it did happen, it happened long ago. And
Ferdinand is dead. And she who was once his love is
an old woman. What does all the past mean to me?
What is going on now between the Director and me
is a new story, which has nothing to do with the past."

And she thought further, that in truth it wouldn't
be so bad to retire some day into the noble villa with
its great park. What wealth, what glamour! What an
outlook for Hugo's future! Truly, he was no longer
young, and that must be considered to some degree,
especially when one was as pampered as she had been
recently. Yes, during this very summer, during these
last weeks, he seemed to be aging more rapidly than
ever. Was not perhaps his love for her to blame? Well,
what was the difference? There were others, younger

ones, and he would be betrayed anyhow: it was evidently his lot. She laughed dryly: it sounded ugly and mean, and she jumped up as if out of a wild dream. "Where am I, where am I?" she asked herself. She wrung her hands entreatingly. "How deeply shall you let me sink? Is there no halting any more? What is it then that makes me so wretched and so contemptible? What makes me reach out into space, and to be no better than Fortunata and other women of her sort?" And suddenly, with a failing heart, she knew what made her so wretched: the foundation on which she had rested in certainty for years was trembling, and the heavens were darkening over her: the only man she had ever loved, her Ferdinand, had been a liar. Yes—now she knew it. His whole life with her had been fraud and hypocrisy: he had betrayed her with Frau Welponer and with other women, with actresses, and countesses, and prostitutes. And when, on sultry nights, the languid charm of propinquity had driven him into Beatrice's arms, then it was the worst and lowest of all his lies, for she knew that on her breast he had thought of the others, all the others, in lust and malice. But why did she know it all of a sudden? Why? Because she was no different, no better than he. Was it Ferdinand whom she held in her arms, the comedian with the red flower, who often enough came home from the public-house at three in the morning, smelling of wine, swaggering, and babbling empty and unclean things, the one who as a young man had subordinated his higher passions to the favor of an old widow, and who in gay company read tender little notes that love-sick fools had sent to his dressing-room? No, that one she had never loved. She would have fled from that one in the first month of her marriage. He whom she loved was not Ferdinand Heinold: he was Hamlet and Cyrano and King Richard, and this one and that one, heroes and scoundrels, conquerors and martyrs, the blessed and the damned. And he who with strange fire had lured her into the summer night out of the secret darkness of their chamber to unutterable ecstasy, was not really he, but some sort of spirit full of hidden power out of the mountains, whose part he was playing without knowing it—for he always played a part, because he could not live without a mask, because he was afraid to see his real features reflected in her eyes. And so she had always betrayed him just as he had betrayed her and had constantly lived a life lost from the beginning, a life of fantastically wild lust—except that no one could have suspected it, not even she herself. But now it was revealed. She was destined to sink lower and lower, and some day—who knew how soon—it would be clear to the whole world that all her bourgeois respectability was a lie, that she was no better than Fortunata, Wilhelmine Fallehn and all the others whom till today she had despised. And her son would know it too; and if he did not believe the affair with Fritz, he would believe a next one—would have to believe it—and suddenly she saw him vividly before her with eyes wide open and full of pain, his arms outstretched in repulsion; and when she wanted to come near him, he turned around in horror, and hurried away with the fleetness of a dream. And she groaned aloud, suddenly wide awake. To lose Hugo? Everything, but not that. Better to die than to have her son no more. To die— yes. For then she would have him again. Then he would come to his mother's grave and kneel down and deck it with flowers and fold his hands in prayer for her. With that thought an emotion crept into her heart that was sweet and at the same time repulsive, and falsely peaceful. Still, deep within her, she heard a murmur: "Have I the right to rest? Haven't I much more to think about? Certainly—tomorrow we shall start out on our journey. Tomorrow—how much there is to do—so much—so much—"

In the quiet dusk that surrounded her, she felt that outside, the world, people, and the landscape had awakened from their afternoon drowsiness. All sorts of distant sounds, indefinite and confused, came to her ears through the closed blinds. And she knew that people were already wandering on the roads, were rowing on the lake, were playing tennis, and drinking coffee on the hotel terrace—yes in her still half dreaming condition, she saw swarms of happy summer-resorters, like tiny puppets, but real as life, bobbing up and down before her. The ticking of her watch on the night table sounded too loud in her ears, and like a warning. Beatrice was curious to know how late it was, but she still lacked the strength to turn her head or even to turn on the light. Some new, nearer sound, evidently from the garden, had become gradually more audible. What could it be? The voices of men, without a doubt. So near? Voices in the garden? Hugo and Fritz? How was it possible that they should both have returned so soon? Well, it was already evening, and Fritz had evidently been drawn back by his love. No doubt they had first rung the bell, and she had not heard it because she was asleep. Then they must have climbed over the fence; naturally they could not suspect that the mistress of the house was at home. Now one of the two was laughing out there. What laugh was that? It was not Hugo's laugh. But Fritz did not laugh like that either. Now the other was laughing. That was Fritz. Now again, the first one. That was not Hugo. He spoke. It was not Hugo's voice. Then Fritz was in the garden with some one else? They were quite near. It seemed as if both had sat down on the bench, on the white one under the window. And now she heard Fritz calling the other one by name. Rudi— Well, then, it was he who was sitting with Fritz under her window. But that was not so astonishing. Recently they had arranged in her presence that Rudi Beratoner should come back very soon. Perhaps he had been here earlier, had seen no one and then had met Fritz, whom love had brought back so soon from Ischl, at the railroad station or some-where else. In any case, there was no reason why she should rack her brains about it. There they were, the two young men, sitting on the white bench under the window of the adjoining room. Now she must get up, dress, and go out into the garden. Why? Did she really have to go into the garden? Had she such a pressing desire to see Fritz again, or was she the least bit anxious to greet the shameless youth who re-cently had aped her dead husband's voice and facial expression with such disgraceful facility? Still there was nothing else for her to do, but to bid the young people good evening. She couldn't keep so still for all the time that they remained out there gossiping about everything they pleased. That it could not be a very pure conversation, she could not doubt. Well, that did not concern her. They should say what they wished.

Beatrice had gotten up and was sitting on the edge of her bed. Then she heard a word with perfect clear-ness, the name of her son. Naturally, they were talking about Hugo, and what they were saying was not difficult to guess. Now they laughed again. But she couldn't understand the words. If she were very near the window, she might be able to understand the conversation, but perhaps it were better to forego that. She might experience some unpleasant surprises. In any case, it would be wisest to get ready as quickly as possible, and to go into the garden. But Beatrice was impelled to slip first very quietly to the closed blinds. She looked out through a small crack and could see nothing but a strip of green; then through another crack, a blue strip of sky. But now, she heard all the better what was being said on the bench. First, it was only the name of her Hugo that she could make out. Everything was so whispered and hushed, as if both of them had in mind the possibility of being over-heard. Beatrice put her ear to the crack and smiled with a sigh. They were talking about school. Very clearly, she heard: "That horrid chap would have liked to flunk him." And then: "A mean dog." She slipped back, dressed quickly in a comfortable house gown; and then, driven by her uncontrollable curiosity, she went back to the window. And now she remarked that they were not talking any more about school. "A Baroness, is she?" That was Rudi Beratoner's voice. And now—pah—what a disgusting word— "He's with her all day long,—and today—" That was Fritz's voice. Against her will, she put her fingers to her ears, went away from the window and made up her mind to go immediately into the garden. But before she had reached the door, she was again driven to the window; she knelt down, put her ear to the crack, and looked out with wide open eyes and burning cheeks. Rudi Beratoner was telling a story—at times he lowered his

voice to a whisper, but from the single words that
Beatrice gathered here and there, it became gradually
clear to her what the affair was about. It was a love
adventure of which Rudi was telling; Beatrice could
make out French pet names which he pronounced in
a sweet, gentle voice. Ah, evidently he was copying the
manner of that person. He did that thing so remarkably well. Who slept in the adjoining room? His sister. Ah, it was the governess— More—more—how did
it work? When the sister slept, the governess came to
him. And then—and then—? Beatrice did not want
to hear it, and yet she listened on and on, with growing eagerness. What words! What a tone! So this
was how these boys spoke about their sweethearts!
No, no, not all, and not about all. What a woman that
must be! Surely she deserved it, that they should speak
like that about her and not otherwise. But why did
she deserve it? After all, what crime had she committed? It was only loathsome when they spoke about it.
When Rudi Beratoner held her in his arms, he was
surely very tender and had pure loving words for her
—as they all had at those moments. If only she could
see Fritz's face! Oh, she could picture it. His cheeks
would burn and his eyes would glow. Now there was
silence for a while. Evidently the story was finished.

And suddenly she heard Fritz's voice. He was asking: "What, must you know everything so exactly?"
A heavy feeling of envy stirred in Beatrice. "What,
do you want an answer to that?" Yes, Rudi Beratoner
was speaking. Well, then, speak louder at least. I
want to hear what you are saying, you rogue, who
have insulted my husband in his grave, and who now
are betraying and reviling your beloved. Louder! Oh,
God, it was loud enough! He was not saying anything

now— He was asking a question—he wanted to know
—if Fritz—had here in town—yes, you blackguard—
run riot with your own profane words! It will not
help you. You shall not learn anything. Fritz is hardly
more than a boy, but he is nobler than you. He knows
what he owes a respectable woman who has shown
him her favor. Isn't that so, Fritz, my sweet Fritz?—
You'll not say anything, will you?

What held her so firmly rooted to the floor, that she
could not get up, hurry out, and put an end to the
shameful conversation? But what would it have
helped? Rudi Beratoner was not the man to be so
easily satisfied. If he did not get his answer today at
this time, then he would repeat his question on the
following day. It was best to remain there and continue to listen—then one knew where one was, at
least. Why so softly, Fritz? Speak out. Why should
you not glorify your happiness? A respectable woman
like myself—that's quite different from a governess.
Beratoner spoke louder. Beatrice heard him say quite
distinctly: "Then you must be a regular idiot." Ah,
let them take you for an idiot, Fritz. Accept the title.
What, you do not believe him, you rascal? You want
to worm his secret out of him at all costs? Have you
any suspicions? Has any one told you already? And
again she heard Fritz's whispering, though it was
quite impossible to understand the words. Now again,
Beratoner's voice, deep and coarse: "What, a married
woman? Go on—would such a one ever—" Will you
not keep still, you wretch? She felt that never in her
life had she hated any one as she hated this youth
who insulted her without knowing that it was she
whom he was insulting. What, Fritz? For Heaven's
sake, louder! "She has already gone away." Ah, ex-

cellent, Fritz, you want to protect me from insulting suspicions. She listened. She drank in his words. "A villa near the lake—her husband is a lawyer." What a rogue! How deliciously he lied! She might really have enjoyed it, if not for the fear that agitated her. What? The husband was horribly jealous? He had threatened to kill her if he discovered anything? What? Till four o'clock this morning? Every night— every—night— Enough, enough, enough! Will you not be still? Aren't you ashamed? Why do you defile me? If your fine friend does not know that it is I of whom you are speaking, still you do know it. Why don't you lie instead? Enough, enough! And she wanted to stop her ears, but instead of doing so, she listened all the more attentively. Not a syllable escaped her any more. And in despair, she heard from the lips of her boy the detailed description of those holy nights that he spent in her arms, heard it in words that beat down upon her like the lashes of a whip, in expressions that she heard for the first time, but that were quickly understood, and that brought bloody shame to her brow. She knew that everything that Fritz was saying out there in the garden was nothing but the truth, and yet she felt that it had already ceased to be the truth, that this contemptible chatter had turned what had been his and her happiness into filth and lies. And to him, she had belonged! He was the first to whom she had given herself since she was free! Her teeth chattered, her cheeks and brow burned, her knees sank weakly to the floor. Suddenly she drew back—Rudi Beratoner wanted to see the house. And how did it happen that the people had already gone away in the finest part of the summer? "I don't believe a single word of your story. A lawyer's wife?

Ridiculous! Shall I tell you who it is?" She listened
with her ears, with her soul, with all her senses. But
no word came. But without looking, she knew that
Beratoner was indicating the house with his eyes; he
was pointing exactly to the window behind which
she was kneeling.

And now came Fritz's answer: "What's the matter with you? You are quite crazy."

Then the other one: "But you needn't say any more.
I have already noticed it. Congratulations! Yes, not
every one has it so convenient. Yes—the—but if I
wanted—" Beatrice could not hear more. She hardly
knew how it happened. Perhaps it was the blood
roaring in her brain that had drowned out Beratoner's
last words. For a long time, the conversation outside
was lost in this roaring, until she could again understand Fritz's words:

"Well, then, keep still. What if she's at home!" It's
a little too late to think of that, my dear boy.

"Well, what if she is?" said Beratoner loudly and
insolently. Then Fritz was whispering again in quick
excitement, and suddenly Beatrice heard both of them
getting up from the bench. For Heaven's sake, what
now? She threw herself flat on the floor, so that it
would be impossible to espy her through the crack
in the blind. Shadows passed before the blinds, steps
crunched on the gravel path, a couple of muffled words,
then a faint laugh further away—and then nothing
more. . . . She waited. Nothing stirred. Then she
heard their voices dying away farther out in the garden—then nothing—for a long time—nothing, until
she was certain they both were far away. They might
have climbed over the fence as they had come, and
might be telling each other their stories outside. Was

there anything left to tell? Had Fritz forgotten anything? He would make up for it now. And in his delightful way, he would find a few more things to add
in order to impress Rudi rightly. Why not? Yes, that
was the gayety of youth. One had his sister's governess,
the other, the mother of his schoolmate, and the third,
a Baroness, who formerly had been in the theatre.
Yes, they had enough to say, these young men—they
knew women and could rightly say that one was like
the other.

And Beatrice wept silently to herself. She still lay
outstretched on the floor. Why get up? Why get up
now? When she would finally make up her mind to
get up, it would be only to put an end to it all. Oh, to
meet Fritz again, and the other one— She could spit
in their faces, beat them with her fists. Wouldn't that
be a solace and a joy?—to rush after them, to scream
in their faces: "You boys, you wretches, aren't you
ashamed, aren't you ashamed?" But at the same time,
she knew that she would not do it. She felt that it was
not worth the trouble, since she had decided and must
remain decided to go on a path on which no scold-
ing and no derision could follow her. Never, never,
could she in her disgrace look any one in the eye
again. She had but one more thing to do on this earth:
to take leave of the one who was dear to her—her son!
Of him alone! But naturally, without his noticing it.
Only she would know that she was leaving him forever—that she was kissing the brow of her dear child
for the last time— How strange it was to think such
thoughts, lying stretched and motionless on the floor.
If some one were to come into the room now, she
would be taken for dead without fail. "Where will
they find me?" she thought. "How shall I do it? How

shall I arrange it, that I shall be lying here senseless, never to awaken again?"

A noise in the front room made her start. Hugo had come home. She heard him going down the hall, past her door, and opening his—and now there was silence again. He had returned. Now she was not alone any more. She got up slowly, with aching limbs. It was almost completely dark in the room and the air suddenly seemed unbearably sultry. She did not understand why she had been lying so long on the floor like that, and why she had not opened the blinds much sooner. She quickly did so now, and before her eyes spread the garden, the towering mountains, and the heavens darkening above her, and she felt as if she had not seen all this for many days and nights. The small world spread out in the evening light, so wonderful and peaceful that even Beatrice felt its calm. At the same time, however, she felt a fear creep gently into her mind. She must not let herself be deceived and confused by this peace. And she said to herself: "What I have heard, I have heard; what has happened, has happened. The quiet of this evening, the peace of this world, are not for me: morning will come, the noises of the day will recommence; people will remain malicious and mean, and love, a filthy joke. And I am one who can never forget it, not in the daytime or in the night, not in solitude, or in new pleasure, not at home or abroad. And I have nothing more to do in this world than to place a farewell kiss on the brow of my beloved son, and go— What can he be doing there alone in his room?" From his open window a faint light shone out over the gravel and turf. Was he already in bed—weary after the joy and exertion of his trip? A shudder ran through her body, strangely com-

posed of fear, horror, and longing. Yes, she longed for
him, but for a different one than the one who lay in
his room and who had the breath of Fortunata's body
about him. She longed for the former Hugo, for the
fresh, clean boy, who had once told her about the kiss
of a little girl at the dance, for the Hugo who had
driven with her one beautiful summer day over the
country-side—and she wished for that time to return,
when she herself was different—a mother, worthy of
that son, and not a good-for-nothing woman, about
whom spoiled boys dared gossip lewdly, as about any
wanton. Ah, if there were only miracles! But there
were none. Never could that hour be unmade when,
with burning cheeks, on aching knees, with thirsty
ears, she had listened to the story of her disgrace—and
her happiness. Even in ten, in twenty, in fifty years,
as an old man, Rudi Beratoner would still remember
this hour, when in his youth he had sat on a white
bench in the garden of Frau Beatrice Heinold, and
his schoolmate had told him how night after night,
until early morning, he had lain in bed with her. She
shuddered, she wrung her hands, she looked up to the
heavens, whose clouds remained still as death and
showed no surprise at her lonely agony. All sorts of
noises from the street and lake came up to her in faint
confusion; the mountains rose up darkly to the beckoning night, the yellow fields lay dully glowing in the
twilight that was creeping in all around. How long
would she remain here so motionlessly? What was
she awaiting? Had she forgotten that Hugo might
disappear out of the house just as he had come, to one
who meant more to him than she? There was not
much time to lose. Quickly she unbolted her door,
went into the small salon, and stood before Hugo's

room. For a moment she hesitated, listened, but heard nothing; then she opened the door hastily.

Hugo was sitting on his divan and stared up at his mother with wide eyes, as if he had been frightened out of a restless sleep. Over his face played strange shadows from the uncertain light of the electric lamp, standing with its green shade on the table in the center of the room. Beatrice remained for a moment at the door, Hugo threw his head back; it seemed as if he wanted to get up, but he remained seated, his arms extended, his hands resting flat on the divan. Beatrice felt the tension of this moment with heart-rending pain. An unequaled fear gripped her soul; and she said to herself, "He knows all. . . . What will happen?" she thought in the same breath. She went to him, forced herself to look happier, and asked: "Were you asleep, Hugo?"

"No, Mother," he answered, "I was just lying down." She looked into a pale, miserable childish face; unutterable sympathy, in which her own suffering was buried, arose within her; still trembling, she laid her hand on his tangled hair, then put her arm around him, sat down beside him, and gently began: "Well, my child—" Then she did not know what to say next. His face was violently distorted; she took his hands, he pressed hers distractedly, stroked her fingers and looked away; his smile was like a mask, his eyes reddened, his breast began to heave, and suddenly he slipped from the divan, lay at his mother's feet, put his head in her lap, and wept bitterly. Beatrice, shaken to the very depths, and yet happy in a way, for she felt that he had not become estranged from her, at first did not say a word, let him weep while she played quietly with his hair, and asked herself in terror:

"What can have happened?" And she comforted herself immediately: "Perhaps nothing unusual. Perhaps
nothing except that his nerves are giving way." And
she remembered very similar convulsive attacks that
her dead husband had suffered for seemingly negli-
gible reasons—after the excitement of a great rôle,
after an experience that had wounded his artistic van-
ity, or entirely without ground, at least without any
that she could discover. And suddenly she began to
wonder whether Ferdinand did not sometimes cry out
on her lap the disappointments and griefs that he had
suffered at the hands of some other woman. But why
did that trouble her? What he had done, he had ex-
piated, and all that was far away, so far away! Today
it was her son who wept in her lap, and she knew that
he wept because of Fortunata. With what pain did
that realization grip her heart! Into what depths did
her own experience sink when she found herself in
the presence of her son's mental agony! Whither did
her disgrace and pain and desire for death flee, before the burning wish to help her dearly beloved child,
who wept in her lap? And in overflowing desire to aid
him, she whispered: "Don't cry, my boy. Everything
will be all right again." And when he shook his head,
as if in denial, she repeated in a firmer tone: "It will
be all right again, believe me." And she realized that
she had directed these words of consolation not only
to her son, but to herself. If it were in her power to
help her son out of his despair, to fill him with new
courage for life, that promise and strength must arise
out of this knowledge alone, and even more from his
gratitude and the feeling that he could belong again
solely to her. And suddenly the picture rose up before
her of that fantastic landscape in which she had

dreamed she was walking with Hugo, and a thought full of promise came to her: "If I were to undertake the voyage with Hugo, that I had been planning before that dreadful hour—and if we were never to return home from that journey?—And if out there, in foreign lands, far from all whom we know, in a purer atmosphere, we were to begin a new, a better life?—"

Then he suddenly raised his head from her lap—his eyes wandered, his mouth was distorted, and he cried hoarsely: "No, no, it will never be all right again!" And he got up, looked absently at his mother, took a few steps towards the table as if he were seeking something there, then walked up and down the room a few times with sunken head, and finally remained standing motionlessly at the window, his eyes turned to the night outside. "Hugo," called his mother, who had followed him with her eyes, but did not feel capable of getting up from the divan. And again, imploringly: "Hugo, my boy!" Then he turned to her again with that forced smile that was more painful than his weeping. And tremblingly she asked again: "What has happened?"

"Nothing, Mother," he answered in a sort of exaltation.

Now she stood up decidedly and went over to him. "Do you know why I came to you?" He merely looked at her. "Well, guess." He shook his head. "I wanted to ask you if you wouldn't like to go on a short trip."

"A trip," he repeated, seeming not to understand.

"Yes, Hugo, a trip—to Italy. We have time; school does not open for three weeks. We can be back long before that. Well, what do you think of it?"

"I don't know," he answered. She put her arms

around his neck. How much like Ferdinand he
looked! Once he had played the part of such a young
boy and had looked exactly like him. And she joked:
"Well, if you don't know, Hugo, I do know very well
that we are to take a journey. Yes, my boy, there's
no more to say about it. And now dry your eyes, cool
your forehead, and we'll go out together."

"Go out?"

"Yes, certainly. This is Sunday and there is no supper at home. Besides, we are to meet the others down
at the hotel. And the moonlight party on the lake,
don't you know that it is to take place today too?"

"Won't you go alone, Mother? I could come for you
later."

An extravagant fear suddenly seized her. Did he
want her out of the way? Why? For pity's sake! She
forced back the frightful thought. And controlling herself, she said: "Aren't you hungry?"

"No," he answered.

"Neither am I. How would it be to go first for a
little walk?"

"For a walk?"

"Yes, and then take the little detour to the hotel."

He hesitated for a while. She stood there in strained
expectation. Finally, he nodded. "Good, Mother, get
ready."

"Oh, I'm ready, I only need to get my coat." But
she did not budge. He seemed not to notice this, went
to his wash-basin, poured water out of the pitcher
into his hands, and cooled his forehead, eyes, and
cheeks. Then he ran his comb quickly through his
hair a few times. "Yes, make yourself handsome," said
Beatrice. And she remembered sadly how often she
had said these words in long past times to Ferdinand

when he was preparing to go out—God knew
where—

Hugo took his hat and said smilingly: "I am ready,
Mother."

She hurried into her room, got her coat, and didn't
fasten it until she was again in Hugo's room. "Now,
come," she said.

As both were leaving the house, the maid was just
returning from her Sunday holiday. But although she
greeted her mistress obsequiously, Beatrice noticed
from the almost imperceptible way in which that person lowered her eyes, that she knew all that had been
happening during the past weeks in this house— Still
she cared little about that. Everything was indifferent
to her now, next to the feeling of happiness, the long
lost feeling, that she had Hugo at her side.

They walked on through the meadows under the
mute blue night of the sky, close to each other, and
as rapidly as if they had a goal. At first they said
nothing. But before they entered the darkness of the
forest, Beatrice turned to her son and said: "Won't you
take my arm, Hugo?" Hugo took her arm and she felt
better. They walked on in the heavy shadows of the
trees, through whose thick branches the light from
some villa lying in its depths broke from place to place.
Beatrice let her hand slip over to Hugo's, she fondled
it, lifted it to her lips, and kissed it. He did not hinder
her. No, he knew nothing about her. Or was he just
making the best of it? Could he understand it, though
she was his mother? Soon they arrived at a broad
greenish-blue strip of light that lay before the gate of
Welponer's villa. Now they could see each other face
to face, but they looked ahead into the dark that immediately swallowed them up again. In this part of

the forest, the darkness was so thick, that they had
to slow their steps in order not to stumble. "Look out,"
said Beatrice from time to time. Hugo only shook his
head and they held firmly on to each other. After a
while they reached a path that, as they well knew from
happier hours, led down to the lake. They turned
down this path and again came into a faintly lighted
place where the trees stood back and left an open
meadow over which hung the still, starless sky. From
here, a weatherbeaten wooden stairway on one side of
which an unsteady hand railing offered some support,
led down to the road below, that to the right lost itself in the night, but to the left led again to the town
from which countless lights shone up to them. In mute
agreement, Beatrice and Hugo turned their footsteps
in this direction. And as if their walk together through
the dark, though speechless, still brought her closer
to him, Beatrice said in a light, almost joking tone:
"I don't like it when you cry, Hugo." He did not
answer, but looked absently away from her over the
steel-gray lake that now seemed to extend like a narrow strip beneath the mountains. "Formerly," began
Beatrice again, and there was a sigh in her voice, "formerly you told me everything." And while she said
that, she felt again as if she were saying these words
to Ferdinand and as if she would learn all the secrets
of her dead husband, that he had so disgracefully kept
from her, when he was yet on earth. "Am I becoming
insane?" she thought. "Am I already mad?" And as
if to recall herself to the present, she snatched Hugo's
arm with such force, that he drew back frightened.
But she went on: "Wouldn't it be easier for you, Hugo,
if you were to tell me about it?" And she clung to
him again. But while her own question continued to

sound within her, she felt that it was not only the
wish to relieve Hugo's soul that put this question into
her mouth, but that a peculiar kind of curiosity had
begun to rage in her, of which she was deeply
ashamed in her heart. And Hugo, as if he guessed the
secret disgrace of her question, answered nothing, and
in fact, let his arm slip out of hers again, as if by accident. Disappointed and left alone, Beatrice walked
beside him along the gloomy street. "What good am I
on this earth," she asked herself, "if I am not his
mother? Is today the day to lose everything? Am I
nothing more than a loose word in the mouths of
spoiled boys? And that feeling of belonging to Hugo,
of our common safety up there in the gracious dark
of the forest, was all that only an illusion? Then life
is no longer bearable, then everything is really over.
But why does the thought frighten me? Was it not
long ago decided? Did I not make up my mind earlier
to put an end to it all? And did I not know that nothing else remained for me to do?" And trailing behind
her, like jeering ghosts, hissed the terrible words that
she heard today through the crack in the blind, and
that meant her love and her shame, her happiness and
her death. And for a moment, she thought in sisterly
fashion of that other one, who once had run along the
sea-shore pursued by evil spirits, weary with tormenting lust.

They were nearing the village. The light that now
fell over the water just a few hundred feet away came
from the terrace where the lively party were eating
their evening meal and waiting for them. To enter
once more into such a gay circle seemed madness to
Beatrice; yes, entirely out of the realm of possibility.
Why was she walking down this road? Why did she

still remain at Hugo's side? What cowardice had it been, that had made her wish to bid him farewell, him, to whom she was no more than a tiresome old woman who wanted to force herself in on his secrets? Then, suddenly, she saw his eyes again turned on her with a look of entreaty, that awakened new fears and hopes in her.

"Hugo," she said.

And in tardy response to a question that she herself had already forgotten, he said: "It cannot be all right again. Telling will not help. It cannot."

"But, Hugo," she cried, as if newly emancipated, now that he had broken his silence. "Surely it will be all right; we are going away, Hugo, far away."

"What good will that do us, Mother?" Us?—Does that include me too? But isn't it better that way? Aren't we nearer to each other that way? He walked faster; she kept at his side—suddenly he stopped, looked out at the lake, and sighed deeply as if consolation and peace came to him from the solitude over the water. A few lighted row-boats were gliding out there. "Might that already be our party?" thought Beatrice casually. Certainly tonight they would have no moonlight. And suddenly an idea came to her: "How would it be, Hugo," she said, "if we were to go out rowing alone?" He looked up at the sky, as if seeking the moon. Beatrice understood the look and said: "We don't need the moon."

"What are we going to do out there on the dark water?" he asked weakly. She took his head in her hands, looked into his eyes, and said: "You shall tell me about it. You shall tell me what has happened to you, as you always have done formerly." She guessed that out in the friendly silence of the dark lake, his

shyness, that now kept him from telling his mother
what had happened, would leave him. Since she felt
no resistance in his silence, she turned in decision
towards the boat-house where her boat lay. The
wooden door was not locked. She went into the dark
boat-house with Hugo, unchained the boat hastily,
as if there were no time to lose, then she swung over
into the boat, and Hugo followed her. He took one
of the oars, pushed away with it, and a second later,
the open sky was over them. Now Hugo took the
other oar and rowed along the shore, past the Lake
Hotel, so near, that they could hear voices on the
terrace. It seemed to Beatrice that she could hear
the voice of the architect above the others. But she
could not discern single figures or faces. How easy
it was to flee from humanity! "What do I care what
they are saying about me, what they think, or know—?
You simply push your boat away from the shore, you
go so near to people that you can hear their voices,
and—it already makes no difference! When one is
not coming back—" It sounded deep within her, and
she trembled a little—she sat at the rudder and steered
the boat towards the middle of the lake. The moon
had not yet come up, but the water around them surrounded the boat with a dull circle of light, as if it
had preserved the sunlight within itself. At times a ray
came from the shore, in which Beatrice imagined she
saw Hugo's face becoming steadily fresher and freer
from care. When they were quite far out, Hugo let
the oars drop, took off his coat, and opened his collar. "How much like his father he looks," thought
Beatrice in painful surprise. "But I did not know him
when he was so young. And how beautiful he is. His
features are nobler than Ferdinand's—and yet I never

knew his real features, nor his voice. They were always the voices and faces of others. Am I seeing him today for the first time?" And she shuddered violently. But Hugo's features, now that the boat was entirely in the black shadow of the mountains, began gradually to grow hazy. He began to row again, but very slowly, and they hardly moved at all. "Now is the time," she thought, but she did not know for a moment for what it was time, until suddenly as if awakened out of a dream, the burning wish returned to her mind to know Hugo's experience. And she asked: "Well, then, Hugo, what has happened?" He merely shook his head. But with growing excitement, she felt that he was no longer so firm in his refusal to speak. "Just speak to me, Hugo," she said. "You can tell me everything. I already know so much. You can hardly imagine—" And as if she might banish the last trace of the spell, she whispered into the night: "Fortunata."

Through Hugo's body went a shudder, so powerful that it seemed to break the boat in two. Beatrice asked further: "You were with her today—and is this how you come back? What did she do to you, Hugo?" He was silent, rowed on rhythmically, and gazed into space. Suddenly, Beatrice was enlightened. She pressed her hands to her forehead, as if she did not understand why she had not guessed it earlier, and bending closer to Hugo, she whispered quickly: "The distant captain was there, was he not? And he found you with her?"

Hugo looked up. "The captain?"

Now for the first time, she realized that the man whom she meant was not a captain. "I mean the Baron," she said. "Was he there? He found you? He insulted you? He beat you, Hugo?"

"No, Mother, the one you mention was not there. I do not know him at all. I swear it to you, Mother."

"Then, what is it?" asked Beatrice. "Doesn't she love you any more? Is she tired of you? Did she laugh at you? Did she show you the door? Is that it, Hugo?"

"No, Mother." And he was silent.

"Well, then, Hugo, what is it? Do tell me."

"Don't ask me, Mother, don't ask me any more. It's too horrible."

Now her curiosity burst into flame. She felt that from somewhere in the confusion of this day so full of puzzles, so full of old and new questions, she must find the answer. She groped in the air with both hands, as if she wanted to gather something that was scattered there. She slipped down from the seat at the rudder, and sat at Hugo's feet. "Now, then, speak," she began. "You can tell me everything. You need not be shy, I understand everything. I am your mother, Hugo, and I am a woman. Can you realize that? You must not be afraid that you can wound me, or offend my modesty. I have experienced much these past days. I am still not an—old woman. I understand everything. Too much, my son—you must not think that we are so far apart, Hugo, and that there are things that you must not say to me." She felt in her confusion how she was giving herself up, how she was decoying him. "Oh, if you knew, Hugo, if you only knew—"

And the answer came: "I know, Mother." . . .

Beatrice trembled. Yet she felt no shame, only a relieved consciousness of being nearer to him and belonging to him. She sat at his feet at the bottom of the boat and took his hands in hers. "Tell me," she whispered.

And he spoke, but told her nothing. With heavy incoherent words he merely declared that he could never be seen among people again. What had happened to him today threw him forever out of the realm of the living.

"What has happened to you?"

"I was not in my right mind—I don't know what happened. They made me drunk."

"They made you drunk? Who, who? You were—not alone with Fortunata?" She remembered that she had seen him recently in the company of Wilhelmine Fallehn and the circus-rider. Then were they there? And with choking voice, she asked again, "What has happened?" But without Hugo's answer, she already knew. A picture painted itself before her eyes in the night, from which she wanted to turn in horror, but it followed her relentlessly and insolently behind her closed eyes. And in new, frightful suspicion she opened her eyes again, and turning them directly to Hugo sitting there in the darkness with tightly pressed lips, she asked: "Is it only since today that you know? Did they tell you over there?"

He made no answer, but a shudder ran through his body, so wild that it threw him weakly to the bottom of the boat beside Beatrice. She groaned aloud once in despair; and trembling forlornly, she grasped Hugo's feverishly shaking hands that he had stretched out to her. Now he left them in hers, and that did her good. She drew him nearer to her, pressed against him, and an agony of longing came from the depths of her soul and flowed mystically over to him. And both of them felt as if their boat, though it stood almost still, were moving on and on in growing speed. Whither was it taking them? Through what dream without aim? To what world without law? Did it ever have to go back to land? Dared it ever? Together they were bound on their everlasting journey; Heaven held no promise of morning for them in its clouds; and weakly succumbing to the anticipation of everlasting night, they gave each other their dying lips. The boat glided on, oarless, to farther shores, and Beatrice felt that she was kissing one whom she had never known before, one who was her husband for the first time.

As she felt consciousness returning, she had enough strength of mind left to beware of a complete awakening. Holding both Hugo's hands tightly in hers, she stepped to the side of the boat. As it listed, Hugo's eyes opened in a look touched with a fear that bound him for the last time to the common lot of man. Beatrice drew her beloved, her son, her partner in death, to her breast. Understanding, forgiving, emancipated, he closed his eyes. But hers took in once more the gray bank rising up in the menacing dusk, and before the indifferent waves pressed between her eyes, her dying look drank in the shadows of the fading world.

"NONE BUT THE BRAVE"

Translated from the German of
LEUTNANT GUSTL

by

RICHARD L. SIMON

I

How long is this thing going to last? Let's see
what time it is . . . perhaps I shouldn't look at my
watch at a serious concert like this. But no one
will see me. If any one does, I'll know he's paying just as little attention as I am. In that case I certainly won't be embarrassed. . . . Only quarter to ten?
. . . I feel as though I'd been here for hours. I'm just
not used to going to concerts. . . . What's that they're
playing? I'll have a look at the program. . . . Yes,
that's what it is: an oratorio. Thought it was a mass.
That sort of thing belongs in church, and in church
only. There's one advantage that church has over a
concert: you can leave whenever you want to.—I wish
I were sitting on the aisle! Steady, steady! Even ora-
torios end some time. Perhaps this one's very beautiful, and I'm just in the wrong mood. Well, why not?
When I think that I came here for diversion . . . I
should have given my ticket to Benedek. He likes this
sort of thing. Plays violin. But in that case Kopetzsky
would have felt insulted. It was very nice of him;
meant well, at least. He's a good fellow, Kopetzsky!
The only one I can really trust. . . . His sister is singing up there on the platform. There are at least a hundred women up there—all of them dressed in black.
How am I to know which one is Kopetzsky's sister?
They gave him a ticket because she was singing in
the chorus. . . . Why then, didn't Kopetzsky go?—
They're singing rather nicely now. It's inspiring!

395

Bravo! Bravo! . . . Yes, I'll applaud along with the rest of them. The fellow next to me is clapping as if he were crazy. Wonder if he really likes it as much as all that?—Pretty girl over there in the box! Is she looking at me or at the man with the blond beard? . . . Ah, here we have a solo! Who is it? Alto: FRÄULEIN WALKER, SOPRANO: FRÄULEIN MICHALEK . . . that one is probably the soprano . . . I haven't been at the opera for an awfully long time. Opera always amuses me, even when it's dull. I might go again the day after tomorrow. They're playing *Traviata*. No, day after tomorrow I'll probably be dead! Oh, nonsense; I can't even believe that myself! Just wait, Doctor, you'll stop making remarks like that! You'll get what's coming to you! . . .

I wish I could see the girl in the box more clearly. I'd like to borrow an opera glass. But this fellow next to me would probably eat me if I broke in on his reveries. . . . Wonder where Kopetzky's sister is sitting? Wonder if I'd recognize her? I've met her only two or three times, the last time at the Officers' Club. Wonder if they're all good girls, all hundred of them? Oh, Lord! . . . ASSISTED BY THE SINGING CLUB— Singing Club . . . that's a good one! I'd always imagined that members of a Singing Club would be something like Vienna chorus girls; that is, I might have known they'd be nothing like them at all! Pleasant recollection! That time at *Green Gate* . . . What was her name? And then she once sent me a postcard from Belgrade . . . that's a good place too! Well, Kopetzsky's lucky right now, sitting in the café, smoking a good cigar!

Why's that fellow staring at me all the time? I suppose he notices how bored I am . . . I'll have you know that if you keep on looking fresh like that I'll meet you in the lobby later and settle with you! He's looking the other way already! They're all afraid of my eyes. . . . "You have the most beautiful eyes I've ever seen!" Steffi said that the other day. . . . Oh Steffi, Steffi, Steffi!—It's Steffi's fault that I'm sitting here bored by the hour. Oh, these letters from Steffi postponing engagements—they're getting on my nerves! What fun this evening might have been! Think I'll read Steffi's letter again. There, I've got it. But if I take it out of my pocket, I'll annoy the fellow next to me.—I know what's in it . . . she can't come because she has to have dinner with "him." . . . That was funny a week ago when she was at the garden party with him, and I was sitting opposite Kopetzsky; she was continually flirting with me. He didn't notice a thing—why, it's amazing! He's probably a Jew. Works in a bank. And his black mustache. . . . Probably a lieutenant in the reserve as well! Well, he'd better not come to practice in our regiment! They keep on commissioning too many Jews—that's the cause of all this anti-Semitism. The other day at the club, when the affair came up between the Doctor and the Mannheimers . . . they say the Mannheimers themselves are Jews, baptized, of course . . . they don't look it—especially Mrs. Mannheimer . . . blonde, beautiful figure. . . . It was a good party, all in all. Wonderful dinner, excellent cigars. . . . They must have piles of money.

Hooray! It'll soon be over! Yes, the whole chorus is rising . . . looks fine—imposing!—Organ too! I like the organ. . . . Ah! that sounds good! Fine! It's really true, I ought to go to concerts more often. . . . I'll tell Kopetzsky how beautiful it was. . . . Wonder whether I'll meet him at the café today?—Oh Lord, I don't feel like going there; I got enough of it yesterday! A hundred and sixty gulden on one card—it was stupid! And who won all the money? Ballert. Ballert, who needed it least of all. . . . It's Ballert's fault that I had to go to this rotten concert. . . . Otherwise I might have played again today, and perhaps won back something. But I'm glad I've promised myself to stay away from cards for a whole month. . . . Mother'll make a face again when she gets my letter!—Ah, she ought to go and see Uncle. He's rich as Crœsus; a couple of hundred gulden never worried him. If I could only get him to send me a regular allowance. . . . But, no, I've got to beg for every crown. Then he always says that crops were poor last year! . . . Wonder whether I ought to spend a two weeks' vacation there again this summer? I'll be bored to death there. . . . If the . . . What was her name? . . . Funny, I can't remember a single name! Oh, yes: Etelka! . . . Couldn't understand a word of German . . . nor was it necessary. . . . There was nothing to say! . . . Yes, it ought to be all right, fourteen days of country air and fourteen nights with Etelka or some one else. . . . But I ought to be with Papa and Mamma for at least a week. She looked badly last Christmas. . . . Well, she'll be over her worries by now. If I were in her place I'd be happy that Papa's been retired on pension.—And Clara'll be married some time. Uncle will contribute something. . . . Twenty-eight isn't so old. . . . I'm sure Steffi's no younger. . . . It's really remarkable: the fast girls stay young much longer. Maretti, who played in *Sans Gêne* recently,—she's easily thirty-seven, and looks . . . Well, I wouldn't have said no! Too bad she didn't ask me. . . .

Getting hot! Not over yet? Ah, I'm looking forward

to the fresh air outside. I'll take a little walk around the
Ring. . . . Today: early to bed, so as to be fresh for
tomorrow afternoon! Funny, how little I think of it; it
means nothing to me! The first time it worried me a
bit. Not that I was afraid, but I was nervous the night
before. . . . Lieutenant Bisanz was a tough opponent.
—And still, nothing happened to me! . . . And it's
already a year and a half since then! Well, if Bisanz did
nothing to me, the Doctor certainly won't! Still, these
inexperienced fencers are often the most dangerous
ones. Doschintzky's told me that on one occasion a
fellow who had never had a sword in his hand before
almost killed him; and today Doschintzky is the fencing instructor of the militia.—I wonder whether he was
as good then as he is now? . . . Most important of all:
keep cool. I don't feel the least angry now—but he was
impudent—unbelievably impudent. He'd probably not
have done it if he hadn't been drinking champagne.
. . . Such insolence! He's probably a Socialist. All the
enemies of law and order are Socialists these days.
They're a gang. . . . They'd like to do away with the
whole army; but they never think of who could help
them out if the Chinese ever invaded the country.
Fools! I'll have to make an example of one of them. I
was quite right. I'm really glad that I didn't let him
get away with that remark. I'm furious whenever I
think of it! But I behaved superbly. The Colonel said
it was absolutely correct. I'll get something out of this
affair. I know some who would have let him get away
with it. Muller certainly would have taken it "objectively," or whatever they call it. This being "objective"
is a lot of nonsense. "Lieutenant"—just the way in
which he said "Lieutenant" was annoying. "You will
have to admit—" . . . —How did the thing start?

How did I ever start talking to a Socialist? . . . As I
recall it, the brunette I was taking to the buffet was
with us, and then this young fellow who paints hunting
scenes—what is his name? . . . Good Lord, he's to
blame for it all! He was talking about the manœuvres;
and it was only then the the Doctor joined us and said
something or other I didn't like—about playing at war
—something like that—but I couldn't say anything
just then. . . . Yes, that's it. . . . And then they were
talking about the Military School. . . . Yes, that's the
way it was. . . . And I was telling them about a patri-
otic rally. . . . And then the Doctor said—not immediately, but it grew out of my talk about the rally—
"Lieutenant, you'll admit, won't you, that all of your
friends haven't gone into military service for the sole
purpose of defending our Fatherland!" What a nerve
of any one to dare say a thing like that to an officer! I
wish I could remember exactly how I answered him—
Oh, yes, something about "fools rushing in where
angels fear to tread" . . . Yes, that was it. . . . And
there was a fellow there who wanted to smooth over
matters—an elderly man with a cold in the head—but
I was wild! The Doctor had said it in a tone that meant
he was talking about me, and me only. The only thing
he could have added was that they had expelled me
from college and for that reason I had to go into military service. . . . Those people don't understand our
point of view. They're too dull-witted. . . . Not every
one can experience the thrill I did the first time I wore
a uniform. . . . Last year at the manœuvres—I would
have given a great deal if it had suddenly been in
earnest. . . . Mirovic told me he felt exactly the same
way. And then when His Majesty rode up at the front
and the Colonel addressed us—only a nincompoop

wouldn't have been thrilled by it. . . . And now a
boor comes along who has been a bookworm all his
life and has the temerity to make a fresh remark. . . .
Oh, just wait. Just see how fit you'll be for the
duel! . . .

Well, what's this? It must be over by now. . . .
"Ye, his Angels, praise the Lord"— Surely, that's the
final chorus. . . . Beautiful, really beautiful! And here
I've completely forgotten the girl in the box who was
flirting with me before. . . . Where is she now? . . .
Already gone. . . . That one over there seems rather
nice. . . . Stupid of me—I left my opera glasses at
home. I wish the cute little one over there would turn
around. She sits there so properly. The one next to her
is probably her mother. . . . I wonder whether I ought
to consider marriage seriously? Willy was no older
than I when he married. He's done well by himself—
and always a pretty wife at home. . . . Too bad that
just today Steffi had no time! If I only knew where she
were. I'd like to have a little *tête-a-tête* with her. There'd
be a fine how-do-you-do! If he'd ever catch me, he'd
palm her off on me. When I think what it must cost
Fleiss to keep the Winterfeld woman!—and even at
that, she's unfaithful to him right and left. Some day
she'll get the fright that's coming to her. . . . Bravo,
bravo! Ah, it's over. . . . Oh, it feels good to get up and
stretch. Well! How long is he going to take to put that
opera glass into his pocket?

"Pardon me, won't you let me pass?"

What a crowd! Better let the people go by. . . .
Gorgeous person. . . . Wonder whether they're genuine diamonds? . . . That one over there's rather attractive. . . . The way she's flirting with me! . . .
Why, yes, my lady, I'd be glad to! . . . Oh, what a

nose!—Jewess. . . . Another one. It's amazing, half of
them are Jews. One can't even hear an oratorio un-
molested these days. . . . Now we're crowding together. Why is that idiot back of me pushing so? I'll
teach him better manners. . . . Oh, it's an elderly man!
. . . Who's that bowing to me over there? . . . How
do you do. Charmed! I haven't the slightest idea who
he is. . . . I think I'll go right over to Leidinger's for
a bite. Maybe Steffi'll be there after all. Why didn't she
write and let me know where she's going with him?
She probably didn't know herself. Oh, it's fierce, this
day-to-day existence. . . . Poor thing— So, here's the
exit. . . . Ah! that one's pretty as a picture! All alone?
She's smiling at me. There's an idea—I'll follow her!
. . . Now, down the steps. . . . Oh, a Major—a recent
graduate—very nice, the way he returned my salute.
I'm not the only officer here after all. . . . Where did
the pretty girl go? . . . There she is, standing by the
banister. . . . Now to the wardrobe. . . . Better not
lose her. . . . She's nabbed him already. What a hussy!
Having some one call for her, and then laughing at
me out of the side of her face! They're all worthless.
. . . Good Lord, what a mob there at the wardrobe.
Better wait a little while. Why doesn't the idiot take my
check?

"Here, Number 224! It's hanging there! What's the
matter—are you blind? Hanging there! There! At
last. . . . Thank you." That fatty there is taking up
most of the wardrobe. . . . "If you please!" . . .

"Patience, patience."

What's the fellow saying?

"Just have a little patience."

I'll have to answer him in kind. "Why don't you allow some room?"

"You'll get there in time." What's he saying? Did he say that to me? That's rather strong! I won't swallow that. "Keep quiet!"

"What did you say?"

That's a fine way to talk! This has got to stop right now.

"Don't push!"

"Shut your mouth!" I shouldn't have said that. That was a bit rough. . . . Well, I've done it now.

"Exactly what did you mean by that?"

Now he's turning around. Why I know him!— Heavens, it's the baker, the one who always comes to the café. . . . What's he doing here? He probably has a daughter or something in the chorus. Well, what's this?—What's he trying to do? It looks as though. . . . Yes, Great Scott, he has the hilt of my sword in his hand! What's the matter? Is the man crazy? . . . "You, Sir! . . ."

"You, Lieutenant, just be altogether quiet."

What's he saying? For Heaven's sake, I hope no one's heard it. No, he's talking very softly. . . . Well, why doesn't he let go of my sword? Great God! This is getting rough. I can't budge his hand from the hilt. Let's not have a rumpus here! Isn't the Major behind him? Can any one notice that he's holding the hilt of my sword? Why, he's talking to me! What's he saying!

"Lieutenant, if you dare to make the slightest fuss, I'll pull your sword out of the sheath, break it in two and send the pieces to your Regimental Commander. Do you understand me, you young fat-head?"

What did he say? Am I dreaming? Is he really talking to me? How shall I answer him? But he's in earnest. He's really pulling the sword out. Great God! he's doing it! . . . I can feel it! He's already pulling

it! What is he saying? For God's sake, no scandal!—
What's he forever saying?

"But I have no desire to ruin your career. . . . So
just be a good boy. . . . Don't be scared. Nobody's
heard it. . . . Everything's all right. . . . And so that
no one will think we've been fighting I'll act most
friendly towards you. . . . I am honored, Sir Lieutenant. It has been a pleasure—I am honored."

Good God, did I dream that? . . . Did he really say
that? . . . Where is he? . . . There he goes. . . . I
must draw my sword and run him through— Heavens,
I hope nobody heard it. . . . No, he talked very softly
—right in my ear. Why don't I go after him and crack
open his skull? . . . No, it can't be done. It can't be
done. . . . I should have done it at once. . . . Why
didn't I do it immediately? . . . I couldn't. . . . He
wouldn't let go the hilt, and he's ten times as strong
as I am. . . . If I had said another word he would
actually have broken the sword in two. I ought to be
glad that he spoke no louder. If any one had heard it,
I'd have had to shoot myself on the spot. . . . Perhaps
it was only a dream. Why is that man by the pillar
looking at me like that?—Did he really hear it? . . .
I'll ask him . . . ask him?!—Am I crazy?—Do I look
queer?—I must be pale as a sheet— Where's the swine?
I've got to kill him! . . . He's gone. . . . The whole
place is empty. . . . Where's my coat? . . . Why, I'm
already wearing it. . . . I didn't even notice it. . . .
Who helped me on with it? . . . Oh, that one there.
I'll have to tip him. . . . So. But what's it all about?
Did it really happen? Did any one really talk to me
like that? Did any one really call me a fat-head? And I
didn't cut him to pieces on the spot? . . . But I
couldn't. . . . He had a fist like iron. I just stood there

as though I were nailed to the floor. I think I must have lost my senses. Otherwise, I would have used my other hand. . . . But then he would have drawn out my sword, and broken it, and everything would have been over. . . . Over and done with! And afterwards, when he walked away, it was too late. . . . I couldn't have run my sword through him from the back.

What, am I already on the street? How did I ever get here?—Its so cool. . . . Oh, the wind feels fine! . . . Who's that over there? Why are they looking over at me? I wonder whether they really heard it. . . . No, no one could have heard it. . . . I'm sure of it—I looked around immediately! No one paid any attention to me. No one heard a thing. . . . But he said it anyhow. Even if nobody heard it, he certainly said it. I just stood there and took it as if some one had knocked me silly. . . . But I couldn't say a word—couldn't do a thing. All I did was stand there—quiet, absolutely quiet! . . . It's awful; it's unbearable; I must kill him on the spot, whenever I happen to meet him! . . . I let a swine like that get away with it! And he knows me. . . . Great Heavens, he knows me—knows who I am! . . . He can tell everybody just exactly what he said to me! . . . No, he wouldn't do that. Otherwise, he wouldn't have talked so quietly. . . . He just wanted me to hear it alone! . . . But how do I know that he won't repeat it today or tomorrow, to his wife, to his daughter, to his friends in the café— For God's sake, I'll see him again tomorrow. As soon as I step into the café tomorrow, I'll see hm sitting there as he does every day, playing Tarok with Schlesinger and the fancy flower merchant. No, that can't happen. I won't allow it to. The moment I see him I'll run him through. . . . No, I can't do that. . . . I should have done it

right then and there! . . . If I only had! I'll go to the
Colonel and tell him about the whole affair. . . . Yes,
right to the Colonel. . . . The Colonel is always
friendly—and I'll say to him—Colonel, I wish to report, Sir. He grasped the hilt of my sword and wouldn't
let go of it; it was just as though I were completely un-
armed. . . . What will the Colonel say?—What will
he say? There's just one answer: dishonorable dis-
charge! . . . Are those recruits over there? Disgusting. At night they look like officers. . . . Yes, they're
saluting!—If they knew—if they really knew! . . .
There's the Hochleitner Café. Probably a couple of officers in my company are there now. . . . Perhaps one
or more whom I know. . . . Wonder if it wouldn't
be best to tell the first one I meet all about it—but just
as if it had happened to some one else? . . . I'm already growing a bit crazy. . . . Where the devil am I
walking? What business have I out here in the street?
—Where should I go? Wasn't I going to the Leidinger
Café? Haha! If I were to sit down with them I'm sure
every one would see what had happened to me. . . .
Well, something must happen. . . . But what? . . .
Nothing, nothing at all—no one heard it. No one
knows a thing. At least for the time being. . . . Perhaps I ought to visit him at his home and beg him to
swear to me that he'll never tell a soul.—Ah, better to
put a bullet through my head at once. That would be
the cleverest way of all—the cleverest!—there's just
nothing else left for me—nothing. If I were to ask the
Colonel or Kopetzsky, or Blany, or Freidmair:—they'd
all tell me the same thing. How would it be if I were to
talk it over with Kopetzsky? Yes, that seems the most
sensible thing to do. But what about tomorrow—tomorrow—yes, that's right, tomorrow—at four o'clock,

in the armory, I'm to fight a duel. But I can't do it, I'm
no longer qualified for duelling. Nonsense, nonsense,
not a soul knows it, not a soul!—There are hundreds of
people walking around to whom worse things have
happened. . . . What about all those stories I've heard
about Deckener—how he and Rederow fought with
pistols. . . . And the duelling committee decided that
the duel could take place at that. . . . But what will the
committee decide about me?—Fat-head, fat-head, and
I just stood there and took it—! Great Heavens, it
makes no difference whether any one knows it or not!
The chief thing is: I know he said it! I feel as though
I'm not the same man I was an hour ago—I know that
I'm not qualified for duelling, and that I must shoot
myself. I wouldn't have another calm moment in my
life. I'd always be afraid that some one might know
about it in some way or another, and that some time
some one might tell me about this evening's affair!—
What a happy man I was an hour ago! . . . Just because Kopetzsky gave me a ticket, and just because
Steffi postponed her date—destiny hangs on things like
that. . . . This afternoon, all was sailing smoothly, and
now I am a lost man about to shoot himself. . . . Why
am I running this way? No one is chasing me. What's
the time there? 1, 2, 3, 4, 5, 6, 7, 8, 9, 10, 11. . . . Eleven,
Eleven. . . . I ought to go and get something to eat.
. . . I'll certainly land somewhere. I might go and sit
down in some little restaurant where no one would
know me.—At any rate, a man must eat even though
he kill himself immediately after. Haha! Death is no
child's play. . . . Who said that recently?—It makes
no difference.

I wonder who'll worry about me most, . . . Mamma
or Steffi? . . . Steffi, Great God, Steffi! . . . She won't

allow any one to notice how she feels. Otherwise "he"
will throw her out. . . . Poor little thing!—At my
regiment. . . . No one will have the slightest idea why
I did it. They'll all have their theories on why Gustl
committed suicide. But no one will hit upon the real
solution: that I had to shoot myself because a miserable baker, a low person who just happened to have a
strong fist . . . It's too silly—too silly for words!—
For that reason, a fellow like myself, young and fit.
. . . Well, they'll all say he didn't have to commit
suicide for a silly reason like that. It's a pity! But if I
were to ask any one right now, they'd all give me the
same answer. . . . And if I were to ask myself. . . .
Oh, the devil, we're absolutely helpless against civilians.
People think that we're better off just because we carry
swords, and if one of us ever makes use of a weapon,
the story goes around that we're all born murderers.
The paper will carry a story:

"Young Officer Suicide" . . . How do they always
put it? . . . "Motive Concealed" . . . Haha! . . .
"Mourning at his Coffin." . . .—But it's true. I feel as
if I were forever telling myself a story. . . . It's true.
. . . I must commit suicide. There's nothing else left
to do—I can't allow Kopetzsky and Blany to come tomorrow morning and say to me: Sorry, we can't be
your seconds. I'd be a fool if I'd give them the chance
—fool that I am, standing quietly by and letting myself be called a fat-head. . . . Tomorrow every one will
know it. Fancy myself believing for a moment that a
person like that won't repeat it everywhere. . . . Why,
his wife knows it already! Tomorrow every one in the
café will know it. All the waiters will know it. Schlesinger will know it—so will the cashier girl— And
even if he promised that he wouldn't tell anybody,

he'll certainly tell them the day after tomorrow. . . .
And if not then, in a week from now. . . . And if he
were to get apoplexy tonight, I'd know it. . . . I'd
know it. And I could no longer wear a cape and carry
a sword if such a curse were on me! . . . So, I've got
to do it—I've got to do it—what else?—Tomorrow
afternoon the Doctor might just as well run his sword
through me. . . . Things like this have happened before. . . . And Bauer, poor fellow, lost his mind and
died three days later. . . . And Brenitsch fell off his
horse and broke his neck. . . . And furthermore,
there's nothing else to do, not for me anyhow, certainly not for me!—There are men who would take
it more lightly. . . . But God, what sort of men are
they! . . . Fleischsalcher slapped Ringeiner's face
when he caught him with his wife, whereupon Ringeiner quit and is now somewhere out in the country,
married. . . . There are women, I suppose, who'll
marry people like that! . . . On my word, I'll never
shake hands with him if he ever returns to Vienna!
. . . Well, you've heard it, Gustl:—life is over for you
—finished, once and for all. I know it now, it's a simple
story. . . . So! I'll be altogether calm. . . . I've always
known it: if the occasion were ever to arise, I'd be
calm, altogether calm. . . . But I would never have
believed that it would come to this. . . .—That I'd
have to kill myself just because a . . . Perhaps I didn't
understand him correctly. . . . He was talking in an
altogether different tone at the end. . . . I was simply
a little out of my mind on account of the singing and
the heat. . . . Perhaps I was momentarily demented,
and it's all not true. . . . Not true, haha! Not true!—
I can still hear it. . . . It's still ringing in my ears,
and I can still feel in my fingers how I tried to move

his hand from the hilt of my sword. He's a husky brute. . . . I'm no weakling myself. Franziski is the only man in the regiment who's stronger than I.

Already at the bridge? . . . How far am I running? If I keep on this way I'll be at Kagran by midnight. . . . Haha! . . . Good Lord, how happy we were last September when we entered Kagran. Only two hours more, and Vienna! . . . I was dead tired when we got there. . . . Had slept like a log all afternoon, and by evening we were already at Ronacher's. . . . Kopetzsky and Ladsiner. . . . Who else was along with us at the time?—Yes, that's right . . . that volunteer, the one who told us the Jewish stories while we were marching. Sometimes they're pleasant fellows, these one-year men. . . . But all of them ought to become substitutes. For what sense is there to it: all of us slave for ages, and a fellow like him serves a year and receives the same distinction as we. . . . It's unfair!— But what's it to me? Why bother about it all? A private in the hospital corps counts for more than I do right now. . . . I no longer belong on the face of the earth. . . . All is over with me. Honor lost—all lost! . . . There's nothing else for me to do but load my revolver and . . . Gustl, Gustl, you're not thinking this thing out properly! Come to your senses! . . . There's no way out. . . . No matter how you torture your brain, there's no way out!—The point is, now that the end is here, behave like an officer and a gentleman so that the Colonel will say: He was a good fellow, we'll always think well of him! . . . How many companies attend the funeral of a lieutenant? . . . I really must know that. . . . Haha! Even if the whole battalion turns out, even if the whole garrison turns out, and they fire twenty salutes, I'll never wake

up! Last summer, after the Army Steeplechase, I was
sitting in front of the café with Engel. . . . Funny,
I've never seen the fellow since. . . . Why did he have
his left eye bandaged? I always wanted to ask him,
but it didn't seem proper. . . . There go two artillery-
men. . . . They probably think I'm following that
woman. . . . Does she *have* to solicit me? . . . Oh,
Lord! I wonder how that one can possibly earn a living. . . . I'd sooner . . . However, in time of need a
person will do almost anything . . . In Przemsyl—I
was so horrified that I swore I'd never look at a woman
again. . . . That was a ghastly time up there in Galicia. . . . Altogether a stroke of fortune that we ever
returned to Vienna. Bokonny is still in Sambor, and
will stay for ten years more, getting old and gray.
. . . What happened to me today would never have
happened if I'd remained there myself, and I'd far
sooner grow old in Galicia than . . . Than what?
Than what— What is it? What is it? Am I crazy—
the way I always forget?—Good God, I forget it every
moment. . . . Has it ever happened before that a man
within two hours of putting a bullet through his head
digresses on all conceivable matters that no longer
concern him? I feel as if I were drunk. Haha, drunk
indeed! Drunk with death! Drunk with suicide! Ha,
trying to be funny! Yes, I'm in a good mood—must
have been born with one. Certainly, if I ever told anybody they'd say I was lying.—I feel as if I already
had the revolver at my head. . . . Now, I'd pull the
trigger—in a second all is over. . . . Not every one gets
over it so easily—others brood over it month after
month. My poor cousin, on his back two years, couldn't
move, had the most excruciating pains, what a time!
. . . Care is the only thing necessary; to aim well, so

that nothing unforeseen happens, as it did to that substitute last year. . . . Poor devil, didn't die, but became blind. . . . What ever happened to him? Wonder where he's living now. Terrible to run around the
way he—that is, he can't run around, he's led. A chap
like him—can't be more than twenty years old right
now. He shot at the girl more accurately. . . . She was
dead at once. . . . Unbelievable, the reasons people
have for killing. How can any one be jealous? . . .
I've never been jealous in my whole life. At this very
moment Steffi is sitting comfortably at the dance hall;
then she will go home with "him." . . . Doesn't mean
a thing to me. . . . Not a thing. She has a nicely fur-
nished place—a little bathroom with a red lamp—
When she recently came in, in her green kimono. . . .
I'll never see the green kimono again— Steffi, herself,
I'll never see again— And I'll never go up the fine
broad steps in Gusshaus Strasse. Steffi will keep on
amusing herself as if nothing had happened; she shan't
tell a soul that her beloved Gustl committed suicide.
But she'll weep—oh, yes, she'll weep. A great many
people will weep. . . . Good God, Mamma!—No, no,
I can't think about it. Oh, no, I can't bear to. . . .
You're not to think about home at all, Gustl, you understand? Not—at—all.

   This isn't bad. I'm now on the way to the Prater.
Midnight. . . . That's another thing I didn't think of
this morning, that tonight I'd be taking a walk in the
Prater. . . . Wonder what the watchman there thinks.
. . . Well, I'll walk on. It's rather nice here. No fun
to take a bite; no fun in the café. The air is pleasant
and it's quiet. . . . Indeed, I'll have a great deal of
quiet—as much as I could possibly want. Haha!—But
I'm altogether out of breath. I must have been running

like crazy. . . . Slower, slower, Gustl, you'll miss nothing, there's nothing more to do, nothing, absolutely nothing! What's this, am I getting a chill?— Probably on account of worrying, and I haven't eaten a thing. What's that beautiful smell? . . . Are the blossoms out yet?—What's today?—The fourth of April. It's been raining a great deal the last few days, but the street is almost entirely bare and it's dark. Hooh! Dark enough to give you the shivers. . . . That was really the only time in my whole life I was scared —when I was a little kid that time in the woods. . . . But I wasn't so little at that. . . . Fourteen or fifteen. . . . How long ago was it?—Nine years. . . . Easily. At eighteen I was a substitute; at twenty a lieutenant and next year I'll be . . . What'll I be next year? What do I mean; next year? What do I mean; next week? What do I mean; tomorrow? . . . What's this? Teeth chattering? Oh!—Well! let them chatter a while. Lieutenant, you are altogether alone right now and have no reason for showing off. . . . It's bitter, oh, it's bitter. . . .

I'll sit on that bench. . . . Ah. . . . How far have I come?—How dark it is! That behind me there, that must be the second café. . . . I was in there last summer at the time our band gave a concert. . . . With Kopetzsky and with Rüttner—there were a couple of others along. . . . —Lord, I'm tired. . . . As tired as if I'd been marching for the last ten hours. . . . Yes, it would be fine to go to sleep now.—Ha, a lieutenant without shelter! . . . Yes, I really ought to go home. . . . What'll I do at home?—But what am I doing in the Prater?—Ah, it would be best never to get up at all—to sleep here and never wake up. . . . Yes, that would be comfortable! But, Lieutenant, things aren't going to be as comfortable as that for you. . . . What next?—Well I might really consider the whole affair in orderly sequence. . . . All things must be considered. . . . Life is like that. . . . Well, then, let's consider. . . . Consider what? . . . —No, the air feels fine. . . . I ought to go to the Prater more often at night. . . . That should have occurred to me sooner. It's all a thing of the past—the Prater, the air and taking walks. . . . Well, then, what next?—Off with my cap. It's pressing on my forehead. . . . I can't think properly. . . . Ah. . . . So! . . . . Now, Gustl, collect your thoughts, make your final arrangements! Tomorrow morning will be the end. . . . Tomorrow morning at seven . . . seven o'clock is a beautiful hour. Haha!—At eight o'clock when school begins, all will be over. . . . Kopetzsky won't be able to teach —he'll be too broken up. . . . But naturally he'll know nothing about it. . . . He may not have heard of it. . . . They found Max Lippay only in the afternoon, and in the morning he had shot himself, and not a soul heard of it. . . . But why bother about whether Kopetzsky will teach school tomorrow. . . . Ha!—Well, then, at seven o'clock— Yes. . . . Well, what next? . . . Nothing more to consider. I'll shoot myself in my room and then—basta! The funeral will be Monday. . . . I know one man who'll enjoy it: the Doctor. The duel can't take place on account of the suicide of one of the combatants. . . . Wonder what they'll say at Mannheimers?—Well, he won't make much of it. . . . But his wife, his pretty, blonde . . . She was worth considering. . . . Oh, yes, I would have had a chance with her if I'd only taken a little better care of myself. . . . Yes, with her it might have been something altogether different from

Steffi. . . . Be on your toes all the time: that is, court
in the proper way, send flowers, talk decently . . . not:
meet me tomorrow afternoon at the barracks! . . .
Yes, a decent woman like her—that might have been
something. The captain's wife at Przemsyl wasn't decent. . . . I could swear that Lubitzsky and Wer-
mutek . . . and the shabby substitute—she was unfaithful with him too. . . . But Mannheimer's wife.
. . . Yes, that would be entirely different. That would
have been an experience that might almost have made
me a different man—she might have given me more
polish—or have given me more respect for myself—
But always that kind . . . and I began so young—I
was only a boy that time on my first vacation when
I was home with my parents in Graz. . . . The Reidl
woman was also along—she was Bohemian. . . .
Must have been twice as old as I—came home only the
following morning. . . . The way Father looked at
me. . . . And Clara. I was most ashamed of all before
Clara. . . . She was engaged at the time. . . . Wonder why the engagement never materialized. I didn't
worry much about it at the time. Poor thing, never
had much luck—and now she's going to lose her
only brother. . . . Yes, you'll never see me again,
Clara—it's all over. You didn't think, little sister, did
you, when you saw me at the station on New
Year's Day that you'd never see me again?—And
Mother . . . Good God! Mother! . . . No, I can't allow myself to think of it. Ah, if I could only go home
first. . . . Say I have a day's leave. . . . See Papa,
Mamma, Clara again before it's all over. . . . Yes, I
could take the first train at seven o'clock to Graz. I'd
be there at one. . . . God bless you, Mamma. . . .
Hello, Clara! . . . How goes everything? . . . Well

this *is* a surprise. . . . But they'll notice something.
. . . If no one else, at least Clara will. . . . Surely,
Clara. . . . Clara's a smart girl. . . . She wrote me
such a sweet letter the other day, and I still owe her
an answer—and the good advice she always gives me.
Such a wholehearted creature. . . . Wonder whether
everything wouldn't have turned out differently if I'd
stayed at home. I might have studied political economy
and gone into my uncle's business. . . . They all
wanted me to do that when I was a kid. . . . By this
time I'd be happily married to a nice, sweet girl. . . .
Perhaps Anna—she used to like me a lot. . . . I just
noticed it again the last time I was home—in spite of
her husband and two children. . . . I could see it, just
the way she looked at me. . . . And she still calls me
"Gustly," the same way she used to. . . . It will hit
her hard when she finds out the way I ended up—
but her husband will say: I might have known as
much—a no-account like him!—They'll all think it
was because I owed money. . . . It's not true. I've paid
all my debts . . . except the last hundred and sixty
gulden—and they'll be here tomorrow. Well I must
see to it that Ballert gets his hundred and sixty gulden
—I must make a note of that before I shoot myself.
. . . It's terrible, it's terrible! . . . If I only could run
away from it all, and go to America where nobody
knows about it. In America no one will know what
happened here this evening. . . . No one will care.
Just recently I read in the paper about Count Runge,
who had to leave because of some nasty stories that
were going around about him. He now owns a hotel
over there and doesn't give a hoot for the whole bunch.
. . . And in a couple of years I might return. . . .
Not to Vienna, of course. . . . Nor to Graz . . . but

I could go out to the farm. . . . And Mamma and Papa would a dozen times rather have it that way—just so long as I stay alive. . . . And why worry about the other people at all? Who ever cares about me?— Kopetzsky's the only one who'd ever miss me. . . . Kopetzsky—the one who gave me the ticket today . . . and the ticket's to blame for it all. If he hadn't given it to me, I wouldn't have gone to the concert, and all this would never have happened. . . . What happened? It's just as if a whole century had passed—and it's only two hours ago. Two hours ago some one called me a fat-head and wanted to break my sword. Great God, I'm starting to shout here at midnight! Why did it all happen? Couldn't I have waited longer until the whole wardrobe had emptied out? And why did I ever tell him to shut up? How did it ever slip out of me? I'm generally polite. I've never been so rude, even to my orderly. . . . But of course I was nervous: all the things that happened just at the same time. . . . The tough luck in gambling and Steffi's eternal stalling—and the duel tomorrow afternoon—and I've been getting too little sleep lately, and all the noise in the barracks. . . . I couldn't keep on standing it forever! . . . Before long I would have become ill—would have had to get a furlough. . . . Now it's no longer necessary. . . . I'll get a long furlough now—without pay —Haha! . . .

How long am I going to keep on sitting here? It must be after midnight. . . . Didn't I hear the clock strike midnight a while ago?—What's that there? A carriage driving by? At this hour? I can already imagine . . . They're better off than I. Perhaps it's Ballert with his Bertha. . . . Why, of all people, Ballert? —Go ahead, right on! That was a good looking car-

riage His Highness had in Przemsyl. . . . He used
to ride in it all the time on his way to the city to see
Rosenberg. He was a good mixer, His Highness—
chummy with every one, a good drinking companion.
Those were good times. . . . Although . . . It was in
a lonely section and the weather was hot enough in the
summer to kill you. . . . One afternoon three men
were overcome by the heat. . . . Even the corporal in
my own company—a handy fellow he was. . . . During the afternoon we used to lie down naked on the
bed. Once Wiesner came into the room suddenly; I
must just have been dreaming. I stood up and drew
my sword—it was lying next to me. . . . Must have
looked funny! . . . Wiesner laughed himself sick.
He's now the riding master—sorry I didn't go into the
cavalry myself. The old man didn't want me to—it
would have been too expensive—but it makes no difference now. . . . Why?—Yes, I know: I must die,
that's why it makes no difference—I must die. . . .
How then?—Look here, Gustl, you especially came
down here to the Prater in the middle of the night so
that not a soul would bother you—you can think over
everything quietly. . . . That's all a lot of nonsense
about America and quitting the service, and you
haven't brains enough to start on another career. And
when you reach the age of a hundred and think back
to the time that a fellow wanted to break your sword,
and called you a fat-head and you stood there and
couldn't do a thing—no, there's nothing more to think
about—what's happened has happened.—That's all
nonsense about Mamma and Clara—they'll get over it
—people get over everything. . . . Oh, Lord, how
Mamma wept when her brother died—and after four
weeks she never thought of it again. She used to ride

out to the cemetery . . . first, every week, then every month, and now only on the day of his death. To-morrow is the day of my death—April 5.—Won-der whether they'll take my body to Graz— Haha! The worms in Graz will enjoy it!—But that's not my prob-lem—I'll let others worry about that. . . . Well then, what else is there to worry about? . . . Oh yes, the hundred and sixty gulden for Ballert—that's all de-cided—then I have no debts to meet.—Are there let-ters to write? Why? To whom? . . . Say good-bye? The devil I will—it's clear enough that a man's gone after he's shot himself! Every one will soon notice that he's taken his leave. . . . If people only knew how lit-tle the whole thing bothers me, they wouldn't feel sorry— No use pitying me. . . . What have I had out of life?—One thing I'd like to have experienced: be-ing in war—but I would have had to wait a long time for that. . . . Outside of that I've experienced every-thing. Whether a person's called Steffi or Kunigunde makes no difference. . . . And I've heard all the best operettas—and *Lohengrin* twelve times—and this eve-ning I even heard an oratorio—and a baker called me a fat-head.—Good God, I've had enough! Life's opened up all its secrets to me. . . . Well then, I'll go home slowly, very slowly, there's really no hurry.—I'll rest for a few minutes on the bench here in the Prater, and think about—just nothing at all. I'll never lie down in bed again. I'll have enough time to sleep.— This wonderful air! There'll be no more air. . . .

2

WELL, what's this?—Hey, there, Johann, bring me a glass of fresh water. . . . What's this? . . . Where? . . . Am I dreaming? My head. Oh, Good Lord. . . . I can't see straight!—I'm all dressed!—Where am I sitting?—Holy God, I've been sleeping! How could I have been sleeping? It's already growing light. How long have I been sleeping? I mustn't ask—must look at my watch—can't see a thing. . . . Where are my matches? Won't a single one of them light? . . . Three o'clock, and I'm to have my duel at four.—No, not a duel—a suicide! It has nothing to do with a duel; I must shoot myself because a baker called me a fat-head. . . . What, did it actually happen?—My head feels so funny. . . . My throat's all clogged up— I can't move at all—my right foot's asleep.—Get up! Get up! . . . Ah, that's better! It's already growing light, and the air . . . Just like that morning when I was doing picket duty when we were camping in the woods. I woke up feeling differently that time. There was a different sort of day ahead of me. . . . I wonder whether I get it all straight. There's the street—gray, empty—just now I'm the only person in the Prater. I was here once at four o'clock in the morning with Pansinger.—We were riding. I was on Colonel Miro-vic's horse and Pansinger on his own nag.—That was May, a year ago—everything was in bloom—every-thing was green. Now it's still cold, but Spring will soon be here—it will be here in just a few days.—Lilies-

420

of-the-valley, violets—pity I'll never see them again. Every one else will enjoy them, but I must die! Oh, it's miserable! And others will sit in the café eating, as if nothing had happened—just the way all of us sat in the café on the evening of the day they buried Lippay. . . . And they all liked Lippay so much. . . . He was more popular in the regiment than I.—Why shouldn't they sit in the café when I kick off?—It's quite warm —much warmer than yesterday and there's a fragrance in the air—the blossoms must be out. . . . Wonder whether Steffi will bring me flowers?—It will never occur to her! She'll just ride out to . . . Oh, if it were still Adele . . . Adele! I'm sure I haven't thought of her for the last two years. . . . As long as I lived I never saw a woman weep the way she did. . . . That was absolutely the tenderest thing I ever lived through . . . she was so modest, so unassuming.— She loved me, I swear she did.—She was altogether different from Steffi. . . . I wonder why I ever gave her up. . . . It was too tame for me, yes, that was the whole thing. . . . Going out with the same person every evening. . . . Then perhaps I was afraid that I'd never be able to get rid of her—she always whimpered so.—Well, Gustl, you could have waited a long time until you found any one who loved you as much as Adele. Wonder what she's doing now. Well, what would she be doing—probably has some one else now. This, with Steffi, is much more comfortable. I am with her only when I want to be—some one else can have all the unpleasantness—I'll take the pleasant part. . . . Well, in that case I certainly can't expect her to come to the cemetery. Wonder if there's any one who'd go without feeling obliged to. Kopetzsky, perhaps—and that's all! Oh, it's sad, to have no one. . . . Nonsense!

There's Papa and Mamma and Clara. It's because I'm
a son and a brother. . . . What more is there to hold
us together? They like me of course—but what do
they know about me?—That I'm in the service, that
I play cards, and that I run around with fast women.
. . . Anything more? Yes—that I often get good and
sick of myself—though I never wrote anything to
them about that—perhaps the reason is because I have
never realized it myself. Well, Gustl, what sort of
stuff are you muttering to yourself? It's just about
time to start crying. . . . Disgusting!—Keep in step.
. . . So! Whether a man goes to a rendezvous or on
duty or to battle. . . . Who was it said that? . . . Oh
yes, it was Major Lederer. When they were telling
us that time at the canteen about Wingleder—the one
who grew so pale before his first duel—and vomited.
. . . Yes, a true officer will never betray by look or
step whether he goes to a rendezvous or certain death!
—Therefore, Gustl—remember the major's words!
Ha!—Always growing lighter. . . . What's that whistling there?—Oh yes, there's the North Railroad
Station. . . . It's never looked so long before. . . .
There are the carriages. Nobody except street cleaners
around. They're the last street cleaners I'll ever see—
Ha! I always laugh when I think of it. . . . I don't
understand myself. . . . Wonder whether it's that
way with everybody, once they're entirely sure. Four-
thirty by the clock at the North Railroad Station. . . .
The only question now is whether I'm to shoot myself
at seven o'clock railroad time or Vienna time. . . .
Seven o'clock. . . . Well, why exactly seven? . . . As
if it couldn't be any other time as well. . . . I'm
hungry— Lord, I'm hungry— No wonder. . . . Since
when haven't I eaten? . . . Since—not since yester-

day at six o'clock in the café! When Kopetzsky handed
me the check—coffee and two rolls.—Wonder what
the baker will say when he hears about it? . . .
Damned swine. He'll know—he'll realize what it
means to be an Austrian officer—a fellow like that can
be beaten in the open street and think nothing of it.
And if an officer is insulted even in secret, he's as
good as dead. . . . If a rascal like him would only
fight a duel—but no, then he'd be very careful—he
wouldn't take a chance like that. The fellow keeps
on living quietly and peacefully while I—it's the end
for me! He's responsible for my death. . . . Do you
realize, Gustl, it is he who is responsible for your
death! But he won't get off as easily as that!—No, no,
no! I'll send Kopetzsky a letter telling him the whole
story. . . . Better yet: I'll write to the Colonel. He'll
make a report to the officer in command. . . . Just like
an official report. . . . Just wait—you think, do you,
that a matter like this can remain secret!—You're just
wrong.—It will be reported and remembered forever.
After that I'd like to see whether you'll venture into
the café!—Ha!—"I'd like to see" is good! There are
lots of things I'd like to see which unfortunately I
won't be able to— Out! It's all over!—

At this moment Johann must be coming to my
room. He notices that the Lieutenant hasn't slept at
home.—Well he'll imagine all sort of things. But that
the Lieutenant has spent the night in the Prater—that,
Good Lord, will never occur to him. . . . Ah, there
goes the Forty-fourth! They're marching out to target practice. Let them pass.—So, I'll remain right here.
. . . A window is being opened up there.—Pretty
creature.—Well I, at least, would want to put something around me, going to an open window. Last

Sunday was the last time. I'd never have dreamt that
Steffi would be the last. Oh God, that's the only real
pleasure. Well, now the Colonel will ride after them
in two hours in his grand manner. These big fellows
take life easy.—Yes, yes, eyes right! Very good. If
you only knew how little I care about you all. Ah,
that's not bad at all: there goes Katzer. Since when
has he been transferred to the Forty-fourth?—How do
you do, good morning! What sort of a face is he making? Why is he pointing at his head?—My dear fellow, your skull interests me not at all. . . . Oh, it's
that way. No, my good chap, you're mistaken: I've
just spent the night in the Prater. . . . You will hear
about it in the evening paper.—"Impossible!" he'll say,
"Early this morning as we were marching out to target
practice I met him on the Prater Strasse"— Who'll be
put in command of my platoon? I wonder whether
they'll give it to Walter. Well that would be a fine
how-do-you-do! A fellow totally devoid of imagina-
tion—should have been a plumber.—What, the sun
coming up already!—This will be a beautiful day—a
real Spring day. The devil—on a day like this!—Every
cab driver will be in the world at eight o'clock this
morning and I—well, what about me? Now really,
it would be funny if I lost my nerve at the last minute
just because of cab drivers. . . . What's up now?—
Why's my heart thumping this way?—Not on account
of the cab driver. No, oh no, it's because I haven't
eaten since yesterday. But Gustl, be honest with yourself: you're scared—scared because you have never
tried it before. . . . But that doesn't help. Being scared
never helped anybody. Every one has to experience it
once. Some sooner, some later, and you just happen
to have to experience it sooner. As a matter of fact you

never were worth an awful lot, so the least you can do is to behave decently at the very end. In fact I demand that you do. I'll have to figure it out—figure out what? . . . I'm always trying to figure out. . . . It's lying in the drawer of my table—loaded—just: pull the trigger—certainly not very complicated!

That girl over there's already going to work . . . the poor girls! . . . Adele also used to have to go to work—I called for her a few times in the evening. When they have a job they don't play around so much with men. If Steffi had only listened to me. I always urged her to become a modiste. . . . Wonder how she'll find out about it?—The newspaper! She'll be angry that I didn't write to her about it. I believe I'm beginning to lose my mind. Why bother about whether she'll be angry or not? How long has the whole affair lasted? . . . Since January. . . . No, it must have begun before Christmas. I brought her some candy from Graz, and she sent me a note at New Year's. . . . Good Lord, that's right, I have her letters at home. Are there any I should have burned? . . . 'Mm, the one about Fallsteiner. If that letter is found—the rascal will get into trouble. Why should that bother me! —Well it wouldn't be much of an exertion. . . . But I can't look through all that scrawl. . . . It would be best to burn the whole bunch. . . . Who'll ever need them? They're all junk.—My few books I could leave to Blany—"Through Night and Ice"—too bad I'll never be able to finish it. . . . Didn't have much chance to read these last few months. . . .

Organ playing? In the church there. . . . Early Mass—haven't been to one in an age. . . . Last time it was in February when the whole platoon was ordered to go. But it didn't mean anything.—I was

watching my men to see if they were religious and
behaving properly. . . . I'd like to go to church . . .
there's something substantial about it after all. . . .
Well, this afternoon I'll know all about it. Ah, "this
afternoon" is good!—what shall I do—go in? I think
it would be a comfort to Mother if she knew! . . . It
wouldn't mean as much to Clara. . . . Well, in I go.
It can't hurt! Organ playing—singing—hm!—what's
the matter! I'm growing dizzy. . . . Oh, God, Oh,
God, Oh, God! I want somebody whom I can talk
to before it happens!— How would it be—if I went
to confession! The Father would certainly open his
eyes if he heard me say at the end, "Pardon, Reverend
Father; I am now going to shoot myself!" . . . Most
of all I want to lie down there on the stone floor and
cry my eyes out. . . . Oh, no, I don't dare do that.
But crying sometimes helps so much. . . . I'll sit
down a moment, but I won't go to sleep again as I
did in the Prater! . . .—People who have religion are
much better off. . . . Well, now my hands are beginning to tremble! If it keeps on this way, I'll soon become so disgusted at myself that I'll commit suicide
out of pure shame! That old woman there— What is
she still praying about? . . . It would be a good idea
to say to her: You, please include me too. . . . I never
learned how to do it properly. Ha! It seems that dying makes one stupid!—Stand up! Where have I
heard that melody before?—Holy God! Last night!—
It's the melody from the oratorio! Out, out of here, I
can't stand it any more. 'Pst! Not so much noise letting that sword drag—don't disturb the people in their
prayers—so!—It's better in the open. . . . Light. . . .
The time's always growing shorter. Wish it were over
already!—I should have done it at once in the Prater.

. . . I should never go out without a revolver. . . .
If I'd had one yesterday evening. . . . Good Lord!—
I might take breakfast in the café. . . . I'm hungry.
It always used to seem remarkable that people who
were doomed to die drank coffee and smoked a cigar
in the morning. . . . Heavens, I haven't even smoked!
I haven't even felt like smoking!—This is funny: I
really feel like going to the café. . . . Yes, it's already
open and there's none of our crowd there right
now . . . and if there were—it would be a magnificent sign of cool headedness! "At six o'clock he was
eating breakfast in the café and at seven he killed
himself." . . .—I feel altogether calm again. Walking
is so pleasant—and best of all, nobody is compelling
me. If I wanted to I could still chuck the whole business. . . . America. . . . What do I mean, "whole
business"? What is a "whole business"? I wonder
whether I'm getting a sunstroke. Oho!—am I so quiet
because I still imagine that I don't have to? . . . I
do have to! I must! No, I will! Can you picture yourself, Gustl, taking off your uniform and beating it,
and the damned swine laughing behind your back?
And Kopetzsky not even shaking hands with you?
. . . I blush just to think of it.—The watchman is
saluting me. . . . I must acknowledge it. . . . "Good
morning!" There, I've said "Good morning" to him!
. . . It always pleases a poor devil like him. . . . Well,
no one ever had to complain about me. . . . Off duty
I was always pleasant. . . . When we were at the
manœuvres I let off the officers of the Kompagnie Bri-
tannika. One time at drill I heard an enlisted man
behind me say something about "the damned drudg-
ery" and I didn't even report him.—I merely said to
him, "See here, be careful—some one else might hear

it, and then you'll be in hot water." . . . The Burghof.
. . . Wonder who's on guard today?—The Bosniacs
—they look good. Just recently the Lieutenant Colonel
said, "When we were down there in '78, no one would
have believed that they'd ever come up to us the way
they have." Good God, that's a place I'd like to have
been! Those fellows are all getting up from the bench.
I'll salute. It's too bad that our company couldn't have
been there—that would have been so much more wonderful—on the field of battle for the Fatherland,
than . . . Yes, Doctor, you're getting off easily! . . .
Wonder if some one couldn't take my place? Great
God, there's an idea—I'll leave word for Kopetzsky or
Wymetal to take my place in the duel! . . . He won't
get off as easily as all that!—Oh well, what difference
does it make what happens later on? I'll never hear
anything about it!—The trees are beginning to bud.
. . . I once picked up a girl here at the Volksgarten
—she was wearing a red dress—lived in the Strozzi-
gasse—later Roschlitz took her off my hands. . . . I
think he still keeps her, but he never says anything
about it—probably ashamed of it. . . . Steffi's still
sleeping, I suppose. . . . She looks so pretty when
she's asleep—just as if she couldn't count to five!—
Well, they all look alike when they're asleep!—I ought
to drop her a line. . . . Why not? Every one does
it . . . writes letters just before—I also want to write
Clara to console Papa and Mamma and the sort of stuff
that one writes!—And to Kopetzsky. My Lord, I'll
bet it would have been much simpler if I'd said good-
bye to a few people . . . and the announcement to
the officers of the regiment.—And the hundred and
sixty gulden for Ballert. . . . Still lots of things to do.
Well, nobody insists that I do it at seven. . . . There's

still time enough after eight o'clock for being deceased! Deceased! That's the word   Then there's nothing else that a fellow can do.

Ringstrasse—I'll soon be at my café. . . . Funny, I'm actually looking forward to breakfast. . . . Unbelievable.—After breakfast I'll light a cigar, then I'll go home and write. . . . First of all I'll make my announcement to the officers of the regiment; then the letter to Clara—then the one to Kopetzsky—then the one to Steffi. What on earth am I going to write her? . . . *My dear child, you should probably never have thought* . . . Lord, what nonsense!—*My dear child, I thank you ever so much.* . . . —*My dear child, before I take my leave, I will not overlook the opportunity.* . . . —Well, letter writing was never my forte. . . . *My dear child, one last farewell from your Gustl.* . . . —What eyes she'll make! It's lucky I wasn't in love with her. . . . It must be sad if one loves a girl and then. . . . Well, Gustl, let well enough alone: it's sad enough as it is. . . . Others would have come along after Steffi, and finally there would have been one who'd have been worth something—a young girl from a good, substantial family—it might have been rather nice. . . .—I must write Clara a detailed letter explaining why I couldn't do otherwise. . . . *You must forgive me, my dear sister, and please console our dear parents. I know that I caused you all a good deal of worry and considerable pain; but believe me, I always loved all of you, and I hope that some time you will be happy, my dear Clara, and will not completely forget your unhappy brother.* . . . —Oh, I'd better not write to her at all! . . . No, it's too sad. I can already feel the tears in my eyes, when I think. . . . At least I'll write to Kopetzsky. . . . A man to man farewell,

and he'll let the others know. . . .—Already six o'clock
—Oh no, half-past-five—quarter to.—If that isn't a
charming little face!—The little dear, with her black
eyes. I've met her so often in the Florianigasse!—
Wonder what she'll say?—And she doesn't even know
who I am—she'll only wonder why she doesn't see me
any more. . . . Day before yesterday I made up my
mind to speak to her the next time I met her.—She's
been flirting enough. . . . She was so young—but I'll
bet no angel at that! . . . Yes, Gustl! Don't put off till
tomorrow what you can do today. . . . That fellow
over there probably hasn't slept all night.—Well, now
he'll go home comfortably and lie down.—So will I!
—Haha! This is getting serious, Gustl! Well if there
weren't a little fear connected with it, there'd be nothing to do at all—and on the whole I must say in behalf of myself that I have been behaving very nobly.
. . . Where'll I go now? There's my café. . . .
They're still sweeping. . . . Well, I'll go in.

There's the table where they always play Tarok.
. . . Remarkable, I can't imagine why that fellow
who's always sitting next to the wall should be the
same one who . . .—Nobody here yet. . . . Where's
the waiter? . . . Ha!—There's one coming out of the
kitchen. . . . Quickly putting on his apron. . . . It's
really no longer necessary! . . . Well, it is, for him.
. . . He'll have to wait on other people today.

"Good morning, Lieutenant."

"Good morning."

"So early today, Lieutenant?"

"Oh that's all right,—I haven't much time, I'll just
sit here with my cloak on."

"Your order, Sir?"

"A cup of coffee."

"Thank you—right away, Lieutenant."

Ah, there are the newspapers . . . are they out as early as this? . . . Wonder if there's anything in them about me? . . . Well, what would there be—Think I'll look and see if there's anything about my committing suicide! Haha!—Why am I still standing up? . . . Sit down by the window. . . . He's already brought in the coffee. There, I'll pull the curtain. I feel uncomfortable with people gaping in. But no one is passing by. . . . Ah, this coffee tastes good—it wasn't a bad idea, this breakfast! . . . I feel like a new man. —The whole trouble was that I didn't eat anything last night. Why has the fellow come back as soon as this? Oh, he's also brought some rolls. . . .

"Has the Lieutenant already heard?"

"Heard what?" For God's sake, does he know something about it already? . . . Nonsense, it's absolutely impossible!

"Herr Habetswallner—" What, what's that? That's the baker's name. . . . What's he going to say now? . . . Has he been here already? Was he here yesterday telling them the whole story? . . . Why doesn't he tell me more? . . . He's going to. . . .

"—had a stroke last night at twelve o'clock."

"What?" . . . I mustn't shout this way. . . . No, I can't allow anybody to notice it. . . . But perhaps I'm dreaming. . . . I must ask him again. . . .

"Who did you say had a stroke?"—Rather good, that!—I said it quite innocently!—

"The baker, Lieutenant. You must know him. . . . Don't you remember the fat fellow who played Tarok with the officers here every afternoon . . . with Herr

Schlesinger? Don't you remember the one who used to sit opposite Herr Wasner—the one in the artificial flower business!"

I'm completely awake—everything seems to check up—and still I just can't believe him.—I'll have to ask him again. . . . Altogether innocently. . . .

"You say that he was overcome by a stroke? . . . How did it happen? Who told you about it?"

"Who could know it sooner than we here, Lieutenant?—That roll you are eating there comes from Herr Habetswallner's own bakery. His delivery man who comes here at half-past-four in the morning told us about it."

Look out! I mustn't give myself away. . . . I feel like shouting. . . . I'll burst out laughing in a minute. In another second I'll kiss Rudolph. . . . But I must ask him something else! Having a stroke doesn't mean that he's dead. . . . I must ask him—if he's dead. . . . Altogether calmly—why should the baker concern me?—I must glance over the paper while I'm asking the waiter.

"You say he's dead?"

"Why certainly, Lieutenant, he died immediately."

Wonderful, wonderful! . . . It's all because I went to church. . . .

"He went to the theatre last night. On the way out he fell on the stairs—the janitor heard him fall. . . . Well, they carried him to his home, and he died long before the doctor ever arrived."

"That's sad—too bad. He was still in the prime of life." I said that marvelously—not a soul would notice. . . . And I have to do everything to keep from shouting my lungs out and jumping up on the billiard table. . . .

"Yes, Lieutenant, it is very sad. He was such a lovable gentleman; he's been coming to this place for the
last twenty years—he was a good friend of the boss.
And his poor wife. . . ."

I don't think I've felt as happy as this as long as I've
lived. He's dead—dead! Nobody knows about it, and
nothing's happened!—What a piece of luck that I
came into the café. . . . Otherwise I'd certainly have
shot myself—it's like a benediction from heaven. . . .
Where did Rudolph go? Oh, he's talking to the furnace man . . . —Well, he's dead—dead. I just can't
seem to believe it! I'd better go and take a look at him
myself.—He was probably overcome by a stroke of
anger—couldn't control himself. . . . Well, what difference does it make what he was! The main thing
is he's dead, and I can keep on living, and everything's
all right! . . . Funny, the way I keep on crumbling the
roll—the roll Habetswallner baked himself! It tastes
very good too, Herr Habetswallner. Splendid!—Ah,
now I'll light a cigar. . . .

"Rudolph! Hey, Rudolph! Don't argue so much
with the furnace man."

"What is it, Lieutenant?"

"Bring me a cigar." . . .—I'm so happy, so happy!
. . . What am I doing? . . . What am I doing? . . .
Something's got to happen, or I'll be overcome by
a stroke of joy! In a few minutes I'll wander over
to the barracks and let Johann give me a cold rub-
down. . . . At half-past-seven we have drill and at
half-past-nine formation.—And I'll write Steffi to
leave this evening open for me! And this afternoon at
four. . . . Just wait, my boy, I'm in wonderful
trim. . . . I'll knock you to smithereens!

THIS BOOK
is published by the publishers of

JEAN RICHARD BLOCH
—And Company : A Night in Kurdistan

WILLIAM BOLITHO
Twelve Against the Gods · Camera Obscura · Overture-1920

ERNEST DIMNET
The Art of Thinking

WILL DURANT
*The Story of Philosophy · The Mansions of Philosophy
Transition : The Case for India · Studies in Genius*

ALFRED ALOYSIUS HORN
Trader Horn

JOHN COWPER POWYS
Wolf Solent · In Defence of Sensuality

FELIX SALTEN
Fifteen Rabbits · Bambi · The Hound of Florence

ARTHUR SCHNITZLER
*Fräulein Else · Casanova's Homecoming · Rhapsody
Beatrice · None But The Brave · Theresa
Daybreak · Dr. Graesler · Little Novels*

FRANZ WERFEL
Class Reunion · Verdi · The Man Who Conquered Death

And Others

from THE INNER SANCTUM *of*
SIMON *and* SCHUSTER
Publishers · 386 Fourth Avenue · New York